Intrigued

BERTRICE SMALL

Intrigued

KENSINGTON BOOKS
http://www.kensingtonbooks.com

KENSINGTON BOOKS are published by

Kensington Publishing Corp.
850 Third Avenue
New York, NY 10022

ISBN 0-7394-1552-2

Printed in the United States of America

For my dearest friend,
Elaine Duillo.
Thanks, sweetie!

Prologue

SEPTEMBER 3, 1650

James Leslie, fifth Earl and first Duke of Glenkirk, lay dying on the battlefield at Dunbar. Around him he could still see and hear clearly many of the brave, loyal men who would join him in death this day. The Scots were being brutally beaten by an army but half their size, yet with mindless arrogance they had moved the previous day from their position of strength on the hills surrounding Dunbar's plain to boldly make their encampment directly before the English. It was a fatal mistake, for the terrain was impossible to defend, as the Scot Covenanter army of King Charles II quickly discovered. Of the twenty-three thousand who had seen the day begin, only nine thousand remained to see it end amid the smoking ruins of the Royal Stuart's hopes.

Among the survivors was Red Hugh More-Leslie, the Duchess of Glenkirk's personal captain, who, seeing his master fall, had leapt over the dead and wounded to cradle James Leslie in his arms.

"We'll get ye out of here, my lord," Red Hugh said.

James Leslie shook his head faintly, saying but one word before he died. *"Jasmine."*

Cursing and weeping alternately, Red Hugh gathered the surviving men of Glenkirk to him. Of the hundred and fifty who had come to Dunbar, thirty-six remained. Putting their duke's body over his horse, and taking mounts where they could find them, the Glenkirk men quickly departed the battlefield, swiftly heading northeast. Cromwell's men were not noted for showing respect to the dead, or to the survivors; but Red Hugh would not allow his master's body to be pillaged or savaged. James Leslie would be buried on his own lands, as had all those lords of Glenkirk who had come before him, except his own father.

And most of the past Glenkirk earls had died in battle, Red Hugh remembered. In battles precipitated by the Stuarts, the captain thought grimly. Solway Moss in 1542 had taken the second earl, and his heir, along with two hundred men and boys from the estates of Glenkirk, Sithean, and Grayhaven. Red Hugh's own great-grandfather had died at Solway Moss with the Leslies. His grandfather, the first Red Hugh, had survived to help bring the others home. Now history repeated itself in a particularly ugly way.

His mistress, the duchess, had known before they had left Glenkirk last month that she would not see her beloved Jemmie alive again. Red Hugh More-Leslie had seen the resignation and sorrow in her eyes as she bid them all farewell. But the duke had lived a good life. He had been an honorable man. And seventy-two years was a goodly span, Red Hugh reasoned, as they rode toward home.

Messengers would have to be dispatched to his two youngest sons in Ulster, to his daughters and sons in England, and to the daughter in the New World. They would be saddened, he knew, but the youngest of them, Mistress Autumn, would be absolutely heart-broken. She had been visiting in England this summer but been un-able to return to Scotland because of the warring factions. What would happen to her now? he wondered to himself. Her father's pet, the lass had been, and spoiled more than any of them, being the last. Well, 'twas not his business. Lady Autumn Rose Leslie was now re-sponsibility of her brother, now the second duke, and her mother, now the dowager duchess. Certainly they would know what to do with her.

After several long, hard days of travel, the towers of Glenkirk Castle came into view. For a moment Red Hugh stopped and stared, one thought, and one alone, clear in his head. James Leslie was dead, and life as they had all known it would never be the same again. Raising his big, gloved hand, Red Hugh signaled his men to move onward. The duke's personal piper walked slowly before them playing the rich and reedy tones of *Lament for Glenkirk*, which rose up, alerting the castle that James Leslie was coming home for the very last time. And after a few moments he could see the widowed duchess standing on the drawbridge, stoically awaiting them. Nay, naught would ever be the same again, Red Hugh thought sadly.

Part One

ENGLAND AND FRANCE, 1650–51

Chapter

1

"I hate Master Cromwell, and his pocky Roundheads!" Lady Autumn Leslie declared vehemently. "There is no fun in England or Scotland anymore, thanks to *him*."

"*Autumn!* Dammit! How many times have I warned you to mind your chattering tongue?" her brother, Charles Stuart, Duke of Lundy, said irritably.

"Oh, Charlie, who is to hear me but the servants?" Autumn answered her elder brother pertly.

"Not all the servants can be trusted these days," the duke replied in soft tones. "Nothing is now as it was. This is not Glenkirk, where the loyalty is first to your father and only secondly to the state. The king will one day be back on his throne, but until then we must be discreet. Remember, sister, who my father was, and my uncle, King Charles, God assoil his soul. Remember that while I am the not-so-royal Stuart, I am a Stuart nonetheless. Cromwell and his ilk will never trust me, nor should they, but I must protect my family until this madness is lifted from the land, and my cousin, Charles the Second, returns to England to govern us in peace."

"But what are we to do until then?" Autumn demanded. "These Puritans are dreadful people, Charlie. They are joyless with their edicts. No dancing! No bowls upon the green! No Maying on May Day! *No Christmas!* Nothing that would bring a person pleasure, or happiness. And Scotland is, I fear, just as bad. Still, once I am back at Glenkirk it will be a little better, especially when the winter sets in, and no one can know what we do. Papa pays little heed to the Covenanters and their dolorous ways. When do you think I can go home?"

The duke shook his head. "I do not know, Autumn. With Cousin Charles on Scotland's throne now, and a battle brewing between him and Cromwell, I cannot honestly say when it will be safe for you to travel north. Are you not happy here at Queen's Malvern with us?"

"I love it here!" Autumn replied. "I always have, Charlie."

"Then what is it that makes you so restless?" he asked.

"Charlie! I am going to be nineteen at the end of next month," Autumn wailed. "And I have no betrothed, no husband, no man at all who takes my fancy. I am quite as bad if not worse than our sister Fortune. At least she had the opportunity to find a husband, but what chance have I amid all this civil strife? There is no court, and even family gatherings are mandated as to size now by the Parliament. How am I to find a husband before I am too old?"

"Nineteen is hardly old," he chuckled, reaching out to take her hand up to kiss it. "You are a beautiful girl, little sister, and one day the right man will come along to sweep you off your feet, steal your heart, and make Papa and all your brothers jealous."

"I wish I could be as certain of that as you, Charlie," Autumn said. She sighed deeply. "Bess was still sixteen when you married her, and Rosamund was seventeen when she wed our brother Henry. I am old, Charlie! Eighteen going on nineteen, and not a suitor in sight, nor is there likely to be one. I hate Master Cromwell!"

Charles Frederick Stuart laughed, unable to help himself. His baby sister was deliciously dramatic, and yet she did have a point. Theirs was hardly a fit society nowadays for a duke's daughter to find a husband. There were men a-plenty who would have Autumn for her wealth and beauty, no matter her age; but it had always been his family's policy to allow its daughters to wed for love. Certainly Autumn should have the same chance as their two elder sisters had had.

"Mother will know what to do," he told Autumn in an attempt to reassure her.

"If I can ever get back to Glenkirk," she replied gloomily.

"The gossip is that there has been a battle in Scotland, and Parliament's forces have won out over King Charles the Second's army. Rumors, however, aren't fact. Perhaps I shall go into Worcester later this week and see what I can learn," the duke said.

"Worcester? You are going into Worcester? When?" The young Duchess of Lundy came into the room with two of her children. "You must see if you can find us some thread, Charlie. We have not a bit and are at a loss to mend, or hem, or make Sabrina and her brothers new clothing. They are outgrowing everything. At least we have cloth, thanks to your frugal family, but without thread we are helpless."

Bess Stuart was a lovely woman with light brown hair filled with golden highlights and warm gray-blue eyes. The youngest daughter of the Earl of Welk, she and Charlie Stuart had fallen in love at first sight. She had just turned sixteen, and he at twenty-six was considered a rake and a rogue by those at the court who knew him. Still, his amber eyes had met Bess Lightbody's sweet gaze, and his heart was immediately engaged. He began to play her most assiduous court.

The Earl of Welk and his wife had been horrified that Charles Frederick Stuart, the late Prince Henry's bastard offspring with the beautiful but notorious Jasmine Leslie—herself the dubious member of an infamous family—a young man openly accepted and beloved by the king and all his kin, despite his shameful birth, should seek to pay his addresses to their youngest daughter. They sent Bess home to Dorset, certain that would end the matter. They had underestimated their opponent.

Bess had not been gone from court a week when she was recalled by royal command to be one of the queen's maids-of-honor. The Earl of Welk sought to *protect* his daughter from the young Duke of Lundy's insistent advances by seeking a suitable marital alliance with a thoroughly respectable family, preferably one with similar religious and political leanings. Upright, modest, prudent people by whom his daughter could be guided in order to become a dutiful and obedient wife. Again he did not take his adversary seriously enough.

Learning from Bess of her father's plans, Charlie had sought aid from his uncle, King Charles I. Understanding his nephew's plight, the king had called the Earl and Countess of Welk into his presence.

"My nephew, the Duke of Lundy, has told me that he wishes to wed your daughter Elizabeth," the king began. "He has asked me to act for him in this matter. While your antecedents, my lord, hardly make your daughter a suitable match for Charlie, we are of a mind to allow it, for we love the lad right well. *And* he has never before asked a favor of us, unlike so many others who people our court. Bring your daughter to us tomorrow at this same hour. If she agrees to the match, we will permit it." The king smiled one of his very rare smiles, then waved the Earl and Countess of Welk from his august presence.

They backed away, bowing and curtsying, but once outside the king's privy chamber the Earl of Welk gave vent to his anger. He sent his wife to the queen's apartments to fetch their daughter and bring her to their small London house, where he would speak with her. Bess was not going to marry that bastard, he vowed silently to himself. And the king's inference that the Lightbody blood was not the equal of a bastard, royal or no, infuriated him.

When the women finally joined him, he told his daughter of their audience with the king. Then he said, *"But you will not wed him, Bess! You will tell the king you do not want to marry his nephew. Do you understand me?"*

"I will say no such thing, my lord," Bess answered. "I love Charlie, and he loves me. I will tell the king, aye, I will have his nephew for my husband, and gladly!"

"You will not!" the Earl of Welk shouted at his daughter.

"I will!" she replied defiantly.

"I will beat you black and blue if you continue to challenge my authority over you, daughter," he told her angrily.

"If you do, I shall show the king the stripes you have inflicted upon my back," she threatened.

"*Oh!*" The Countess of Welk collapsed into a chair, her countenance pale, her hand fluttering over her heart.

"Now look what you have done to your mother," the earl said.

"She is only surprised that I have spoken up as she has herself longed to do all these years of her marriage to you, my lord," Bess bluntly told her father. "Please, sir, be fair. Charlie has never before sought to wed a lady. He loves me enough to ask the king's aid in making our dream come true. We love one another."

"Are you with child?" her father demanded angrily.

"*Oh!*" The Countess of Welk closed her eyes in despair.

"*What?*" Bess looked astounded at her father's words.

"Have you allowed this Stuart bastard liberties?" her father said. "Have you lain with him? My question is plainspoken, girl."

"Your query is outrageous and insulting, sir," Bess said. "I have not allowed the duke *any* liberties. Nor have I shamed myself or him by behaving in a wanton manner, laying with him without benefit of clergy. How dare you even suggest such a thing, my lord!"

"I am your sire, and it is my right to make certain that you are chaste, particularly here at court, where gossip can ruin a maid's reputation even if it isn't the truth," the earl replied. "I only seek to protect you, Bess. You are my youngest child."

"I thank you for your concern, my lord," Bess said dryly. "Now with your permission I must return to St. James. The queen allowed me but two hours away, and my time grows short." She curtsied and departed her parents.

Having no choice, the Earl and Countesss of Welk grudgingly accepted their daughter's decision in the matter. Charles Frederick Stuart and Elizabeth Anne Lightbody were married in the king's own chapel at Windsor Castle on the third day of May in the year 1639. They had withdrawn immediately from the court, visiting only rarely thereafter, content to remain in the countryside at Queen's Malvern, Charlie's estate. And to everyone's surprise, the ebulient and charming not-so-royal Stuart was a loyal and devoted husband.

"What color thread?" the duke asked his wife in response to her request.

"Whatever you can find," Bess said. "But try and find some light color. There will be black for certain, for these Puritans are forever mending their garments until they are more thread than fabric. However, try and find something light," Bess instructed him.

"Can I go to Worcester with you, Papa?" the duke's eldest son, Frederick, asked his father.

"I should welcome your company, Freddie," his father replied.

"When?" the boy queried.

"In a few days' time," the duke promised.

"Let me go too," Autumn said. "I'm so bored."

"Nay," her brother said. "It is not safe on the road for a young woman these days, sister."

"I could dress like a boy," Autumn answered him.

"No one, little sister, would ever mistake you for a boy," Charlie said, his eyes lingering a long moment on his sister's shapely young bosom. "It would be impossible to disguise *those* treasures, Autumn."

"Don't be vulgar, Charlie," she snapped at him.

Bess giggled, unable to help herself. Then, managing to control herself, she said, "We'll find something fun to do, sister, while Charlie is in Worcester. The apples are ready to press, and we can help with the cider making. Sabrina loves cider making."

"Your daughter is nine, Bess. At nine little girls love just about everything. Why did the pocky Parliament have to behead King Charles and declare this *commonwealth?* I want to go to court, but there can be no court without a king. God's blood, I hope your cousin young King Charles comes home to rule us soon! Everyone I speak to is sick unto death of Master Cromwell and his ilk. Why doesn't someone behead him? They called old King Charles a traitor, but it seems to me that those who murder God's chosen monarch are the real traitors."

"*Autumn!*" her brother pleaded, anguished.

"Oh, no one is listening, Charlie," Autumn said airily.

He shook his head wearily. He had never thought when his mother asked him to allow Autumn to visit this summer that she would prove to be such a handful. He kept thinking of her as his *baby* sister, but as she had so succinctly pointed out to him earlier, she was going to be nineteen in another month's time. He wondered why his mother and stepfather had not found a suitable husband for Autumn; but then he remembered the difficulties they had had marrying off his two elder sisters. And who the hell was there in the eastern Highlands for the Duke of Glenkirk's daughter to marry? Autumn had needed to go to court, but these last years of civil war had made such a visit impossible, and then his uncle Charles had been executed. Now what English court there was existed in exile, sometimes in France, sometimes in Holland. He didn't know what they were going to do with this sister, but he suspected they had better do it soon, for Autumn was ripe for bedding and could easily find her way into mischief.

The day he had planned on going to Worcester a messenger from Glenkirk arrived before dawn. It was early October. The clansman had had a difficult time eluding the parliamentary forces in Scotland but, moving with great caution, he had finally managed to cross over the border. From there he had made his way easily to Queen's Malvern. Grim-faced and obviously quite exhausted, he told the duke his news was for Lady Autumn first. The duke sent for his wife and sister, who came quickly, still in her dressing gown, hearing her visitor was a Glenkirk man.

"Ian More! Has my father sent you to escort me home?" Autumn asked excitedly. "How is my mother? 'Tis good to see one of our own."

Wordlessly—and, the duke noted, with tears in his eyes—the messenger handed the letter to Autumn. " 'Tis from yer mam, m'lady."

Eagerly Autumn broke the seal of the missive and opened it. Her eyes scanned the parchment, her face growing paler as her eyes flew over the written words, a cry of terrible anguish finally escaping her as she slumped against her brother, obviously terribly distraught, the letter slipping from her hand to fall to the carpet. She was shaking with emotion.

The clansman picked up the parchment, handing it to the duke, who now had an arm about his sister. Charlie quickly read his mother's words to her daughter, his handsome face contorting in a mixture of sorrow and anger. Finally laying aside the letter, he said to the clansman, "You will remain until you are rested, Ian More, or does my mother wish you to stay in England?"

"I'll go back as soon as the beast and I have had a few days' rest, m'lord. Forgive me for being the bearer of such woeful tidings."

"Stable your horse, and then go to the kitchens for your supper. Smythe will find you a place to sleep," the duke told the messenger. Then he turned to comfort his sister, who had begun to weep piteously.

"What is it?" Bess asked her husband, realizing that the news the Glenkirk man had brought was very serious.

"My f-father i-is d-d-dead!" Autumn sobbed. "Ohh, damn Master Cromwell and his parliamentary forces to hell!" She pulled from her brother's gentle embrace and ran from the family hall where they had been seated.

"Oh, Charlie, I am so sorry!" Bess said. She looked after her young sister-in-law. "Shall I go after her?"

The duke shook his head. "Nay. Autumn considers such a public show of emotion on her part a weakness. She has been that way since her childhood. She will want to be alone."

"What happened?" Bess queried her husband.

"Jemmie Leslie died at Dunbar in defense of my cousin, King Charles. He should not have gone, not at his age, not with the history of misfortune the Stuarts always seem to visit on the Leslies of Glenkirk, but you know what an honorable man he was. He has paid for his loyalty with his life. Mama writes that she will come to England before winter to live in the dower house at Cadby, which is hers. She asks that Autumn remain with us, or go to Henry until she comes. My half-brother, Patrick Leslie, is devastated by his papa's death, and chary of the responsibilites he must now take on as Glenkirk's new master. Mama feels he will better assume those obligations if she is not there for him to fall back upon. She is right, of course."

"But how will she be able to travel under the circumstances?" Bess fretted.

He chuckled. "She will find a way, I guarantee you, Bess. When Mama wants something, little dares to stand in her way. It is Autumn we must worry about. She is not above going to find Cromwell and attempting to kill him herself. We will have to dissuade her from any and all thoughts of instant revenge."

"And just how will you do that?" his wife asked him.

"Autumn is loyal first to the family. I shall tell her that any foolishness on her part will reflect on all of us. On the Leslies of Glenkirk, and on me and mine in particular, on India and Oxton, on the Southwoods, and the cousins at Clearfield and Blackthorne, on poor, plump old Great-Aunt Willow and her brood, *on us all*. She will swallow her anger, even if it kills her, for their sakes. That much I can guarantee. And when Mama arrives she will know just what to do to distract Autumn from any thought of revenge. Mama has always been clever that way," the duke said. "She is the only one who can control my little sister. Papa, heaven help him, adored and spoiled her terribly."

Autumn kept to her bedchamber for the next several days, her maidservant, Lily, bringing her meals which, for the first two days, were sent back uneaten. On the third day Autumn nibbled a bit from her tray, and by the end of the week she was once again eating. She came from her room to speak with Ian More before he began his long ride back to Scotland, and Glenkirk.

"Were you at Dunbar?" she asked him as they sat before the fire in the family hall.

"I was, m'lady," he answered her somberly.

"How many went, and how many came home?" she asked.

"Hundred and fifty rode out. Thirty-six rode home, m'lady," was his reply. " 'Twere only luck any of us came back."

"My father had no luck that day," Autumn noted aloud.

"Stuarts ain't nae been fortunate for our people, m'lady. Worse, this new king dinna even look like a Stuart. He be a dark laddie, m'lady, but he hae his family's charm. Yer da was nae happy to follow the Stuarts, but he were a man of honor, Jemmie Leslie, God bless him!"

Autumn nodded. "Aye," she said. Then she handed Ian More a sealed packet. "Give my mother this when you return. I will await her coming here at Queen's Malvern."

"Will we ever see ye at Glenkirk again, m'lady?" he asked her, his plain face concerned.

Autumn shook her head wearily. "I do not know, Ian More. I honestly do not know. It certainly did not occur to me when I left Glenkirk last April that I should never again see it. I know not what will happen to me now that my father is dead."

"The new duke will look after ye, m'lady," Ian said firmly.

"*Patrick?*" Autumn laughed for the first time since she had learned of her father's death. "Patrick will have all he can do to look after himself and Glenkirk, Ian More. Papa's death will have shocked my brother by its suddenness, but even more horrific for him will be his precipitous ascent to all the responsibility Glenkirk entails. Patrick will have no time for me. I am better off, though not greatly so, remaining in England with Charlie and Henry."

A small smile touched the clansman's lips. Lady Autumn Leslie was far more astute than he would have previously given her credit for; but then, lassie or nae, she was a Leslie. Leslie women were ever noted for being resourceful, and intelligent. Obviously the lass was finally growing up, and about time, he considered. He arose from his seat opposite her and bowed neatly. "I'll deliver yer message to yer mam as quickly as I can, m'lady. Hae ye any word for yer brother?"

"Tell him I wish him good fortune, and God bless," Autumn replied. "Tell him I hope we will meet again one day."

Ian More felt tears pricking his eyelids. *Damn Covenanters!* he thought irritably. Why could they not all be content to leave everything as it was instead of fighting, and costing Scotland more sons and future generations? Why did their beloved duchess and her daughter have to flee from their home? *Damn the Covenanters! Damn the Puritans, and damn the royal Stuarts as well!* He swallowed hard. "I'll deliver yer kind words to Duke Patrick," he told the girl. "Take care of yerself, m'lady."

"And you also, Ian More," Autumn replied. "God be with you on your return journey. Take no chances."

"I won't, m'lady," but they both knew he lied. Ian More would do whatever he had to, to return to Glenkirk and deliver his messages as quickly as he could.

It was almost the end of October when the Duke of Lundy and his eldest son finally traveled into the town of Worcester, a good day's ride from Queen's Malvern.

"We'll be back in time for your birthday, and I promise to bring you a fine gift," he told his sister.

"I'm not going to celebrate my birthday any longer," Autumn told him dourly. "At least not until I am a married woman. I shall remain eighteen until then, Charlie, but if you should like to bring me a gift because you love me, then I shall accept it," she told him, a twinkle in her eyes.

"You shall have your gift because I love you, sister," he assured her. He was relieved to see that Autumn was shedding her initial grief over her father's death. She would never forget Jemmie Leslie, but she realized life must continue onward. Hopefully their mother would arrive before winter set in, and together she and Autumn would heal. Charles Frederick Stuart could but imagine the sorrow the Duchess of Glenkirk was experiencing now. She had lost two husbands before she was twenty. His own father, Prince Henry Stuart, who had been her lover, had died two months after his own birth. She had been reluctant to remarry, but Jemmie Leslie would not take no for an answer. They had been wed for thirty-five years. How would she go on without him?

He rode to Worcester with his seven-year-old son by his side, surrounded by his own men-at-arms. Worcestershire was royalist country, but it did not hurt to be careful. About them the countryside lay peaceful in the midautumn sunshine. The fields were harvested, and the gleaners busily at work in them. The orchards had been picked clean of their apples and pears. Cattle and sheep grazed on the fading green hillsides. They reached the town just before sunset, putting up at The Crown and Stag, a large, comfortable inn where the duke was well known.

They went to church the following morning in the cathedral by the river. Freddie was wide-eyed at the great altar, the soaring arches, and the magnificent stained-glass windows. Afterwards they set about to find the thread his wife had requested. It was more difficult than he had anticipated, but finally in the shop of a small and insignificant mercer they found thread. A great deal of black, as Bess had warned him, but still a goodly supply of white and colors. The Duke of Lundy bought as much as the mercer would let him have, paying a premium gladly for it, however. Still, who knew when he would get into town again, or if this mercer would even still have thread.

He spent the rest of the day showing his young son about the beautiful town. Frederick Stuart had never been to Worcester before. In fact, he had been nowhere other than his relations' homes. Seeing his son had a good supper, Charlie put the lad to bed. Then he went to join his friends, which was his true reason for coming to Worcester. When they could, the local gentlemen met to exchange news and gossip about the civil war, and the latest of Cromwell's edicts. The men sat together in a discreet private room, safe from spies and protected by the innkeeper, who was an ardent royalist.

"They say Dunbar was a debacle, and the king was beaten by an army a quarter the size of his," Lord Hailey remarked. "How the hell could such a thing happen? The rumor is, the king will leave Scotland and go to his sister's court in Holland, or to his mother in Paris."

"In answer to your first question, Hailey, the Scots left their position of strength in the hills to come down to the plain. They did it once before at the first battle of Dunbar, several hundred years ago. They do not, it seems, learn from their mistakes. They lost that first battle for the same reason," the Duke of Lundy told his companions.

"How do you know so much about it, Charlie?" asked his friend, Lord Moreland.

"My mother sent a messenger down from Scotland to tell my sister that her father had been killed at Dunbar. The messenger was one of the few survivors from my stepfather's troop. He told me all about the battle. When Jemmie Leslie fell, his people took his body and withdrew. You know the reputation Cromwell's men have for piking the wounded, and stealing everything they can from the bodies. The Glenkirk men didn't intend to leave their duke to such tender mercies. They took his body, gathered up the horses, and made their way home."

"Jemmie Leslie dead? I can hardly believe it," Lord Moreland said.

"God rest him," Lord Hailey, who had been the Duke of Glenkirk's contemporary, replied. "I remember him trying to court your mother, and hunting with your grandfather and uncles. He was a good man! Damn Cromwell and his revolution!"

"You sound like my sister," Charlie said with a small chuckle, "although she refers to 'Cromwell and his pocky Roundheads.' "

"Not publicly, I hope," Lord Hailey said, concerned.

"I have warned her about curbing her tongue," the duke said. "It will be better when our mother arrives."

"Your mother is coming down from Scotland? God's blood, man! She'll never make it with all those parliamentary troopers running amuck about the countryside. Can you not stop her?" Lord Hailey demanded.

"Nay, I cannot," Charlie said simply. "She'll travel well protected, I assure you. As for the rumors of my cousin, Charles, fleeing Scotland, put no stock in it. Charles has not yet been properly crowned. He will remain at least until that notable event has taken place."

"But Cromwell's people hold Edinburgh," Lord Moreland reasoned, draining his tankard of wine.

"Scots kings are traditionally crowned at Scone, and our forces hold Scone," the duke answered.

"And when the king is formally crowned, will Scotland rise up to aid him?" Lord Plympton said.

"I don't know," Charlie said quietly, and he refilled his own tankard. "Scotland has been torn for years by religious strife. I would not be surprised if they had not had enough of war and desire nothing more than peace. If this desire is stronger than their nationalism, and loyalty to King Charles II, then we in England must take up the king's banner to rid ourselves of these Roundheads and Puritans."

The air was blue with the haze from their pipes as the men smoked their Virginia tobacco, drank wine and October ale, and talked among themselves. The English were, they knew, just as tired of war. Would anyone have the energy to overthrow Cromwell and the Parliamentarians? Most of them had not trusted the Scots Stuart kings who had followed old Queen Bess almost fifty years ago. Still, this second Charles Stuart had been born in England and was well liked. He was, to their minds, the Stuarts' first real English king. There were those sitting among them who considered that if the late Prince Henry, who had been King James I's eldest son, had been permitted to wed with the beautiful widowed Marchioness of Westleigh, now Jasmine Leslie, it would have been this Charles Frederick Stuart seated with them here tonight who would have been their king. And he would not have alienated the parliament and their Puritan allies the way his uncle, Charles I, had done. Charles Frederick Stuart would not have lost his head.

"So," grumbled Lord Plympton, "we must sit here helpless while we are governed by a bunch of commoners who have had the temerity to dissolve the House of Lords and claim to have abolished our monarchy. Bah, say I, to all of them!"

His companions laughed. They felt just as helpless as did their companion, but for now they were forced to wait for their king. Suddenly the door to their private room flew open to admit the plump and breathless Lord Billingsly.

"Get you home, those of you who can!" he gasped. "There are Roundhead troopers been seen in the area. And the rumor is, they are being led by Sir Simon Bates, the coldhearted devil who slaughtered Sir Gerald Croft's family over in Oxfordshire!"

"Who told you that, Billingsly?" Lord Moreland demanded.

"I saw the Roundheads myself as I rode toward the town. Believe you me, I got behind the nearest hedge as fast as I could," came the honest reply. "I'm not of a mind to make my wife a widow yet, gentlemen."

"She'd be the merriest widow in England, Puritans or no," murmured Lord Moreland to the Duke of Lundy.

"Damnation!" Charlie swore. "I can't leave for Queen's Malvern until the morning, for there is no moon to light the road. Bess is alone with Autumn and the children."

"Billingsly may be mistaken," Lord Moreland soothed his friend.

"I'm not!" came the indignant response. "Get home as quickly as you can, my lord duke, though they did not seem to be headed in your direction. Still, I would want to be with my family if they came my way."

"I'll go at first light," Charlie said.

"What about your little lad?" Moreland asked.

"Freddie comes with me," the duke said. "His mother would have a fit if I left him behind, even for safety's sake. Jesu! I hope those bastards don't come near Queen's Malvern. My sister will be unable to keep her temper, especially with her father now dead at Cromwell's hands. God have mercy on us all, gentlemen. We'll meet again when we can, though the lord knows when that will be."

The duke, his son, and their men departed Worcester just before first light the following morning. At that same time a cowherd in a field at Queen's Malvern saw the troop of soldiers coming toward him in the distance and ran as fast as he could for the house, shouting as he went to warn anyone within hearing of his voice.

"Roundheads! Roundheads!" the cowherd yelled at the top of his voice. "Roundheads coming over the hill!" He dashed through the kitchen gardens into the buttery with his news.

A serving wench ran up the stairs from the kitchens to warn the rest of the house. The duchess hurried from her bedchamber to the nurseries. The nursemaids already had Sabrina and little Willy up, and were dressing them as quickly as they could.

"Take the children into the gardens and hide," Bess said.

"No, Mama!" Sabrina cried. "I want to be with you!"

"You will go to the gardens with Mavis and Clara," the duchess said firmly, and hurried from the nurseries.

"What is happening?" Autumn came from her room with Lily in her wake.

"Roundheads," Bess said.

"In Worcester?"

"They send out raiding parties now and again to frighten the royalist population," her sister-in-law replied. "Perhaps you should go with the children."

"Nay, I'll stay with you, Bess. What of the valuables?"

"We buried them months ago in the rose gardens," Bess replied with a twinkle. "They'll probably steal what's here anyway, but they can. I'll risk no life or limb of any of our people in defense of *things.*"

There came a thunderous knocking on the door of the house as the two young women hurried down the staircase. Smythe, the majordomo, ran to answer the fierce summons, unbarring the door and drawing it open.

"Ye took yer own good time," the Roundhead trooper said, pushing Smythe into the hall. Then, raising his musket, he smashed it savagely into the majordomo's head.

The Duchess of Lundy screamed with horror as the faithful servant fell to the floor, blood pouring from his wound. She ran forward. "What have you done?" she cried. "He meant you no harm! Who is your commanding officer? I shall report you for this act of barbarity!"

The trooper raised his musket and fired his weapon. A bright blossom of scarlet bloomed over Bess's heart, and she collapsed to the floor quite dead. Autumn froze where she stood in the shadows of the hallway. She instinctively knew that her ability to remain silent was her key to survival. She could feel Lily behind her, shaking with fright. The trooper knelt over Bess's body and began pulling her rings from her fingers.

A second man stepped through the doorway of the house, but he was elegantly if soberly garbed. "What are you about, Watkins?" he demanded. He was tall with cold eyes.

"Just a bit of looting, sir. 'Tis permitted," he said, looking up at the gentleman.

Autumn stepped forward. "Are you this man's superior?" she said in haughty tones.

The gentleman bowed, removing his hat. "I am, madame."

"He has murdered two people in cold blood!" Autumn almost shouted. She bent and snatched Bess's rings from the surprised trooper. "Give me those, you thieving murderer!" Straightening herself up, she glared at the gentleman. "That is the Duchess of Lundy, whom this monster killed when she protested the murder of her servant. Smythe but opened the door, and this creature pushed into the hallway and battered him to death. How dare you allow your men to enter a peaceful house and wreak such havoc, sir!" She shoved her sister-in-law's rings into her pocket.

"And you are, madame?" the gentleman asked sternly.

"Lady Autumn Leslie, daughter of the Duke of Glenkirk, sister to the Duke of Lundy, whose house this is," Autumn replied. "Is it the policy of this so-called commonwealth to invade the houses of its citizens to loot and kill? And who the hell are you that you have such little control over your men?" she shouted at him.

"Sir Simon Bates, madame, at your service," he responded, his eyes sweeping over the young woman. She was very beautiful, her dark hair tumbling about the quilted burgundy satin of her dressing gown.

"What are you going to do about this animal?" Autumn demanded.

"He will be punished, I assure you, madame," Sir Simon responded.

"An eye for an eye," Autumn said grimly. "I want it done now! Give me your pistol, sir, and I will do it myself!"

"Would you really?" Sir Simon was suddenly amused. The girl was distraught, of course. She would not really kill Watkins in cold blood, but to appease her, he handed her his pistol. She probably wouldn't even know how to use a weapon. Then, to his great surprise, Autumn cocked the pistol and, jamming the barrel between the trooper's eyes, shot him dead. *"My God!"* he said, astounded, as she calmly handed him back his pistol.

Watkins's body hit the floor with a muffled thump.

"You thought I wouldn't do it, didn't you?" Autumn said quietly.

"Who taught you to shoot?" Sir Simon asked her, amazed by what had just happened.

"My father, whom your people killed at Dunbar," Autumn answered him coldly. "Are you going to arrest me? I don't care if you do!"

"I should," Sir Simon said slowly, "but I will not, madame. As you have so succinctly put it, *an eye for an eye*. Besides, Watkins was of little import. He was but cannon fodder, and would have been killed sooner or later. And then, too, there is the matter of the pistol, which I gave you. While I did indeed not believe you would actually shoot the scum, I must accept my responsibility for Watkins's execution."

"Remove him from this house," Autumn said in hard tones. "I will not allow him to be buried on the same lands in which poor Bess will be interred. Dig your grave by the side of the public road. This animal has widowed a good man and orphaned three children, sir. Take him, and be gone from Queen's Malvern!" Autumn could feel her legs beginning to tremble, but she stiffened her spine. These Roundheads and their arrogant captain would not make her cry.

"Where is the plate?" Sir Simon asked.

"How should I know?" she replied angrily. "I am but a guest in this house, sir. My sister-in-law was prepared to let you take whatever you desired. She said no life was worth mere *things*, but you have taken two innocent lives. And having done so, you are now prepared to rob the dead?" She shrugged scornfully. "Take whatever you want, sir. I will not impede your thievery."

"Madame, your tongue is sharper than my sword," he told her.

She stared coldly at him, and he realized with surprise that one of her eyes was a clear leaf green and the other a bright turquoise blue. Fascinated, he wished suddenly that they had met in another time and place. He bowed politely to her. "I will leave this house in peace, madame, but I must take some of your livestock to feed my men."

Becket, who was Smythe's assistant, came running into the hall, shouting, "They've fired the east wing, m'lady!" He stopped short, seeing the three bodies, two of whom he recognized. "Oh, Jesu, God!" he said, and his glance went to Autumn. "M'lady?"

"Form a bucket brigade and do what you can to save the house," Autumn said grimly. Then she turned to Sir Simon. "Take your dead and anything else you want, *but go!* You have done enough damage here for a lifetime, but your life will be worth nothing when my brother returns and sees his wife murdered, his house a ruin!"

"Your brother is a Stuart, is he not?" Sir Simon said.

Autumn nodded.

"Then I feel no guilt for what has happened here today, Lady Autumn. You Scots and your Stuarts have been a blight upon England since you inherited old Bess's throne. I feel no shame for the death of a Stuart, madame," he told her coldly.

Autumn slapped him as hard as she could, leaving a large red welt upon Sir Simon Bates's handsome face. "My sister-in-law, sir, was English, as is my brother, for all his paternity. Charles was born here in this house. As for Bess, she was the Earl of Welk's youngest daughter. He is one of your own. I shall be certain to tell him exactly how his innocent child died at the hands of your Roundheads, Sir Simon. You think to terrify us with these raids, but all you have succeeded in doing is hardening our resolve to restore the monarchy. *God Save the King!*"

"If I were not aware that you are suffering from shock, madame, I would slay you myself for the traitor you are," he replied, rubbing his injured cheek. "Others will not be so caring of you, lady."

"If I had a weapon, sir, I should slay you for the traitor you are," Autumn answered him bravely.

Sir Simon laughed in spite of himself. What a bewitching little wildcat Lady Autumn Leslie was. He envied the man who would one day bed her, and wished he might be that man. "Good day, madame," he said, bowing once again as he put his hat back on his head. Then he bent to hoist Watkins's body over his broad shoulder, departing through the open door.

She stood stock still, watching the Roundheads and their captain as they rode down the gravel driveway of Queen's Malvern, driving several sheep and cattle ahead of them, and chickens, turkeys, ducks, and geese squawking indignantly as they were tied and slung over saddles. Her gaze moved to the east wing, where the servants were gallantly battling to save that part of the house and prevent the fire from spreading any farther.

"Autumn, what has happened?" Her niece, Sabrina, was unexpectedly by her side. Then, seeing her mother, Sabrina screamed. *"Mama!"* She clutched at Autumn, burying her face in her aunt's skirts. "Mama," she sobbed.

"She is dead, Brie," Autumn said, and hearing the words aloud from her own lips, she collapsed onto the floor, cradling her niece while they both wept uncontrollably.

It was there Charles Frederick Stuart found them when he finally reached his home less than an hour later.

Chapter

2

*B*ess! His beautiful blue-eyed Bess lay crumpled in a heap upon the dark polished wooden floor of the entry; the blood on her bodice dried black now; her eyes wide, the image of shock and disbelief still lingering in them. Within his chest his heart was suddenly crushed, and then an emptiness such as he had never felt swept over Charles Frederick Stuart. His glance took in Smythe, also dead. His sister and his daughter huddled together weeping with sorrow. His eldest son was frozen by his side, his small hand clutching his father's.

"What has happened here?" He pushed the words up through his constrictred throat, his tongue almost becoming entangled in them. He wanted to shriek his outrage, and howl to the heavens at this terrible injustice. *Bess! Bess! Bess!* Her name echoed in his brain.

Autumn looked up, her eyes swollen and red. "Roundheads," she said, and nothing more. Then she began to shake, finally collapsing unconscious next to her dazed and benumbed niece.

The Duke of Lundy picked up his young daughter. She was cold but half-conscious with her shock. The servants were beginning to crowd into the hall. Many were sobbing with both fright at what had happened and relief to see the duke, their master, returned from Worcester.

Becket, with a wave of his hand, called forth young Sabrina's nursemaid, Mavis, taking the child from her father and transferring her into the woman's arms. "Take Lady Sabrina to her bedchamber and see to her welfare," he said in a very no-nonsense voice. "You two!" He pointed at a pair of young footmen. "Remove Smythe from the entrance to be prepared for burial. Lily! Don't just stand there gaping, girl. See to your mistress. Samuel! Peter! Carry Lady Autumn to her chamber! Clara, take Master Frederick upstairs. My lord, if you will come with me, I will try and explain what has happened here this morning. Where is the duchess's tiring woman? Sybll, stay with your mistress until the master decides what is to be done. The rest of you, back to your duties!

The duke followed Becket to the relative quiet of his library. The servant poured him a generous dollop of smoky, peat-flavored whiskey, shoving the crystal tumbler into his master's hand.

"Forgive my boldness, my lord, but with Smythe dead I felt, as his assistant, that I had to make some order out of the chaos. I am at your service, and will tell you what little I know. Just after dawn a cowherd spotted a troop of Roundheads making their way toward Queen's Malvern. He gave the alarm. Her ladyship ordered the children hidden with their servants in the gardens. When I had finished overseeing this duty I discovered some of the blackguards had entered the east wing and, finding nothing they might loot, fired it. I ran to tell her ladyship, but she was already dead. Lady Autumn orderd a bucket brigade and sent me back to oversee it. I fear I can tell you nothing else."

"Did my daughter see her mother murdered?" the duke asked.

"She was not in the hallway, my lord, when I was there," Becket replied. "There was, however, a third victim, a Roundhead soldier. I must assume the captain of the troop removed him. He was obviously quite dead. He lay on his back, a bullet hole directly between his eyes, my lord. The Roundhead captain was a gentleman, my lord." Becket refilled the duke's tumbler, which was already empty.

"Then my sister is the only person who can tell us all that happened here this morning," the duke said slowly. He focused his gaze on Becket. "Your loyalty is appreciated, Becket, and you will, of course, assume Smythe's position permanently. Have my wife's women lay her out in her wedding gown. Have a grave dug in the family graveyard. We will bury her tomorrow. Inform me when my sister is conscious and able to speak with me."

"Yes, my lord," Becket said, and then he withdrew.

Alone, Charles Frederick Stuart put his head in his hands and wept. How could this have happened? The county of Worcester was a royalist enclave, a place of safety from Cromwell and his bloody Roundheads. Not any longer, obviously. And that fool, Billingsly, who had told him the Roundheads were headed in a different direction! *Bess!* His sweet Bess was dead and gone. He would never again hear her voice or lay with her in their bed. Never again would he caress her little round breasts that had always responded so well to their shared passion. *Bess was dead.* Taken from him in a war of rebellion that had seen his uncle murdered by the Parliament and his cousins in exile.

He had avoided taking sides in this civil strife even as his mother had advised, even as his brother, Henry Lindley, was doing. The royal Stuarts had always loved him and treated him with exceptional kindness from the moment of his birth. Still, for his family's sake he had remained neutral. Now, however, he had no choice. Now he would take sides, for with his wife's murder the Roundheads had forced his hand. So be it, Charlie thought grimly, but no matter how many of them he killed—*and he would kill*—it would not bring back his lovely young wife. Bess was gone from him forever.

He stood by her graveside the next day in an autumn rain, his three children by his side. His sister, however, had not yet been revived from her swoon, although she was showing signs of returning consciousness. Sabrina and Frederick were somber. Baby William did not understand what had happened. He would have no memories of Bess at all but those they gave him, the duke thought sadly. He took comfort in the fact that Bess was buried next to her great-grandparents, Adam de Marisco and Skye O'Malley. They would watch over her, he knew.

Autumn Leslie finally revived the morning after her sister-in-law's burial. Charlie came and sat by her side, taking her small hand in his.

"Do you remember what happened, lass?" he asked her.

Autumn nodded; then she told him.

"Becket said the trooper was shot," Charlie gently probed. "Did his captain execute him?"

"Nay," Autumn told him. "I did."

"*You?*" The duke was not certain whether he should believe her or not. It had been, after all, a terrible experience.

"I said I wanted him killed for murdering Smythe and Bess," Autumn explained. "Sir Simon laughed at me, but he handed me his pistol and told me to go ahead and kill him. He didn't think I would, Charlie. He thought me a silly girl, hysterical with what had happened; but I took his weapon and slew the monster who had killed Bess and Smythe! Sir Simon was very surprised. I told him to arrest me, but he said the trooper was cannon fodder and would have died sooner or later. He said he accepted the responsibility for his death, for it had been he who had foolishly given me his pistol. Then he took the body and left. It was then that Sabrina came and saw her mother lying there. Oh, Charlie! I hate this Commonwealth, these Roundheads, and pocky Cromwell. *I hate them!*"

He sighed deeply. "We buried Bess yesterday," he said.

"How long have I been unconscious?" Autumn gasped.

"Three days," her brother answered.

"My God!" She was stunned by his revelation.

"As soon as you are well enough to travel, Autumn, I will take you to Cadby. Perhaps Mother will be there by the time we arrive. Then I am taking the children to Glenkirk to Patrick, for safety's sake."

"Charlie! What do you mean to do?"

"Fight for my king," her brother answered her. "I mean to join my cousin, King Charles II, in Scotland, little sister."

She nodded, understanding completely. "You have been left with no other choice," she said. "What of Queen's Malvern?"

"I will close it up and leave but a skeleton staff to watch over it. I shall pay the servants for two years, and they shall all have their places when this is over, should they want them. They are safer without my presence than with it, now that the Roundheads have decided all Stuarts are the enemy. They will learn that they have made a bad mistake, making an enemy of me," Charles Frederick Stuart said.

"Mama will not be happy with your decision," Autumn said softly.

"I know," Charlie answered, "but I cannot allow my wife's death to go unavenged, nor can I now stand by as the monarchy is rent asunder by these traitors. Cromwell and his ilk are little better than the others, sister. My uncle was a good man but a bad king. Those who had his favor, and surrounded him, keeping him from the truth, were every bit as abusive of their power as the men who now claim to govern England. But these men have murdered God's annointed king and persecuted our good Anglican church. I see now, as I did not see before, that they must be stopped!"

"I am in complete agreement with you, brother, but you know what Mama will say. Particularly now that our father is dead in defense of the Stuarts."

"I will send a messenger to Cadby, saying that you are coming to be with Mama," the duke said. "The rest of it I prefer to tell Henry and his family myself. It is not something one can write in a letter, although I must send a message to Bess's parents in Dorset. Welk and his wife are now openly Puritans, but they are still Bess's family."

"Do not tell them what you intend to do with the children," Autumn said. "They will want their daughter's offspring, but they must not have them, Charlie. They must not be allowed to make Brie and Freddie and wee Willie into joyless, condemning psalm-singers."

He nodded. "I shall tell them only the truth—that Bess was murdered by a Roundhead trooper in defense of one of her servants. It will be enough," the duke said with a grim smile.

On the following day the duke sent one of his own servants off to Dorset to inform his in-laws of their daughter's demise. The messenger was instructed to return at his leisure with the Earl of Welk's response. Becket would then write to the Earl of Welk, explaining that his master and his children had departed Queen's Malvern, that they would be traveling, and that the duke had not said when he would return. Charlie knew that when he explained his plan to his mother and brother Henry, they would understand and not betray either his whereabouts or that of the children to Johnathan Lightbody.

The day after the messenger had been dispatched to Dorset, the Duke of Lundy, his youngest sister, his children, and several servants departed Queen's Malvern. Gazing back at the beautiful house with its ivy-covered and ancient brick walls, they all wondered if they would ever see it again. To protect their destination, the servants would not be dismissed until December, when they would be given their two-years' stipend and the assurance of their places when the duke returned home to Queen's Malvern one day.

"The east wing doesn't look too bad," Autumn said softly.

The duke stared at the blackened walls and smashed lead-paned windows. "The servants rescued most of the paintings," he said bleakly. Then he turned his horse toward his brother's estate, a two-day ride across the countryside.

Cadby, home to the Marquess of Westleigh, was a fine old brick house set above the banks of the river Avon, its green lawns running down to the water. Henry Lindley greeted his brother warmly and hugged his sister, exclaiming over her beauty effusively.

"We'll have to find you a fine husband," he teased her.

"*Where?*" Autumn demanded. "Certainly not in the England of today, unless, Henry, you expect me to wed a sober-sided Puritan."

"Heaven forfend!" her eldest brother exclaimed.

"Is mama here yet?" Charlie asked his sibling.

"She arrived two days ago and is already well ensconced in the dower house," Henry answered. "God's blood, Charlie! I have never seen her so despondent. When you sent word you were coming, I rejoiced. Perhaps your presence, and that of Autumn, can cheer her up." Then, suddenly, the Marquis of Westleigh looked about, saying, "Where is Bess?"

"That is why we are here," the duke told his elder brother. "Freddie and I were in Worcester. Roundheads, led by that devil, Sir Simon Bates, invaded Queen's Malvern one morning. Bess, and my majordomo, Smythe, were killed in cold blood. Autumn shot the trooper who did it." Then he continued to tell Henry in detail what had transpired that terrible day.

"Sabrina and William?"

"Saw nothing, thank God! I am taking them all to Patrick, and then I shall join the king," Charlie said quietly.

Henry nodded. "I understand," he said. "You have no choice now in the matter. Ahh, Charlie, I am so sorry!"

"Sorry for what?" Their mother, Jasmine Leslie, entered the room, and immediately her daughter flew into her mother's embrace.

"Mama!" Autumn burst into tears.

"What is this? What is this?" Jasmine demanded, first hugging her child and then setting her back to look into her face. The now Dowager Duchess of Glenkirk was as beautiful at sixty as she had been at forty, but the look in her eyes was bleak.

"Come into the Great Hall," Henry said, "and Charlie will tell us everything, Mama." He quickly instructed his servants to see the children to the nurseries with his own brood, and bring wine and biscuits for his family. His wife, he explained, was not home, being out tending to some sick tenants, but even as they settled themselves in the Great Hall of Cadby, Rosamund Wyndham Lindley hurried in with a smile, greeting her guests and fussing at her servants to bring the refreshments in a more timely fashion.

"They do take advantage of Henry," she said with a twinkle. Rosamund was Henry's second wife, and the mother of his children. The marquess's first wife, his beautiful cousin, Cecily Burke, had died six months after their wedding, when she fell from her horse as she took a particularly high jump, breaking her neck. Cecily had died instantly, and Henry had gone into shock, refusing to leave Cadby, seeing only his brother, Charlie, and his older sister, India, as he mourned his young wife.

Two years after Cecily's death, the Marquess of Westleigh was invited to the wedding of the Earl of Langford's heir. Charlie, who had also been invited, prevailed upon his elder sibling to go.

"You can't mourn forever," he said bluntly. "Mama certainly never did."

So Henry Lindley had gone to the wedding at RiversEdge and, to his astonishment, met the girl who was to be the love of his life. Rosamund Wyndham was, at almost sixteen, not ready to consider marriage, but the Marquess of Westleigh knew what he wanted. God rest his sweet Cecily, but he was finally ready to get on with his life. He courted Rosamund with a mixture of charm, humor, and determination. Unable to resist him, Rosamund wed Henry Lindley shortly after her seventeenth birthday. She had ruled his heart and his house ever after.

They were barely settled about the roaring fire when the dowager duchess, mentally counting heads, said, "Where is Bess?"

"She is dead," Charlie told his mother, and then proceeded to relate the entire tale.

When he had finished Jasmine Leslie looked at her youngest child, amazed. "You shot a Roundhead trooper?" she said.

Autumn nodded.

"God's blood!" the dowager duchess exclaimed. "I remember a time when my grandmother did a similar deed to save my life, and that of my children. 'Twas a brave act, as was yours. I am proud of you!"

"Surely, Mama, you do not condone murder," the Marquess of Westleigh said, shocked at what his sister had done.

"The man was scum and had murdered both Bess and a trusted servant," the dowager duchess said. "Autumn was protecting herself, for who knows what this Sir Simon Bates would have done otherwise. The fact that he accepted responsibility for the trooper's death shows my daughter proved to this villain that she is a strong girl, and not to be taken advantage of by any!"

"Sir Simon Bates is known to be totally ruthless. What if he holds the death of this man over Autumn, over the family?" Henry said in worried tones.

"How can he?" Autumn spoke up. "The only people in the hallway of the house were the trooper, Sir Simon, and myself. What proof could he possibly offer for my act? I am but an innocent and unmarried maiden, and certainly incapable of such a terrible deed. If we should ever see Sir Simon again, and he accused me, I should believe he was attempting to extort moneys from us, as we are known to be a wealthy family. Or perhaps the threat of such a tale would be an attempt to force me into marriage with him. A wealthy, well-connected wife could not harm Sir Simon's future when the king is restored to his kingdom. Particularly a wife whose brother is the king's first cousin." Autumn smiled sweetly at her astounded relatives, but her mother laughed.

"You are quick, my child," she said with a chuckle. She turned to Henry. "You fret too much, my dear. Autumn is perfectly correct. There is no proof that she killed that trooper, and no other witnesses than herself and this Sir Simon Bates. I expect he is still in a bit of a shock that a slip of a girl could be so brave, and remember, he did give her his weapon and encourage her to dispatch Bess's murderer. He'll say nothing, I assure you all. And now, Charlie"—she looked directly at her second son— "what are you about?"

"I have closed Queen's Malvern up and I am taking my children to Glenkirk. Then I will declare for the king, Mama." He stood before the fireplace, legs apart, his hands upon his hips in a gesture of defiance.

Jasmine sighed deeply. "Of course you will, Charlie. You are Henry Stuart's son, and but for an accident of birth would have been England's king. You have attempted to remain neutral in this strife. But you can no longer be undecided, and Cromwell's ilk has forced your hand. I understand, my son. I am not happy about this turn of events, but I do understand. You can do nothing else now. But why take the children to Scotland?"

"Because left here, they would endanger Henry and his family. Cromwell's people have not hesitated to use children as pawns. We cannot forget poor little Princess Elizabeth, imprisoned in Carisbrooke Castle, who has only recently died because these godly Puritans did not properly care for the poor girl. Nay, Charlie's children will be safer, and more than likely forgotten, at Glenkirk."

"And when his in-laws come calling, which they will," Henry asked, "what the hell are we to say to them?"

"You will lie, Henry," his mother instructed him, "and say you do not know where your niece and nephews are. You will admit that

Charlie came here, but you will say you know not where he was going, for he refused to tell you, fearing to endanger your family. It is a small lie, and a perfectly plausible explanation. The Earl of Welk has neither power nor the funds to pursue the matter. Common sense will tell him the children are safe in their father's care. He may bluster and blow, but there is nothing he can do but accept that with his daughter's murder, his grandchildren are gone until this nonsense is settled," the Dowager Duchess of Glenkirk concluded firmly.

"He will come," Henry said gloomily, "and you will deal with him, Mama, for you know I am very bad at lying."

She laughed. "So was your father, my dear, but you will have to deal with Welk, for I shall more than likely not be here."

"*What?*" Both the duke and the marquis spoke at once.

"England is a very dour place right now, my dears. My responsibility as a mother is not done until Autumn is properly wed. We will find no bridegroom here for her, but perhaps in France or Holland we will. Do not argue with me, my lads. Your sister turned nineteen yesterday and is no longer in the first flower of her youth. Her beauty and her wealth will, of course, find us the right man, but there is little time before she will be considered past her prime, and it will be harder to make a brilliant match," the dowager duchess told them.

"We are going abroad?" Autumn smiled suddenly. "Oh, yes, Mama! That is the answer! Charlie said you would have the solution to my problem, and you have found it!" She hugged her mother happily.

"So," Jasmine Leslie said, "you have been discussing this situation with your sister, Charlie."

"Rather, Mama, she has been bemoaning the fact that she was about to turn nineteen, a fact we entirely overlooked, being on the road."

"I told you," Autumn said firmly, "that I would celebrate no more natal days until I was wed."

Her family all laughed, but Autumn was adamant and shook her head at them.

"When will you leave?" Henry asked their mother.

"In a week or two, when my servants are rested from our flight from Scotland," the dowager duchess answered. "It was not an easy trip, what with being stopped half-a-dozen times a day by Cromwell's people and having the coach searched over and over. And remember, my servants are not young any longer." She arose from the chair in which she had been sitting. "Come with me, Autumn. You look worn from your adventures and should rest before the evening meal." With her daughter in tow, Jasmine left the Great Hall of Cadby.

"When her servants are rested," Henry repeated. "She could barely stand when she got here several days ago. Patrick sent a troop of men-at-arms with her, and a damned good thing too. They managed to skirt around Edinburgh, but in the Borders they had a bit of a run-in with a troop of Roundheads. Her coach outran them, but it was quite a struggle. Her driver took a musketball in the shoulder, but he never faltered. Fergus More-Leslie is a tough bastard," the marquis said admiringly. "And Adali! My God, Charlie, the man is close to eighty, but he took the reins from Fergus so he could bind up his wound, and he brought the coach through the worst of the attack. None of them are young anymore. Yet here they are, leaving home and hearth for a new adventure."

"It has always been said that Mama is more like our great-grandmother than any of her children or other grandchildren," Charlie noted. "Are the Glenkirk men still here?"

"Aye," the marquis replied.

"Good! They can accompany me and the children to Scotland, then. We'll take Mama's coach for the children and their servant. I've just brought Biddy. I had to leave Clara and Mavis behind. Both have lads at Queen's Malvern. Who knows how long my bairns will be at Glenkirk. I couldn't be burdened with a household under the circumstances," Charlie explained.

"Can this Biddy ride a horse?" the marquis asked.

"Aye. Why?" his brother inquired.

"Don't take the coach, Charlie. You'll make better time and have a better chance of getting through without difficulties a-horse. The

coach is cumbersome. One of the Glenkirk men will take William
with him, leaving the serving woman free to concentrate on her
journey. Brie and Freddie have been riding since they were three. It
will be tiring, but they will survive it, I'm certain," his brother advised.

"Perhaps you're right," the Duke of Lundy replied, nodding
thoughtfully. "Brie and Freddie will think it a game."

"When will you go?" Henry asked.

"I'll give the children two days to rest and then we must be on
our way. I cannot take the chance that Welk will find us here, and I
would be over the border as quickly as possible. The more distance I put between the children and England, the safer I will
feel."

Henry Lindley agreed, and while he loved his younger brother,
he was not sorry to see him depart two days later. He and his wife
had five children of their own who must be considered. And there
were Cadby and its people to be protected as well. Unlike his father,
who had been a charming and swashbuckling gentleman, life had
taught Henry Lindley to be cautious, which was not a bad trait in
this day and age.

The Dowager Duchess of Glenkirk bid her second son a tender
farewell. "Try not to get yourself killed, Charlie," she said. "God's
blood! You so resemble your father! Remember, you are all I have
left of him, Charles Frederick Stuart. I am not of a mind to give you
up yet." She kissed him on both cheeks. "You can reach me by
sending your messages to Belle Fleurs. Even if we are not there,
they will know how to get in touch with me." She kissed him again,
and then turned her attention to her three Stuart grandchildren.
"You must be in charge of your brothers, Sabrina. Obey your uncle
Patrick when you can, though he's likely to let you run wild."
Jasmine kissed the little girl.

"Yes, Grandmama," Lady Sabrina Stuart said, and she curtsied.

"And you, Frederick Henry Stuart, remember who you are. Obey
your uncle and watch over your sister and baby brother," she instructed.

"I will, Grandmama," Freddie said, kissing her hand.

"Gracious! That was as elegantly done as any courtier, laddie," she praised him, and then kissed both his cheeks.

"And now you, William Charles Stuart, obey your elders and try to be a good lad."

"Yeth, Mam," the little boy lisped.

Jasmine smiled softly, then bending, she kissed the child. Straightening, she looked at them a final time and said, "God go with you all, my dears." Then she reentered the house, not wanting to see them ride off.

"Until the Roundheads came, it was a lovely summer, Charlie," Autumn said. "I'm sorry it had such a sad end to it." Then she flung her arms about her brother and kissed him. "I will miss you."

"Don't wed with just any man, little sister," he advised her. "Marry for love and love alone, Autumn." Kissing her, he turned away and mounted his horse, joining his family.

Autumn had already bid her nephews and niece a fond farewell. Now she stood with Henry as the Duke of Lundy and his children, in the company of the Glenkirk men-at-arms, rode away from Cadby. The brothers had said their good-byes previously.

"I hate Cromwell and his pocky Roundheads!" she said softly as the riders disappeared around a bend in the road.

"So you say quite frequently, little sister," Henry remarked dryly. "Come inside now. The day is chill, and if you and Mama are to leave for France shortly, you must be healthy and well."

"Have you ever been to France, Henry?" she asked him.

"Several times," he told her. "You will enjoy it. I believe Mama means to spend the winter in the Loire at Belle Fleurs."

"Oh," Autumn said, sounding disappointed. "I was hoping to go to Paris."

"Do not fret, sister," her brother advised. "Mama will want you to acclimate yourself to France, give you time to get used to speaking French instead of English, have a wonderful and most fashionable wardrobe made for you and, like any good general planning a strategy, learn all she can about the current French court. Her wealth, and her grandfather's French relations, will be invaluable to you, Autumn, which is why she wants you to meet them first. Trust

Mama to do what is right, and I will wager a year from now, if not sooner, you will be a happily married young woman," Henry Lindley assured his sister as, linking his arm in hers, they returned to the house.

It rained for the next week, and Autumn thought often of her brother Charlie, on the road north with his children. Actually, the weather would be of help to them, provided they didn't catch an ague. Only someone in a great hurry, or in desperation, would ride in such weather.

The day before she and her mother were to leave for France, the Earl of Welk arrived, angrily demanding to know what had happened to his daughter's children, and where they were now.

The Marquess of Westleigh welcomed the angry man into his Great Hall and then told him, "My mother will discuss the matter with you, my lord. I know little, if anything, but that my sister-in-law was murdered in cold blood by parliamentary forces. My youngest sister, Lady Autumn Leslie, was there and can tell you what happened that day, but you must speak gently to her. The shock of that day still pains her."

The Earl of Welk was a spare man of medium height and sallow complexion. His severe black garb did little to alleviate an impression of meanness. He turned to the Dowager Duchess of Glenkirk. "Well, madame?"

"My son and our grandchildren were here several weeks ago, but where they are now, my lord, I have not the faintest notion. I told Charles that I did not want to know, in order that I might protect his safety, and that of *our* shared grandchildren. Surely you can understand."

"Your son is not fit to care for *my* grandchildren, madame!" came the angry reply.

"Indeed, my lord, and what makes you think such a thing?" Jasmine demanded in haughty tones. "My son is their father."

"Your son is profligate, a wastrel," the earl answered.

Jasmine laughed. "Even in his callow youth Charlie could neither be called profligate nor wastrel by any. And once he had met your daughter, my lord, once his heart was engaged, there was no one for him but Bess. He was loyal, loving, and faithful to her from the moment they met, and you, my lord, know it well."

"My daughter would be alive had she not been wed to your son," the earl responded.

"Your daughter spent the happiest years of her young life with Charlie and their children. She is dead not because of my son but because of the actions of one of your *godly* parliamentary troopers. They burst into her home and battered her majordomo to death. When Bess protested, this devil, without a word, shot her dead. My own daughter witnessed the entire incident and would, herself, have been killed had the captain of these men not entered the house. When he did, the trooper was stripping the rings from your dead child's stiffening fingers. These are the creatures you and your ilk have loosed on England, my lord! Thieves and murderers of the innocent."

"The Stuarts are not innocent," the earl muttered.

"The Stuarts, for all their royalty, are like the rest of us, John Lightbody. They are human, and subject to human frailty. The king was a bad king, but he was a good man. You were not satisfied with deposing him. Nay, your ilk had to murder God's own annointed, and then mouth piously to excuse your crime. Shame on all of you!"

"It is easy to see where your heart lies, madame," the Earl of Welk said grimly.

"My heart, sir, lies in a tomb at Glenkirk with my husband, who died at Dunbar in defense of king and country. I espouse no cause, nor did my not-so-royal Stuart son. As to our grandchildren, as I have told you, I do not know where Charlie has taken them, but wherever it is, it is for their safety's sake. Their surname would, it now appears, have made them targets of your *godly* parliamentarians. Given the way in which they treated Charlie's little cousin, the Princess Elizabeth, I understand the necessity to hide his own children. Your people did not care properly for the princess. She died of exposure, for you would not allow her chambers to be properly heated; and she died of hunger, for she was ill fed. Is that a fate you wish for Sabrina, Frederick, and wee William, my lord?"

"In the care of my wife and myself, loyal citizens, our three grandchildren would be safe," he told her.

Jasmine laughed scornfully. "You are truly a fool if you believe that, my lord. The children belong with their father, and that is where they are. Do not make an enemy of my son, sir, for one day, I guarantee you, the king will be restored to his throne, and when that time comes, you will be glad of a friend at court who is the king's dearly beloved cousin."

"The Stuarts will never return to England's throne," the Earl of Welk said.

Again Jasmine laughed. "Oh, but they will, sir. I do not know how long it will take, but they will return to rule England one day. Be certain you are not on their personal list of traitors."

"I shall go to the courts!" the earl cried, frustrated.

"Go then. I'm certain your parliamentary courts will be eager to learn of the unjustified murder of an innocent woman by one of their soldiers, who then attempted to steal from her. Already two of the commandments you hold dear are broken: thou shalt not kill and thou shalt not steal. My daughter is not the only witness to this crime. Sir Simon Bates was captain to the troop that invaded Queen's Malvern. He, personally, executed the soldier involved. He cannot deny it lest he perjure himself. Your *godly* officers would not lie, I am certain."

"Madame, there is something wicked about you, but to my regret your logic is flawless. If you hear from your son, will you contact me?"

"Alas, sir, I will not be able to do so. My daughter and I leave for France shortly. I could not remain in Scotland, for my memories overwhelmed me. The dower house here at Cadby is mine, of course, and I thought to end my days here, but again, I am engulfed by my remembrances. My grandmother left me a small home in the French countryside. My daughter and I shall go there to mourn the loss of James Leslie. My son, Henry, however, will, of course, send any word to you that he receives. Do not wait for it, though, sir. I suspect Charlie will not reveal his hidey-hole to any, lest his children be endangered again." She smiled sweetly at him and held out her hand for him to kiss.

He was dismissed and he knew it. His gloved hand took her beringed one, and his lips offered the customary salute to her rank. "I thank you, madame, for seeing me," he said, "and I bid you good day."

"Good day, my lord," Jasmine replied. "My felicitations to your exemplary lady wife." Then Jasmine turned and departed the Great Hall of Cadby.

The Earl of Welk turned to the Marquess of Westleigh. "Your mother is a formidable woman, my lord."

Henry restrained a smile. "She is, sir," he replied with the utmost seriousness.

"You will contact me?"

"Should I receive any communication from my brother, sir, of course," the marquis responded immediately. Not that he meant to keep such a promise, but he must appear to be sympathetic and co-operative. His own family had to be considered, but he would never betray any of his siblings. His mother was correct in her estimation of Johnathan Lightbody, Earl of Welk. He had neither the power nor the wealth, nor powerful friends who would pursue the issue for him. Still, Henry Lindley considered, there was no use making enemies. With charm and a smile, he bid the Earl of Welk a good day, watching as Lightbody left his home.

"You are clever," his sister Autumn said, arising from her chair by the fire, where she had been seated the entire time. "Mama is clever in a haughty way, as her royal heritage dictates, but you, Henry, are clever in a different way. I will wager that Bess's father actually believes that you will contact him if Charlie should send a message to you. He left you in a far calmer state than our mother left him," she concluded with a chuckle.

Henry smiled a slow smile. "There is no sense making enemies one does not need," he said. "Now Welk will return to his wife with a reasonable explanation for his failure to obtain custody of Charlie's children. The man is a fool to believe our brother would relinquish his offspring to them under any circumstances." He shrugged. "Where is Mama now?"

"Back in her house, overseeing the repacking of her trunks. She will leave some of her possessions there, I believe, as it is now her home in England. Tell me about Belle Fleurs, Henry. You were there once, I know. Is it big? Is it pretty?" Autumn asked her eldest brother.

"Aye, we were there as children," he said, "when Mama was attempting to avoid marrying your father because she was annoyed that King James and his wife had ordered it. She had no idea how deeply he loved her and hid us all there until one day he found us." The Marquess of Westleigh smiled with his memories. "I was close to seven then, and India eight, Fortune five, and Charlie still in nappies. It was long ago, and yet it seems like yesterday," he chuckled. "What fun we had there! Mama allowed us to run wild, which we did. We almost forgot our native tongue. Then our great-grandmother came, with news that our great-grandfather had died; and close on her heels was your father, whom we quickly began to call Papa, because the truth was, we all wanted a father most desperately.

"Belle Fleurs is small and exquisite. I remember it had wonderful gardens. It is near Archambault, which as you know is the home of our French relations. I do not think Mama's been back to Belle Fleurs in over thirty years. I know, however, she has always kept staff on to see the place was kept up. I believe India and her family went there one summer, and Charlie took Bess there for their honeymoon. Still, it has been years since the family went to Belle Fleurs for any extended stay. I imagine it will now be your home, Autumn."

"I will return to England and Scotland when the king is restored," Autumn said.

"You might wed a Frenchman," her brother told her "and besides, no matter what Charlie and Mama say, it will take much skill and not just a few years to remove Master Cromwell from his place and restore Charles II to his throne."

"But the majority of the people hate pocky Cromwell and his minions!" Autumn said.

"The people, dear little sister, have no real power, whatever the politicians may say. The people do what they are convinced to believe is the right thing to do. Power, Autumn, is the headiest aphrodisiac of all. Few can resist its lure. In times past it was the king's own council who held the greatest power. Today it is the Parliament. England has not had quite its cropful of Master Cromwell and his adherents quite yet. Go to France, dearest sister, and make a new life for yourself. What a wonderful adventure you have ahead of you, Autumn! Do not be afraid of it."

"But what will become of you, Henry, and the others?" Autumn wondered aloud, with regard to her siblings and their families.

"In Ulster our brothers have married and continue to do what they can to protect their people from Cromwell's men, although they do little damage in the north. Fortune, Kieran, and their family are safe in Mary's Land. Charlie has gone to join the king. Patrick will not, I am certain, but rather draw in his Glenkirk people for their own safety's sake. India and Oxton, like me, will remain on our estates, attempting to remain neutral but doing whatever we must to protect our lands and families. We aren't important families and with luck will survive this storm intact. And you, darling girl, will go with Mama to France to find your true love, and your fortune."

Suddenly Autumn was weeping against her brother's black velvet doublet. "I l-liked it better in the old days, when we were all together and no one was fighting or afraid," she sobbed.

Henry Lindley, Marquess of Westleigh, sighed softly and stroked his sister's mahogany-colored hair. "So did I, Autumn," he said sadly, "so did I."

Chapter

3

Sir Simon Bates rode alone as his horse traveled up the gravel driveway that lead to Cadby. Several days after the unfortunate incident that had resulted in the death of the Duchess of Lundy, he had returned to Queen's Malvern to see if Autumn was all right. The beautiful young woman had touched him, and he was still amazed that she had had the courage to shoot the trooper who had killed Lady Stuart. Queen's Malvern, however, was bereft of its family. Only the servants remained, and the duke's beautiful horses, grazing in their pastures.

"Lady Autumn has gone to join her mother, the Duchess of Glenkirk," Becket informed Sir Simon in his plummiest tones. He moved to close the house's door.

Sir Simon Bates jammed his booted foot into the opening and said, "And just where is that?"

"I am not certain, sir," Becket replied.

"Surely you know. You *must* know! And where is your master, and his children?" Simon Bates could feel his anger rising at being bested by this servant. He was the government's representative.

"The Duchess of Glenkirk may be with her oldest son, the Marquess of Westleigh, or with her oldest daughter, the Countess of Oxton. All the household was informed was that young Lady Autumn would be joining her mother. As for my master and his children, I have no idea where they have gone. The duke wished it that way, as he felt your attack on his home last week, and the murder of her grace, was because of his connection with the king and his family. Now, sir, if you will remove your boot from the door . . ." Becket finished, looking directly into Sir Simon's fathomless dark eyes.

"Which is closer?" Sir Simon persisted, "Cadby or Oxton?"

"They are equidistant from Queen's Malvern, sir," Becket said.

Sir Simon Bates removed his foot from the door and found it immediately slammed shut in his face. The insult passed unnoticed, for his mind was considering where he might find Autumn Leslie. He cared nothing for where the duke and his offspring had fled. That was the business of the government, and as far as he knew Charles Frederick Stuart was not wanted for any crime against the state. His wife's murder had been an unfortunate accident. Mounting his horse, he considered, and decided that the girl would have gone to her brother for protection, and not her brother-in-law. He turned his horse toward Warwickshire.

Now he could see, as he arrived several days later, that Cadby was every bit as impressive as Queen's Malvern. It was madness that had brought him here. He had no right to be chasing after this girl, he knew, but one look and he had been bewitched by her. He had to know she was well, and could one day be happy again.

Again he was greeted by a protective servant. And then it was Henry Lindley who came from somewhere in the house and cautiously asked him his business here.

"I am Sir Simon Bates," he began, only to be abruptly cut off.

"I know who you are, sir," Henry answered him. "What do you want of us?"

"Your sister—she is well?" He knew he sounded like a perfect fool, but he was suddenly witless and tongue-tied.

"I have three sisters, Sir Simon, but I am assuming you refer to my youngest sister, Lady Autumn. She is with our mother, mourning the loss of her father and our dearest sister-in-law."

"I wonder," Sir Simon ventured boldly, "if I might see her to convey to her my apologies once again."

Henry's first instinct was to have Sir Simon Bates ejected from his house immediately, but he thought better of it. There was no need offending this man, and thereby possibly endangering his family. Autumn would send him packing quickly enough, and she would be gone on the morrow. "I will take you to the dower house, where my mother now lives," the Marquess of Westleigh said. "My sister is there."

Surprised to have been granted his request, Sir Simon Bates followed Henry Lindley from his house and through the gardens, on the other side of which stood a beautiful small stone house, two stories in height. They entered without knocking, the marquis calling out to his mother to come to her salon. An elderly serving man, dressed all in white, a strange cap upon his head, hurried forth.

"My lord Henry." He bowed.

"Adali, this is Sir Simon Bates, and he has come to inquire after my sister's health," the marquis said, a twinkle in his eye.

"Indeed, my lord," Adali replied.

Sir Simon was unable to restrain himself. "What is that you wear upon your head, man?" he asked.

"It is called a turban, sir," was the frosty reply.

"You are a foreigner. I thought so," Sir Simon said.

"I have lived in this land longer than you have been alive, sir," Adali answered him, "but you are correct in your assumption that I was not born here. My father was French and my mother, Indian. I have been in my mistress's service since her birth." He then turned to the marquis. "I will fetch her ladyship, my lord," he said, bowing, and then he withdrew from the room.

"How did your mother come to have a foreigner for a servant?" Sir Simon asked the marquis.

"My mother was born in India. Her father was its emperor," Henry Lindley said quietly, rather irritated by the query.

Fergus More-Leslie entered the salon bearing a tray with a decanter and several goblets. He wore no livery, but rather dark breeches, a white shirt, and a well-worn leather jerkin that matched the deep brown of his equally worn leather boots. "I hae brought ye some whiskey, my lord, and wine for the ladies when they come.

Shall I pour, or will ye want to be doing it?" He set the tray down upon a small table.

"We will wait for Mama and my sister, thank you, Fergus," the marquis said.

"Verra well, my lord," the reply came, and Fergus withdrew from the salon.

"*A Scot?* Your mother has a Scot for a serving man?"

"My stepfather was a Scot, Sir Simon," Henry said tightly.

"Oh, yes, of course." Simon Bates knew he was in over his head. He had been a fool to come here.

The door to the salon opened again, and two women entered. The Duchess of Glenkirk went immediately to her son and embraced him. Then she looked at Sir Simon. "Did Adali understand you correctly, Henry? Is this indeed Sir Simon Bates?"

"I am, your grace," Sir Simon answered eagerly.

Jasmine Leslie turned icy eyes on the man. "I was not addressing you, sir, but since you have had the temerity to speak to me I shall tell you what I think of you."

"*Mama!*" Henry's voice held a warning.

"Do not *mama* me, Henry. This man could not control his troopers and is responsible for Bess's death and that of a loyal servant. *And*, if that were not enough, remember what else he did in giving my poor, innocent daughter a pistol! How dare you come here, sir, and for what reason, may I inquire?"

"To make certain your daughter was all right, your grace," Sir Simon Bates replied. "The incident at Queen's Malvern was regrettable, but these things happen in war, I fear. I am not a monster, madame, and I have sisters of my own." God's blood, how old was this woman? he wondered. She was utterly beautiful, with hardly a line on her face. She was every bit as lovely as her daughter, who stood pale and silent by her side.

"Your reputation precedes you, sir. It is said you have overseen the murder of innocents, and that would certainly seem to be the case in my daughter-in-law's tragic demise," Jasmine said angrily. "You say you have come to ask after Autumn. Surely you can see the grief upon her visage, sir. She will never again be the same innocent girl she was before you and your men forced your way into Queen's Malvern. You insult us, coming here!"

He was shaken by her angry words, but he understood. He turned to Autumn. "Will you forgive me, Lady Autumn?" he said.

"I am going to France tomorrow," Autumn answered him as if he had not just asked her pardon. "I shall never have to see you or England again."

"You are leaving the country?" Sir Simon was surprised.

"My mother inherited a small house in the Loire," Henry said quickly before Jasmine might begin a tirade. "My sister's health, as you can see, is fragile. She will heal better away from all of this sadness, you will agree."

"Where are you sailing from?" he asked them.

"They sail from Harwich," Henry said.

"My men and I will escort you, your grace," Sir Simon said formally.

"That is not necessary, sir," Jasmine told him coldly.

Then her son spoke up again. "I think it an excellent suggestion, Mama. I thank you, Sir Simon, for your consideration. Mama, I have no men-at-arms to go with you, and in these times I fear to hire any. Your own escort could turn on you and rob you. I know you will be safe with Sir Simon, and reach Harwich alive and with your trunks intact. I will even go with you."

"My men are garrisoned at the castle, my lord. We shall meet you on the road tomorrow morning. I will take my leave of you now." He bowed and hurried from the room.

When they heard the front door of the dower house slam closed, Jasmine turned to her son, outraged. "Are you mad?" she demanded.

"Nay," Autumn spoke up. "He is very clever, aren't you, Henry? And he is right, Mama. We cannot travel alone in such dangerous times. What better escort can we have than Sir Simon Bates and his Roundheads? No one will dare to accost us. He does it because, I believe, he is taken by me, but once we reach Harwich I shall never see him again. It is hardly a just punishment for what he did that he should pine of a broken heart for me, but I suppose it is the best we can do."

"You are a foolish girl," Jasmine told her daughter. "This man has dared to have pretensions in your direction, Autumn."

"Which can come to nothing," the girl replied.

"I meant it when I said I would go with you to Harwich, Mama," Henry Lindley said. Then he turned to his sister. "And you will continue to behave as a frail and frightened young girl would, little sister. I believe as long as you do that, Sir Simon will be foiled in his aspirations toward you."

"What you mean," Autumn said with a small chuckle, "is that even Sir Simon Bates would not attempt to seduce a half-wit, eh, brother?"

"Precisely!" he agreed with a grin.

"You shall be the death of me yet," the Duchess of Glenkirk said, throwing up her hands. "Henry, pour me some of that excellent Glenkirk whiskey. My nerves are shattered."

"Oh, Mama, you are as bad as I am, feigning distress," Autumn teased her mother. "If India's adventures in Barbary and Fortune's in Ulster did not do you in, I doubt very much I can."

"I was much younger then, and I had your father," Jasmine replied. She took the tumbler her son handed her and swallowed down a draught of the peat-flavored whiskey. "Excellent!" she pronounced. "I do believe I shall recover after all."

And her children laughed.

They gathered that night in the Great Hall of Cadby, and Jasmine felt a deep sadness, knowing it might be some time before she saw her eldest son's family again. Her daughter-in-law, Rosamund, instinctively understood and attempted to comfort Jasmine.

"Do not grieve, madame. We will come to France to visit you next summer, if these difficulties have not been solved by then. I know how much you love your grandchildren. But certainly this civil strife will be over with by next year, and the king will return."

"Rosamund, we have spoken on this, you and I," Henry chided his wife. "Cromwell will not relinquish his power easily, nor will the men who support him. They have murdered one king and would murder the other were he in their hands. The young king hasn't the power to return yet, and the people of England, while complaining, have not yet had their bellyful of these psalm-singing Puritans so that they will rise up in the king's defense. We will probably go to France to visit Mama."

His wife looked crestfallen. "I can hope it is over soon," she said sadly. "What is going to happen to the children? With everything, and anything that was pleasurable forbidden, how can they meet other young people of their station, and how can we make matches? Henry is already eleven, and I daren't even teach him to dance, lest one of the servants reports it to the authorities!"

"Perhaps you should come to France too," Autumn suggested.

"I will not leave my home," Henry Lindley said, "nor will my family leave it. We ceased going to court years ago. If we cannot hold a few celebrations in this time, then we will find other ways to make matches for the children when their time comes. They are all far too young now anyway. Eventually Cromwell will be sent packing and the king will return. You are brought low, Rosamund, by all that has happened lately. After Mama and Autumn depart for France, we will take the children and go to visit your parents at RiversEdge."

His wife, who was the eldest daughter of the Earl and Countess of Langford, clapped her hands in childlike delight. "Aye, Henry, I should like to visit RiversEdge!"

Autumn smiled to herself. How easy it was for Rosamund. She had a husband she adored and five beautiful children. Her parents were both alive at their family's home. Nothing had really changed for Rosamund, except that her social life was now curtailed because of the Puritans. Cadby had never been threatened and was unlikely to be, although isolation was not a guarantee, as she had learned from the incident at Queen's Malvern.

Still, Rosamund was not being driven from her home and the life she had always known. Autumn had no idea if she would ever return to Glenkirk. She looked at her three nephews, Henry, James, and Robert. By next summer they would have changed, as would their two sisters. She wondered if Henry would be able to bring his family to France, or if he would keep them at Cadby for fear of losing his estates should he leave them. And what would happen to Queen's Malvern? Would it still be there when this was all over, and Charlie came home again?

The next morning dawned clear and cold. They would travel in the Marquess of Westleigh's large, comfortable coach, accompanied by a baggage cart. When they arrived in France, a coach, already purchased by the duchess's agents, would be awaiting them, along with horses for it, for the baggage cart, and for the travelers, who might on some days prefer riding. There would also be servants awaiting them from Jasmine's chateau. The duchess had left nothing to chance. It was important that Autumn like France, for it would more than likely be her home for the rest of her life.

She did not want her daughter becoming involved with some exiled English nobleman. Anyone connected with the Stuart court was suspect, in her mind. Besides, what could an exile offer her daughter? No home. No family. No income. No life. Never! Autumn would marry a Frenchman. The Dutch were too dull and stolid, but a Frenchman would understand Autumn. The Duchess of Glenkirk was a woman who believed firmly in fate. No young man had caught Autumn's fancy in either Scotland or England. The duchess had to believe that her youngest child's fate lay in France. Bidding Rosamund and her five Lindley grandchildren farewell, she climbed into the coach with her two serving women, Rohana and Toramalli, and with Autumn's serving wench, Lily. Toramalli's husband, Fergus, and Adali, would drive the baggage cart. Red Hugh, Jasmine's personal captain, had already departed for France to oversee the preparations for his mistress. He would meet them there.

"I shall write to you as soon as we reach Belle Fleurs, my dear," she told Rosamund. "Enjoy your visit to RiversEdge, but after that stay close to home and keep the children near. My felicitations to your parents."

Rosamund's soft blue eyes were teary. "I wish you would stay," she said. "The dower house is always here for you, Jasmine."

"It is comforting to know that, my dear," came the reply. Then the window of the coach was pulled firmly up, and the vehicle rumbled off down the gravel driveway toward the main road.

As they approached Warwick Castle, they were joined by Sir Simon Bates and his troopers. The Roundhead captain drew his mount up next to the Marquis of Westleigh.

"Good morning, my lord. How far will you travel with us?" he asked politely.

"I will accompany my mother all the way to Harwich, sir," came the pleasant reply. "I am loath to see her go, you will understand."

"Of course, my lord." Sir Simon turned to Autumn. "Good morning, my lady. You are well, I trust."

"Mama says I will marry a Frenchman," Autumn answered. "I do not think I ever met a Frenchman. Have you met a Frenchman, Sir Simon? Are they like us? I wish I could go home to Scotland, but Papa is dead. It makes Mama unhappy to think about him and Glenkirk."

"She was not like this at Queen's Malvern," Sir Simon noted to the marquis. "She was quite spirited with me then."

"She managed to maintain her composure until she saw Mama. It was then she collapsed into tears, whether over her father or over Bess, or perhaps both, we do not know. She has been childlike ever since, but we believe she will recover in the peaceful surroundings of Mama's chateau. Poor Autumn," Henry Lindley sighed, and then he looked straight ahead, preventing further conversation.

Autumn struggled with herself not to break into laughter. She almost felt sorry for Sir Simon, but that she knew him to be a true villian. She gained a certain satisfaction in the fact that he felt guilty over Bess's death and her supposed plight. They traveled for five long days, finally reaching Harwich on the coast. Autumn kept herself from Sir Simon as much as possible, lest she give away her ruse. Still, in the hours before they sailed he sought her out.

"I hope you will be happy in France," he said.

"I was happier before I met you and Bess was killed. I was happier before this civil strife and my father's death. I shall never know that kind of happiness again," Autumn told him.

"You are not mad!" he said, the relief palpable in his voice.

"Nay, I am not mad, sir, just filled with sorrow. I believe the trip has begun to restore me already."

"Perhaps you were mocking me, my lady," he replied.

"Perhaps I was," she agreed.

"You do not like me," he said.

"Why should I?" Autumn demanded. "You are responsible for my sister-in-law's murder. You espouse a cause that has destroyed my world and murdered my king. You and your compatriots have turned England into a dour and dark land. Nay, I do not like you, Sir Simon."

"You are the most beautiful girl I have ever seen," he said, totally heedless of her scorn.

"You lust after me in your heart, sir. You have from the moment you stepped through the doorway at Queen's Malvern," Autumn said, her voice filled with contempt.

"What would a virtuous maid know of lust?" He was suddenly jealous. How could she be chaste and yet have such knowledge?

"Am I a fool then, sir, that I cannot see desire in a man's eyes?" Autumn berated him. "You are the fool, I fear, if you believe that! I despise you, and men like you."

"I could keep you in England," he said suddenly.

"*How?*" Her glance mocked him.

"You committed a murder to which I was witness," he said menacingly.

"*Prove it,*" she taunted him. "You cannot. All you would do is succeed in delaying my voyage. It would be your word against mine. Even your psalm-singing judges in their black garb would not believe that I killed a man. I am a young, unmarried girl of good family. I had no weapon, and this man you allege I killed, where is his body?"

"You are much too clever for a mere woman," he told her. "You have bewitched me, Autumn Leslie! Perhaps that is the charge I should bring against you. *Witchcraft!*"

"Go to hell!" she spat at him. "Try it, and I shall revert to the poor half-wit you believed I had become. Tonight on the tide, my mother and I will sail for France. We shall never again see one another, Sir Simon, and for that I am eternally grateful!" Then, to his surprise, Autumn slapped him as hard as she could. *"That* is for your presumption, sir!"

To her surprise he caught her hand and, turning it palm up, he quickly placed a hot kiss upon it. "We shall indeed meet again, my lady," he promised her softly, and his dark eyes lingered a moment on her beautiful face. Then he turned and was gone.

She could feel the wetness of his mouth upon her flesh, and Autumn shuddered. She hurried from the private sitting room where they were speaking to her small chamber next door to wash her hands. Scrubbing at the spot his lips had touched, she wondered if she would ever remove the sensation of the kiss from her skin. The feeling was one of deep revulsion. Outside, in the inn's courtyard, she could hear Sir Simon and his troopers departing. Autumn drew a deep sigh of relief. His threats had been worthless. He could do nothing.

Jasmine entered the little bedchamber and looked hard at her daughter. "Sir Simon came to bid me farewell, and said he was relieved that your indisposition had only been temporary. What did he mean by his words, and what have you done, child?"

"Nothing," Autumn said. "He said he hoped I should be happy in France. When I spoke he realized I was not suffering any longer." There was no need, Autumn thought, to reveal the entire conversation to her mother, now that the Roundhead captain was gone.

"The captain of the *Fair Winds* says we sail within the hour," Jasmine told her daughter. "The luggage is aboard. Come and say farewell to your brother, child."

They were actually leaving. Suddenly she was overwhelmed by sadness and struggled to hold back her tears. This was difficult enough for her mother without her bursting into tears, Autumn thought.

"Where is Lily?" she asked. She had not seen her maidservant when she had fled to her chamber.

"Lily is already aboard the ship with the others," her mother said. "Adali says she is terrified of the sea voyage. You will have to make certain she remains calm."

"But we shall not be at sea for that long," Autumn replied. "Lily is such a little coward. I am surprised she left Glenkirk."

"She would not have, but for her uncle Fergus," Jasmine told her daughter. "He and Red Hugh are her only living blood kin. Remember that Fergus and Toramalli have raised Lily since she was seven, having no children of their own. As she had no young man to stay for, she screwed up her courage and agreed to come with us. England is one thing, but France an entirely different entity. Do not say she is a coward, for she is not. It has taken all her ability to conquer her fears. She might have returned to Glenkirk and remained in your brother's service. She is a clever girl no matter her timidity, and she saw the advantage in remaining with you, my child. I know you don't know her very well yet, but Rohana and Toramalli have trained her well."

"She is sweet," Autumn admitted. "I just miss my old Maybel."

"I know, but Maybel, poor woman, was becoming bent and crippled with age. She could not have made this trip. I should have replaced her several years ago, but I knew you loved your dear old nursemaid, and she has missed you, Autumn. Still, she is very content, snug in a fine new cottage with a good stone fireplace that your father had built for her. She will never want for anything, and you needed a younger woman to look after you."

"Who were Lily's parents?" Autumn asked. "They are never mentioned at all. How are they kin to Fergus?"

"Fergus and Red Hugh had a much younger sister who ran off with a tinker years ago. She died when Lily was seven, and the tinker sent Lily back to Glenkirk, saying that while she was his child, he had never wed her mother and could not take care of her. Red Hugh was in no position to care for the child, and as it was obvious by then that Toramalli would have no bairns, she and Fergus took Lily in, raising her as their own. Now you know. It wasn't necesary you know before. Come along, Autumn. Your brother will be wondering where we have gotten to if we do not join him soon."

The Duchess of Glenkirk and her daughter departed the small chamber and joined the Marquess of Westleigh in the courtyard of the inn. Seeing them coming toward him, Henry Lindley felt a pang of sadness sweep over him, but he bravely mustered a smile.

"So," he said jovially, "you are ready to depart on your adventure! I hope, little sister, you will not find yourself in all the difficulties that your female relations in the past have managed to find themselves." He chuckled at the dark look his mother shot at him. "Now, Mama," he said, patting her beringed hand, "you will be there watching over Autumn like a dragon, I am quite certain. Besides, she is not like either India, or Fortune in her disposition. She is a much more bidable lass, eh?"

"She has not had the opportunities her sisters had, and besides, Henry, times have changed."

"My lady, your cloak, and my mistress's." Lily hurried up to them with the garments. "Rohana apologizes, but she brought them aboard the ship in error, fearing they would be left behind." The young girl placed the duchess's dark blue velvet cloak, lined in beaver, about her shoulders. Then she set Autumn's garment, which was also lined in thick, warm fur, around her slender frame, carefully fastening the silver frogs down the front of the cloak. Stepping back, she curtsied.

"Thank you, Lily," the duchess said, and then, turning to her daughter, said, "Bid Henry farewell and go aboard the ship." Then she watched as her eldest son, the second of her children, and her youngest daughter, the last of her children, bid each other good-bye.

"You don't have to *do* everything that Mama says," Henry murmured low, "but *listen* to all she says. She is wise. Still, you certainly have enough common sense to know what is right and what is not. Guard your tongue, your virtue, and your reputation, Autumn. Beware of men who praise you too greatly. They will want either your maidenhead, your fortune, or both, and cannot be trusted. Marry only for love and no other reason, sister. Let me know if Mama needs me, or the others."

"I will," Autumn replied. "And I will heed your advice, Henry." She kissed his cheek. "I love you, brother."

He returned the embrace, enfolding her in his arms and kissing her tenderly. "God bless you, little sister, until we meet again."

"Remind Charlie not to get killed," Autumn said softly, "if you can, Henry." Then she extricated herself from his embrace and followed her servant aboard the waiting vessel.

Jasmine turned to her eldest son. "Be careful," she warned him. "Do not get caught up in this foolishness like your brother. Heed me as I know Patrick and the others have. Cromwell and his ilk, with their mean-spiritedness, will not last forever."

"Will you come home when they are gone?" he asked her.

She smiled at him and drew her hood up as the wind gusted about them. "I do not know," she answered honestly. "God only knows Belle Fleurs isn't much bigger than my dower house, but I have always had a weakness for the place. Besides, I like the weather in the Loire better than in England. I shall not say never, Henry. See I am buried at Glenkirk when the time comes, and if that is not possible, then Queen's Malvern, near my grandmother."

"You are not planning on dying on me, madame," he said with a twinkle in his eye.

"Nay, but the time will come, Henry, one day. I want you to know what I want else you do the wrong thing and I am forced to come back and haunt you."

He burst out laughing. "Mama, there is no one like you in the whole world." Then he kissed her heartily on both cheeks. "God speed, and write to me so I know what is happening with Autumn."

"I will," Jasmine promised, and then, kissing her son a final time, she turned and hurried up the gangway of the waiting ship.

The Marquess of Westleigh remained standing upon the dock until the *Fair Winds* had cleared the harbor. Only then did he return to his coach, directing his coachmen to take them home with all possible speed. His mother and sister sailed upon one of the family's trading ships. It would take them down the North Sea into the English Channel, past Brest and across the Bay of Biscay to the mouth of the Loire, and from there up the river to the city of Nantes, where their coach would be waiting for them. The duchess's personal captain had gone ahead to France to make all the necessary arrangements.

It was mid-November and the seas were rough, though the

weather was fair. The wind blew constantly from the north, speeding their travel as they passed the Channel Islands and rounded the Ile d'Ouessant. A northwest wind blew them past Pointe Penmarche, and it began to rain the afternoon their ship sailed between Belle Ile and Le Croisic. Captain Ballard, the ship's master, came to the main cabin, where Jasmine and her daughter were housed. Autumn and Lily, her servant, were lying down, for the pitch of the vessel left them dizzy. Adali dozed in a chair, while Rohana and her sister, Toramalli, sat quietly sewing by their mistress's side. At the discreet knock upon the door, Toramalli jumped up and ran to answer the summons.

"Good afternoon, your grace," Captain Ballard said as he entered. His eye lit upon Autumn. "Is her ladyship all right, madame?"

"A wee touch of *mal de mer*, Captain," Jasmine explained. "My daughter has never been to sea before. She has battled her symptons since boarding, but today it finally overcame her. She will survive."

"Perhaps the knowledge that we will be entering the mouth of the Loire by morning will cheer her," Captain Ballard said with a smile. "We should reach the city by late afternoon, your grace."

"Excellent, Captain," Jasmine replied. "I do want to thank you for coming out of your way like this. You would be well on your way to Mary's Land now had you not had to make this side trip. You will remember to give my daughter, Mistress Devers, the packet of letters I have given you?"

"Indeed, Your Grace, I will. They will make a nice Christmas treat for her, even if these Puritans running our country don't allow for a celebration of our Lord's birth."

Jasmine laughed, but then she warned the captain, "You must be careful, Ballard, in your criticism. If the wrong people heard, they could demand your replacement. My family perfers to manage their own commerce, and not be interfered with by others. The O'Malley-Small Trading Company has survived for almost a hundred years because of our discretion."

"Aye, your grace," he agreed, shamefaced.

"I know your heart is where it should be, Ballard," Jasmine tempered her criticism, "but unlike others, we have always accepted all faiths, and consequently your crew is quite mixed. Among them, however, may be some who are not quite as open-minded as we. Be careful, not just for our sake, but for your own as well."

He nodded again, and then with a bow withdrew.

"These Puritans have caused quite a stir," Rohana said to her mistress. "I never expected that at our ages we should be uprooting ourselves yet another time."

"And how will we find Belle Fleurs, my princess?" Toramalli asked. "It has been more than thirty years since we were last there. Old Mathieu will be long gone. Who has been taking care of the chateau?"

"His grandson, Guillaume," Jasmine answered her serving woman. "He and his wife, Pascaline, have been caring for Belle Fleurs. It will seem very old-fashioned to Autumn, I think, but it was always a welcoming place, eh?"

Her serving woman chuckled, remembering how years before they had fled England with their mistress for Belle Fleurs. And then the duke had come and they had married and departed France, never to return until now. The twin sisters looked at each other and nodded their graying heads. Belle Fleurs had been a good place then, and it would be once again.

It was still raining by morning, but the lurching and tossing of their vessel had almost ceased and, looking out of the porthole, Autumn saw they were already on the River Loire. She could see the land through the mist and fog. *France!* They were in France. Soon she would be involved in the merriment of a royal court, and she could forget Master Cromwell and his sour-faced Puritans, who seemed to hate everything that was beautiful and light. She was feeling infinitely better than she had the night before. Even Lily was up, humming as she packed the remainder of her mistress's garments into her trunks.

"Where is Mama?" she asked aloud to the servants.

"Topside with my Fergus," Toramalli answered her.

Autumn headed to the door.

"You just wait one moment, my lady," Toramalli said in a stern voice. "Lily, get your mistress's cape. She should not go outdoors without it. It's damp, and the wind, light though it may be, will be a chilly wind, you may be certain. Hurry up, girl! You have to learn to anticipate these things."

"Sorry, Auntie," Lily said and, picking up the green velvet cloak with its beaver lining, she draped it over Autumn's shoulders, then fastened it carefully and drew the fur-lined and -edged hood up over her mistress's head. She struggled not to grin, for Autumn, her back to Toramalli, was making faces at Lily. "There, m'lady," Lily said in the most proper voice she could muster as she struggled not to giggle. Then she handed Autumn a pair of silk-lined, scented leather gloves. "You don't want chilblains on them pretty hands, m'lady."

"Certainly not!" Autumn exclaimed. "What would my fine French lord, whoever he is, and wherever he is, think of chilblains!"

Lily snickered, unable to help herself, and Autumn began to giggle.

"Oh, yer a funny pair, you are," Toramalli said. "Lily, get your cape and go with your mistress. Perhaps a good blast of cold air will calm you both down."

The two young women exited the cabin onto the outside deck. Behind them, Toramalli shook her head despairingly. "How you and I managed a six-month voyage from India with the princess without getting silly, I'll never know," she said to her twin sister.

"We were born and raised to serve," Rohana said quietly. "We were slaves, and our outlook was quite different than Lily's is, Toramalli. She will, in time, be an excellent serving woman for the young mistress. They are both Scots, and still young."

"You defend Lily as always," Toramalli said. "Without us she would have been a strumpet like her mother."

"You are unduly harsh, sister. Lily's mother was taken advantage of by a sly tinker. She fell in love. I remember Lily's father well. He was as handsome as midsummer's eve is long. I suspect Fergus's sister wasn't the first lass to follow him."

"If I didn't love Lily as much as I do," Toramalli grumbled, "I would send her packing!"

"No, you wouldn't," Rohana laughed.

Toramalli sighed. "No," she said. "I wouldn't, but the lass will be the death of me, sister!"

The *Fair Winds* docked at Nantes in midafternoon, ahead of the captain's earlier prediction. Red Hugh was waiting for them. He saluted his mistress as he met her on the deck of the ship.

"My lady. All is in readiness for you," he told her. "I thought as you were arriving so late, and it almost dark, you would want to stay the night here in Nantes. I have arranged accommodations at the best in the city, Le Canard Bleu. When you are ready, your coach is waiting on the dock." He pointed.

"Thank you, Red Hugh. Now greet your family and we can be on our way," the duchess said with a small smile.

The big Scotsman grabbed Toramalli and gave her a noisy kiss. "Damn me, woman, if I haven't missed you!" he said.

"You big fool!" she muttered, but her cheeks were flushed with pleasure. "All right, I've missed you too."

In far more restrained fashion, Red Hugh greeted his sister-in-law and his niece. He turned to his brother. "Fergus, lad." Then he said to the duchess, "We're ready, my lady."

Jasmine thanked Captain Ballard again, and with her daughter and servants debarked the *Fair Winds*. The coach Red Hugh had obtained was spacious and beautifully outfitted. A smaller vehicle was also awaiting them at the inn, he told his mistress as he ushered her and the other women inside. Then he and his brother climbed up on the coach's box, and they drove off from the harbor to their inn. Upon their arrival the landlord hurried forth, bowing and smiling. Red Hugh had obviously made quite clear the importance of his mistress to the innkeeper, who personally escorted Jasmine and her party into his establishment.

Inside the inn was clean and warm, and quite spacious. The aromas of food cooking permeated the place, and the smells were utterly delicious, Autumn thought, as they were brought to a gracious apartment on the main floor of the building. Young Lady Autumn was also amazed by the ease with which her mother switched back and forth between the English and French languages. This was done so Lily might understand, for all the others spoke French, even Red Hugh and Fergus.

"Lily, you must learn French, for if this is to be our new home, you cannot communicate without a command of the language. Besides, how will you flirt with the young men if you don't know what they are saying and can't speak with them," the duchess teased. She turned to the innkeeper. "Now, M'sieu Pierre, we will have our supper here in our apartment. Nothing special. The odor from your kitchens is delightful, and I shall leave the choices up to you. We shall eat as soon as the food is ready, for I long for a hot bath and my bed. I am not as young as I once was, and travel is quite exhausting." She favored him with a small smile.

The innkeeper bowed so low his head almost touched the floor. "We shall serve you immediately, Madame la duchesse, and afterwards hot baths shall be brought for both you and your beautiful daughter." He bowed again and backed from the room.

"What a funny man," Autumn said, "but so accommodating."

"He is a clever fellow, and his establishment is well run," Jasmine noted. "Nonetheless, my gold buys the best service. Remember that, Autumn. Gold is power."

"Am I an heiress?" Autumn asked her mother. "I have never before considered such a thing."

"You are an heiress," her mother said. "You have a large dowry that your father arranged, and you will also receive a generous portion from me, my daughter. You are wealthy enough to attract only the best husband." Then she smiled wickedly. "And a few handsome fortune hunters as well, *ma bébé.*"

"Will we go to Paris, Mama?"

"Eventually," Jasmine said. "I must learn firsthand what is really happening here in France. Queen Anne is the regent, but there has been much haggling back and forth over little King Louis. The queen's closest adviser is Cardinal Mazarin, and he is hated by many of the princes of the blood, but their hate is just a disguise for jealousy. They want the power that having the young king in their possession can bring, but he and the queen have kept the boy safe so far."

"At least the French have not killed their king," Autumn said. "How old is little King Louis, Mama?"

"He is twelve, and next year when he reaches his thirteenth birthday he will come into his majority and rule without a regent, although I suspect his mama will still influence him. However, once he is legally in charge, the queen and the cardinal's enemies cannot kidnap the king and claim to be doing it to protect him from Queen Anne and Cardinal Mazarin." Jasmine laughed. "The queen and her allies have been very clever, Autumn. She is to be admired."

"A twelve-year-old king cannot have much of a court," Autumn said, sounding disappointed.

Her mother laughed. "You will have your chance, *ma bébé*," she promised her youngest child.

The door to their apartments opened, and a line of servants entered with bowls and platters from which were emanating delicious smells. The table was set up, and the dishes placed upon the sideboard.

"I shall serve Madame la duchese," Adali told the inn's servants, and they departed.

"We will not stand on ceremony here," Jasmine said. "Sit down, all of you. Adali at the foot, Autumn on my right, and the rest of you wherever you choose." She allowed Red Hugh to set her at the table's head, smiling a small thanks to him.

Adali filled each plate, passing the first to his mistress, the second to Autumn, and then the rest, serving himself last. There were whole artichokes steamed and served with a piquant vinaigrette and a delicate olive oil. A *boeuf bourguignonne* with tiny green onions and slivers of carrot in a rich and succulent gravy; prawns broiled and flavored with fennel; a fat capon stuffed with onions, celery, and sage that Adali carved thin, juicy slices of breast from; a pink country ham. There were two kinds of cheese, a runny Brie and an English cheddar; freshly baked bread, still warm from the ovens; and a crock of newly churned sweet butter, which Adali placed upon the table for them all. On the sideboard there remained an apple tartlet and a pitcèr of heavy golden cream. There was a hearty red wine served, but while she enjoyed two cups of it, the duchess declared that the wines from her family's vineyards at Archambault were better.

When the meal had been thoroughly appreciated by them all and the inn's servants had returned to clear away the debris, two wooden tubs were placed in each lady's bedchamber. They were promptly filled, Fergus and Red Hugh generously helping the innkeeper's staff in the task. Jasmine and her daughter then bathed before retiring. Lily, Rohana, and Toramalli would sleep in their mistress's chambers. The men would sleep in the parlor, where they had eaten. They slumbered heavily for the first time in many nights, their beds steady and not rolling beneath them. When morning came they arose and ate a hearty breakfast. Adali had the previous evening ordered a basket of food for their journey that day.

For the next few days they traveled north along a road that followed the River Loire. Each inn they sheltered in at night was every bit as good as Le Canard Bleu had been, and Autumn complained that she was going to get fat with all this delicious French cooking.

"You do not have to eat it *all*," her mother said.

"Mama, I need to keep up my strength!" the girl protested.

At Tours they crossed the Loire where it met the River Chèr, following a secondary road, finally turning off onto a narrower track leading them deeper into the countryside. On either side of their coach they could see the dormant vineyards, and beyond a small hill was crowned with a beautiful chateau.

"That is Archambault, where my cousins reside," Jasmine told her daughter. "When we are settled I shall take you to visit."

"How far are we from Belle Fleurs?" Autumn asked.

"Not very," her mother said even as their carriage and the baggage coach turned off onto a thin ribbon of a path, rumbling and lurching down the rutted and frozen dirt path. Bare branches scraped against the vehicle, almost impeding their passage. It had not been so overgrown when she had last been there, Jasmine thought; but then it had been so long ago. She would need to hire several gardeners, but Guillaume would be able to direct her there.

"Mama! Oh, Mama, look!" Autumn was pointing, her eyes alight. "Is that Belle Fleurs, Mama? Is it?"

Jasmine focused, and for a moment all her lovely memories came flooding back. Belle Fleurs had sheltered her and her four oldest children from James Leslie; and then Jemmie had come, and Belle Fleurs had become a place of idyllic love. It would never again be that way for her, Jasmine thought, but it very well could be for Autumn. Reaching out, she took her daughter's hand and gave it a little squeeze.

"Aye, *ma bébé*, that is Belle Fleurs," she said.

Chapter

4

The chateau was set on a tiny peninsula of land, surrounded by the waters of its lake on three sides. On the fourth side a large, beautiful garden was enclosed with a low stone wall. Built in the year 1415, Belle Fleurs was now 235 years old, but its original construction had been sound, and considered quite modern for its day. Constructed of flattened, rough-hewn blocks of reddish-gray schist, Belle Fleurs had four polygonal towers, with dark slate roofs that were shaped like witches' hats, set at each corner of the building. The coach's access to the courtyard was over a heavily constructed bridge through a tall, well-fortified chatelet flanked by rounded and corbeled towers rising high on either side of the entry arch.

As their vehicle came to a stop, a man of middle years hurried forward even before Fergus might come down from the box. Opening the coach's door, he lowered its steps and offered a hand to Jasmine first, and then her daughter. "Welcome, Madame la duchese!" he said. "I am Guillaume. I hope your trip was a pleasant one." He bowed neatly.

"Very pleasant," she answered him, impressed by his air of assurance. "The house is ready to receive us?"

"*Oui,* madame, but I took the liberty of waiting until you arrived to hire more servants. My wife, Pascaline, and I can serve you and your daughter for the next few days. I see you have your own personal staff as well."

"We will need gardeners to trim the trees and bushes along the entrance way," Jasmine said, "and the road needs to be raked smooth. It is far too rutted." She let him lead her into the chateau, followed by the others. They went up a small flight of stone steps past a covered stone porch and found themselves in a wide foyer. "Ahh," she said with a smile, "it is good to be back." Then she turned to her caretaker. "I remember my grandmother telling me that there once was another Guillaume here at Belle Fleurs. Are you related to him?"

"My great-grandparents, Guillaume and Mignon, had the pleasure of serving your grandparents, *Madame la duchese*. It was the lord de Marisco who bought the chateau from a Huguenot gentleman after the St. Bartholomew's Massacre in Paris following Henri of Navarre's wedding to the Princess Margot. The previous owner thought it advisable to retire to La Rochelle. Ah, here is my good wife. Come, Pascaline, and meet our mistress and the young mistress. You will show them and their maidservants to their chambers."

Adali stepped forward. Age had shrunk him somewhat, but he still possessed an air of command about him. "I am Madame la duchese's majordomo," he said. "I have been to Belle Fleurs before. Fergus"—he beckoned the man forward—"and his wife, Toramalli, will want quarters together, and such are available, I know. Madame la duchesse's personal captain will also sleep in the house." He turned and favored the plump Pascaline with a brief smile. "Madame and the demoiselle will eat in the Great Hall tonight. You are prepared, *bonne femme?*"

"*Oui*, M'sieu Adali," Pascaline said with a curtsey. She recognized authority when she saw it. "The meal is a simple one, but nourishing."

"Excellent!" Adali said. "Now, *mes amies,* let us get the baggage unloaded as quickly as possible. I smell rain in the air."

"Adali is in his glory again," Autumn chuckled to her mother. "He is really lost without a house to run, isn't he?"

"This is not Glenkirk," Jasmine said to her daughter. "This is a small chateau as chateaux go. The kitchens are below us, as are the servants' quarters. In addition to the Great Hall, there is a small library on this level, and upstairs only six bedchambers. Not apartments with several rooms, but simple bedchambers. Outside you will, when you have time to explore, find stables, a kennel, a falconry, and a dovecote."

"It is pretty," Autumn said, "but not very grand."

"Nay, it is not grand. It is a chateau for lovers, or for a small family. My cousins' chateau, Archambault, is grand, and eventually I shall take you to see it," Jasmine promised.

They settled themselves in, and during the next few days Autumn was kept busy arranging her chamber to suit herself and unpacking. Her room overlooked the lake, and the single window had a seat built into it where Autumn found she liked to sit looking out through the leaded panes, sometimes unfastening the window to familiarize herself with the scent of the fertile French countryside. The furnishings were simple, of ancient but well-polished golden oak.

There was a large bedstead with a seven-foot oak headboard carved with flowers and vines, a solid canopy of oak overhead that was held up by the headboard, and the two carved wooden posts at the foot of the bed. It was certainly not as big as the one in Mama's room, which was enormous. She had a tall oak cupboard called an armoire in which Lily hung her gowns, and a fine oak chest for the rest of her possessions. There was a single little table on one side of the bed that was set opposite a fireplace flanked with carved stone angels.

The bed hangings, which were hung from tarnished brass rings, were made of a faded rose-colored velvet. The cushion in the window seat was a natural colored linen with rose velvet flowers embroidered onto it. The window had a large shutter that could be closed to keep out the cold air, along with linen and velvet drapes. Beneath the bed was a trundle with a thick mattress for Lily to sleep upon, and on the little nightstand a silver taperstick with its own snuffer attached by a delicate silver link. On each end of the narrow fireplace mantel sat small, square porcelain bowls of potpourri that perfumed the chamber. Despite her reservations regarding the social disadvantages of living in such an isolated and small chateau, Autumn liked her bedchamber, and she liked Belle Fleurs.

Adali, with the aid of Guillaume, hired servants for the chateau. Pascaline would be their cook, but she needed two girls to help her, as well as a boy to scrub the pots and sharpen the knives. A laundress and her helper were employed, as well as three housemaids and three footmen. Two men were hired for work in the stables. A head gardener and half a dozen men would work on the grounds, seeing that the gardens were properly kept and the driveway cleared of brush and tree limbs. Guillaume would oversee all who worked outside, and Adali would manage the inside of the chateau. Red Hugh and Fergus were responsible for gamekeeping, and would protect the duchess and her daughter. Within two weeks the household was running smoothly and Autumn and her mother had settled in quite comfortably.

Then one afternoon in early December, a distinguished gentleman rode up to the chateau. Dismounting in the courtyard, he gave his horse to the attending stableman and entered the house. Adali hurried forward.

"Monsieur le Comte, you are most welcome to Belle Fleurs. I shall tell my mistress you are here. Come into the hall. Marc, wine for monsieur le comte!" Ushering the guest into the Great Hall, he hurried off to fetch Jasmine.

"*Philippe!*" She came into the hall, hands outstretched, a welcoming smile upon her lips.

"*Cousine*, you have not changed a bit in all the years that have separated us," he said gallantly, kissing her on both cheeks.

"Liar!" she laughed.

"I was sorry to hear of your husband's death," he told her.

"And I of Marie Louise's passing," she returned. "Come, Philippe, and sit by the fire. 'Tis a cold day, and you must be chilled from your ride."

They sat together, and he said, "You have come to France to escape Cromwell and his Puritans, I have no doubt."

"You cannot imagine how dreadful it is, Philippe," she told him, and went on to describe the bleak England of Protector Cromwell. "I could bear it for myself, but not for Autumn. There is no society as we once knew it any longer, Philippe. I have come to France to mourn in peace, to escape the joylessness of England today, but most important, I have come to seek a suitable husband for my youngest child. She is just nineteen and probably the most beautiful of all my daughters. There was no one in Scotland for her, and certainly no one in England today who would do. So I have come to Belle Fleurs."

He nodded, understanding. Then he said, "France has been in turmoil these past years, Jasmine. The king was hardly out of leading strings when his father died. Parlement made the queen regent for the boy, but that has caused such difficulty. Anne of Austria is no fool. She has leaned heavily upon the cardinal, but the princes of the blood hate him and are jealous. I am glad you sailed to Nantes. Had you come via Calais you might never have gotten to Belle Fleurs. We have been fortunate in this little region, for we have seen little fighting, but about us all is conflict."

"Has it really been that bad, Philippe? We heard little of it at Glenkirk, and in England all we discuss is the king's murder and the young king's hopes of restoration."

"It *has* been that bad," he said. "Last January the queen mother had the Prince de Conde, the Prince de Conti, and the Duc de Longueville arrested. Then she had to pacify Normandy and Burgundy. She left Paris in the hands of Monsieur while she went to Guyenne to restore their loyalty. Gaston d'Orleans's loyalty is insecure at best and treasonous at worst, but he is her brother-in-law. He has never gotten over the fact that Louis XIII made his wife regent and not him."

"I thought Conde was loyal," Jasmine said.

"He runs with the hares and hunts with the hounds," the Comte de chèr said dryly. "The chief troublemaker in all of this is Jean Francoise Paul de Gondi, the Archbishop of both Corinth and Paris. If there is a treasonous plot, you will be certain to find Gondi involved. For all his public piety, he is a very wicked and ambitious man. He has always believed that the queen mother was not fit, by virtue of her sex, to be the regent. If anyone is responsible for the estrangement between Monsieur and Anne of Austria, it is Gondi. So he lures Gaston d'Orleans, and the cardinal tries to convince the Duc de Bouillon, and his brother, Marshall Turenne, to give their complete loyalty to the queen mother. The marshall had some success in an August campaign in Champagne. The cardinal knew that if Turenne declared for Anne in light of his recent victories, it would be good for the young king. Turenne, however, refused, and so the cardinal made certain his next battle would cost him dearly for his presumption. He was beaten at Rethel only this autumn, but now the two frondes, the first led by Gondi, and the Parisian burghers have joined with that of the princes. Only God knows what will happen now, *ma cousine*. I am not certain that in coming to France you have not jumped from the frying pan into the fire."

"When will the king declare his majority?" Jasmine asked.

"Next September, following his thirteenth birthday. That was what his father wanted, and frankly, *chérie*, if the regency went on much longer, I should fear for King Louis's life. All Anne and Cardinal Mazarin have to do is keep the boy in their hands until his next birthday. Once he is king in fact as well as in name, these rebels cannot continue on lest they be declared traitors. For now they keep France involved in civil wars under the guise of attempting to protect the king from his mother and the cardinal," the comte explained.

"What do you think of Mazarin?" she inquired, curious.

"He learned well from Richelieu. This cardinal is a consummate politician, but he is honestly and entirely devoted to young Louis. The men who struggle against Mazarin are driven by self-interest," Philippe de Saville told her. Then he patted her hand. "There is nothing for you in Paris right now, *chérie*, but here in this region, life goes on as it always has." He chuckled. "No patriotic Frenchman would bring war into the vineyards, *ma cousine*. The early vintage is paramount."

She laughed, then grew more somber. "But are there suitable prospects for my daughter, Philippe?"

"That is a woman's matter, *chérie*. We must ask my sisters, Gaby and Antoinette. They will know, for they have daughters who needed to be married off once. Gaby and 'Toinette are like us, bereft of their mates now, and living with me at Archambault." He chuckled. "They far prefer the spacious home of their childhood to the little dower houses each would have had to accept. Do you have a dower house at Glenkirk?"

"Nay, but there is one at Cadby, and why the architects of these houses think widows need less room simply because they no longer have husbands is beyond me," Jasmine said indignantly.

"Mama. Adali said we had guests." Autumn came into the hall. Her gown was of simple silver-blue damask, both bodice and skirt, with a wide collar of white linen edged in silver lace. Her hair was neat but not dressed, being plaited into a thick braid.

"Tres charmante!" Philippe de Saville said with a smile.

"This is my daughter, Lady Autumn Rose Leslie, *monsieur le comte*," Jasmine said formally. Then she turned to the young girl. "Autumn, this is my cousin, Philippe de Saville, the Comte de chèr. With his permission you will call him *Oncle* Philippe."

Autumn made her curtsey. "How do you do, *Oncle* Philippe," she said, and gave him her hand. "I am pleased to make your acquaintance."

He kissed the elegant hand and bowed. "I am pleased to make your acquaintance, *ma petite*. How lovely you are. We shall have no difficulty in finding you a husband."

"Oh, but I mean to go to Paris to court to seek a husband," Autumn replied frankly. "Certainly no one of importance lives in the provinces, *Oncle*. I am an heiress, you know, and will accept only an aristocrat of good family with his own wealth, so I may be certain he doesn't wed me merely for mine, and will not love me."

Philippe de Saville laughed heartily. *"Mon Dieu, ma cousine,* she is like every other woman in this family. Outspoken, and most frank. *Ma petite,"* he then said to Autumn, "your mama will explain the situation to you, but for the moment there is no real court in Paris because of our civil disturbances. Within the next year, however, that will change. In the meantime you will partake of society here in the region, and you will not find it lacking, I promise you." Rising, he directed his next speech to Jasmine. "Come to Archambault for the twelve days of Christmas, but come before, on St. Thomas's Day. My sisters will probably come to see you before then, so they may begin their plotting." He bowed to both women and then took his leave.

"*No court?*" Autumn looked crestfallen.

"Perhaps it is better that you make your debut into society here first," the mother soothed her daughter, secretly relieved. Autumn couldn't know it, but court was such a bother, and the French court was more formal and devious than England's court. *I don't know if I have the patience for this sort of thing anymore*, Jasmine thought.

"I like Oncle Philippe," Autumn said with a smile.

"You will like his sisters too," Jasmine promised, "and they will be most valuable in introducing you into society here. You are related by blood through your great-grandfather de Marisco, whose mother was the second wife of the Comte de chèr and great-grandmother of Oncle Philippe."

"I never knew I had a French family on your side, Mama. Papa would occasionally mention his uncles in France. Where are they?"

"Nearer to Paris. Eventually we shall meet them when the young king reaches his majority and the country is safe."

"I will need new gowns if I am to go to Archambault," Autumn said slyly. "You would not want me to appear a poor and unfashionable Scots cousin, Mama."

Jasmine laughed. "We will wait until my cousins Gaby and Antoinette arrive, which, if the weather remains pleasant, will certainly be in a day or so. They will know just what to do."

"May I ride this afternoon?" Autumn asked her mother.

"Of course, *ma bébé*, but remember, do not stray far. You do not know your way yet," Jasmine cautioned.

Autumn loved the horse she now rode. He was a tall and slender black gelding she had named, simply, Noir. She had changed from her gown into dark green woolen breeches lined in silk to protect her delicate skin from chafing, a white silk shirt that tied at the neck and had full sleeves, and a dark leather jerkin with carved ivory buttons edged in silver. Her boots, which fit to the knee, were of brown leather. The afternoon, while cool, was not cold, and so she wore no cape or cloak.

She followed a trail behind the gardens beyond the low stone wall into the woods. The trees were now bereft of their leaves, which had fallen and dried. They made a pleasant crunching noise beneath Noir's hooves. Soon the chateau disappeared behind her. About her in the branches, the rooks chattered companionably to each other as they preened. Autumn followed the trail until she came to a brook that rushed swiftly over a rocky streambed. Stopping, she debated whether they might cross it without injury to herself or the horse.

"It is not safe," a voice suddenly cut into her consciousness.

Startled, Autumn looked across the water and saw a man, dressed as casually as she was, sitting beneath a tree, while his own horse browsed nearby. "How do you know?" she demanded of him. "Have you tried?"

"The bottom is uneven, mademoiselle. It would be a pity for such a fine animal as the one you ride to break his leg and have to be destroyed," the gentleman said.

"But I am curious as to what lies beyond this brook," Autumn said, wondering who the man was. Probably a poacher who didn't want her to know what he was up to, and so was attempting to scare her off.

"The water is the dividing line between the lands belonging to the chateau of Belle Fleurs and the lands belonging to the Marquis d'Auriville," the man said. "You would be trespassing, mademoiselle, should you cross over," he told her.

"Who are you?" Autumn said boldly.

"Who are you?" he rejoined.

"I am Lady Autumn Rose Leslie. My mama owns Belle Fleurs, and we have come to live here, for England is not a happy place now."

"Neither is France, mademoiselle. You have merely exchanged one civil war for another, I fear," he said as he arose from his place and stretched lazily. He was a very handsome man with a long face.

"Are you a poacher?" she asked him, not doubting for a moment that he would lie if he were.

"No, mademoiselle, I am not a poacher," he said with an amused laugh. How ingenuous Lady Autumn Rose Leslie was, he thought.

"Then who are you?" she again asked him, thinking that he really was very tall. Every bit as tall as her brother Patrick.

"I am a thief, mademoiselle," he replied.

Not in the least nonplussed, she countered, "What do you steal, monsieur?" He was obviously mocking her. He didn't look like a bandit at all.

"Hearts, *chérie,*" came the startling reply, and then the man turned, caught his mount and, vaulting into his saddle, blew her a kiss as he rode off.

Astounded, Autumn watched as the man and his horse disappeared into the trees on the other side of the stream. She suddenly realized that not only was her heart racing, but her cheeks felt hot. It was all very confusing. Taking his advice, Autumn turned Noir back toward the chateau. If the lands on the other side of the brook *did* belong to someone else, then she really did not have the right to ride there unless she gained the owner's permission first.

When she returned to her home she sought out Guillaume and asked him, "To whom do the lands beyond the brook belong?"

"Why, to the Marquis d'Auriville, my lady," he answered. "Why do you ask?"

"I was curious," Autumn said with a little shrug. "I considered crossing the stream this afternoon but then worried I might be trespassing."

"It is a good thing you did not attempt it, my lady," Guillaume said. "The streambed is very rocky and uneven. Noir could have been injured. I am glad you are so careful with him. He is a fine mount."

The very next day the Comte de chèr's two widowed sisters, Madame de Belfort and Madame St. Omer, arrived at Belle Fleurs shortly after nine o'clock in the morning. With small shrieks of glee they rushed into the Great Hall, chattering nonstop.

"Jasmine! *Mon Dieu, cousine,* you have not changed at all! You have the figure of a young girl, despite all those children you pro-duced for your husbands! And your hair! It is still dark but for those two little silver chevrons on either side of your head!" Gabrielle de Belfort kissed her cousin on both cheeks and plunked her plump figure down by the fire, gratefully accepting a goblet of wine from Adali. "Adali, you are an old man. How could this have happened?" She smiled at him.

"Time, madame, I fear, has finally caught up with me," he said, returning her smile. "You, however, remain summer-fair."

"Very *late* summer," Antoinette St. Omer said dryly. "*Bonjour,* Jasmine. You must cease wearing black as soon as possible. Your skin is too sallow for it. Jemmie, I'm certain, would agree with me. Where is your daughter? We have come to inspect her so we may plan how to help you marry her off. Philippe says she is lovely."

"Adali, go and fetch Autumn. Tell her her *tantes* have arrived." Jasmine turned to her two cousins. "I have told her she is to call you both *tante*, as she has begun to call your brother *oncle*. We are seeking a husband, but first I think Autumn could use a bit of society, for she had none in the wilds of Scotland. By the time she was old enough for it, England was embroiled in civil war."

"There will be plenty of festivities at Archambault shortly, and Philippe loves to entertain despite his widowed state. It was really he who planned all the parties, even when Marie Louise was alive. She was best at running the house and giving him his sons," Antoinette said. While her sister was plump and short of stature, she was tall and spare, with her father's dark brown eyes, and iron gray hair that was fixed in the latest style of short curls.

"Oh, yes," Gaby interjected. "Philippe gives marvelous parties! Everyone in the entire area, and even beyond it, wants to come. Fortunately none of the vineyards is owned by any of the grand no-bles, so we have escaped the war, and our young men have remained at home." She shivered delicately. "War is such a nasty and dirty business. I do not know why men want to play at it. I truly don't!"

"Power does not appeal to my sister," Madame St. Omer said with a wink at Jasmine. "Ahh, here is the child. Come forward, girl, and let me see you. I am your *Tante* Antoinette St. Omer, and this is your *Tante* Gabrielle de Belfort."

Autumn hurried into the Great Hall to join the three women. She curtsied prettily, saying as she did so, *"Bonjour, tantes.* I am happy to meet you."

Madame St. Omer, who had not sat down since she entered the hall, took Autumn's chin between her thumb and forefinger, turning her head first this way and then that. "The skin is good, in fact excellent," she pronounced. Reaching around, she drew the thick braid into her hand and fingered its ends. "The hair is a good color and soft, yet not fine." Releasing the plait, she stared critically at Autumn's face. "The bones are good, the forehead high, the nose straight, the chin in proportion, the lips perhaps a trifle wide." Then she gasped. *"Mon Dieu,* child! Your eyes are different colors! One is the marvelous turquoise of your mama's, but the other is as green as a summer leaf. Where on earth did you ever get eyes like that?" Obviously overcome, she sat down, finally accepting the wine the footman had been waiting to give her and swallowing down a long draught of it.

"I owe my green eye to my paternal grandmother, Lady Hepburn," Autumn said with a chuckle. "I have always thought that my features, being so unique, would fascinate the gentlemen, *tante.* Do you know, or have you ever known a girl with such a feature as my eyes?"

"I have not!" Madame St. Omer answered, "but you may very well be right, *ma petite.* What others might see as a defect may very well prove bewitching to a suitor. You are shrewd, Autumn Leslie, and that is the French in you!" She turned to her sister. "Is she not lovely, Gaby? We shall have such fun planning her wardrobe. . . ." She stopped, turning back to Autumn. "You have jewelry, *ma petite?"*

"I have jewelry," Jasmine spoke up before her daughter might, and her two cousins nodded.

"Oh, what a winter it is going to be," Madame St. Omer said, pleased. "There are several eminently suitable gentlemen who would make excellent husbands for your daughter, *ma cousine.*

Gaby's late husband was related to one: Pierre Etienne St. Mihiel, the Duc de Belfort. And then there is Jean Sebastian d'Oleron, the Marquis d'Auriville; and Guy Claude d'Auray, the Comte de Montroi. These three are the crème de la crème in our area. All have their own estates and are very well endowed financially, so you need not fear they are fortune hunters. Even at court you could not find better matches."

"Are they handsome?" Autumn wanted to know.

"Oui," her aunt said. "I suppose they are, but *ma petite*, it is not a pretty face you must consider first, but a man's character and his purse. Jasmine, *ma chérie*, have you a priest in residence?"

"No, 'Toinette, we do not," came the reply. They were in France now, and she would revert to the faith of her childhood, although such a thing had never made a great difference to her. Still, she had been baptized a Roman Catholic and taught by her cousin, the Jesuit Father Cullen Butler. He had died the year before on her former estates in Ulster, a man in his mid-eighties.

"Your Guillaume has a son who has just been ordained," Madame St. Omer told her. "This would make an excellent living for him. You must see to it, Jasmine. Your daughter, I suspect, has been raised a Protestant, *n'est-ce pas?*"

"Aye, but she was baptized in Ulster shortly after she was born by both a priest and then a minister," Jasmine said.

"But she does not know her catechism, I am certain. If she is to wed a respectable Frenchman, she must be taught these things."

Jasmine nodded. "You are right," she said slowly. "I shall speak to Guillaume immediately. There is a small chapel here in the house somewhere. We will reopen it, and the priest can hold mass each day." She laughed softly. "How pleased Father Cullen would be."

"We will bring our own tailor tomorrow," Madame de Belfort said. "Autumn must have several pretty new gowns for her visit to Archambault. As I recall there is a storeroom beneath the hall, Jasmine. I will wager you will find the materials your grandmother bought stored away there. If not, we shall send to Nantes for some, but *la petite* must be shown to her best advantage. There are, after all, other young, unmarried girls in the region who are fishing for husbands. She will have serious competition.

"Nonsense!" Madame St. Omer contradicted her sister. "There isn't a girl in the region as beautiful, and certainly not as wealthy. We shall have all we can do, keeping the fortune hunters away and seeing that only the right gentlemen are permitted to court Autumn. I am so glad, chèr Jasmine, that you have put this matter into our hands." She smiled at her cousin, displaying her large, almost rabbity teeth.

After the two sisters had taken their leave, with promises to return early the following day, Autumn said to her mother, "The *tantes* are so . . ." She struggled to find the right word but could not.

"Overwhelming?" Jasmine supplied with a smile. "Aye, both Gaby and 'Toinette are all-engulfing in their desire to see that everything is done properly. I remember my grandmother saying that they were very much like their mother, but Autumn, we are fortunate to have their good advice. I want you happy, my child, and your father would too."

Suddenly Autumn's eyes filled with tears. "I miss him, Mama," she said brokenly. "Why did he insist on going to war for the Stuarts?"

Jasmine closed her eyes for a long moment so she might manage her own grief. Then, opening them, she said, "You know why, Autumn. James Leslie was the most honorable man I have ever known. He knew it was a fatal mistake for the Leslies of Glenkirk to defend and follow after the Stuarts, but they were his overlords, and related to him by blood. In his mind, even realizing it was likely to be a disaster, he felt compelled to obey their call, particularly as his own distant Leslie kin were involved up to their hips in the muddle. Your father might have pleaded his age, but he would not, and it was there he and I disagreed. I do not believe his honor would have been compromised by refusing to go. He did. It was easier for him to live with my disapproval than his own self-scorn. So he is dead and in his tomb at Glenkirk, and you and I are here in France, attempting to make a new life for ourselves."

"But what of Patrick?" Autumn fretted.

Her mother laughed now. "Poor Patrick. He always knew that one day he should be the Duke of Glenkirk, but I know he never expected to find himself with all that responsibility so soon. He will survive. Both your father and I were good teachers. Patrick will reach down into himself to find he has both the wisdom and the strength to do what he must. Before I left him I advised him to find a wife to stand by his side. He should have by now had his fill of enjoying the ladies while avoiding his obligations. Now he has no choice in the matter." She laughed again. "When I left Glenkirk I thought never to return, but now I know that I will one day go back. After all, I do want to be buried next to your father when my time comes."

"Oh, do not talk of your death, Mama!" Autumn cried, genuinely distressed, throwing her arms about her surviving parent.

"I intend to live to be an old lady, even as my mother is and my grandmother was," Jasmine soothed her daughter. "I must if I am to see your children and spoil them as Madame Skye spoiled me."

"Grandmama Velvet never spoiled me," Autumn said.

"It is not my mother's way," Jasmine said.

"And I never knew Papa's mother, even though I get my green eye from her," Autumn said. "I remember when I was almost thirteen, her coffin was brought home from Italy. I never knew where she was buried. Papa said it was a secret. Why was that?"

"I suppose it is all right for me to tell you now," Jasmine said. "Your grandmother's great love was her second husband, Francis Stewart-Hepburn, the last Earl of Bothwell. He was King James's first cousin, and poor Jamie was terrified of him, for Francis was everything the king wasn't. He was highly intelligent, handsome, passionate, and clever. He was called the uncrowned king of Scotland, which of course didn't please the king or his adherents. His weakness, however, was that when his royal cousin pushed, Francis, I am told, pushed back twice as hard. The king's counselors had him accused of witchcraft, claiming he was a warlock."

"Was he?" Autumn was fascinated by this bit of history, which she had never before heard.

"No, of course not," Jasmine laughed, "and despite the fact that the courts dragged forth several hysterical women—of low birth, I might add—claiming to be witches who identified him as a member of their coven, nothing could really be proved. What no one knew was that the king had a passion for your grandmother. He raped her one night, and she fled to Bothwell, who had been her friend. They fell in love, and eventually, after Lord Bothwell had been exiled and driven from Scotland, your grandmother, who was a widow, joined him, and they were married. It was actually your father who engineered his mother's escape, and then pretended to know nothing when the king grew angry. Jamie never knew the part your father played.

"When we came to France some years back for the wedding of Princess Henrietta Maria to our king, Charles the First, I met your grandmother for the very first time. She asked your father when she died to bring her body and Lord Bothwell's home to Scotland to be buried on the grounds of the old Glenkirk Abbey. He had already predeceased her. Bothwell's body was removed secretly from its grave in the garden of their villa in Naples. His bones were placed in your grandmother's coffin with her, and they were, as she had requested, interred together. Your father did not tell me until the coffin was returned to Scotland. Patrick knows now, for I told him before I left Glenkirk, so he would be certain to see the grave was always tended properly. Now you know, Autumn."

"I think that is the most romantic story I have ever heard!" Autumn said with a gusty sigh.

"And that is not even the entire story," Jasmine said with a smile, "but it is much too long a tale for today. Now we must consider preparing you for society, and the possibility of your finding a husband. I shall give you one word of advice, *ma bébé*. Do not marry just to marry. Do not choose a man because everyone else says he is the *right* man. Marry for love, *ma fille*. Marry only for love!"

"Why would you marry for any other reason, Mama?" Autumn cuddled next to her mother as they sat before the fire.

"Marriage," Jasmine began, "is a sacrament, and that is what I was taught, but it is a business arrangement as well. There is property and wealth involved with people of our station. More often than not, love is not considered before marriage. It is hoped that it will come after marriage."

"But what if it doesn't?" Autumn asked.

"Then it is hoped that at least the couple involved can respect one another and live together in harmony. My first marriage was arranged by my father. I did not meet Jamal Khan until our wedding day. Fortunately my husband and I fell in love as we grew to know each other. My grandparents arranged my second marriage with Rowan Lindley, but he and I were in love before we wed. My third marriage, to your father, was ordered by King James. You know the story, so I need not go into it with you. Your father and I were fortunate in that we loved one another dearly. I allowed your sisters their heart's desires, and it has turned out well for both of them. Now you, my youngest daughter, my last child, must find a mate. Choose wisely, Autumn. Your marriage will last until his death, or yours."

Autumn nodded, then asked, "Am I to become a Catholic, Mama?"

"You were baptized one, although you were not raised in that faith. Such things are not important to me, but here in France they are. I will speak with Guillaume about his son, who is a priest, so you may be taught the faith you must practice and must teach your children one day," Jasmine told her daughter.

Then, that same day, she spoke with Guillaume about his son. "Has he found a place yet?"

"No, Madame la duchese, he has not," answered Guillaume.

"Since I intend making my home here at Belle Fleurs, we must really have a priest," Jasmine explained. "There is a chapel here in the house, isn't there?"

"*Oui*, madame, behind the hall next to the library," came the reply, "but it has not been used in years," Guillaume said.

"I shall tell Adali to have the serving girls open it up and clean it. What is your son's name?"

"Bernard," Guillaume replied. He could barely stand still, for he wanted to go and tell his wife, Pascaline, of this stroke of good fortune that had befallen them.

"Tell Père Bernard that I shall expect him here before week's end to take up his duties. He will live in the house until a small cottage can be built for him. I will explain his responsibilities to him when he arrives and is settled. Go and tell your *bonne femme* now, for I can see in your eyes that you are anxious to do so." Then Jasmine smiled.

Guillaume bowed several times. *"Merci*, Madame la duchese, *mille merci!"* He hurried off in the direction of the kitchens.

They had settled in, and now Jasmine was bringing a priest to the house. France was really going to be her home, she considered. *I never thought to leave Glenkirk when I married Jemmie. I have lived so many places in my life. I wonder if this is my final home, or whether fate will surprise me again in my old age.* Then she laughed softly at herself. A change made life interesting. She had gotten too complacent with her life at Glenkirk. She had not left there since they had come home from Ulster, and Autumn had been a little baby. Oh, occasionally she would come down into England for an English summer with her mother, but Queen's Malvern had changed with Charlie's marriage to Bess. She had been content to remain in her own home.

Now, however, life was taking her by the hand and leading her down a new path. She hoped she had done the right thing, bringing Autumn to France. What if she didn't find a husband to love? What would happen to her daughter then? Jasmine sighed deeply. She had always considered herself independent and self-reliant. Now she wished Jemmie Leslie, her beloved husband, was still by her side. All these decisions she had made regarding her children she had made with his help and advice. They had looked over their combined family together. She hadn't done it alone at all. Not until now.

"Damn the Stuarts!" she said softly. "And damn you, Jemmie Leslie, for going off and leaving me alone! Your loyalty to me should have been greater than your loyalty to the Stuarts. What did they ever do for you? Nothing!" Then she began to cry bitter tears.

"My princess, drink this." Her faithful Adali was by her side, pressing a small crystal of cordial into her hand.

She swallowed the potent liquid down and then said, "What am I to do without him, Adali? What if I have made the wrong move in this chess game of life?" She looked up at the old man, now past eighty.

The kindly brown eyes met hers without hesitation. "His loss is great indeed, my princess, but we survived before him and we will survive now. There was nothing for your daughter in Scotland or England. If her fate is here, we will know it soon enough. If not, we will go where we are directed, even as we have always done. You are strong, my princess. You have always been strong. Rohana, Tora-malli, and I have been by your side since your birth to aid you. None of us will desert you now."

"We are old, Adali," she said. "I am past sixty."

He made an elegant swirl of motion with his hand. "Age, my princess, is but a number. Oh, the body grows old, but it is what is in the heart that keeps us young."

She was forced to smile now. "Then like Grandmama, I shall remain forever young, Adali, even if I eventually turn into a wizened crone." She swallowed down the rest of the cordial. "I think I have finished feeling sorry for myself now. Thank you."

He bowed slightly from the waist. "I overheard the two *mesdames*, and I have been to the storerooms in the cellar below the kitchens. It is filled with trunks holding absolutely magnificent fabrics. The trunks were cedar, and lined in copper. The fabrics are free of mildew, or mold. They will, of course, need airing to disperse the cedar fragrance, but other than that, they will be fine. I shall have them brought to the hall. The chapel was locked, and I could not find the key for it, but relying on some of my old skills, I managed to open the door. We shall take the lock to the blacksmith and have a new key made."

"You will not let me rest, Adali, will you?" Jasmine said with a chuckle, and she patted his arm lovingly.

"Time will not wait for us, my princess, no matter how much we wish it," Adali said. "We have work to do if young Autumn is to be ready for her debut into French society."

The Duchess of Glenkirk arose from her chair by the fire. "Very well, Adali, lead on," she told him, and together they departed the Great Hall.

Chapter

5

"Mademoiselle must have at least a hundred petticoats."

"One hundred petticoats?" Autumn was astounded by the tailor's pronouncement. "M'sieu Reynaud, why do I need so many petticoats?"

"Mademoiselle," came the pained reply, "the farthingale is passé. It is the petticoat that is fashionable now. They give body to the skirts, and you certainly do not want your skirts drooping about you in a bedraggled and ragtag manner, like some merchant's daughter, or"—he rolled his eyes dramatically—"a street urchin. *Non! Non! Non!* One hundred petticoats is absolutely the least number you can have. Silk, of course. It has the best texture," he explained.

"Starched lawn will not do for some of them?" Jasmine asked.

"If Madame la duchese wishes to scrimp . . ." The tailor raised a disapproving eyebrow and shrugged his bony shoulders.

Jasmine laughed, not in the least intimidated by the tailor. "I will agree to one hundred silk petticoats for my daughter, M'sieu Reynaud, but she must also have twenty-five lawn petticoats as well. They are cooler on a summer's day. Not for evening wear, of course, but for morning or afternoon, you understand."

"But of course, Madame la duchese," the tailor said with a small smile. "Madame is absolutely correct. I bow to her fashion sense."

"He bows to her well-filled purse," murmured Madame St. Omer in low tones. "Why have I never before noted what a terrible snob Reynaud is? But he is the best tailor in all of France, even Paris. Worse! He is well aware of that fact, the little beast."

"Oh, hush, sister, lest he hear you!" Madame de Belfort whispered back nervously. "You know how he is, and if you insult him, he will not do Autumn's wardrobe for her. Without him what chance has she?"

"Have you had the opportunity to inspect the fabrics I have?" the Duchess of Glenkirk asked the tailor.

M'sieu Reynaud burst into rapturous cries of approval. "Madame, never in my life have I seen such quality! The velvets! The brocades! The silks! The cloth of gold and of silver! And the ribbons and laces, madame! Where on earth did you obtain such magnificence?"

"My grandmother left them here many years ago," Jasmine said. "They were in my storerooms, m'sieu."

"*C'est* impossible! They have no odor of rot about them, or any sign of mildew staining the fabric!" the tailor cried.

"The trunks were cedar, lined with copper," Jasmine explained.

"Amazing!" he replied. Then he was all business once again. "Michel, my tape, *s'il vous plait*. If we are to have anything ready in the ridiculously short time Madame St. Omer has insisted upon, we must begin today. I shall measure mademoiselle myself."

Autumn stood quietly upon a small stool as the tailor swiftly took her measurements, his sharp voice snapping off the figures to his assistant, who quickly wrote them down and then repeated each figure to be certain he had gotten it correctly. Any mistake could be fatal to the wardrobe about to be made. When all the measurements had been taken and written down the tailor spoke again.

"What colors are preferred?"

"I think my daughter . . ." Jasmine began, only to be cut off by the volatile tailor.

"Madame la duchesse, I speak to she who must wear these gowns," he fiercely chided her. "If *mademoiselle* is unhappy, then she is not at her best with the gentlemen. *N'est-ce pas?*" Turning his back on the mother, he addressed Autumn. "Tell me the colors you like best, mademoiselle."

Autumn thought a moment, and then replied, "My hair is dark and my skin translucent. I like rich, clear colors. Emerald green. Turquoise, and peacock blue. Lilac and deep violet. Ruby red. Colors such as those complement me, M'sieu Reynaud. Necklines today are horizontal. I want mine as low as we dare, and no modest little kerchiefs for evening wear either. I want lace on *all* my petticoats and chemises, and I will not wear a corset of *any* kind. Is that understood?"

The tailor smiled, surprised, but appeared well pleased by her answer. "Mademoiselle is absolutely correct," he agreed.

"*Sacré bleu!*" Madame St. Omer exclaimed, amazed.

"If the necklines are too low, she will gain a reputation without ever having done a thing but enter the room," Madame de Belfort fretted.

"Mademoiselle will set fashions, not be shackled by them," M'sieu Reynaud said approvingly. "She is perfect, and my gowns shall be perfect! We shall have our first fitting in two days' time, madame," he said to the Duchess of Glenkirk. "You agree?"

"I shall rely upon you, M'sieu Reynaud," Jasmine replied with a smile. "We are completely in your hands."

The tailor bowed. "I shall not fail you, madame," he told her passionately. "My people will come later today to gather up the materials. They shall take them all, for who knows what we shall do, eh?"

The Duchess of Glenkirk nodded. "Of course," she said. "I have already inventoried everything. Adali, escort m'sieu and his assistant out, and see that the fabrics are ready when they are called for later."

"Yes, my princess," Adali responded. Then he accompanied the tailor and Michel from the Great Hall of the chateau.

"Hah!" Madame St. Omer said, well pleased. "He is a difficult little man, *cousine*, but he likes Autumn and will therefore do even better than his best for her." She turned to the young girl. "You clever minx," she chuckled. "You did not blush and play the *jeune fille*. Had you done so, he would have simply made you ordinary gowns. Now he will kill himself to be certain you are the best-dressed young woman at the Christmas revels at Archambault! You will snare a fine, wealthy and titled husband, and Reynaud will be delighted to take all the credit for it," she chortled. "He will be your friend for life!"

"If I don't like what he does, I shall tell him," Autumn said. "Like my sisters, I am particular about my clothing."

"Temper any criticism with lavish praise," Madame St. Omer suggested. "That way you will not insult him, and believe me, *ma petite*, your wardrobe is of paramount importance. We French are enamoured of fashion, and this fussy little man is an *artiste* with fabrics."

Two days later, Belle Fleurs was alive with the tailor and his staff, come for Autumn's first fitting. Lily helped her mistress into ten silk petticoats and the first skirt was then draped over them.

"It is not right," the tailor said pettishly. He pulled upon his chin thoughtfully. "*Pourquoi? Pourquoi?*"

"Lily, take the skirt off and give me one of those," Autumn said, pointing to one of the lawn petticoats. "Good, now put it over the top of the silk ones and let us refit the skirt." She looked to Reynaud. "What do you think?" she asked him.

He nodded approvingly. "Much better, mademoiselle. You have the fashion sense. One less silk petticoat, I think, and it is perfect."

Lily reached beneath her mistress's skirts and unfastened the tabs on a silk garment, drawing it down so Autumn might step out of it.

"It is perfect!" the tailor said, clapping his hands together. He turned to the duchess and Madame St. Omer. "Mesdames?"

"Excellent, M'sieu Reynaud," came the expected approval, as Autumn winked at her mother over the tailor's periwig.

Five other skirts were fitted that morning, and then came the bodices, which were more difficult. Autumn had insisted that both bodice and skirt be of the same color.

"In my grandmother's day bodices were far more beautifully decorated with jewels, crystals, and gold threads," she said. "How sad that my bodices must be so plain, with only ribbons and lace to embellish them."

The tailor nodded in complete agreement. "It is the times, mademoiselle," he said. "One does not dare to be lavish in the midst of civil war. At least we are not as dull as England is now." Then he gave her a mischievous smile. "I have a few tricks, mademoiselle, that I have given to no one, but to you only will I impart them. Mademoiselle will be the most fashionable young lady at Archambault, I promise her." He turned to the Duchess of Glenkirk. "I shall have twelve gowns, six for day wear, and six for evening, delivered to the chateau at Archambault by the time madame arrives. And each day afterwards, except Christmas day, of course, I shall deliver two more gowns. Your daughter will be well garbed, I assure you. When you have concluded your visit, leave everything, and my people shall deliver mademoiselle's new wardrobe back here to Belle Fleurs."

"You are both generous and efficient, M'sieu Reynaud," Jasmine told him. "See Adali, and he will advance you any funds you may need."

The tailor bowed respectfully to her. Then he and his staff gathered up their materials and the half-finished gowns, quickly departing. To be offered payment of any kind in advance was indeed a bonus, for the rich were just as likely not to pay, or keep a tradesman waiting months or even years for remuneration.

"You should not have offered to pay him anything until all was satisfactory," Madame St. Omer scolded her cousin, the duchess.

Jasmine shook her head. "Now," she replied wisely, "he will keep his promises in hopes of being compensated in full when the last gown is delivered. He will not disappoint me, and I will not disappoint him, *cousine*. I may have lived in the Highlands all these years, but human nature does not change, 'Toinette."

Antoinette St. Omer laughed. "You sound like Mama," she replied. "If Reynaud keeps his word, we shall have to have a separate chamber for all of your daughter's wardrobe."

Autumn was almost sick with excitement as they rode to Archambault on December 21. "What if my gowns aren't there? Damnation, Mama, I shouldn't behave like some silly chit of a girl. What is the matter with me?"

"You're excited, that's all. Sixteen or nineteen, Autumn, this is your first foray into real society," Jasmine responded.

They were warmly welcomed at the chateau by the comte and his widowed sisters.

"Tonight," Philippe de Saville said, "we shall be just family."

When they entered the Great Hall of the chateau that evening, however, there was a handsome young man whom Jasmine did not recognize as any member of the comte's immediate family.

"Oh! Oh! Here they are now," Gaby de Belfort twittered nervously. "Autumn, *chérie*, do come and meet my late husband's nephew. This is Pierre Etienne St. Mihiel, the Duc de Belfort." She reached out and drew Autumn forward. "Etienne, this is Lady Autumn Rose Leslie, my *cousine*'s child. I have told you about the Duchess of Glenkirk."

The duke bowed over Autumn's outstretched hand, his cool lips just touching the skin. "Mademoiselle," he said, and then he looked up at her. A lock of his blond hair fell over his forehead and his brown eyes scanned her with open interest.

"M'sieu le duc," Autumn replied. He was really quite handsome, but she could sense that he knew it.

"And this is Autumn's mama," Gaby pattered on.

The Duc de Belfort greeted the Duchess of Glenkirk.

Jasmine nodded pleasantly at the young man. She wondered how much depth there was to him. "My *cousine* has mentioned you in passing, monseigneur," she told him.

"I can but hope she spoke well of me, Madame la duchese," he replied.

"How could she not?" Jasmine said, and then she turned away to speak with Madame St. Omer.

"I like your gown," the duke said to Autumn. "It's the exact color of the fine burgundy I make." His eyes appeared to struggle to see beyond her neckline, which was low enough to tempt but not low enough to reveal.

"*Merci,*" she replied. "Is your burgundy as good a wine as they make here at Archambault? I have drunk Archambault wine all my life. My father would have no other vintage at Glenkirk."

He smiled. "You will judge yourself one day soon, mademoiselle. In the spring I hope you and your mama will visit Chateau Reve. Do you ride? You must, of course. Perhaps we could ride tomorrow if the weather is pleasant," the duke suggested to her.

"You are staying at Archambault, monseigneur?" Autumn asked him.

"Yes," he replied.

A footman was at their side, offering them silver goblets of wine.

"He is handsome," Jasmine said to her daughter later that night, as they sat before a fire in their apartment. "Gaby absolutely adores him. She says his chateau is simply gorgeous."

"He says he will ask us to visit in the spring," Autumn told her mother. "He is nice, but I suspect he knows he is."

"My *cousine* asked him to come early so he might gain an advantage with you. I think she may have miscalculated, *ma bébé*."

"I don't know what's the matter with me, Mama." Autumn said with a deep sigh. "When you met Papa, were you so disinterested? When did you know he was the one for you?"

"When I met your father, my stepsister, Sybilla, had decided she was going to be the next Countess of Glenkirk, for your father was not a duke then. But Jemmie didn't want Sibby, and I was to marry Rowan Lindley. After I was widowed, and after Charlie was born, your father finally got around to trying to court me. He had always held a certain fascination for me. The spark was there; I just did not allow it to burst into flame. By the time I was your age, Autumn, I had had two husbands and two children." She patted her daughter's hand. "I know it seems the entire emphasis of our coming to France is on finding you a husband, *ma bébé*, but if no man takes your fancy, you must not marry just for the sake of marrying. You must be happy, Autumn, and if being unwed makes you happy, then so be it!"

"Oh, Mama! I like the gentlemen well enough. I just can't seem to find one I like enough that I don't want to lose him. In all my life I have only met one man who intrigued me enough that I wanted to know him better, but he was unsuitable," Autumn told her mother.

Now Jasmine was fascinated. She had never before heard her daughter mention any gentleman who attracted her. "Who is this gentleman, *ma bébé* and where did you meet him?" she gently inquired.

"I met him here in the forest one day," Autumn explained. "I expect he was a poacher, though he denied it. I have no idea what his name is, or who he is. He said he was a thief, and when I asked him what he stole, Mama, he said the oddest thing. He said he stole *hearts.*"

Jasmine laughed softly. "I think I should certainly be fascinated by such a gentleman, Autumn," she told her daughter. "A man that clever is unlikely to have been either a thief or a poacher. I wonder who he was. Well, if he is a gentleman, you shall undoubtedly see him, for your uncle Philippe has invited every family of stature and wealth in the entire region for a great party he is giving on Twelfth Night. In the meantime you shall have to make do with St. Mihiel. You could practice flirting with him, *ma petite.*"

"Mama! Girls today do not put on such affectations," Autumn said. "Perhaps when you were young, but no longer."

"When I was young," her mother replied, "girls were not allowed the privilege of choosing their husbands for love, and most today are not either. In my day, *ma petite*, your parents chose your husband, and that was the end of it. You wed their choice, and lived with it. Perhaps if you cannot make up your mind, Autumn, I should simply choose the man I think the best mate for you, and we'll be done with it. You haven't the faintest idea of what girls do today, but I will wager flirting is still very much part of courtship."

"I think it's silly," Autumn said frankly.

"You will catch more gentlemen with honey, *ma petite*, than you will with sour wine," Jasmine advised.

On Christmas Day they were joined by Guy Claude d'Auray, the Comte de Montroi, a charming young man with dancing blue eyes and light brown hair filled with golden highlights. He made Autumn laugh, and he quite obviously irritated Etienne St. Mihiel. She was finally beginning to enjoy herself. She had never had young men pay her such attention, for she had lived a very protected life at Glenkirk. It had been a life that had suited her quite well. It was fun, however, to have Etienne and Guy paying her court, vying for her complete attention, arguing over who would dance with her next. One day she found herself giggling and tapping the arm of one of her swains teasingly with her feather fan.

"You are flirting, *ma fille*," her mother murmured softly.

"*Mon Dieu*, I am!" Autumn said, surprised. But then she turned her concentration back to her duke and her count.

"Only one more to come," Antoinette St. Omer said softly, watching Autumn as she danced with the duke.

"*If* he comes," the comte remarked dryly. "You know how independent Sebastian is, and he has an abhorrence of virgins besides."

"Well, he had best get over *that* if d'Auriville is to have an heir one day," Madame St. Omer replied sharply. "Proper brides are virgins, Philippe. I do not know where Sebastian d'Oleron gets such odd notions. He is hardly in the first flush of youth and will soon be too old to sire an heir. Such a charming man, but so stubborn."

The Comte de Saville's Twelfth Night fête was to feature dancing and a midnight banquet. The guests were to come in costume, and there would be a masque performed by a troupe of traveling players invited for the occasion.

"I am coming as the sun," Autumn announced to her swains.

"Then I shall come as the moon," Etienne said quickly, and he grinned smugly at the Comte de Montroi.

Guy d'Auray was not in the least put out. "I shall come as a comet who circles the sun," he told them.

Autumn clapped her hands together. "Oh, Guy! How clever you are to have thought of such a guise, and so quickly," she told him.

The comte bowed elegantly to her. "*Merci, chérie*," he said.

"Who gave you leave to call her *chérie?*" the duke demanded.

"You may both call me *chérie*," Autumn quickly replied in an effort to prevent further argument.

The two young men glared at each other.

"Gracious, Mama," Autumn later said to her mother. "They are so competitive. I almost expected them to get into a duel over me." Her eyes danced mischievously at the thought.

"Duels are illegal, Autumn, and the penalty is death for those caught," her mother warned her. "Do not tease your suitors into breaking the law. It is hardly a way to make your decision."

"What decision?" Autumn replied.

"Why, which of them you will marry," Jasmine responded.

"I don't want to marry either of them, Mama," the young woman returned. "Etienne is charming and Guy such fun, but I am not in love with either of them. I don't think I could be."

"It is too soon," her mother said. "You don't know either of them particularly well yet, but by spring you should."

Autumn nodded. "Perhaps you are right, Mama. I must give myself more time to know them better."

The Duchess of Glenkirk, in mourning, did not wear a costume to her cousin's Twelfth Night fête. Instead, she wore a gown of deep violet that M'sieu Reynaud had made for her, along with an exquiste silver and amethyst masque. The gown's only ornamentation was a collar of silver lace. Her daughter, however, was garbed magnificently in a cloth-of-gold gown with a transparent overgown of gilt sprinkled with tiny gold beads and diamante. The dress was set low on the shoulders to reveal Autumn's creamy skin and beautiful young bosom. The sleeves were puffed to the elbow, with topaz-studded ribbons, and then fitted below to the wrist. Her shoes were painted gold, and the heels studded with tiny diamonds. Her hair had been affixed into an elegant chignon, sprinkled with gold dust, and dressed with small looped strands of tiny gold beads, yellow diamonds, and topaz. Atop her head sat a delicate gold crown representing the sun, each ray tipped with a yellow diamond. From her ears hung yellow diamonds. About her neck was a chain of small yellow diamonds and rose gold, from which dangled a large, round Golconda diamond cut with so many facets that it flashed fire with every move Autumn made.

"*Ravissante!*" her uncle declared when she first came into the Great Hall. "No other woman here tonight will outshine you."

"You do not think it a bit too bold?" fretted Madame de Belfort, looking anxiously between Jasmine and her brother.

"Nonsense!" Madame St. Omer said before anyone else could speak. "It is a daring costume, and when baiting a trap one uses the most delicious cheese available. Bravo, *ma petite!* You will drive the gentlemen wild tonight!"

Jasmine laughed. "She certainly will, 'Toinette," the duchess agreed with her cousin, and then she patted Gaby de Belfort's plump hand in an effort to comfort her. "Autumn isn't sixteen, Gaby. To garb her as a *jeune fille* would be totally inappropriate."

Etienne St. Mihiel and Guy d'Auray hurried into the hall, almost knocking each other over in their eagerness to reach Autumn. The duke was dressed in silver, a crescent studded in aquamarines upon his head. His companion was in deep blue and silver, a comet's tail of gold and silver for his headpiece. Autumn admired both of them equally, although each thought he had gotten the better of the other. As the music started they began to argue over who should dance with her first. It was then a gentleman, garbed as a bandit in a black cloak, a wide-brimmed felt hat with several white plumes, and a black mask, stepped between the duke and the comte, bowed to Autumn, and led her off onto the floor.

"Who is that?" Jasmine asked.

"Unless I miss my guess," Antoinette chuckled, "it is d'Oleron himself. I suspected curiosity would eventually get the better of him."

Jasmine watched her daughter with interest, smiling to herself as she remembered her youth.

"You are bold," Autumn told her partner as he led her through the intricate steps of the dance.

"Your costume, *chérie*, is hardly modest," he replied. "You glitter and glow like a beacon as you offer yourself to the highest bidder." He twirled her about gracefully.

"I have no need for the highest bidder, m'sieu," Autumn said in a tight voice. "I am an heiress of great worth."

Her partner laughed, genuinely amused. "Are you indeed, mam'selle?"

Autumn stopped in the midst of the dance and stamped her foot at him. "Yes, I am!" she snapped.

"Do not make a scene, *chérie*," he advised as he drew her back into the figure. "You have a temper, but I like a woman with a temper. It shows character. I do not wish to marry some passionless creature."

"*Marry?*" Autumn was astounded by his words. "What do you mean *marry*, m'sieu?"

"You have come to France to find a husband, or at least that is the gossip," he told her, and he laughed again when she blushed. "I am, to the relief of my relations, now in the market for a wife. I think you will do quite nicely, Lady Autumn Rose Leslie."

That voice. It was *his* voice. "*You!*" she said. "It is you! The gentleman in the forest who said he was a thief."

The music stopped, and her partner bowed elegantly. "Jean Sebastian d'Oleron, Marquis d'Auriville, at your service, mademoiselle." He caught up her hand, and kissed it, but he did not let it go. Instead he led her across the Great Hall into a small alcove.

"I would not marry you if you were the last man on earth!" Autumn said angrily. "I should rather die a virgin!"

"There is no chance of your dying a virgin, *chérie*, but you surely cannot prefer those two bumbling suitors who dog your every move."

"Etienne is a duke and you are only a marquis," Autumn said. "As for Guy d'Auray, he amuses me. I don't even know you."

"You will," he told her confidently. "Now as for St. Mihiel, he may be a duke, but my blood is far bluer than his." He backed her against the stone wall of the alcove. "Have you ever been kissed?" he asked her curiously. One of his arms stretched out to confine her, while the fingers of his other hand brushed against her full mouth. "Your lips are like rose petals," he said softly.

Breathe! her inner voice said. *Breathe dammit!* She could hear her heart thumping madly in her ears. Had she ever been kissed? No! She most certainly had not, but she was most certainly going to be. The roving hand tipped her face up to his, and his lips touched hers tenderly. Autumn sighed deeply, unable to help herself.

He drew away. "It is better if you close your eyes, *chérie*," he suggested gently. "Let us try again now." His mouth took possession of hers even as her eyes closed slowly.

She soared. It was wonderful. It was everything she had always imagined a kiss should be. It was even more! And he had absolutely no right to be taking such liberties. Autumn raised her foot and stamped her diamond-studded high heel into his boot. "How dare you, monsigneur!" When he leapt back, swearing softly, she slapped him; then, pushing past his satin-clad bulk, she hurried back into the main part of the hall.

Sacré bleu, but his foot hurt where she had assaulted him! When he got his footwear off it was likely to be black and blue. What a wildcat! There was no doubt in his mind now that this was the girl he wanted to make his wife. When he had seen her that day in the forest he had known it, but he had bided his time. There were several things he had had to do before he could court a respectable young girl like Autumn. His mistress, Marianne Boucher, had to be pensioned off, and their daughter put with the nuns to be educated. He had made arrangements to pay the child's school fees, and when she was ready to marry one day, he would dower her if he approved of the match. He knew Marianne would see he did, for she was a practical woman. He had bought her a house in the town of Tours, near their daughter's convent. She would be comfortable. More important, she understood her time in his life had come to an end. He would now marry and raise a family.

Jean Sebastian d'Oleron, limping slightly, made his way across the Great Hall to where his host stood, undoing his mask as he came. He bowed to the comte. "Philippe. I thank you for inviting me tonight." He bowed. Then he turned to the three older women. "Mesdames." He bowed again.

"Allow me to introduce my cousin, the Dowager Duchess of Glenkirk," Philippe said.

The marquis took Jasmine's hand and, raising it to his lips, kissed it. "I can see, madame, where your daughter gets her beauty. I would like to call upon you when you return to Belle Fleurs. Do not promise your daughter to another until we have spoken."

Madame de Belfort gasped audibly. Madame St. Omer smiled archly.

"I cannot promise my daughter to any man without her permission, monseigneur," Jasmine explained. "It is tradition in our family that our daughters choose their own husbands, *m'sieu le marquis*. As long as the gentleman is suitable, the choice is theirs . We prefer to marry for love, and no other reason."

"Eccentric perhaps, Madame la duchese, but I would agree that love is the only reason to wed." He bowed and kissed her hand again. Then, turning, he left the Great Hall of Archambault.

"Mon Dieu," Madame de Belfort said, fanning herself vigorously. "My nephew had best look to his interests if he is to have Autumn to wife."

"Do not bother to alert him, Gaby," Jasmine said. "Autumn has already told me that while she enjoys their company, neither Etienne nor Guy is for her. I have suggested she get to know them better before she makes her decision. My daughter is young. She may be a bit immature, but she knows her mind and is a sensible girl."

"But d'Oleron is so . . . so . . ." Gaby floundered for the right word.

"So deliciously dark and dangerous," Madame St. Omer said with a twinkle in her brown eyes. "Oh, to be nineteen again, and as beautiful as Autumn! What a man our elusive marquis is, sister!" She smacked her lips with distinct relish.

"Oh, 'Toinette," her sister wailed. "What are we to tell Etienne? He is truly enchanted with Autumn."

"You will tell him nothing, *cousine*," Jasmine said. "It is up to Autumn to decide, and to tell the others when she does. I do not want my daughter determining whom to marry for all the wrong reasons. Or refusing to marry because she feels pressed by all of us."

"You have favored d'Oleron all along," Gaby hissed at her sister. "Poor Etienne!"

"I have indeed favored d'Oleron," her sister admitted frankly. "It is time he married, and not to some silly, weak little mademoiselle, but a girl who burns with passion. Autumn is that girl, although in the end she may not want d'Oleron or any of the others. Etienne St. Mihiel is a man who would find to his regret that Autumn could not be molded into the French wife he truly desires. Such a union would be a disaster!" She kissed her sister's cheek. "Let them sort it out themselves, Gaby. It will all work out eventually." She turned to her cousin. "What do you think of him, Jasmine?"

"Nothing yet, 'Toinette. He is bold, *oui*. He is very handsome. *Absolument!* Autumn is intrigued, but only time will tell."

"How do you know Autumn is intrigued with him?" Madame St. Omer asked curiously. "She only met him tonight, and you have not spoken to her since they danced."

"Nay, *cousine*, I believe the marquis is the man Autumn told me she met in the forest while out riding. He puzzled her, and yet he excited her." Jasmine laughed softly. "She thought he was a poacher, but he told her he was a thief—of hearts."

Madame St. Omer chuckled. "That sounds like Sebastian."

"How do you know him?" Jasmine wondered.

"His late mother was my best friend," Antoinette St. Omer explained. "She was also my husband Raoul's first cousin. His sister's child. I have known Sebastian since he was born. Both his parents are dead. They had gone to Paris on a visit. When they returned home both had contracted the plague. They died within a day of each other. Sebastian was only sixteen, but he took on the responsibilities of his estates at Auriville, and his vineyards are every bit as good as Archambault's."

"How old is he?" Jasmine asked.

"Thirty this August past," came the reply.

"Why has he not married before?"

Madame St. Omer hesitated a moment, and her sister spoke up.

"He was married," Gaby de Belfort told Jasmine. "It was a shameful scandal!"

"It was not Sebastian's fault," Madame St. Omer responded quickly. "When he was seventeen he was wed to Elise Montpensier, the only daughter of the Comte de Montpensier. What can I say about Elise? She looked like an angel, but she was a daughter of the devil. No sooner were they wed than she began taking lovers. She had no discrimination. A nobleman, a stableboy. It made no difference to her. All she desired was a strong, tireless cock. When she found herself with child, she could not be certain it was Sebastian's. So she went to an old witch woman in the forest to rid herself of the baby. Whatever it was the hag gave her killed Elise and her child. They had not been married even a year, Jasmine. He has not married since."

"Do not forget Marianne Boucher and her daughter," Gaby said sweetly. "She has been his mistress for seven years, and he has acknowledged her daughter, Celine, as his child." She smiled at her sister. "Etienne is far more discreet than to publicly acknowledge his bastards."

Jasmine laughed as her two cousins glared at each other, each determined to make her candidate for Autumn's hand the winner in this contest. "Well," she told them, "at least we know the gentlemen can father children. What of M'sieu Guy?" she teased them.

"A daughter and twin sons," Philippe chuckled.

"*O la la!*" Jasmine replied admiringly, and the two sisters were forced to laughter themselves.

"What a quartet of busybodies we are," Madame St. Omer said. "But I will admit to being eager to find what the outcome of this all is to be. Perhaps Autumn will have none of them."

"I doubt my daughter could find better suitors anywhere else," Jasmine told them, pleasing her relations mightily, for they really wanted to help in this delicate matter. "Tomorrow," she continued, "we shall return to Belle Fleurs and give Autumn some time to herself. She has had far too good a time at Archambault and needs a bit more solitude to regain her sense of proportion. I shall tell Etienne and Guy they may not call upon us for at least a month. It is a good plan, eh?"

Her three cousins agreed, nodding their heads in unison.

Jasmine and Autumn returned to their home the following day.

"I am glad to be back," Autumn admitted to her mother. "I hardly had time to sleep, or a moment to myself these past three weeks."

"You do not miss the excitement, or your two eager beaux?" Jasmine smiled at her daughter.

"Etienne and Guy are entertaining, but I began to grow weary of their constant rivalry. I suppose some women would find it flattering, but I found it annoying. Particularly in light of the fact that I was never really alone with either of them, nor had I allowed them even so much as a kiss. It was becoming tiresome, Mama."

"And what of the Marquis d'Auriville, *ma bébé?*"

Autumn colored becomingly. "The marquis?" she said weakly.

"*Oui,* m'sieu le marquis," her mother said. "I saw him lead you off to dance, and when you returned several minutes later you were flushed. Did he kiss you?"

Autumn nodded. "He says he is going to marry me." She bit her lower lip in vexation. "You know how I dislike being told what I am going to do, Mama. And yet . . ."

Jasmine laughed softly. "He fascinates you, doesn't he?"

"Aye, he does," Autumn admitted.

"Did you enjoy his kiss?"

"Aye, but I am not certain why. Was it because it was my first kiss? Or was it because he excites me? If having Etienne and Guy squabble over me wasn't bad enough, this marquis confuses me even further. Would I like it if the duke or the comte kissed me?"

"You will only know if you kiss them too," her mother said.

"Are you advising me to kiss every suitor I have?" Autumn had to laugh. "I do not think other girls have mothers who would suggest such a thing to them. Indeed, Mama, I think I am most shocked by you."

"Nonsense, *ma petite!* There is nothing scandalous in what I propose. If you are to make a comparison between these three gentlemen, you must certainly kiss all three. How else are you to know? And not to know is a far worse fate. Of course, it must go no further than kissing, Autumn. A simple kiss is harmless, but anything else would be forbidden, *ma fille.* And most important of all, make no hasty decisions."

Winter set in, but it was a far milder winter than Autumn was used to in Scotland. January passed, and they were left in solitude until its last day, when Sebastian d'Oleron came riding up the driveway to Belle Fleurs. His horse slowly crossed the bridge and passed through the chatelet into the chateau's courtyard. A stableman hurried to take his animal when he dismounted. A tall man with a silver-flecked russet beard came forward.

"You are . . . m'sieu?"

"The Marquis d'Auriville," Sebastian said. "I have come to call upon Lady Autumn."

"I will escort you inside, m'sieu le marquis," Red Hugh said.

Inside Adali hurried forward, garbed in his usual white trousers and long coat, a small turban upon his head.

"The Marquis d'Auriville to see the young mistress," Red Hugh said. "Best to see if her grace approves first." The last was said in English.

Sebastian d'Oleron's face gave no indication that he had understood the Scotsman. The marquis was well educated and spoke several languages, English being among them. He was rather fascinated by this polyglot household of servants. He knew very little about Autumn, except that he wanted her and intended to have her.

"Will you come into the hall, m'sieu le marquis, and I will fetch my mistress?" Adali said. He bowed, then turned and led the way.

The marquis liked the Great Hall of the little chateau. It was warm and inviting with its country oak furnishings, its warm fires, the ancient tapestries hanging upon the stone walls, the Turkey carpets, the fragrance of potpourri.

"Please, will you sit by the fire, monseigneur? Marc! Wine for the marquis." Adali bowed and then withdrew, leaving their guest comfortably ensconced with a goblet in his big hand. Adali found his mistress in the chapel with Autumn, who was being taught her catechism by the young priest, Father Bernard. "Madame, the Marquis d'Auriville has come to call upon the young mistress," he said.

Jasmine rose, raising a restraining hand to her daughter. "I will go. When you have finished your lessons, Autumn, you may join us in the Great Hall. Please see to your coif before you come." She walked quickly from the chapel. "M'sieu le marquis," she greeted her guest as she came into the hall. "*Non! Non!* Do not get up. I will join you. Adali, some wine, please." She smiled at him. "How clever of you to give my daughter some time after all the festivities we so enjoyed at Archambault. I suggested to the duke and the comte that they not call on us until midwinter, but you were gone and I could not speak with you. Now here it is the last day of January, and you have come."

"I want your daughter for my wife," he said.

"You do not know my daughter, nor does she know you," Jasmine replied. "I told you that the choice is hers, and it is. If you want Autumn, monsigneur, I am afraid you will have to court her properly, and you will probably have to put up with at least two rivals, as you already know." Jasmine restrained a smile, seeing his irritation.

"I am not like those two wastrels," he said. "I personally oversee my vineyards. I have little time for niceties, Madame la duchese. It is almost time to prune the vines, to add lime and fertilizer. The growing season will be upon us before you know it. I cannot dance attendance upon a pretty girl while my vineyards go to ruin."

"I am no expert in such things, monseigneur, but I believe you may safely give up the month of February to come courting," Jasmine told him with a small smile. "Tell me now, did you not court your first wife?"

"No, Madame la duchese, I did not. The marriage was arranged by my parents prior to their deaths. When I was seventeen I married Elise. Her dower consisted of some excellent land matching my estates, which I planted new vines upon. You have been told the gossip, of course, and you know that while the vines flourished, the marriage did not. I have been a widower for thirteen years."

"Autumn's father was a widower when I married him. He had been for many years," Jasmine told him. "We had three sons, and two daughters. The children of his prior marriage had died with their mother. I brought four children to our marriage. We are a large family."

"I have cousins and a sister who is a nun," he offered.

"And your mistress and her daughter?" Jasmine pressed gently.

"I have bought Marianne a house, pensioned her, and Celine is in school with the nuns. Marianne understands that our liaison is now over. She is a practical woman, Madame la duchese," the marquis told his companion. "When I wed again, I will be faithful, even as I was faithful to my first wife."

"Then I have no objections to your paying your addresses to my daughter, Sebastian d'Oleron, but if you want Autumn, you will, I fear, have to court her properly. She is young and inexperienced, as I'm certain you realized when you kissed her. But you opened Pandora's box with that kiss, I fear. Now she wants to know whether other men kiss the way you did." Jasmine chuckled.

He laughed, and as he did he wondered why he was not upset by the duchess's revelation. He had wed Elise and found her to be totally promiscuous. Instinct told him that the lovely Autumn was entirely different. Her curiosity was only temporary. The lips that had softened beneath his belonged to him, as she would soon learn.

Chapter ✤ 6 ✤

Autumn came into the hall, her heart fluttering nervously. God's blood, he was so handsome! He was tall and lean and hard. She wanted to touch his thick, coal black hair. She wanted his mouth on hers again. She had thought of nothing but those two kisses for weeks. She doubted the kisses of Guy d'Auray and Etienne St. Mihiel could possibly equal the kisses of the marquis, but she certainly intended to find out before she committed herself in marriage to any man.

"Adali says we have a guest, Mama," she said, feigning innocence.

He rose, Jasmine noted, restraining himself from going forward to greet her. He bowed formally. "Mademoiselle Leslie."

"M'sieu le marquis," she answered, and held out her hand to him to be kissed.

He complied and, releasing the dainty hand, said, "Your mother has given me her permission to court you, mademoiselle. Do I have your permission also?"

Clever, clever man! Jasmine thought. *You already know her.*

"Why do you desire to court me, m'sieu?" Autumn asked sweetly.

"Because I am seeking a wife, and you excite me," he told her frankly. "It would appear to be a good beginning."

"I must love the man I wed," Autumn replied.

"I am a widower, mademoiselle. I have learned from bitter experience that I too must love the wife I next take," he told her. "It may well be that we will discover we do not suit one another, after, of course, we have gotten to know each other a bit better. That is what courtship is all about."

Gray. *No, silver!* His eyes were silver. "You may court me, m'sieu le marquis," she told him, "being advised that there are two others who are courting me as well."

"*If* I decide I want you, Autumn Rose Leslie, they will have no chance," he said softly.

"*If* I decide I want you, Sebastian d'Oleron," she quickly countered, "they will have no chance."

Oh, my, Jasmine thought, as she quietly observed her daughter with the marquis. The sparks that flew between the two hurled her back in time for a moment. Such similar sparks had ignited a lifelong love match for her and James Leslie. *Oh, Jemmie, if you could only see her now. If only you were with me instead of in your tomb at Glenkirk.* She felt tears pricking at her eyelids and blinked them back. Very soon, she realized, she would be alone for the first time in her life, and this time there would be no new love. Yet she was content in that knowledge. She had had three husbands, each unique and each loving. She had her marvelous memories to fall back on. Now it was time for her youngest child to find love.

"Mama, the marquis would like me to ride with him now. May I?" Autumn's little heart-shaped face was begging her to assent, although the tone of her voice was calm and well-modulated, as if it really didn't matter at all to her.

"Of couse, *ma petite*. Go along and change your garments, remembering that the day is chill and the sun not particularly warm," Jasmine said.

"*Merci*, Madame la duchese," the marquis said to Jasmine.

"I shall call you Sebastian," she said to him. "And you may address me as Madame Jasmine from now on, *mon brave*."

Autumn had run from the Great Hall to exchange her gown for riding clothes.

"Tell me about her father," Sebastian said to Jasmine. "How did he die? There is so much I need to know about her."

The question endeared him to Jasmine, although he could not know it. Neither the young duke nor the count had ever inquired into Autumn's family. Obviously her fortune was all they needed to know about her.

"My husband died at Dunbar, fighting for King Charles. He was a very brave, very loyal man. It was that loyalty that cost him his life, for he was too old to have been involving himself in such a battle. Autumn will tell you that the Leslies always find themselves in difficulties when they throw in their lot with the royal Stuarts. They are bad luck for our family. Belle Fleurs belonged to my grandparents. My grandfather de Marisco's mother took the Comte de Chèr as her second husband and gave him several children. That is how we are related, through my great-grandmother de Saville.

"Belle Fleurs seems to be the place I come to escape. When I was last here it was with my four oldest children. I had not yet married Jemmie Leslie, Autumn's father." She smiled wistfully. "King James had ordered our marriage, but Jemmie and I had a difference of opinion, so I came to France with the children."

"You obviously settled your differences," the marquis said with a small smile.

Jasmine laughed. "Indeed we did, although we had many others over the years of our marriage, the last being when he insisted on going to fight for the Stuarts, damn him! Forgive me, Sebastian. The wound is new and very painful. Tell me about your home."

"It is the chateau nearest to Archambault," he began. "It is called Chèrmont. It has been in my family—the lands at least—for as long as any can remember. The chateau itself is over two hundred years old, and very beautiful. It was built, I am told, on the ruins of an earlier dwelling. It is smaller than Archambault, but larger than your home. Autumn will be very happy there, Madame Jasmine."

"Happy where?" Autumn came back into the hall dresed in her riding breeches. She had wasted no time in changing from her gown.

"Chermont, my home," the marquis said.

"I have not said I would marry you, m'sieu le marquis," she told him pertly. "I have only said I would ride with you."

"Go along," Jasmine told them before the difference degenerated into a full-blown argument.

They walked from the hall out into the courtyard, where Red Hugh was waiting with their horses. After he had helped Autumn to mount, he climbed upon his own horse. As they walked their animals over the chateau's little stone bridge he followed behind them at a discreet distance. Hearing the hoofbeats behind her, Autumn stopped and turned about.

"What are you doing?" she demanded of Red Hugh.

"I am your escort, m'lady," he told her calmly.

"I do not need an escort," Autumn said in a tight little voice.

"It is your mother who gives me my orders, m'lady, as you very well know. I am certain m'sieu le marquis understands."

"I do," Sebastian d'Oleron said. "If you were seen riding with me alone, *chérie*, and our betrothal not yet announced, it could cause gossip. I am sure you do not want any gossip."

"Why should I care? Particularly if the gossip is not true," Autumn remarked. "It makes no difference to me what people may say, as long as I know my honor is intact, monsigneur."

"Honor and reputation are closely related, *chérie*," he explained. "If one is tarnished, then so is the other. People are quick to believe the worst of even the most saintly person. As my intentions toward you are most honorable, I find no insult in your escort."

Autumn clamped her lips together to quell the further protest welling up inside her. With Red Hugh tagging along behind them, how was she going to get him to kiss her again? She clapped her heels to her horse's sides and cantered off. To her surprise, the marquis was right by her side, and behind them she heard Red Hugh's horse. They rode to the top of a gentle hillock overlooking the river chèr. There was a fine view of Archambault on a neighboring hill, and all around below them the vineyards lay sleeping in the weak winter sun.

"The vines are so beautiful, even without their leaves and fruit," Autumn said. "They look like an army of gnarled brown gnomes. There is such peace here. Where is Chermont?"

"Down the river a few miles to the south. It is nearer to Chenonceaux, the royal estate, than Archambault or Belle Fleurs," he explained.

"Does the king come there?" she wondered.

"In the past the court has," he answered her. "Little King Louis has been much too busy learning the lessons of statehood and running away from those who would protect him to have had much time for chateaux like Chenonceaux. It is a very romantic place. When we are married I shall take you there, *chérie.*"

"Must I keep reminding you, monsigneur, that I have not said I will marry you?" Autumn laughed.

"Must I keep reminding you, *chérie*, that you will, and sooner rather than later. You are as ripe and as sweet as a summer peach. I want to eat you up!" he teased her, his silver eyes glittering dangerously.

"I think you are an impossible man," she replied, blushing, to her great annoyance.

"Of course I am," he agreed with a grin, "but then, you are an impossible girl, *chérie*. We are ideally suited. We will have wonderful fights, and then we will make passionate love afterwards, eh?"

"I have never made love, passionate or otherwise," she said bluntly, determined to keep him off balance.

"Of course you haven't," he responded calmly. "I shall be your first and your only lover, Autumn Rose Leslie."

"Not necessarily, monseigneur," she told him sweetly. "My mama has outlived three husbands and a royal lover. My grandmother had two husbands. My other grandmother had two husbands, a royal lover, and was in a Turk's harem for a time. My great-grandmother de Marisco had six husbands and several lovers in her day. So you see, monseigneur, you might do better to wait until I have outlived several husbands to wed me. Wouldn't you prefer to be the last, rather than the first?"

"How many sisters do you have?" he demanded. Her outrageous tale was, of course, a delicious fabrication to tease him.

"Two," she said.

"How many husbands has each had?" he continued.

"One apiece," she admitted, but then added, "they are yet young!"

He laughed. *"Petite menteuse,"* he accused.

"I am not a liar!" she protested. "Neither India nor Fortune is old. They would slay you if you said so."

The marquis turned about and called to Red Hugh, "How old are mademoiselle's sisters?"

"The eldest is over forty and the other close to it," he answered. "Her grace will know, monsigneur."

"And they are happily married?"

"God bless us, monseigneur, aye, they are. Lady India down in Gloucester and Mistress Fortune across the ocean in the New World. Both as happy as clams in a bed of seaweed," Red Hugh volunteered cheerfully.

The marquis turned back to Autumn. "If your sisters are content with only one husband each, *chérie,* then so must you be, despite your grandmothers and great-grandmother de Marisco," he told her.

"I am not my sisters," she said airily. "Besides, they had more experience in society than I ever had. Before I wed I shall have my little adventures, Sebastian d'Oleron."

"Oh, very well, kiss your other two admirers. You will quickly see that I am the man for you and end this nonsense. Shall we wed in April, *chérie?"*

"No!" she almost shouted.

"Have you noticed that the Comte de Montroi has the beginnings of a second chin?" he asked her pleasantly, changing the subject.

Autumn giggled. She had indeed noted it. Guy was inordinately fond of sweets. "You are terrible," she told him.

"And I would wager that de Belfort wears a corset," the marquis continued. "He is a man who enjoys his food and his wine, *chérie.* In two years' time he'll be going to bed an hour after sunset, and sleep will be all that is on his mind, I guarantee you, *ma petite."*

Autumn laughed aloud at his observation. "Is there anything you can say that is good about my other suitors, monseigneur?"

"Their blood is blue. They are wealthy. They are both decent and very, very dull," he answered with a grin.

"What makes you the best candidate for my hand?" she asked.

"My blood is bluer, my coffers fuller, and I will never go to bed an hour after sunset unless it is to make passionate love to my beautiful wife the whole night long," he said in tones so low only she might hear him. Reaching out, he placed a large hand over her two smaller ones as they gripped the reins of her mount. His look was smouldering.

She could feel her heart hammering suddenly. Chills ran up and down her spine. Her throat was momentarily tight. After what seemed an eternity her voice returned. "Surely you have faults?" she managed to say. "You cannot be perfect."

"I do not tolerate fools, *chérie*. I can be reckless. When I want something, *truly want it*, nothing stands in my way," he told her as he gently squeezed her hands before releasing them.

"I have a temper," she replied.

"I know."

"I do not like being told what to do."

"I know."

"I will only marry for love."

"So you have told me several times," he said. "Are you not the tiniest bit in love with me yet, *chérie?*"

"You are very overwhelming, monseigneur. You tend more to anger me than anything else," she admitted to him.

"Aha!" he said. "You do indeed feel something for me. Anger is the opposite of passion, so I may have hope."

"I am beginning to think you are mad," Autumn told him.

"I am, *chérie*. I am madly in love with you!" he declared.

"That is ridiculous!" she snapped. "How can you be in love with someone you barely know? Why, Etienne and Guy have had more acquaintance with me than you have, monsigneur."

"That day I first saw you in the forest, across the rocky streambed, I knew you were the girl for me," the marquis replied. "Do you not believe in love at first sight, *chérie?*"

"*No!*" Autumn said firmly. "I most certainly do not!"

He laughed. "I see you will be the practical one in our marriage, *ma petite*. I suppose that is not a bad thing. I hope our children will be like you."

"Take me home," Autumn said, turning her horse's head about. "No! Go home, m'sieu le marquis! Red Hugh will see me back to Belle Fleurs. I shall tell Mama I wished it that way."

"I will come again, *chérie*," he told her, not aruging with her abrupt decision.

"If it pleases you," she responded.

"I would please you, Autumn Rose Leslie," came the reply.

Her horse stopped in its tracks and Autumn looked directly at him. God's blood! He was so damned handsome, but he was confusing her with his mixture of dominance and foolishness. "I will be pleased to have you call on me again, Sebastian d'Oleron, even as I will be pleased to see Etienne and Guy. In the end, however, if none of you suit me, I shall dismiss you all. Do you understand? I should rather be happy and a maiden than wed and miserable."

He nodded, his expression serious. "I understand, *chérie*," he said, but then he grinned. "When all is said and done, though, you will fall in love with me and wed me." Placing his fingertip to his lips he blew her kiss, then rode off.

"A determined gentleman," Red Hugh noted as they returned to the chateau. "You would appear to be well matched, m'lady."

Autumn laughed. "He is quick of wit and considerate of me, I will agree. But he is every bit as stubborn as I am. If I wed him, would we be constantly at each other's throats?"

"Yer parents were, occasionally, in their youth," Red Hugh volunteered. "It made their marriage stronger. Their love became deeper as they learned the fine and delicate art of compromise, m'lady."

"I will wager that is not a word in the marquis's vocabulary," Autumn told her companion.

They reached the chateau. Autumn went into the hall to tell her mother she was home again.

"Where is the marquis?" Jasmine asked.

"I sent him home when he became tiresome," Autumn replied.

"Do not worry, Mama, he will be back. Now I must go and bathe. I stink of my horse and do not wish to sleep with the scent."

When she had departed the hall Jasmine spoke. "What do you think, Hugh? Will it be a match?"

"If the marquis has anything to say about it, aye, your grace, it will. He is quick. Flattering one minute, battling with her the next. Such treatment intrigues her. She will resist until she either tires of him or lusts after him. Who can say which it will be."

"Do you like him?" Jasmine inquired.

"Aye! He's a real man, like our duke, God assoil his good soul. He would not be afraid to get his hands dirty. The other two have charm, your grace, but I think them effete compared to the marquis. Her ladyship, like her sisters, needs a real man, not some pretty, clever gentleman to dance attendance on her. She would soon be bored."

Autumn, however, did not have time to become weary of her three suitors. Suddenly the trio was at Belle Fleurs daily, at first keeping her amused with their rivalry over her hand. The Comte de Montroi made her laugh with his quick wit and clever tongue as he made mock of the others, his blue eyes dancing with mischief. Etienne St. Mihiel was the main butt of his teasing, for the duke was deadly serious in his pursuit of Autumn. He found nothing funny about the situation, which had put him into contention with two other gentlemen. Etienne was very used to obtaining his way, and the thought that he might lose this lovely heiress was very distressing to him. Then, one afternoon, the comte enraged the Duc de Belfort with his jests, and the two almost came to blows.

"You and Sebastian are too closely related to Autumn," he mocked them.

"What do you mean?" the marquis said.

"You and de Belfort are related to her *tantes*," the comte replied. "I am certain the consanguinity involved would prevent either of you from marrying Autumn. Therefore I win by default," he chuckled.

"Impudent puppy!" snapped Etienne St. Mihiel. "She will never wed with you as long as I live!"

"*Non*, she will not, because she will marry me," the marquis told them both with a grin.

"I think this is a question for Père Bernard," Autumn noted.

The young priest came, and the situation was explained. A small ghost of a smile flitted over his plain face. Then he said, "I do not believe the bonds of blood between Mademoiselle Autumn and the two gentlemen in question are so strong that the problem would be considered by the Church as an impediment to marriage between her and either of them. You are all worthy contenders for her hand. I shall look forward to performing the ceremony when she decides."

"We will be married by the bishop in Tours, not some country priest," Etienne St. Mihiel said proudly. "The bishop is my first cousin."

Not to be outdone, the comte retorted, "I am related to Archbishop Gondi in Paris. He would gladly perform my marriage to Autumn."

"I will be delighted to have you perform the ceremony between me and Autumn," the marquis said softly to Père Bernard.

"*Merci*, monseigneur," the priest answered.

"How certain you all are that I will have any of you," Autumn told them, irritated. "You are not the only eligible gentlemen in France. You are all becoming tiresome. I do not want to see you en masse again. You may call upon me individually, monsieurs, for how else can I get to know any of you, when you spend all your time with me bickering amongst yourselves over which one of you is to marry me? How often must I tell you? The decision is mine. It does not belong to any of you.

"You will come to call upon me in rotation, according to your rank. Etienne, I shall see you tomorrow. Then, the following day, the marquis, and finally the comte. Do not get your rotation confused else you aggravate me further and I dismiss you entirely. Now go home!" Turning away, Autumn departed the Great Hall, leaving her surprised suitors openmouthed. She was very hard-pressed not to laugh aloud at the looks upon their faces when she scolded them. *Even Sebastian.*

"It is outrageous!" the duke said angrily. "I shall make my offer to her mother and we will be done with this charade."

"You're a fool, de Belfort," the marquis told him. "Madame Jasmine herself has told us the decision is her daughter's alone. You cannot offer for Autumn without Autumn's consent. She is wealthy in her own right, and her blood is every bit as blue as ours. Bluer, if the fact be known, for she had an emperor for a grandfather. Neither our titles nor our riches impress her. She will wed for love alone, *mon brave*. All our wealth and rank cannot overcome that fact."

"Then I will make her love me," the duke said determinedly.

"Hah!" the comte responded to his friend's remark. "Do you even know what love is, Etienne?"

"I have loved many women in my day," was the response.

"*Made love,*" Guy d'Auray corrected him. "There is a difference between the two. If you do not know it, you have already lost her."

"*Adieu,* monsieurs," the marquis said. "I shall see you at my wedding, if not before." He bowed to his two rivals and withdrew.

Autumn watched him go from the window of her mother's bedchamber.

"What have you done?" Jasmine asked from the bed where she was laying down, recovering from a mild headache.

"Sorted them out," Autumn replied. "They were like a trio of puppies squabbling over a bone. Namely me! It is not flattering; it is irritating. They will now come one at a time until I make my choice or they get bored. How can I learn what they are like otherwise?" She explained to her mother what she had proposed.

"Clever, *ma bébé,*" Jasmine said.

"I am not certain whether my solution will prove more annoying in the long run," Autumn admitted.

Her mother laughed. "No, you were correct to do what you did. You will get to know them quickly now and can decide which two to discard. If you have not already decided."

"You know I have, Mama," Autumn said. "I do not, however, want him thinking I was won too easily." She smiled. "He is very arrogant."

"It is part of his charm," her mother replied.

"And I have not yet kissed Etienne or Guy," Autumn said.

"You really should, for comparison's sake," Jasmine agreed.

Autumn giggled. "Did you talk to India and Fortune like this, Mama?" she wondered aloud.

Jasmine laughd briefly. *"Non, ma bébé,* I most certainly did not. India was so positive that she knew everything, and Fortune was so practical it didn't seem necessary. At least until she chose Kieran. Then it was too late, for she was wildly in love." Jasmine sat up and patted the bed for her daughter to sit by her side, and when Autumn had complied, she continued. "You were born that October, just a few weeks after Fortune and Kieran wed. My last child. A great surprise to both your father and to me, as we thought we were past that time in our lives. But you were welcome! Oh, yes, Autumn Rose Leslie, you were so welcome!

"I should never say this to your sisters or your brothers, but I think you have been my favorite child, simply because of when you were born to me. You gave Jemmie and me the opportunity to be parents a final time, for your brothers and sisters were either all grown or close to it. They did not really need us any longer, but you surely did, and we were glad of it. How could we be old, grand-children or not, if we were still raising our youngest child?" She patted Autumn's hand.

"What will you do when I am wed, Mama?"

"You will not be far from me, *ma bébé,"* Jasmine said. "I shall live quite comfortably here at Belle Fleurs. Perhaps some day I shall even go back to my dower house at Cadby for a visit, or to Glenkirk, when my heart no longer hurts so greatly. If that time ever comes."

"I wonder if it will, Mama."

"I still mourn them all in my heart. Jamal Khan, my first husband. Rowan Lindley. Henry Stuart. And now your father," Jasmine replied. Then she smiled. "What a wonderful life I have had, *ma bébé!"*

"You make it sound as if it is over, Mama," Autumn said, alarmed.

Her mother chuckled. "Nay, not over. It is just a new beginning, but I cannot yet see where I am going, Autumn."

"I cannot see where I am going either," the girl told her mother. "I am half in love with Sebastian, not that I have indicated it to him, but he does fascinate me so, Mama. But is it enough that I should wed him? You must help me in this decision, for I have so little experience."

"If you are certain that it is Sebastian, then you must dismiss the other two, Autumn. It is not fair to keep them dangling."

"Not yet, Mama," Autumn said. "I shall not be cruel, but I need a bit more time. Besides, Sebastian is so very annoying in his confidence. He needs a good set-down before I decide for certain."

It was almost March before the people in the region of the Loire and the chèr learned that a treaty had been signed on January 30 in Paris between the two frondes, making Gaston d'Orleans their single leader. The boy king's uncle, egged on by Archbishop Gondi, and the Parlement, demanded Cardinal Mazarin's exile. Mazarin resisted until his life was threatened; then, reluctantly, he gave in to the pleas of both Queen Anne and young Louis, leaving Paris on February 6, 1651.

Now Gaston d'Orleans claimed that the king had been kidnapped. On the night of February 9 and 10, the archbishop surrounded the Palais Royale. Confronting her brother-in-law, Queen Anne showed him the sleeping king first and then awakened her son, so he might see what was going on about him. Thereafter the king had a horror of disorder and no liking for Paris at all, or the Parisians who had crowded about his bed, reaching out to touch him with their grubby fingers, stinking of garlic.

Less than a week later the king released the princes of the blood, who had been imprisoned for the past few months. A week after that the French Parlement registered a royal decree that no foreigner, even a naturalized citizen, be able to hold the office of a royal minister. Cardinal Mazarin, from his sanctuary in Bouillon, then fled to the electorate of Cologne for his own safety; but he remained in contact with Queen Anne, who was almost a prisoner in Paris. The Parlement next began a trial against the cardinal, attempting to prove him a traitor.

Easter was celebrated on April 9. Spring had come to the chèr, and Autumn knew she would have to make a decision soon. She had still not allowed either Etienne or Guy to kiss her, although both men had tried, even pleading with her. It was, Autumn considered, as if she was afraid their kisses would prove every bit as exciting as Sebastian's, and that was something she didn't want to know yet. "I don't know what to do," she said aloud one afternoon as she walked with Guy d'Auray in the gardens of the chateau.

"Do about what?" he asked her, curious.

"Kiss me!" Autumn said suddenly.

The Comte de Montroi needed no further encouragement. Taking Autumn into his arms, he kissed her slowly and sweetly.

It was lovely, Autumn thought, but it was not exciting. Drawing away from him, she sighed deeply and bit her lower lip in distress.

"Ahhh," he said, knowledge dawning quickly in his blue eyes. "I am not the one, am I, *ma belle?*"

Autumn shook her head. "No, Guy, you are not. I am sorry!"

"Do not be," he told her. "Love is a precious and very rare commodity, Autumn. It should not be denied, nor should it be feigned. It is d'Auriville, isn't it?"

"I think so," she admitted.

He smiled gently at her. "We shall remain friends, *oui?*"

"Oui!" she said, returning the smile. "Oh, Guy, the girl who captures your heart will be a very fortunate mademoiselle."

"Indeed she will," he concurred with a twinkle. Then he bowed, taking her hand to kiss. *"Adieu, ma belle.* I shall not come for awhile, and when I come again it will be as your *bon ami,* eh?"

Autumn nodded and watched as he left her.

"Nicely done, *ma fille,*" her mother's voice said, and Jasmine came from behind a tall hedge where she had been seated upon a marble bench. "You have made a good friend, Autumn, for as gallantly as he behaved, he will always be a little bit in love with you, and ready to come to your aid should you need him. I do not believe Etienne St. Mihiel will react as nobly. He is a young man used to getting what he wants; but you must send him away yourself."

"He will be here tomorrow," Autumn said. "I shall kiss him and then dismiss him as well."

But as her mother had suspected, it was not as easy to send the Duc de Belfort away. They walked in the gardens as she had with the comte. There was no opportunity to kiss him, and suddenly Autumn knew it didn't matter if she did or not. It was Sebastian d'Oleron, the Marquis d'Auriville, she wanted, and so she spoke.

"I have made my decision, Etienne," she began. "I am not in love with you, nor do I believe I could ever love you. I hope you will understand and that we may remain friends, for we have family in common." Looking up at him for the first time, Autumn was shocked by the fury she saw boiling up in his brown eyes.

"You dare to refuse me?" he demanded. "I have been patient with this little game you have been playing because I know you to be innocent and inexperienced. And have you dismissed your other suitors as well, or am I to be the only laughingstock, mademoiselle?" He had stopped now. His face was plainly angry.

"I told Guy yesterday, monseigneur," Autumn said quietly.

"And d'Oleron?" His tone barely concealed his outrage.

Autumn hesitated, and the duke pounced on her indecisiveness.

"So! It is to be d'Oleron," he said, his voice scathing.

"I did not say so," Autumn quickly responded, her courage returning. How dare Etienne question her!

"Then you are turning him away also?" came the query.

"I did not say that either," Autumn snapped.

"Then it is d'Oleron!" the duke insisted. "He shall not have you if I cannot!" Then Etienne St. Mihiel pulled Autumn against him, his mouth descending crushingly upon hers. Feeling Autumn's tender young breasts pressed against his chest, his lust boiled over. He attempted to force her to the ground, where he might ravish her. It was then he was yanked most unceremoniously off his feet and spun about to face Red Hugh, who towered over the duke by several inches.

Autumn stumbled backward, just barely regaining her footing. She vigorously wiped her mouth with her sleeve, attempting to rid herself of his noxious kiss. It had been a hateful and unpleasant kiss.

"How dare you lay your hands on me, *cochon*," Etienne St. Mihiel shouted furiously at Red Hugh. "I will have you arrested for this assault!"

"That would not be wise, monseigneur," the big Scotsman said.

"Then I should be forced to tell a justice that you attempted to rape my young mistress in an effort to force her into a marriage after she had refused your suit. You would be the laughingstock of the entire region. The parents of other eligible young maidens would certainly think twice before allowing you to court their daughters. I am sure that you do not want that, monseigneur. After all, you do need a wife." Red Hugh smiled pleasantly and, reaching out, straightened the duke's doublet, which had become rumpled in the altercation.

Etienne St. Mihiel leapt back as if he had been scalded. He shot Red Hugh a venomous look. Then he turned to Autumn. "I shall not call upon you again, mademoiselle," he said coldly.

"Do not be angry, Etienne," Autumn coaxed him. "We can be friends. Guy was content to accept that."

"You have forfeited my friendship, mademoiselle," the duke told her icily. "If we should be invited to the same affair, do not, I beg you, approach me, for I shall cut you."

"You shall not have to," Autumn advised him. "I shall avoid you at all costs, monseigneur. I am glad I followed my instincts, for you are really quite a dreadful man." Then Autumn turned and left him.

Red Hugh bowed to the duke. "I will see that your horse is waiting for you in the stableyard, monseigneur," he told him. Then he escorted the outraged gentleman from the gardens.

Autumn watched from a window of the chateau, discreetly hidden behind a curtain. "Good riddance!" she said aloud.

The next day the marquis did not come. At first Autumn was fearful that something might have happened to him. Then, learning that he was seen out in his vineyards helping to tie some new vines to their supports, she was outraged.

"You must understand that this is a man who loves his lands," Jasmine told her daughter. "He is not so much the gentleman that he cannot work. I certainly approve."

"But he is supposed to be courting me," Autumn grumbled. "I will wager he has heard I have dismissed the duke and the comte. He thinks he has me, and because he does, he has dared to ignore me. Oh, I just hate his arrogance!" She stamped her foot irritably.

"You do not know he is aware that you have sent his rivals away. I doubt that either of them would publicly brag about it, particularly the Duc de Belfort. I think he just felt he was needed in his vineyards today."

"But under our rotation agreement it also means I shall not see him for another several days," Autumn complained.

"Are you so anxious then to see him?" her mother asked.

"Of course! Now that I have sent Guy and Etienne away, Sebastian's courtship of me may begin in earnest. I want to know if we are to be married or not, Mama. Another six months and I shall be twenty!"

Before Jasmine could answer her daughter Madame St. Omer hurried into the Great Hall. "Thank heavens you are both here!" she said. "You will never believe what I have just learned. The king and his mother are at Chenonceaux! We are not, I am told, to acknowledge their presence there publicly, but all the families along the Cher are expected to go and pay their respects to His Majesty! You must come too, Jasmine, and you must bring Autumn with you! Ohh, it is so exciting! I am behaving even worse than Gaby! I had to leave her at home, for she is so thrilled she cannot stop talking!" Then she looked more closely at her two relations. "What has happened?" she demanded to know. "You both have that *look.*"

"Autumn has refused the suits of the comte and the duke," Jasmine told her cousin.

"Ahhh," breathed Madame St. Omer. "Then it is to be my candidate, d'Oleron. I am not surprised, *ma petite* Autumn. I could see from the first that you were taken with one another, but it has certainly taken you long enough to come to that decision. Does he know?"

"He didn't come today," Autumn said. "He is working like a common laborer in his vineyards, I am told."

Her *tante* chuckled. "He is like that, *ma petite.* The land means everything to him. His family has always been so. Did not your papa revere his own Glenkirk?"

"But he took time to court Mama," Autumn said.

"And when Sebastian learns he is your sole surviving suitor, *chérie,* he will take time also, I promise you," Madame St. Omer replied.

"Now we must think about what you will wear when you meet the king."

"The king is a child," Autumn said. "He is probably more interested in his toy soldiers than what I or any of us, for that matter, will wear to Chenonceaux. I have wanted to see the chateau, however. I understand that it stretches the entire width of the river."

"The king, I am told, is mature for his age," her aunt replied. "He would have to be to survive the past eight years. I am astounded they were able to leave Paris, but I understand that Gaston d'Orleans, the king's uncle, arranged the trip because the king is suffering from being in the city too much. He far perfers the country."

"But why Chenonceaux?" Autumn said. "Surely there are chateaux nearer to Paris."

"Indeed there are, *ma petite,* but this is to be a *secret* trip, and closer to Paris, the secret could easily be revealed. Besides, the prince is terrified that Cardinal Mazarin will kidnap the king if he learns where the boy is. Possession of the royal majesty is power." She turned to Jasmine. "Bring your Adali, *ma cousine.* I am told both the queen and her son love pomp and show. They will also be impressed that the emperor of India's daughter has been living in Scotland and England all these years and now has chosen France for her sanctuary."

"I will take your advice," Jasmine answered. "When shall we go? I would, you will understand, prefer to travel with the family."

"Meet us on the river road three mornings from now," Madame St. Omer replied. She looked at Autumn. "I hope by then you have put poor d'Oleron out of his misery, *ma petite.*"

"He has but to come to Belle Fleurs," came the reply.

"He will come," her *tante* said, nodding her head wisely, *"He will come."*

Part Two

AUTUMN 1651–1655

Chapter

7

The king could scarcely contain his excitement. He had never before been to Chenonceaux, and the pristine beauty of the chateau excited him. The magnificent gallery that extended across the river was to him a marvel. Louis had never been particularly fond of Paris, and the incident of the previous February had done little to endear the city or its populace to him. He disliked the archbishop intensely. His uncle and his cousins were equally in his disfavor, although he hid his distaste well. *Just a few more months*, the young king thought, *and then I shall reach my majority*. He wondered why his father had chosen the age of thirteen for him to inherit; but then, perhaps his father had known the difficulties he would face and had not wanted to tempt fate too greatly.

A week. It was all his uncle Gaston would allow him. He wanted to ride and to hunt, but instead he was forced to stand politely, greeting a stream of loyal and doting nobles who were frankly delighted to have him here. It was a bore. The boy smiled and gave his hand to be kissed over and over again. One day he would build a palace where all his nobles would come to live so he might keep an eye on them. Then there would be no more treasonous behavior and petty wars.

"My son," his mother the queen spoke. "Here is a most especial lady come to pay you her respects."

The young king focused his gaze upon the lovely woman who came forward and curtsied with exquisite grace. She was accompanied by a gentleman in clothing such as he had never seen.

"This, Louis, is the Dowager Duchess of Glenkirk. Madame la duchesse is the daughter of an Indian king, although she has lived in Scotland for many years. She has come to her chateau, Belle Fleurs, to mourn her husband, who was killed defending the rights of your cousin, King Charles II.

The young king, rather than allowing his hand to be kissed, instead kissed Jasmine's hand. "How kind of you to come to see me, Madame la duchese," he said. His fine, dark eyes swept over her. Yet in mourning, she was still impeccably and elegantly garbed in a gown of midnight blue silk, its sleeves tied with pearl-studded ribbons, her collar a soft cream-colored lace. Her dark hair, with its silvery chevrons on either side of her head, was simply dressed in a chignon.

"I am honored, Your Majesty, to make your acquaintance. Is it permitted that I present Your Majesty with a small token of my respect?"

The king nodded, his eyes bright with sudden curiosity and excitement. He had not expected a gift.

Adali handed his mistress a small square ebony box, banded in pure gold. Jasmine opened the box and then presented it to the king. Within, upon a bed of black velvet, lay an oval-shaped diamond. It was fully as big as the round made by the king's thumb and second finger. Louis gaped, frankly amazed. He had never before seen anything like this perfect pale yellow stone.

"It is called a tiger's eye, Your Majesty. It was given to me by my first husband, Prince Jamal Khan of Kashmir," Jasmine told the boy. "I hope you will enjoy it. Its color is quite unique."

The king took the box from her and looked more closely at the diamond. It was even more magnificent close up. "Madame, I do not believe I have ever been presented with such a wonderful gift. *Mille merci.*" Closing the box, he handed it to one of his servants; then his gaze went to Adali. "Who is this who accompanies you, madame?"

"My steward, Adali, who has served in my household since my birth, Your Majesty. His father was a French mariner," Jasmine explained.

Adali bowed low to the king.

Louis nodded with a smile at Adali. "How good it must be, madame," he noted sharply, "to have a servant one can truly trust."

"Adali is my right hand, Your Majesty. I would trust him with my life, and have many a time. Now, if Your Majesty will indulge me but a moment more, I should like to introduce my daughter, Lady Autumn Rose Leslie." She drew the girl forward.

Autumn curtsied low to the king. Louis stepped quickly forward and tipped the girl's face up so he might see her better. It was a gesture worthy of a much older man, Jasmine thought, but then, she had heard the boy was extremely mature for his age.

"Exquisite," he said, and raised her up. Then, turning to his mother, he said, "I have had enough for now, *Maman*. I should like to escort Lady Autumn across the gallery without the benefit of a royal retinue so I may learn how she likes our country. Uncle!" He looked directly at Gaston d'Orleans. "You shall see our guests are entertained. I will rely upon you." Then, tucking Autumn's hand in his, he led her off.

Autumn was astounded and did not know what to say. She had never before been in the company of a king. This was the sort of adventure her sisters and her mother had had. She smiled brilliantly at the others as they passed, reserving a particularly bright smile for the Duc de Belfort.

"Who is he?" Louis demanded to know.

"A suitor who did not take his dismissal well," she replied, amazed she could speak.

The king chuckled. "Are you a coquette then, mademoiselle?"

"I should hope not!" she quickly replied, lest he gain the wrong impression of her.

"Why are you in France?" Louis wanted to know.

"My papa was killed fighting for King Charles," Autumn explained. "I am the youngest in my family, and sadly neither Scotland nor England is a fit place for a demoiselle of my station to seek a husband any longer. Mama is mourning Papa. She owns a chateau nearby, Belle Fleurs. We came to France to escape Master Cromwell and his pocky, treasonous Roundheads. And, hopefully, to find a husband for me."

"And you rejected the gentleman who was glaring so hard at you?"

"The Duc de Belfort, Your Majesty. I have also rejected the Comte de Montroi, but not the Marquis d'Aurville," Autumn told him.

"How fortunate you are able to to choose your mate, or will it be your mama's choice, *ma belle?*" he wondered. "I shall be matched with some princess from Spain or Italy, of course. Then I shall be expected to get heirs upon her, but at least that is the enjoyable part."

"Your Majesty is yet a boy," Autumn said. "Surely you cannot have already . . ." She stopped, blushing.

"'I had my first woman when I was eleven," he told her, amused by her blushes. "A man should begin taking his pleasure as early as he can if he is to learn how to please women, *ma belle*. Are you a virgin?"

"Yes!" Autumn squeaked, not certain whether to be shocked or to laugh.

"Ah, how fortunate your husband will be, *ma belle*. I have not yet had the pleasure of initiating a virgin into the delights of Eros, but done properly, I am assured it is a wonderful experience for both man and maid. How old are you?"

"N-Eighteen," Autumn fibbed.

"Diane de Poitiers, the lady who was responsible for making Chenonceaux the exquisite creation it is, was my ancestor Henri the Second's mistress. She was twenty years his senior, but he adored her and was faithful to her until death. You are only five years older than I am, *ma belle*."

Autumn wasn't entirely certain what the king meant by telling her the story. Finally she said, "She must have been a remarkable lady."

"I suspect that you are remarkable also, *ma belle*," the king murmured, stopping and gently pressing her against the stone wall of the gallery, between two windows that overlooked the river. His fingers stroked her face. "You are very beautiful, Mademoiselle Autumn," he told her. He ran his fingertips across her mouth. "Kiss them!" he commanded.

Autumn's eyes widened with shock. *"Your Majesty!"* she gasped.

"Louis," he said softly. Then, pressing himself against her, the king kissed Autumn. It was a deep and passionate kiss, his tongue slipping along her lips, attempting to force entry into her mouth.

Autumn wasn't certain what to do. This bold boy was a king, but she had to admit his behavior was that of a much older man. She half-struggled against him, pulling her head away. "Your Majesty! Louis, please! I have not your experience, and you are frightening me!"

He looked surprised by her words even as his hand fondled one of her breasts. She had said she was a virgin, but surely she had played little love games with her suitors. He squeezed the sweet breast in his grasp. "I want to see you naked," he told her. "You are delicious in your innocence, and you excite me. Stay here with me, Autumn. This chateau is meant for lovers, and I would be your lover."

She was astounded by the young king's impudent and brazen speech. Suddenly regaining her courage, she pushed him firmly away. "I must assume Your Majesty is jesting with me, else I should be forced to be mortally offended by Your Majesty's words. You are certainly not suggesting that a virgin with my noble bloodlines, an heiress of my worth, squander her most precious possession, *her virtue,* on a brief liaison. When I come to my marriage bed I shall be pure for my husband. I shall not shame myself, or him, with loose behavior either before or after our marriage." She reached out and put a hand on the king's silk-clad arm. Your Majesty, there is a tiny part of me that is flattered to have caught your royal attention, but that little bit of me shall not overcome my desire to do what is right and moral . . . *Louis."*

The king sighed so deeply that Autumn could not restrain a small giggle. Not in the least offended, the king grinned at her. "Mama would approve of you, Mademoiselle Autumn. So would the cardinal."

They continued on now, walking across the River chèr through the windowed gallery that stretched from one side of the lovely stream to the other. Autumn thought it was the most beautiful place she had ever been, and said so.

"You do not live upon the river?" the king asked her.

"No, Belle Fleurs is located a mile or so from the chèr, but the chateau sits, surrounded by water on three sides, on a lake that is fed by a tiny tributary of the river. My French relations, the de Savilles have a great chateau, Archambault, set above the chèr."

"Do you like living in the country?" he wondered.

"I have lived in the country my entire life," Autumn told him. "I have been to large towns, but I do not like them. I prefer to live in the country, where I may see the seasons change."

"One is closer to God in the countryside," the king noted. "I do not like cities either. When I rule in my own right, I shall leave Paris and build myself a great palace in the countryside. It is there my court shall be settled, and nowhere else."

"Do you think your nobles will like being in the country all of the time?" Autumn asked him.

"They will have no choice. I am the king. They will have to do what I say, or suffer the consequences. You see, mademoiselle, my entire life has been fraught with disorder, and I do not like disorder. The princes of the blood, Conde, Conti, de Longueville, among others, have squabbled back and forth, sometimes for me, other times against me. In Paris, Gondi, the archbishop, foments trouble all of the time, setting the people against me one day, the princes the next. Only the good offices of my mother and Cardinal Mazarin have kept me safe and within sight of my majority. In a few months I shall be king in fact as well as name. I cannot wait!

"I shall build my palace one day, and make it the most exciting place in the world to be. I shall not have to force them to come. They will want to come, because to not be at my palace with me will be worse than exile. I shall make my palace the most fashionable place on the face of the earth. And when they all gather there, I shall have total control, mademoiselle! No rebellions shall be fomented, for those who displease me shall be expelled from the heaven on earth that I will create!"

"What a wonderful dream!" Autumn told him. "Do you know where you will build this marvelous palace, Louis?"

"I have a hunting lodge outside Paris in a place called Versailles. I very much like it there. That is where I shall set my new palace. And when it is habitable, will you come and see me? With your husband, of course, Mademoiselle Autumn. The proprieties must be observed with you, I now know."

"Build your palace, Louis, and I will come," she promised him. "I do not like cities, but I think I would like a lively court."

"Let us seal our bargain with a kiss then," the king said.

Autumn shook her finger at him. "You are very naughty," she told him. Then, pursing her lips, she leaned forward to kiss him.

The king, however, wrapped his arms about her and again kissed her with great passion. His dark eyes were dancing with mischief as he released her, blushing and protesting. "I don't know how to kiss any other way," he explained.

Autumn shook her head. "I hope," she said, "you will rule France as well as you kiss, Louis."

"Your Majesty, forgive my intrusion. Your mother is looking for you." The Marquis d'Auriville bowed low to the king. "I will escort my betrothed back to her family for you."

The king, who was taller than Autumn by several inches but not yet fully grown, replied, "And you, monseigneur, are . . . ?"

"Jean Sebastian d'Oleron, Marquis d'Auriville, Your Majesty." He bowed low again. "I am at your service."

"You are to marry Lady Autumn?"

"Yes, Your Majesty." The marquis smiled.

"When is the wedding day?"

"I have not yet decided," Autumn spoke up nervously. "I should very much like some of my family to come from England."

"*Mais oui,*" the king replied. "Mademoiselle's mama approves of this match?" he demanded.

"But of course, Your Majesty. I have not courted Autumn without her mother's approval. It would not have been proper," Sebastian said.

"I do not know if I want Mademoiselle Leslie to marry yet," the boy king told the marquis. "I may desire her company while I am here at Chenonceaux, and afterwards in Paris. Paris is deadly dull."

"I do not want to go to Paris now," Autumn said nervously.

"I am certain the king does not mean for you to accompany him, *chérie*," the marquis said. "His mama, who is looking for him, will make any arrangement with your mama, I am certain. Is that not so, Your Majesty?" Sebastian smiled blandly at Louis.

"My mother only desires what makes me happy," the king replied.

"That is as it should be," came the answer from the older man. "You are the king. But I think, perhaps, your mother has all she can do to keep you safe until Your Majesty's thirteenth birthday in September. Without the good cardinal, who has been banished by Your Majesty's enemies, it is difficult for her. There should be no distractions that upset her, eh?" He smiled again at the king.

"When you are married to Mademoiselle Leslie, and I desire her presence, will you bring her to my court, monseigneur?" the king asked.

"Your Majesty has but to command," the marquis answered him.

"Then we will withdraw our objection to your marriage," Louis responded quite grandly. He took Autumn's hand up and kissed it. "I must go now and find my *maman. Adieu, ma belle* Autumn." Then Louis turned and hurried back down the gallery.

Autumn heaved an almost audible sigh of relief.

Sebastian chuckled. "Now that you have kissed four gentlemen, *chérie*, are you at last able to say I am the man for you?"

"How dare you tell the king I was your affianced?" she demanded. "I have not said I would marry you!" Her pretty cheeks were flushed.

"But is that not why you dismissed de Belfort and Montroi, *chérie?*"

"Perhaps I mean to dismiss you as well," Autumn threatened.

"I think I must kiss you again to bring you to your senses," he told her mischievously, reaching out to pull her into his arms.

Autumn struggled halfheartedly, beating her little balled-up fists against his dark green velvet doublet. "You are so arrogant!"

"And you, *chérie*, are so adorable," he told her. Then his mouth captured hers and, unable to help herself, Autumn slipped her arms about his neck. His lips were warm and smooth. They pressed firmly against hers. She felt as if he were drawing her very life force from her body, but she didn't care in the least. When his hand made contact with her breast, she pulled away gasping, wide-eyed. "I saw him touch you like this, *chérie*. Did you like it?"

"*Yes!*" she whispered back to him breathlessly.

Her honesty aroused him. He felt himself growing hard and groaned. "*Mon Dieu! Mon Dieu!* You have no idea what you do to me, *chérie!*"

"Yes, I do!" Autumn answered him, her hand slipping beneath his doublet to caress the bulge in his breeches. "I am a virgin, but I am not without certain knowledge, monseigneur."

He caught up the little hand and kissed the palm passionately. "If I do not take you back to your mother now, *chérie*, you are going to lose your maidenhead in a bridged gallery spanning the River chèr. I am only a man. I do not want a hurried coupling, however, *ma petite*. When I claim the prize of your virginity I want your heart to soar and your body to vibrate with the pleasure I can give you. Come!" He pulled her along, back in the direction of the main section of the chateau.

"I have not said I would marry you, Sebastian d'Oleron!" she cried as she almost ran by his side.

"You told the king you would, and so you must!" he replied.

"I will not be forced!" she shouted.

He stopped and, facing her, demanded to know, "What must I do to win you, Autumn Rose Leslie? Tell me, and I will do it. May God and His Holy Mother help me, but I love you!"

"I want to be courted properly," she said in dulcet tones.

"What in the name of all that is holy have I been doing?" he demanded of her, his look perplexed.

"You have been playing boys' games with de Belfort and Montroi, Sebastian. You have all been attempting to see who could best the other. I have not been involved at all in any of this. Now that I have decided that you are the most interesting of my three suitors, you may court me; and when I have decided that you please me, I will set a wedding date, monseigneur," Autumn told him sweetly.

"I should have taken you and put a child in your belly," he said, half-angry. The minx was utterly maddening.

"It would do you no good," Autumn said. "My father's mother was in the throes of labor and would not wed her betrothed husband until he returned a piece of her property that her father had foolishly included in the marriage agreement. Had my grandfather Leslie not given in, my father would have been bastard-born. He was wise enough, however, to see the error of his ways. So Papa was born only minutes after the priest had pronounced my grandparents man and wife. We Leslie women do not like being herded like cattle; nor can we be trained like horses or dogs. You had best understand that if you really wish to wed me."

He had to laugh, and he did. "You will not make me a good French wife, *chérie*, will you?"

"I shall make you a very good wife, Sebastian." She smiled wickedly up at him. "If I marry you, *cheri*."

"Have you ever been spanked?" he said threateningly.

Autumn turned and pressed herself against his length. "No," she said softly. "Will you spank me when we are wed?" Her lips were dangerously close and very tempting. "Will you bare my bottom or, if I wear them, leave my silk drawers on, monseigneur?" She rubbed herself against him teasingly. "I have never been spanked," she cooed.

Gritting his teeth, he pushed her away, and taking her hand again, led her back into the great salon where the king was holding court. He said nothing, and Autumn could not refrain from a tiny giggle.

"We are going to have such grand fun, *mon coeur*," she told him.

"Madame," Sebastian said to Jasmine, "I have brought your daughter back. I found her close to being compromised by our boy king, who even at the age of twelve and a half already has a reputation for his sensual appetites. I had to tell the king we were betrothed. He wanted Autumn to remain here with him, and then go on to Paris. She will tell you the rest." He looked at Autumn, who was now facing him as she stood next to her mother. "I shall come tomorrow morning and we will ride. Is that to your liking, *chérie?*"

"*Oui*, Sebastian," Autumn said meekly, fluttering her dark lashes at him.

He leaned over and spoke only for her ear. "I am going to begin soaking my hand in brine each day to toughen it up, *chérie*. You had best prepare yourself for a spanking very soon. *Without your drawers.*"

"*Oui*, Sebastian," she murmured, and he laughed.

The Marquis d'Auriville bowed to Jasmine, then to Madame de Belfort and Madame St. Omer. "Mesdames," he said. The three ladles curtsied to him, and he left them.

"What happened with the young king?" Jasmine said to her daughter.

"I would not have expected a boy of that age to be so mature," Autumn replied, still surprised. "Nothing really happened. I was kissed, and my right breast was fondled. I gently but firmly put the young gentleman in his place. We were speaking quite companionably when d'Auriville decided I needed to be delivered from His Majesty. They fenced back and forth verbally, then the king returned to the salon. Why are men like dogs with a bone where a woman is concerned?" Autumn wondered.

"Oh, dear," Gaby de Belfort fretted nervously. "I hope that the king was not offended by your behavior, or the marquis's."

"Do not be a fool, sister," Antoinette St. Omer said impatiently. "The king is like all boys his age, eager for his first conquest. There is no harm in it. Autumn handled herself quite well, as any sensible, proper young girl would have."

"He said he had his first woman over a year ago," Autumn told them.

Madame St. Omer chuckled. "I'm sure he did," she said. "But that was not a conquest, Autumn. That was a woman provided for His Majesty, and probably by the cardinal, who recognized his master's penchant for all things sensual. By giving the boy respectable whores to amuse himself with, he is kept occupied and out of difficulties. Ah, Mazarin is a clever fellow. They say the queen is secretly married to him."

"But he is in exile," Autumn noted.

"A temporary thing, I assure you," her aunt pronounced. "He will most certainly be back when Louis reaches his majority. Now, *ma petite*, tell me: How does a king kiss?"

"*Sister!*" Gaby de Belfort was pink with her blushes.

Autumn laughed. "Quite like any other man, but monsieur le marquis," she said. "Sebastian is by far the best kisser I have ever known. There are four to date, *tante*. Louis was a bit determined, however, as if he had something to prove to himself."

"I think," Jasmine said, "that we had best go home now. We have paid our respects to the king and his mother. It will be dark before we reach Belle Fleurs. I do not like being on the road after dark." She also did not want this continuing conversation overheard and gossiped about.

"Indeed," Madame St. Omer agreed. "Let me see where Philippe has gotten to and tell him. Ah, there he is, with Madame Delacroix. She is a widow and has designs on our brother, I am certain. Look how she is flirting with him, the hussy!" She hurried off to fetch her sibling, a determined look in her eye.

" 'Toinette fears another wife for Philippe would force us back to our little dower houses. She far prefers the grandeur of our beloved Archambault," Gaby de Belfort said with unusual frankness.

"Philippe will not remarry," Jasmine said. "He is far too comfortable as a widower, and he has his sisters for company. If he wishes to relieve the usual male itch, I do not doubt there are plenty of ladies willing to accommodate him."

Gaby chuckled. "*Oui, ma cousine*, you are most correct," she said. "I tell my sister that, but she worries that someone like Madame Delacroix will entrap our brother before he realizes what has happened. Philippe, being the gentleman he is, would then follow through, rather than hurt a woman's feelings. That is why she is so protective of him."

Adali had gone ahead to see that the coaches were brought forward. They were waiting as Autumn and the two older women exited the chateau. As he helped Madame de Belfort into her carriage, the Comte de Saville and his other sister hurried from Chenonceaux to join her. Adali then climbed into the Belle Fleurs coach with his mistress and Autumn, and without further delay they were off, back onto the river road that paralleled the Cher toward their own homes.

When they arrived back at Belle Fleurs, Autumn instructed Lily to lay out her riding clothes for the morning. "The marquis is coming!" she told her servant. "He is to court me, and then I shall marry him."

"Don't know what took you so long to come to that decision," Lily said pithily. "Any fool could see he's the man for you, m'lady. The others have been so fearful you would turn him away."

Autumn chuckled. "I wanted to be courted like an ordinary girl, Lily. Three suitors at one time is too much for any girl. All they did was argue amongst themselves over me, but I was ignored!"

"You'll not be ignored now," Lily observed. "That Frenchie you've chosen is no laddie, m'lady. His eyes are hot when he looks at you. They say the French are grand lovers." She giggled.

Autumn swatted Lily lightly. "I don't think Mama would like to hear you speaking that way, or Toramalli, for that matter. I think you are becoming more knowledgable as your proficiency in the French language increases, Lily. I think you learn more from the footman Marc than you learn from Père Bernard," she teased.

Lily had the good grace to blush, and Autumn laughed. "Oh, m'lady, you're naughty, you are."

Mother and daughter sat by the fire in the hall that evening. Each was comfortably attired in a quilted velvet dressing gown with fur-lined slippers upon their feet, for the evening was chill. They had toasted bread and cheese over the fire as they had done when Autumn was a child at Glenkirk. They sipped sweet, pale gold wine and ate the last of the winter pears, sliced upon a plate and drizzled with honey.

"I wish we could be like this forever," Autumn told her mother. " 'Tis so safe, and we have no cares at all for the moment."

"You are nineteen and it is past time you grew up," Jasmine said. "Your father and I overprotected you, for you were our baby."

"I was never unhappy over it," Autumn replied with a smile.

"Nay, you were not," her mother agreed. "Now tell me why this sudden reluctance to grow up, Autumn? Is it Sebastian? Are you having second thoughts? You know the choice is yours. If you conclude he is not the man for you, I will support your decision."

"Becoming a wife is an important step," Autumn said slowly.

Jasmine stroked her daughter's mahogany-colored hair with a gentle hand as the girl sat by her knee, looking up at her mother. "Do not think so hard on being a wife. Think of falling totally in love with the marquis, of what it will be like to be his lover. These things come first, Autumn. Only afterwards, when you have decided that you cannot be without him, that you want to spend your life with him and have his children, only then do you think of being a wife."

"But what exactly is *that* kind of love, Mama? How will I know it when I find it? I feel so foolish having to ask you such a question. I saw the love that existed between you and Papa. Yet I am not quite certain of just what it is, or what it feels like." She sighed deeply. "What if I think Sebastian is the man for me and afterwards discover that he isn't? I shall be trapped, Mama!"

"I cannot really explain what true love is, Autumn. All I can tell you is that you will know it when you find it. I did. Your sisters did, and you will too. Are you afraid of the marquis?"

"Nay," Autumn replied. "I actually like him, but he does infuriate me with his arrogance!"

Jasmine laughed. "He is in love with you and fears losing you," she explained. "So he puts on a masque of masculine superiority, which I will agree can be most infuriating. All men do it. Even your father. Why do you think I ran away from him when the king ordered our marriage? He was so overbearing and dismissive of my wishes. He was James Leslie, the Earl of Glenkirk. He was doing his duty as the king's loyal servant. I was outraged! Did he love me? Or was he merely marrying me because the king had ordered it? Did he want me? Or was his desire to have the guardianship of my not-so-royal Stuart greater than his desire for me? He never said. All he said was that I was to choose the day and he would be there. It was hardly flattering."

Autumn giggled. "What was the scandal you caused that is always alluded to but never spoken of by the family?" she asked. "The one that involved both you and Papa."

"I am aware of what you mean," Jasmine said, and then she laughed softly. "I suppose you are old enough to know. Shortly after I came to England from India, and was living with my de Marisco grandparents, Uncle Robin gave his famed Twelfth Night revel. Your father, who was his friend, was staying at Lynwood House. My stepsister, Sybilla, had decided she wanted to be the next Countess of Glenkirk, but Jemmie could not see Sibby for the trees. That night he and I, who were both widowed, decided we were in need of a little comforting. We were discovered together in his bed. When he did not immediately offer marriage, my stepfather demanded it. Before Jemmie might answer, I said I would not wed him. That was the end of the matter for me. My grandparents immediately arranged my marriage with Rowan Lindley. I, unaware that Jemmie had fallen in love with me, was quite happily wed. Consequently, when the king ordered our marriage several years later, after Rowan had been killed, I did not know how Jemmie Leslie felt. But I wanted to be loved because I had been loved by three wonderful men, and I knew that marriage without love would be bleak in comparison with my former liaisons."

"So you came to love Papa?" Autumn asked.

"I think I had loved him all along, since that impetuous intrigue," Jasmine responded. "I had put those feelings aside, for I had decided that they would go nowhere. How wrong I was!"

"But that still doesn't answer my questions about love," Autumn told her mother.

"No one can answer those questions, *ma fille*. All I can tell you is that you will know love when you find it. There are no other assurances, Autumn. You must believe that, and trust me in this." Jasmine patted her daughter's shoulder comfortingly. "Now, my darling girl, go upstairs, and get some sleep. I will wager that the marquis will be here quite early to ride with you. Now that he has the entire field to himself, he will want to sweep you off your feet and into his bed as quickly as he can."

Autumn rose to her feet and leaned over to kiss her mother. "Good night, Mama," she said, and departed the hall for her bed-chamber. While Lily was able to pull out her trundle and fall into a quick, deep sleep, Autumn lay awake. What was love, she had asked her mother, hoping for a clear and definitive answer, yet Jasmine had been unable to give her that answer. Was it that sensation she had felt when her eyes had first met those of Sebastian d'Oleron's, across a forest brook? She had told her mother she wasn't afraid of him, but she was afraid of the confused, unfamiliar feelings he aroused in her.

Autumn climbed from her bed and slipped across the room to her window. The moon glistened silver upon the dark surface of the lake. She didn't understand the feelings that roiled within her. Perhaps that was why, she suddenly realized with great clarity, she had held him off, while half-encouraging the Duc de Belmont and the Comte de Montroi. She had been like a child offered a selection of sweets who, finally choosing one, was now uncertain if she really wanted it at all.

Why is this so difficult for me? she wondered. *India knew when she met her true love. Fortune, if the stories are to be believed, certainly knew. But that was before I was even born. What is the matter with me? Mayhap Sebastian is not the one, but oh! he is so handsome, and how he makes my heart beat faster when we meet.* She chuckled softly to herself. He had been jealous, seeing the boy king trying to make love to her. And knowing that, Autumn suddenly felt a great sense of satisfaction. Padding back across the floor, she climbed into her bed again and fell into a deep sleep.

In the morning she was very particular about her toilette. Her green light wool breeches were brushed thoroughly, Lily complaining that they would shine if she had to add another stroke to the fabric. Autumn pulled them on over her silk drawers. Beneath her white silk shirt with its full sleeves she wore a white flannel waist-cote, its v-neck threaded closed by means of a pale blue silk ribbon.

Light wool socks, the same color as her knee breeches, were put on beneath Autumn's brown leather riding boots. Seated, she allowed Lily to undo her plait, brush her hair out, and rebraid it. Taking her doeskin jerkin up she fastened the silver and bone buttons and took her riding gloves from the serving woman.

The door to her bedchamber opened and her mother was there. "He is not here yet, and we must go to early mass, Autumn," she said. "Father Bernard will be unhappy if you shirk your duty to God."

Autumn did not argue, and afterwards they went into the hall, where the first meal of the day had been laid out. He was there, awaiting them. Her heart began to hammer erratically.

"You will join us, Sebastian?" Jasmine said, seeing her daughter was unable to exhibit any show of manners.

"I thought you would have already eaten by now," he said.

"Mass first, and then the meal," Jasmine chided him gently. "Autumn must eat. I know my daughter, and she will keep you out riding for a good part of the day. Adali will see you have bread, wine, and cheese to take with you. Sit down! Sit down!"

"*Bonjour, ma petite,*" he said softly, raising her hand to his lips. "You slept well after your adventures at Chenonceaux?"

"It was just a little adventure, monseigneur," she replied, retrieving her hand from his and seating herself.

"It might have become a bigger adventure but for me," he said.

"Ah, yes," she responded. "You rescued me from the clutches of an overamorous twelve-and-a-half-year-old boy." Autumn helped herself to a hard-boiled egg and began to peel it.

"A king," he corrected her, "who, if the rumor is accurate, has already fathered a bastard on one of his whores."

"Even the king would not resort to rape, monseigneur," Autumn said through gritted teeth. "It was a kiss, a brief touch. I was fully capable of managing the situation. I wonder if His Majesty bothered to ask his mother why she was searching for him?" She smiled sweetly and dipped her egg in the salt.

"Nonetheless," Jasmine interjected, "I am pleased that Sebastian followed you and was there should you have needed his assistance."

She lifted the filigreed silver dish before her and said, "Will you have an egg, monseigneur? And do try some of that most excellent Dijon mustard. Wine? Or perhaps you would like to try some tea, a lovely hot beverage from my own native land. The family trading company imports it from India. It is becoming most popular, and is much nicer than the Spanish chocolate or Turkish coffee."

"Madame is most gracious," the marquis said. "Perhaps I should court you instead of your daughter."

Jasmine laughed heartily. "You flatter me, but I should advise you that I am not in the market for a husband, Sebastian. A son-in-law, but definitely not a husband!"

Autumn listened to their patter and found herself growing increasingly irritated. She swallowed down her egg and a piece of bread smeared with butter. She drank her tea in dark silence, and when she had finished she said as she stood, "I am ready to ride, monseigneur." Then she stamped down from the highboard, and from the hall.

The marquis leapt up, bowing to Jasmine and then following her. The duchess laughed, and then she signaled Adali. "Tell Red Hugh he need not accompany Autumn today," she said. "Hurry!"

Adali bowed and ran from the hall on slippered feet. He was surprisingly agile for an elderly gentleman.

In the courtyard Autumn mounted her horse, gathering the reins into her gloved hands. Urging her mount forward by means of a gentle kick, she trotted from the courtyard across the arched stone bridge.

Behind her the marquis looked about for Red Hugh, but the big Scot was nowhere to be seen. Then Adali came up to him, puffing slightly, and said, "We are entrusting you with the young mistress, monseignuer. Do not abuse that trust." The marquis nodded, his handsome face serious, and mounted his own horse to ride off after Autumn.

She had followed the woodland trail, and by the time he caught up with her she was leading her horse across the stream where they had first met. Safe on the other side, she turned around and smiled triumphantly at him. Then, remounting the beast, she continued on through the trees until she came to a sunny, open meadow. Autumn cantered across it. Almost to the other side, she heard his horse coming up quickly behind her.

Stopping, she waited for him, and when he finally reached her side she said, "It took you long enough, Sebastian. Where is Red Hugh?"

"I was told his presence was not required today. You have been put in my complete charge," he told her with a grin.

Autumn laughed aloud, her bad mood now gone, ridden off in the glorious spring day. "You are a brave man," she told him. "These are your lands? I remember you told me the day we met that the lands across the stream belonged to the Marquis d'Auriville. How can that be if your home lies south of Archambault?"

"My chateau and my vineyards lie south, but my holdings stretch behind and beyond Archambault. Even their lands belonged to my family in ancient times. They gave the land that is now Archambault to a second son. The de Saville and the d'Oleron families have a common ancestor, one Lucien Gaullus Sabinus. The legend goes that he was a tribal chief who sided with the Romans. He was given citizenship and a Roman name for his loyalty. The lands that had been his were divided in the eighth century, when the family had only two children, both sons, and the younger had the opportunity of a rather excellent marriage, provided he could offer his bride something substantial. I have several hundred yards more of river frontage, my estate having descended from the older son."

"Sabinus. Sebastian!" she said. "Your name is your ancestor's."

"You know Latin?" he asked her.

"I am an educated woman, Sebastian. I speak my native English, French, and Italian. I have studied both Latin and Greek. I read. I write. I can do simple mathematics. I have been taught geography, logic, and a great deal of history, including that of my mother's India. I was born in Ireland. Baptized both a Catholic and a Protestant. That is a complicated story in itself. I have been raised to be very liberal in my thoughts, both sacred and secular. I am studying with Father Bernard, but I strive not to upset him. His mind is narrow, as are most priests'."

He laughed at her candor. "You will not be a perfect French wife, I can see that even now," he told her, "but I will have no other girl for my mate, Autumn. You do not frighten me at all with your frankness."

"I am the youngest in my family," she continued, "born to my parents when they both believed themselves past having children. That is why I was born in Ireland. Mama did not realize she was with child, and thought her barren years had set in at last. When she finally realized her moon link was broken not for good, but because she was with child, they were across the sea from Glenkirk. I have five older brothers. Two are dukes, one a marquis, and the two youngest, barons. I have two elder sisters. India, the oldest, is the Countess of Oxton. The next, Fortune, whom I do not remember, lives in the New World, with her husband. Fortune might have had a great estate in Ulster; she fell in love with the wrong brother, but the right man," Autumn explained.

"Another story, for another time," he said.

Autumn nodded with a smile.

"When you told me your mother had outlived three husbands and a royal lover; that both your grandmothers had two husbands, and one of them also a royal lover, and had been in a Turk's harem; that your great-grandmother had had six husbands and several lovers; you were teasing me, *chérie*, were you not?" he asked her.

"No," Autumn replied briefly.

"I shall ask your mama," he said.

"You are free to do so, monseigneur, but I do not lie," Autumn responded. "The truth I have spoken is so fantastic that I will permit you to question it, but be warned, Sebastian: You will only question my veracity once with my permission. Should you ever mistrust me again, I shall leave you, even if we are married. Now, you know all about me. I would know all about you."

"I was born and raised at Chermont," he said. "I have never left the region. My sister is a nun and my parents are dead. I am a very dull fellow, Autumn. You should know this if we marry. My passion is for my lands, for my wine, and now for you. I will never deceive you, and I will spoil you as no woman has ever been spoiled. I will adore the children you give me. Can you live such a quiet life?"

"I have lived so quietly all my life. My home, Glenkirk, is in the southeastern Highlands. I occasionally traveled with my mother to England in the summers, but I have never been to London or even Edinburgh. I have been sheltered and kept from worldly society. I do hope that once we have several children, you will take me to court. The king said he is going to build a wonderful palace at Versailles. I would like to see that, Sebastian. Will you take me to court one day?"

"You will have to marry me if I am to take you to court," he told her. "Are you saying you will marry me?"

"Of course I am going to marry you," Autumn said. "Why am I allowing you to court me? Why did I send de Belfort and Guy away? Do you think me some vixen to tease and taunt you? *Men!* Why do you never understand?"

"Then we are betrothed?" he asked her.

"Well, not until you have given me a ring," she replied. "Your intentions must certainly be public, monseigneur."

"And when you have your ring will you set a wedding date?" he demanded of her.

"I thought late summer," she murmured dreamily.

"If I do not kill you before then, *chérie,*" he replied through gritted teeth.

"You must not kill me; at least not until you have made love to me," Autumn responded. "Remember, you once told me I should not die a virgin." She encouraged her horse into a canter. "Come along, Sebastian! We must return to Belle Fleurs and tell Mama that everything has now been settled between us."

He began to laugh. He couldn't help it. She was unlike any girl he had ever met, and she was probably going to drive him mad; but he would have no other wife. He kicked his horse and followed after her.

The round emerald was leaf green in color. It was surrounded by rich, round turquoises and round-cut, blue-white diamonds. The stones were set in Irish red-gold. It was the most beautiful ring Autumn had ever seen. Even Jasmine, whose collection of jewelry was famed, was impressed with the ring's beauty and nodded her approval.

"The stones match your eye colors," Sebastian told Autumn as he slipped the ring on her slender finger. "I had it made especially for you, *chérie.*" Then he kissed the hand that wore the ring. "Now, we are formally betrothed, and my intentions are most public, *n'est-ce pas?*"

She smiled up at him, and there were tears in her eyes. "Thank you," she managed to say to him.

"I shall leave you two to yourselves," Jasmine said quietly. "You will stay the night, Sebastian?"

"I will, madame."

"Adali will show you your room then, when you are ready," she said and, curtsying to them, Jasmine left the hall.

"Shall I keep watch, my princess?" the elderly majordomo asked.

"Tell him where he is to sleep, and say Autumn will show him later. They need to be alone, Adali. I think we both remember why."

Adali nodded. "So long ago, and so far away," he replied. "That I should live to see your children and their children has been the greatest blessing of my life, my princess. How many have gone? Yet Rohana, Toramalli, and I remain to serve you."

"Which is a blessing for me, old friend," Jasmine told him. "I am going to bed now. Do what you must, and then seek yours."

Adali reentered the hall, smiling at the sight of Autumn and Sebastian, their heads together, speaking in low tones. "Mademoiselle," he began, "I am becoming too old to keep the hours of young lovers who are courting. The marquis will have the blue room on the other side of your mama's. Will you show him when you are ready, so I may put these old bones into my featherbed?"

"Of course, Adali," Autumn said, trying not to show too much delight. *"Bonsoir,* and sleep well."

Adali bowed politely to the young couple and departed the hall.

"Are they not worried that I might seduce you?" Sebastian teased her and kissed the tip of her nose.

"I think they are hoping *I* seduce *you,*" she teased back. "That way I cannot change my mind and we *must* marry."

"Do you want to be seduced?" he asked, nuzzling her dark, perfumed hair.

"No," Autumn told him. "I want our wedding night to be a perfect memory, monseigneur, but if you choose to instruct me now in some of the niceties of love, I should not object."

"Yet you were bold enough to touch me once," he said, curious to know what had emboldened her.

"My campanions as a child were mostly boys from our village," she explained. "Remember, I am the baby of the family, and all my siblings but for my eldest Leslie brother, Patrick, had left Glenkirk by the time I was brought from Ireland. As we grew older and my playmates began to gain an interest in the lasses, they began to compare their organs. It never concerned them if I was there, although they never dared to approach me, being the lord's daughter. But I was frankly curious. They would jest with each other, and sometimes even with me, I think to see what I would say, and if I might be shocked. Then my brother Patrick found out. He beat several of the lads for their impertinence. Then, after having given me a talk-ing-to regarding the male organ, he sent me to Mama to learn the rest. When Papa heard of it, he was at first outraged, but Mama showed him the humor in the situation. That is why I touched you. Mama explained that a woman's touch can both soothe and excite. I wanted to soothe you because you were being so kind."

"Have you ever *soothed* any other gentlemen, Autumn?" He wanted an answer, partly out of curiosity, partly because he was jeal-ous.

"Gracious, no!" she exclaimed. "Mama also explained such a touch was only for one's betrothed husband or husband. You surely do not think I go about handling manhoods with no discrimination, Sebastian!" Then she giggled. "I should have been wed long since if I did that, and not necessarily to a man I loved."

He laughed, unable to help himself. She was such a mixture of intelligence and innocence. He realized that only her isolated up-bringing had kept her safe from an earlier seduction. Had she been brought to a licentious royal court, she would been easy prey for li-bidinous and salacious courtiers with an appetite for fresh young flesh. "I see," he said with great understatement. He took her little hand and, turning it over, kissed the palm. "I like it when you soothe me, Autumn."

A shiver ran up her spine and then back down again. "Perhaps we should retire," she said nervously.

"Perhaps not," he said softly, and arose from the oak settle where they had been sitting. "Let us sit before the fire," and he drew her up to stand with him. "That is a fine, thick sheepskin, *ma petite.*" He maneuvered them down to the floor. "There, is that not nicer, and warmer too? Spring nights are yet chill. It's almost as if winter can-not let go. Underneath, however, one senses warmer weather, but a fire is nice in the evenings."

"I saw my parents sit before a fire this way once," Autumn replied. She had also seen a great deal more until Adali, on his cat's feet, had clapped a hand over her open mouth and carried her off to her nursemaid, chuckling as he did so. Would Sebastian make love to her that way? she wondered silently.

They sat in silence, watching the flames dance and dart. The fire was red, orange, and golden, with the occasional blue flame. It crackled and growled softly to itself as it burned. Autumn noticed that the fireplace was flanked by stone angels with beautifully carved faces. She wondered why she hadn't espied it before, but then she had never viewed the fireplace from this particular angle before. His arm slid suddenly about her, and her first instinct was to stiffen, but then she relaxed and lay her dark head against his shoulder. For the moment words seemed unnecessary.

One arm about her, Sebastian reached out with his other hand and caressed the curve of her slender neck. The hand moved slowly and delicately about the curve of her jawline, his fingers brushing lightly across her full lips. Those lips, almost involuntarily, kissed at his fingertips. Grasping her chin gently, he turned her head slightly and kissed her, tenderly at first, the kiss deepening as he felt her returning his passion with her own, shyly, then more boldly.

Autumn sighed with the pleasure his lips were so generously bringing to hers. The pressure of his mouth seemed to almost communicate his desires to her. She felt her lips parting slightly, as did his, their perfumed breaths mingling, adding to their growing arousal of each other. His tongue, to her surprise, if not shock, suddenly pushed through into her mouth to touch her tongue with a fervent and heated caress. She jumped at the first contact; but then, realizing the wave of enjoyment sweeping over her, followed his lead, caressing his tongue in return.

Her lack of fear, her obvious enjoyment, all worked to set his senses reeling. Their lips had yet to unlock. Now his hand moved to undo her bodice, slipping it quickly off and laying it aside. Autumn said nothing, and her eyes were tightly closed. He kissed her eyelids in a gesture of reassurance; then his fingers undid the ribbons that held her chemise closed. His big hand slid beneath the fabric to fondle a small but decidedly shapely breast. He was almost trembling with his excitement and the overwhelming love he was feeling for this exquisite girl.

Autumn purred as the hand fondled her. Her head rubbed against his shoulder. Her torso arched against him, straining against his arm.

She could hear her heart thumping in her ears. She quivered with open anticipation as his hand caressed her gently, teasing at her nipple with the ball of his thumb. Their lips parted, and Autumn drew in a deep breath. Then she sighed gustily.

"You like being touched," he said quietly.

She opened her eyes and looked into his. *"Oui,"* was all she said. Then she closed her eyes again, relaxing against him.

He shifted her slightly and, lowering his head, his mouth closed over her nipple. He sucked hard upon it, his arm tight about her.

Autumn's eyes flew open again, surprise filling them. The tug of his mouth was incredible, engendering feelings within her that she had never known existed. She wasn't even certain she understood them! There was something masterful about him. Yet she quickly realized that he was at her mercy even as she was at his. The tingle of excitement she felt between her legs was absolutely brand new and utterly revealing. She wanted a name for it. She thought she knew that name. "Is this lust?" she asked ingenuously.

He lifted his head from her breast. His eyes were practically glazed with his open desire. *"Oui,"* he said softly. Then his head dropped again to her nipple. He suckled. He licked. He nipped ever so gently, then licked again. His hand squeezed her breast, forcing the flesh upwards so he might put more of it in his mouth. He groaned at the obvious pleasure he was receiving.

Her slender fingers tangled themselves in his thick, dark hair. "Show me what else there is," she demanded of him. "I want to know!"

In answer he lay her back onto the sheepskin. She could see the fire blazing, just above her head, it seemed. His fingers tore at her chemise, ripping it open to bare her torso to his hot silver eyes. He began to kiss the flesh in an almost frantic manner. His mouth seemed to score her flesh wherever it touched. His dark head moved lower, lower, until finally he stopped, and as suddenly began to lick her skin with long, sweeping strokes of his tongue.

"Ahhh," she sighed, feeling a shiver, which was a mixture of both excitement and chill where his tongue had touched. Then she felt his hand pushing up her skirts, fondling the curve of her calf, sliding up, up, until his fingers were brushing at the inside of her thigh.

"You do not wear *les caleçons?*" he said, not certain whether to be surprised or shocked.

"Only when I ride, beneath my breeches," she murmured. "I did not grow up with them, and drawers are difficult to get to when one needs the necessary and is wearing twelve petticoats."

He removed his hand from beneath her skirts. She was really too inexperienced for what he had in mind. *Not tonight.* But one night soon, he thought.

"Why have you stopped?" she asked him, genuinely curious.

He kissed her lips lightly, and began to retie her half-torn chemise, shaking his head at the rip he had inflicted upon the material. "How will you explain this to your serving woman?" he wondered aloud.

"I shall dispose of it so she does not see it," Autumn said. "Why did you stop, Sebastian? I was very much enjoying your attentions."

"Because," he half-lied, standing and pulling her up with him, "I did not think I could control myself where you are concerned, *chérie*. You are far more tempting than I had anticipated, Autumn. Had we gone further, I do not think I could have stopped." He picked up her bodice and helped her into it, fastening the laces and jeweled buttons for her.

"Perhaps I did not want you to stop," she said.

He stood up and pulled her up after him. "You are an innocent, *chérie*. You will have to trust me for now to make such decisions."

"You will be a *very* French husband, *n'est-ce pas?*" she teased him; and then, standing on her toes, she kissed him a quick kiss.

"*Oui*," he agreed with a laugh, "and you, not being a good French wife, will drive me to distraction, eh?"

"*Oui*," she acknowledged with a smile. "Come, monseigneur, if you are not going to continue your seduction of me, then I might as well show you to your chamber. You are next to Mama. I am on the other side of her. Think of how close we are before you sleep." Then she led him upstairs, pointed to a door, and was gone.

With a rueful smile, Sebastian d'Oleron entered his bedchamber. A small fire burned in a corner fireplace. A taper flickered by the bedside, and upon the bed his nightshirt had been laid out. On a small chest at the bed's foot, a basin of water and a cloth sat awaiting him. Undressing, he washed himself as best he could and lifting up the night garment, put it on. As he slipped it over his head and down his long, lean frame, he saw that beneath it was a small slip of neatly folded parchment. Picking it up, he opened it and read, *"I will be at Chermont tomorrow."* It was signed *"d'Albert."*

"Merde!" he swore softly. Why now? Why when he was in the midst of a budding courtship with Autumn? What possible excuse was he going to use to leave Belle Fleurs for even a short time? And it would not necessarily be a short time, since d'Albert was involved. Still, he had no other choice, Sebastian d'Oleron thought to himself as he climbed into his bed. He would have to think of an excuse even if it angered Autumn. Just a few more months, and the king would be installed upon his throne for good and all. Then they could all take their ease.

He awoke just before first light, as was his habit. He dressed quickly and left his chamber. There was no one in the Great Hall, but in the stableyard he met Red Hugh.

"Good morning, monseigneur," the Scotsman said.

"Bonjour, Hugh. Tell Mademoiselle Autumn I have gone back to Chermont to oversee the planting of some new vines. I will be back as quickly as possible. I apologize for leaving without telling her, but I only just awoke a little while ago and realized this task awaited me. They are a new variety of vine. I would be certain they are planted properly in the right field." He smiled, and then without another word mounted his horse, which the stableboy had brought him.

It was a poor excuse, he thought as he rode off, but it would have to do. D'Albert was a part of his life he would hopefully never have to share with Autumn because it would be over and done with by the time they wed in late summer. Reaching the main road, he pushed his mount into a canter. Soon he was passing the entry to Archambault. Then, finally, as the sun climbed above the horizon, he reached Chermont. He slid from his mount as a groom took the horse to lead him into the stables, and entered the chateau. In the hall he found d'Albert, already up, breaking his fast with fresh baked bread and cheese, a goblet of wine in his hand. He gestured with the goblet in greeting.

The marquis joined him at the highboard, asking as he sat down, "How did you know where I was?"

"Your valet. Was it a secret, Sebastian?" He shoved a piece of bread into his mouth.

"I'm getting married, d'Albert, I have been courting my soon-to-be wife," the marquis said. He took a deep swallow of wine.

"What's she like?"

"Beautiful, adorable, a Scot, and utterly impossible," came the answer. "She's going to be furious to find me gone when she awakens."

"Sorry," d'Albert replied sanguinely, "but you have some work to do for the master, monseigneur. The lady is still at Chenonceaux, but they depart tomorrow for Paris. The popinjay is terrified of losing his nephew. Nothing can be written down. You will have to memorize everything so you may tell the lady."

"And how the hell am I supposed to do that, d'Albert? If you had come a few days ago, before I went to Chenonceaux with all the rest of the local gentry to pay my respects, I might have been able to steal a private moment with the lady," the marquis told his companion. "Now it will be very difficult, if not impossible."

"You have to do it," d'Albert said. "The next few months are critical to the success of the master's plans. If the king is to be crowned, as his late father wished it, we must act now, before that popinjay d'Orleans and his troublesome friends in Paris cause any more difficulties. You have no idea how hard it has been to keep those wolves and foxes at bay these past eight years. They have wanted nothing more than possession of the king so they might circumvent his father's will and rule France in his name. Do you know what a disaster that would have been?"

The Marquis d'Auriville nodded in agreement. Then he said, "The lady likes perfumed gloves. I could take her a pair and say I meant to bring them to her the other day."

"Do you have such an item?" d'Albert asked.

"*Oui.* I intended giving a pair to my soon-to-be mother-in-law. I shall simply take the pair for the lady and send to Nantes for another pair." He arose from the table. "Come along now, d'Albert. We will go to my library, where you will instruct me. If they are leaving tomorrow, I shall have to go this afternoon."

"Shall I tell the master you are marrying?" d'Albert asked as they walked from the hall.

"*Oui,* and tell him once I have a wife I can no longer play this game. It would be too dangerous. I do not want to involve Autumn. Besides, she renders me vulnerable, which makes me too risky an ally. He will understand. We plan to wed in late summer."

"I will tell him, but you know if he wants you to continue in his secret service, monseigneur, you will have no choice," d'Albert replied. "Besides, it is for France!"

Sebastian d'Oleron laughed. "Tell me what I must know," he responded. *For France?* He almost laughed again. The only difference between the princes of the royal blood and Cardinal Mazarin was the fact that the cardinal was truly devoted to the young king and his best interests. That that devotion brought him the power the others wanted was irrelevant in his eyes.

In the late afternoon he approacheed Chenonceaux. By incredible good fortune he met the king and his mother returning from the hunt with their retainers. Sweeping his hat from his dark head, he bowed from his saddle, and the king greeted him.

"Monsieur le Marquis d'Auriville, is it not?" Louis said. "What brings you back to Chenonceaux, and how is the beautiful Lady Autumn? She has promised to come to court when I build my new palace."

"So she has told me, Your Majesty. We are to be wed in late summer, at the end of August. I returned because I have a gift for your mother. I forgot to bring it with me the other day. I did not want you leaving Chenonceaux without it, Your Majesty," He smiled his charming smile.

"You are gracious, monseigneur," Queen Anne said as she brought her horse abreast of them, squeezing between her son and the marquis. "Come and join us for some wine. Then you may give me your gift."

"I thank you, Your Majesty," he replied jovially, suddenly dropping his voice to quickly say, so only she might hear, *"I have a message for you from d'Albert."*

Queen Anne nodded imperceptibly and then turned to her son.

They entered the inner court of the chateau and from there moved into the beautiful palace. In the Great Hall the servants scurried to and fro with wine and sugar wafers. They chattered about the hunt, which had taken up a good deal of their day. When d'Orleans began to hold forth in his pompous manner, the marquis found himself drawn aside into a corner by the queen.

"Quickly!" was all she said.

"You have done well, recalling Pierre Seguier to be chancellor, taking the royal seals from Chateauneuf, and giving them to Mole. Now you must name the Comte de Chavigny, who holds the confidence of Conde, as your first minister. This will infuriate d'Orleans. Gondi will find himself isolated, as it will appear the princes of the blood royal have regained royal favor. In another month Conde's influence must be decreased. You will meet with the bishop to promise him a cardinal's hat. The political factions will be totally confused by all of this. In July you must appear to sacrifice all to Conde's ambitions and dismiss the cardinal's three allies, Servien, Lionne, and Le Tellier, in order to lull Conde into a false sense of security. By month's end you must somehow manage to pick a quarrel with Conde, making him the aggressor. I shall get further instructions to you before then." As he finished speaking, the marquis presented Queen Anne with the exquisitely wrapped gift and bowed low to her.

The queen made a great show of opening the silk wrapping with its cloth-of-gold ribbon. She lifted out a pair of gloves with a cry of delight. "My dear marquis, how absolutely beautiful," she said as she tried on the gloves, holding out her hands to admire them. They were of the softest cream-colored kidskin, embroidered with pearls and tiny pink crystals, and lined in rose-colored silk. She sniffed. "They are scented! It is my favorite violet! Ohh, you could not have given me a lovelier gift! Louis! Come and see the beautiful scented gloves monsieur le marquis has brought me!" She smiled up at Sebastian and said low, "I understand and shall await *his* next message. Thank you. I did not think he had friends here among the vineyards."

"He has friends everywhere, madame. Never doubt it. I know at times it must seem as if you are alone, but you are not. Courage! It is but a few months more, and the king will be in full command. It is toward that day we all endeavor." Then the marquis kissed the queen's hand and bowed once again.

"Let me see your new treasure, *Maman*," the king said, coming up to them and taking his mother's hand. "Ah, exquisite! The workmanship is marvelous. Where did these gloves come from, monsieur le marquis?"

"They are made in Florence, Your Majesty, but I purchased them through a merchant in Nantes who imports them," Sebastian replied.

"I will want his name. I have not ever seen gloves so fine." The king turned his head slightly. "Maurice, obtain the information needed from the marquis before he leaves us." Then he looked to Sebastian again. "Will you stay for dinner, monseigneur?"

"If Your Majesty will forgive me, I must return to Belle Fleurs. I left before dawn. Autumn will be expecting my return today. If I leave now, I can just get back before nightfall. With Your Majesty's permission I beg leave to withdraw." He bowed to the young king.

"She is very beautiful and equally tempting, monseigneur," Louis remarked. "I cannot say I blame you. I should far prefer her company to that of a king. You may withdraw with our thanks for the lovely gift you have brought my mother." Louis inclined his head slightly, indicating that the interview was over.

The marquis bowed again to the king and Queen Anne, then backed away until the royals turned from him. One of the king's secretaries, Monsieur Maurice, came and was given the information regarding the source for the gloves in the town of Nantes. As he hurried from the chateau he was approached by Prince Gaston d'Orleans himself.

Blocking the marquis's way, the prince said, "Why did you come here today, monsieur?"

"I had a pair of scented gloves for the queen that I meant to bring the other day but did not. Hearing you were leaving tomorrow, I returned with my gift this afternoon. Why do you ask, monsieur le prince? Is something wrong?"

"Why would you bring her a gift?" the prince demanded.

"Why would anyone bring a queen a gift? In hopes that if one day a royal favor was needed, it would be given, although I hardly believe a pair of kid gloves is worth much," he chuckled. "Why do you ask?"

"The king is in danger," the prince said, lowering his voice in a conspiratorial fashion. "The queen cannot be trusted, and her minion, the cardinal, lurks just beyond tomorrow, waiting to rule France."

"I would not know about such things, monsieur le prince. I am a simple man whose family has lived here along the chèr for over two thousand years. We were here when Rome came, when the Vikings came, and now when King Louis has come. My passion is for my lands, for the vines I tend, the wine I produce. Politics is not for a man like me. I am soon to wed. My next concern will be for an heir to Chermont. What happens in Paris is long past by the time we hear about it along the River chèr." He bowed to Gaston d'Orleans. "God will protect the king, monsieur le prince. Have faith, and do not worry." Then he turned and moved into the courtyard where his horse was awaiting him.

"Fool!" the prince said. "A simple country bumpkin for all his ancient title and name. I am beginning to see plots where none exist. Damn Mazarin to hell! He has me so on edge!"

The marquis mounted his horse and rode from Chenonceaux. The prince could know nothing, of course, but still such was the mood of the conspirators that even the most innocent event frightened them. He smiled to himself, almost amused. The cardinal was obviously a force to be reckoned with by those whose motives were disloyal. He had never met Jules Mazarin but had become involved in the cardinal's intricate network of informants and spies through his sister, who was a Cistercian nun. Jeanne Marie admired the cardinal's devotion, piety, and honesty. Having been raised a sensible country girl, she also liked the cardinal's practical nature.

She was his elder by five years, and he had not seen her in ten years when she one day appeared at Chermont for a "visit." She was, she said, inspecting a proposed site for a new convent her order was considering building in the area. She would, she said, stay with him, so they might catch up on old times. This was said in the company of her companions, half a dozen dour-faced nuns who could not possibly know that he and Jeanne Marie had never had any "old times" worth reliving. He had been five when she had gone to the nuns. He had been ten when she decided she wanted to dedicate her life to God's work.

He had, of course, welcomed his sister and her party to Chermont, offering them a small wing of the chateau for their privacy. His priest, Père Hugo, was delighted to have a congregaton at the early mass for a change. Then Jeanne Marie took him aside one morning, explaining what had been going on in Paris ever since King Louis XIII had died. Queen Anne, allied with the cardinal, struggled to keep the little king out of the hands of wicked men whose only desire was for personal power. His sister was dramatic in her speech, but he knew from the gossip that had filtered into the region that she was telling him the truth.

Then Jeanne Marie surprised him. The cardinal, she explained, had long ago assembled a network of people of goodwill whose sole desire was to see the little king safey educated and enthroned on his thirteenth birthday. But, she explained, there was a lack along the chèr of a good agent.

The conspirators wanted to keep young Louis ignorant of France, ignorant of God's will, ignorant of the world. They wanted to make him as selfish as they were. They wanted him seeped in pleasure so that it would be all he desired out of life. They wanted him useless so they might rule for him. The cardinal and the queen could not allow such a thing to happen to the boy who had been born to his parents when France had given up all hope of an heir. The boy the people called *le Dieudonne,* "the Godgiven one."

"You are a good man, Sebastian," his sister had said.

"How can you know that?" He had smiled at her. "We have hardly ever known one another, Jeanne Marie."

"When our father died you paid my full dowry to the convent. You send gifts of grapes and wine yearly, as well as a generous purse, brother. And there are those who correspond with me here who tell me of you and your exploits, although I cannot say I approve of your mistress in Tours. Still in all, you are a man of honor, and God-fearing. The cardinal needs men like you, Sebastian. Will you aid him?"

"What would I be required to do?" he asked her. "You know I will not endanger the family, or Chermont."

"You will be given a contact, and he will pass messages from the cardinal to you that you, in turn, will pass along to others. It is very simple. There is little if any danger involved. There are not so many of your kind that the cardinal can afford to lose them. As I have told you, he has no one in this area. It is likely you will hear from no one for months on end, but once in a while you may be required to act for His Eminence. You will be here when that time comes, my brother."

So he had agreed to act as the cardinal's eyes and ears in his own small region, and Jeanne Marie had been right. He was not called upon often. Until the cardinal had left France several months ago. After that, d'Albert had been on his doorstep several times. He usually passed his messages, which he memorized so there would be nothing to connect him to this intrigue, onto another person, always unknown to him. D'Albert had told him the cardinal believed it was better that his people not know one another. This was the first time he had been in a position to deliver a message to the final recipient.

Returning to Chermont, he assured d'Albert of his success and then mentioned Gaston d'Orleans. "I think he thinks me little better than some stupid farmer," the marquis said with a chuckle.

"Probably," d'Albert agreed. "His sense of self-importance is enormous. What did the queen say to you?"

"That she understood the cardinal's instructions and will await his next message. She is in a dangerous position now, isn't she?"

"She is," d'Albert said, "but she will survive if for no other reason than to see the crown placed on her son's head come September. I'll leave before dawn, monseigneur. I do not know if we will meet again."

"I understand," Sebastian d'Oleron said. "I will now return to Belle Fleurs to pacify my betrothed, who will want to know why I thought the planting of new vines more important than her. I shall have to bring her an outrageous gift to assuage her irritation."

To his surprise, however, he found Autumn quite reconciled to his absence, even as he offered her a small open box within which resided a pair of round ruby earbobs set in gold. "For you, *chérie*. I really do not think the vines more important than you are to me, but they are our livelihood. I would leave our heir an estate even richer than the one I inherited." He kissed her lips tenderly.

"I agree," she told him quietly.

"You do?" He was surprised. Had she not only recently complained about his devotion to his estates?

"*Oui*. Mama has explained it all to me. Now I understand. It is so easy for a woman to simply believe everything is as it is, and not question how it became that way." Autumn smiled at him.

He smiled back. He realized that he hated lying to her, yet she was but a girl. She could know nothing of the political intrigues that had been washing over France these past years. Here, amid the peace of the vineyards, Autumn felt safe, and he wanted her to continue to feel that way. He pushed aside his guilt. It was unlikely that the cardinal would ever call upon him again. Autumn need know nothing of the schemes and machinations in which he had been involved.

But as the day grew closer for the young king to assume his majority, France boiled with plots. In March the Parlement had begun a trial against the cardinal in absentia. Mazarin had had his assistant, Monsieur Colbert, prepare an inventory of the cardinal's wealth, which he then used to recruit reliable soldiers into his service. Once Louis was safely enthroned, the cardinal knew he would be recalled. The king of Spain publicly offered the cardinal a place in his government. Jules Mazarin publicly refused, saying he would be a servant of France in his thoughts and desires until his death.

The cardinal was willing to play a waiting game, for he understood better than any his opponents' weaknesses. There was a great divergence of interests between the princes of the blood royal and those of Paris, a lack of common ground even among the aristocrats and the imminent declaration of Louis's majority. Time was on his side, not on the side of his enemies. In Paris the queen would manipulate those about her as he had taught her; and Louis, he knew, was equally skilled at deception, a fact his foes could not anticipate, for they thought the king a mere child. They would soon learn that age had little to do with intellect, or the ability to wield power successfully.

This was the France to which Autumn Leslie had come, but because she was living safely at Belle Fleurs she knew nothing of the turmoil. "I love my earbobs," she told him. "They are every bit as fine as Mama's ruby earrings. *Merci*, monseigneur." Then she kissed him in return.

How sweet she was, he thought as he put his arms about her and cuddled her against his chest. Autumn murmured softly as his hand brushed her breast, and she nuzzled his neck. "I am glad you understand my position," he said softly, kissing her ear.

"I think we should choose a wedding day," Autumn said, surprising him greatly with her sudden decision.

"What has brought this on?" he said, setting her back and looking into her face. Her odd eyes, the one blue and the other green, fascinated him.

"I do not think I can wait to lay with you much longer," she replied bluntly. "When you touch me I both ache and burn, but I know not for what. It is very disconcerting, Sebastian! I think I need to couple with you, or at least that is what I can gather from speaking with Mama and her women. Do you not long to possess me entirely?"

He drew a very deep breath and then exhaled. "*Mon Dieu, chérie, oui!*" Then he enfolded her in his arms once again. "Autumn, my first marriage was a disaster arranged with the best of intentions by my parents and my wife's parents. But from the moment she tasted passion, Elise wanted more. I could not satisfy her lusts, and she turned to other men with absolutely no discrimination at all. I love you! I want you! But I am also afraid."

Autumn drew away from him, and he could see the look of absolute determination in her eyes. It was a look he had never before seen. "It is I who should be afraid, monseigneur," she said. "What if I discover I do not like coupling?" Then she chuckled. "But that is unlikely. The women of my family are noted for their passion . . . and their loyalty. We do not betray our husbands. Since I wish to be well married before I reach my twentieth birthday at the end of October, I think we should set our wedding day for the last day of August. And because I see the question in your eyes, *chérie*, I will tell you that I do love you, Sebastian d'Oleron. I should not have set a wedding date if I was not certain of that fact."

"Why do you love me?" he demanded fiercely.

"Because your heart is good; you are loyal; you love your lands. Because you are outrageously handsome and you set my heart to beating wildly each time you enter my view. Because I have lain awake at night imagining what our children will look like. If that is not love, or at least its beginnings, Sebastian, it is good enough for me. I cannot conceive of marrying another man, but I know most certainly that I want to marry you. Love, I have discovered, is like fog. It is elusive. You cannot pin it down. You just know, and I do."

He kissed her hungrily, and then he smiled down into her face, his eyes alight with his joy. "I knew that first day in the forest," he told her again. "I knew, but I was afraid!"

Autumn reached up and gently stroked his smooth face. "You do not have to be afraid ever again, monseigneur." Then she kissed him, yielding herself completely to his desires.

He felt, for the first time, the absence of restraint on her part. She seemed to melt into him, and her lips were soft beneath his, offering him everything. The marquis shuddered with his growing desire for Autumn. His hands tangled with the silkiness of her dark hair, holding her face so he might cover it with his kisses. His mouth touched her closed and shadowed eyelids, her forehead, her cheeks, the tip of her nose, traveling back again to the lips that were his forever.

She slipped her arms about his neck, pressing herself hard against him. She sighed and soared with the pleasure he was giving her with his hot kisses. She made neither cry nor resistance as they slid to the floor before the fire. She wasn't afraid as his hand slipped beneath her skirts, pushing them up so that she felt the evening air on her skin. His hand caressed her belly, her legs, the insides of her thighs. His fingers tangled themselves in the dark bush that covered her Venus *mont*. A single digit ran itself insinuatingly along the deep slash that divided her nether lips. Autumn trembled.

"I will stop," he said low.

"No!" was all she replied.

She was already moist with her excitement. He pressed the finger between the plump folds of soft flesh, seeking her little *bouton d'amour*, easily finding it and rubbing it gently. He could feel it beginning to swell beneath his ministrations. She began to squirm beneath his hand. Suddenly she cried out softly, her body stiffening first and then relaxing with a gusty sigh. Leaning over, he kissed her mouth, his tongue darting between her lips to play but a moment with her tongue. His finger was still between her nether lips. He began to play with her once more.

"*Again?*" she asked, surprised but not displeased.

"We will take it a step further this time," he told her. She was so deliciously wet. He desperately wanted to put his head between her soft little thighs and taste her, but he knew she was not ready yet for such delightful sport. Instead he firmly but carefully began to push the digit into her love channel. She gasped, surprised, but he soothed her with little kisses and soft reassurances, ceasing his forward movement for a moment, then pressing forward again.

Autumn didn't think she could breathe, but then she drew a long, deep breath. The invasion of his finger was so intimate, so possessive. She was not so innocent that she didn't realize the long slender finger was imitating his manhood. She arched herself against his hand, wanting him to delve more deeply, yet just the tiniest bit afraid. The finger seemed to encourage her to open to him like a flower, but then he stopped. "No! No!" she cried softly. "More, monseigneur. *More!*"

But the finger withdrew gently. "*Non, chérie,* your maidenhead I will take as it should be taken. With my manhood." He kissed her lips again and drew her skirts down.

"Then take it now!" she said recklessly. "I want to feel you within me, Sebastian! I do not understand it, but I need you!"

Sitting up, he gathered her into his arms and stroked her disheveled dark hair soothingly. "You are so new to passion, *ma petite,*" he said. "Do not doubt that I want you, for I do with all my heart, but on our wedding night you and I will begin to explore all the boundaries of desire. Not before then. I shall not again, before our wedding night, touch you, Autumn. It is all I can do to restrain myself from ravishing you, and you would obviously ravish me, given the knowledge, eh, *chérie.*"

She laughed weakly. *"Oui!"* she told him, totally unashamed.

They lay together silently for some time before the fire in the hall, and then finally she arose reluctantly. He followed her, and together they ascended the stairs to their separate bedchambers. Before her door he took her into his arms to again kiss her. She kissed him back, then smiled, shaking her head.

"Why is it that your kisses make me want to rip my clothes off?" she wondered aloud. "I want to rip your clothes off too."

He laughed. "You are a lustful wench," he told her.

"But only for you, monseigneur," she reassured him earnestly, looking up into his handsome face.

The silver eyes looked back at her. *"I know,"* he replied, meaningfully. "And I know you are nothing like Elise, *ma petite.* Now listen to me, Autumn. Tomorrow I will return to Chermont. I cannot remain here at Belle Fleurs, for I desire you too greatly, as you desire me. I will want you and your mama to come to my chateau in a few days to see where you will be living, and the house of which you will soon be mistress. If you spend the next two months preparing for our wedding, it will go quickly. August thirty-first is a good time, for it is just before the harvest. We are agreeed, then?"

"We are agreed," Autumn answered him with a smile.

Chapter

9

"You are getting as bad as I am, my dear Gondi," the prince said. "You see conspiracies where there are none."

"Better to be circumspect, Gaston, than careless," came the dry reply. "Mazarin certainly has a network of spies and informants. He would be a fool if he didn't, and we both know he is not a fool. He would also not be so well informed if he was not being sent information. It is too late in the game to destroy his network, but there is one way to dismantle and undo his influence with the king."

"How?" Gaston d'Orleans demanded.

"The queen," came the reply. "Power is like a game of chess, Gaston. If we check the queen, we have the king."

"Are you mad?" the prince cried. "You cannot kill the queen! Even I, who have always disliked her, would not dare put such a stain on my immortal soul. Tell me, Gondi, do you ever consider your immortal soul?"

"Perhaps I shall one day, when I receive that cardinal's hat I have been promised," Gondi answered him. "I am not speaking murder, my poor prince. I am simply suggesting that if the queen was not about to influence young Louis—and we all know from where her ideas emanate—the king might be more amenable to our influence. The laws of France may stipulate a king can be crowned at thirteen,

Gaston, but he is still an inexperienced lad. He needs our guidance. *France* needs our guidance."

"What do you propose?" Gaston d'Orleans queried his companion.

"The queen will see her son crowned next month even if she must personally slay dragons to attain that goal. Let Louis be instated officially. It is to our advantage that he be so. If we attempt to stop the king's investiture, we will be called traitors. But once the crown rests officially upon those dark curls, we will become advisers, and confidantes of His Majesty, the king."

"And my sister-in-law?" the prince demanded.

"Will disappear into retirement, my dear Gaston. Away from Paris. Away from her son. It must be a luxurious sequestration. I would not have the king thought cruel to his dear and faithful *maman*. Where was that chateau you visited after Easter? On the Loire?"

"Chenonceaux, on the chèr, near Tours."

"A lovely place, I am told," Gondi replied silkily.

"But if the king knows she is there . . ."

"But he will not, Gaston, nor will the country lordlings about the region know she is there. She will be imprisoned, but most comfortably. I have great respect for her station. Her priest will be allowed to accompany her, but her servants will be pensioned off. Better our own people serve her. You do understand why?"

The prince nodded silently.

"The reason we will give for her sudden departure is that, having fulfilled her duty to her late husband, she is now allowing their son his freedom to rule as he sees fit, being an intelligent lad, and wise beyond his years. It is just the sort of twaddle she would say," Gondi chuckled, well pleased with his plan. "Now that we have gotten rid of Mazarin, the playing field is ours, Gaston! All ours!"

"You forget that my nephew is not a child any longer, Gondi."

"Neither is he a man, and he is most devoted to his dear *maman*. He will do what we tell him for her sake, and her safety," Gondi said.

"And if he does not?" the prince asked bluntly.

"There is always his brother, le petit Monsieur."

"*Jesu!* You speak treason, Gondi!" Gaston d'Orleans said, shocked. He had not realized before how truly ruthless his companion was.

"It will never come to that, my dear Gaston," Gondi soothed the prince in dulcet tones. "Louis, for all his station, is a young boy, like other young boys. He will be delighted to be freed of the restraints placed upon him by Mazarin and his mother. He will believe he is finally and really king. He can be kept amused in any number of ways. Let him begin to design that palace he is always babbling about that he wants to build at Versailles. We will put the best model makers in Paris at his disposal. They will make his dream come alive before his very eyes. It will take months and months of work. While he is playing, we will be ruling in his name. And there are other ways to keep him from troubling us. Have you not noticed that the young king has a very powerful libido? I am told that pretty little serving wenches are not safe from his lustful adavances these days. We will see only the loveliest of girls serve the king's needs *in all ways*," he concluded with a rich chuckle. "And, of course, we must arrange a good marriage for the boy, Gaston. Another ploy to amuse our Louis." Gondi's foxlike face was wreathed in a smile, and he rubbed his hands together, delighted with himself and his own cleverness.

"Perhaps," Gaston d'Orleans said slowly and thoughtfully, "perhaps you are adroit enough to make this happen, Gondi." A long and elegant finger stroked his chin. His blue eyes were contemplative. "My nephew, however, is most attached to his *maman*. He may not accept her absence easily. Eventually you will have to tell him where she is. Whatever you think, Gondi, Louis is the king. There will come a day when no man can stand in the way of what the king desires. What will you do then, *mon ami?*"

"The mother will write the son, telling him of her pleasure in her retirement. Eventually we will supply her with gambling partners. You know how she loves to gamble. We will give her her own troupe of ballet dancers for her amusement. She will urge Louis to keep his mind on the business of his realm and not concern himself with her. After awhile such reassurances will content him. He will no longer care or ask."

"If you are keeping her whereabouts such a secret," the prince said sensibly, "how can we give her gambling partners and dancers?"

"We will keep the secret for a year or two, no more. By then the boy will be ours," the cleric replied.

"And Mazarin?" the prince countered. "Do you really think he will be content to remain quiet while the queen disappears and we take control of my nephew? He has an army at his disposal! He will invade France. Then what will happen?"

"If he invades France, particularly when he is forbidden her borders, he is guilty of treason, my dear Gaston. He will be in the same position we have been in all these years. He will not dare to kidnap the king from us. Besides, at the first hostile move on his part, the queen's very life will be in danger. I will make certain that he understands that. His love for Anne of Austria is well known, for all his cardinal's robes. Now, tell me, Gaston, what chateaux are near Chenonceaux? I want to know whom we may trust and not trust."

"The nobility of the region have ancient names but are little more than farmers, *mon ami*. They care nothing for politics, just the weather, which determines a good vintage year or a poor one." He laughed scornfully. "When we were there last spring they came to pay their respects. Each of them done up in his or her best finery, at least five years' out of date fashionwise, except a lovely young Scots girl, who is living in exile from the Commonwealth at a small chateau nearby. She was most fashionably garbed, as was her widowed *maman*. My nephew took her off to walk along the river gallery. He was followed at a discreet distance by the girl's affianced." The prince chuckled. "Louis returned rather quickly, but the girl and her gentleman came later. An amusing little incident that I should have forgotten, but that the same gentleman returned several days afterwards. He came, he said, to bring the queen a small token that he had meant to bring on his previous visit. Scented gloves, I believe. My sister-in-law went into raptures over them. I thought it a bit odd, but when I questioned the gentleman he proved to be a bit of a dunce, I thought."

"Who was he?" Gondi asked, curious.

"The Marquis d'Auriville," was the reply.

The cleric thought a moment, then said, "I have never heard of him, Gaston."

"Why would you?" the prince replied. "He is a farmer, unimportant. There is no reason any of us would know him." A discreet cough made Gaston d'Orleans turn his head slightly. "Yes, Lechaille, what is it?"

"Your Highness asked me to remind him of his supper with the queen. Your Highness will want to change his garments. We just have the time to do so if Your Highness comes now." The valet bowed.

"Where the devil did he come from?" Gondi demanded, startled to see the servant.

"Show him," the prince commanded Lechaille.

The valet touched the wall, and a small door sprang open.

Gondi was astounded. "He might have been listening the whole time, Gaston," he said, concerned.

"Were you listening to our conversaton, Lechaille?" the prince asked.

"No, Your Highness. I was laying out your garments, and preparing the water for your ablutions," the valet said calmly.

"You see, Gondi, it is as I said earlier. You worry too much." He arose from his chair. "I bid you good evening. I must go and get ready to join my sister-in-law and her son for the evening meal. Escort monseigneur out, Lechaille. Then come back and help me," the prince said.

"How long have you been with the prince?" Gondi asked the servant as he was conducted from the prince's apartments in the Palais Royale.

"I have been with His Highness for two years, monseigneur. Before that my uncle, Pierre Lechaille, served His Highness for almost forty years, and my grandfather served the prince's father, King Henri the Fourth."

"And what did your father do?" Gondi asked, curious.

"My father, monseigneur, died before my birth," was the brief answer. "The courtyard is beyond that door, and you will find your coach waiting for you, monseigneur," Lechaille said, bowing, and then turning away to hurry down the corridor.

With a shrug, Gondi exited the building. The prince was right: He was seeing plots where none existed. The valet was a loyal servant from a long line of loyal servants. The cleric clambered into his coach and was quickly gone.

Lechaille hurried down the hallway toward his master's apartments. Entering them, he said to his son, who was his assistant, "Find d'Albert as quickly as you can, René." Then he entered the prince's dressing chamber, saying as he went, "I have seen your friend off, Your Highness."

Taking up his cloak, the younger man ran quickly from the prince's apartments and dashed from the Palais Royale. He moved through the streets of the city toward an inn he knew d'Albert frequented when he was in Paris. To his relief, the cardinal's agent was having his supper when he entered Le Coq d'Or. "Wine!" René called out, and slapped a coin upon the counter of the inn's taproom. Then, taking his pewter cup, he moved to stand by the large open fireplace, his back to d'Albert's table. "My father needs to see you," he murmured low.

"Tonight," was the reply.

"It will be late," René replied.

"I will be here," was the answer.

René swallowed his wine down and departed the inn to hurry back to the palace before he was missed.

Well after midnight, Robert Lechaille entered Le Coq d'Or. He immediately spotted d'Albert, who surreptitiously signaled him toward the inn's back stairs. There, out of the hurly-burly of the taproom, they met, and the prince's valet told him of the discussion he had heard late that afternoon between his master and Gondi.

"You must get word to him as quickly as possible," Lechaille said. "What they are planning is treasonous no matter that they couch it in clever phrases!"

"Did they say when?" d'Albert asked.

The valet shook his head in the negative.

"I do not know what he can do, other than warn the queen," d'Albert said slowly, "but I believe the conspirators will not harm her physically. We have people quite near Chenonceaux, and at least we know she would be safe. Also, we can rescue her from there with little difficulty," the cardinal's agent told the valet.

"I could warn her!" Lechaille replied.

"If you do, your use to us is over, Robert. You would endanger your own life and probably the life of your son," d'Albert told him. "He needs you where you are. This will not be over until the king is able to recall him, and we vanquish these troublemakers. It will all take time, and we have that time. Now, promise me you will do nothing foolish. You do trust me, don't you, Robert?"

The valet nodded. "I do, d'Albert, even if I do not know your first name," he said with a small, wry smile.

"Françoise," was the amused reply. "I'll get the message routed out of Paris tonight. Now go back to the Palais Royale and continue to keep watch for us."

The two men shook hands, and Lechaille said, "God speed, Françoise!" Then he moved back down the staircase and was gone.

Alone, d'Albert sighed. He hated riding at night, but there was no help for it. The dawn was several hours away, and even at a snail's pace he could be several miles out of the city before the sunrise. It was a long journey to the duchy of Cologne, but he would make it personally, speed being important. It was the end of August when d'Albert finally rode into the cardinal's residence in Cologne.

Jules Mazarin, hearing his servant's news, said, "There is no help for it. I must return to France."

"My lord, do not, I beg you," d'Albert pleaded. "They will kill you. I have never known such ruthlessness as Gondi exhibits."

"Who do we have near Chenonceaux? Is there anyone?" the cardinal replied, ignoring his servant's plea.

D'Albert considered a moment, and then said, "There is the Marquis d'Auriville, but he is about to wed, and he told me he will serve no longer. His chateau, Chermont, is several miles upriver from Chenonceaux. He is a good man, monseigneur, loyal to the king, but he is in love and fears to endanger his bride."

"If he is a good man, d'Albert, then he will continue to serve until it is no longer necessary," the cardinal replied quietly. "You will make the arrangements, returning to France ahead of me and arranging for me to stay at Chermont. I will travel incognito." Reaching for the bellpull, he yanked it, saying to the servant who answered his call, "Ask my cousin, Seigneur Carlo, to join us." The cardinal arose and went to his map chest, drawing out a large chart and laying it open across the table.

"When I came to Cologne I crossed from France into the duchy of Luxembourg, and thence to Cologne. It was the most direct route for me at the time. It would not be expected that I should reenter France under any circumstances, but on the chance those particular borders are being watched, I shall take an entirely different and unexpected route. By voyaging down the Rhine I can cross into France at Strasbourg, here." He pointed to the map, and then his finger began to trace a route. "To Colmar, to Vesoul, to Dijon, to Nevers, to Bourges, and from there across the countryside to Chermont." He turned to look at d'Albert. "What do you think, old friend?"

"You will be recognized," d'Albert said.

"Nay, I will not," the cardinal replied. "I shall travel as a simple gentleman with a few men-at-arms to protect me."

"Your absence will be noted here in Cologne. Your residence has hardly been private. D'Orleans's spies will fall over themselves in the rush to tell him you have departed Cologne. Then all of France will be on its guard, monseigneur," d'Albert said fatalistically.

The door to the cardinal's paneled library opened and a masked figure entered. He bowed to the cardinal and said, "You sent for me, cousin? How may I serve you?"

"Remove the mask, Carlo," the cardinal instructed the man, who immediately pulled the mask from his head.

D'Albert gasped, staring openmouthed at the man. Then he looked at the cardinal and back again to his cousin. Finally, shaking his head, he exclaimed, "*Mon Dieu! Mon Dieu!* He could be your twin, monseigneur. If you were garbed identically, I, who have served you so faithfully all these years, could not tell the difference. Who else knows of this man and his presence here, or even of his existence?"

"Only my servant, Luigi, who has been with me since my childhood," the cardinal replied. "My cousin keeps to his apartments. Luigi brings him his meals. When he walks in the garden, I hide myself, so no one will know I have this twinlike relation." The cardinal smiled, amused by d'Albert's astonishment. "Carlo studied for the priesthood, although he never took final orders. I can leave him here in Cologne, and it will be as if I am yet here. Luigi will remain with him to complete the illusion. Hence I am free to return to France to direct my restoration, and protect my queen from those who would harm her. It is a good plan."

"But you will need an army, my lord, to restore you to the king's side," d'Albert protested, fearful for his master.

"I have fifteen hundred horses and two thousand foot soldiers," the cardinal said. "They will cross into France at various points over the next few months. We will meet at a single location to be decided upon. In the meantime, d'Albert, you must go to Chermont to tell the marquis I will be arriving sometime before Christmas. I will be introduced as his distant cousin, Robert Clary, who has been traveling in the east for many years. He will say he believed me dead, since he had not heard from me in so long. That small lie will cover a multitude of sins." He chuckled and smiled again.

D'Albert was astonished. In all the years he had secretly served the cardinal, he had never seen him smile. And now, today, Mazarin had smiled twice! "Monseigneur, I believe that you are actually enjoying this intrigue," he said boldly, "but please, I beg you, for the king's sake, be cautious. Gondi and the others finally believe themselves close to attaining their goal. They will do murder to retain their power, and *le bon Dieu* help any who stand in their way."

The cardinal patted d'Albert's narrow shoulder. "*Le bon Dieu* will protect us all, *mon ami,* for what we do is right in His eyes," he assured his servant. "Now I will arrange for you to rest here a few days, as you have ridden hard and long, I have not a doubt. I must arrange to leave for France as quickly as possible."

"I will ride with you when you go," d'Albert said. "After we cross into France, I will leave you and ride with all speed to the Marquis d'Auriville to tell him that his cousin Robert will soon be coming for a visit. Shall I arrange to inform the queen?"

"Nay," the cardinal replied. "Only you and I and d'Auriville will know the truth. It is better for everyone, and I will be safer."

"What is today's date?" d'Albert asked.

"August thirty-first," the cardinal answered him.

"Monsieur le marquis will surely be wed by now," d'Albert said.

But Sebastian d'Oleron, to his great annoyance, was not married. The Duchess of Glenkirk had been called to Paris with her daughter by their exiled English queen, Henrietta Maria, to attend the young French king's formal investiture, following his thirteenth birthday on September 5. The proclamation of the king's majority would take place on the seventh of September, attended by as many of the nobles in France who could get there. It would be celebrated with great pomp and show, for Anne of Austria had been looking forward to this day since her son inherited his father's throne eight years earlier. She had beaten those who attempted to take her son from her and rule in his name. Now she was triumphant. Only the absence of Jules Mazarin, her faithful partner in this miracle, saddened her. But the Marquis d'Auriville, like many of his neighbors, could not leave his vineyards with the harvest season upon them.

In Paris, Autumn, her mother and her two *tantes* were fortunate in that the de Saville family had a small hôtel on the Rive Gauche, located at Quatre Rue Soeur Celestine. Because they had had no time to send word ahead, the old concierge, Madame Alma, was distraught as their large traveling carriage pulled into the building's courtyard. She shuffled forward, distress upon her worn face.

"Madame St. Omer! Madame de Belfort! Why did you not say you were coming! The dustcovers are upon all the furniture! There is no food! 'Tis a poor welcome to Paris I offer you."

"The servants we brought can lift the dustcovers and fetch food from the market, Alma," Madame de Belfort said soothingly as she alighted from their coach. She hugged the old woman. "It's good to see you again. This is our cousine from England, Madame la Duchesse de Glenkirk, and her daughter, soon to be la Marquise d'Auriville. We have all come for the king's proclamation. Isn't it exciting!"

"You will forgive me for saying it, madame," the concierge answered her, "but one king is very much like another for people like me." Taking a large iron key from her apron pocket, she moved ahead to open the front door of the house. The lock turned silently as the concierge waved them into the building. "Come in! Come in!"

Autumn sneezed. "It's musty," she said as she entered the dimly lit foyer.

"We must open the windows," the old woman, said, and proceeded to shuffle about, doing just that.

Now the serving women, who had traveled in a separate coach, hurried in and began to remove the dustcovers, swiftly snatching them from the furniture. Soon they were all sneezing as the dust flew about, pollenating the salon. Laughing, all the women retreated into the foyer, shaking their skirts out as they went.

"Gracious, how long has it been since anyone has stayed here?" Autumn asked.

"It has been at least ten years, mademoiselle, since any of the de Savilles came to Paris," the concierge said. "Why they keep the house confuses me, as they rarely use it."

"But here we are today for the king's special day, and where would we lay our heads, Alma, if it was not for Quatre Rue Soeur Celestine?" Madame de Belfort replied with a smile. "Of course, if you were not here to look after the *hôtel* for us, we would have to reconsider, wouldn't we?"

"I am here," the old woman said. "Now, I will take one of your women to the market, to see if we can find something for your supper tonight. Ah!" The concierge jumped back as Fergus and Red Hugh entered the house. "Who are these great beasts?" she demanded.

"They are my servants," Jasmine explained, "and gentle as lambkins for all their size, Madame Alma."

The old woman looked the two men up, and then she looked them down again. "I shall take them to the market with me," she said. "How long has it been since I was last seen in the company of a man, I cannot recall. This will set the old wives chattering," she cackled merrily.

"What kind of men are these Parisians," Red Hugh teased the old woman in excellent French, "to overlook such a fine figure of a woman as yourself, Madame Alma?" Then he gave her a kiss on her withered cheek. "I'd follow you to the ends of the earth if you could cook," he concluded.

"I can," she told him with a wink. "Come along now, *mon braves!* There is bread and cheese to buy."

Striding on either side of the little old lady, the two big Scots left the house. Behind them the women were laughing. When they returned from the marketplace, laden with fresh bread, cheeses, a fat capon, plucked and ready to roast, fresh fruit, and other staples, the dustcovers had disappeared, the horses were stabled and the coaches set to one side of the yard, the luggage was unloaded, and smoke was coming from all the chimneys. Obviously everyone had settled in nicely.

In the morning the women dressed in their finest gowns, Jasmine in midnight blue, Autumn in rose, Madame de Belfort in silvery gray, and Madame St. Omer in deep wine. They departed for the Palais Royale to first pay their respects to Queen Henrietta Maria. It was she who had sent the invitations to the royal proclamation.

"How did she know we were in France?" Autumn had asked her mother when they had arrived.

"I send the queen a purse each month," Jasmine explained. "She is very poor and, while the young king's aunt, neither he nor his mother give her enough to really live comfortably. I do not believe they intend being mean, but the queen is used to living as a queen. She does not know how to live any other way, and now she must. She is very much in debt. So each month I send her a purse. It is not so much as to be embarrassing to her, or ostentatious. Just a token, a reminder of my loyalty. Remember, Autumn, in different circumstances this lady would have been my sister-in-law. Then, too, she has young children to bring up. The Duke of Glocester is just eleven, and little Princess Henriette Anne only six. The poor lady has lost her husband, as well as Princess Elizabeth last year. Her lot is not a happy one.

Autumn had been quite surprised at her mother's response, especially given the fact that she thought the Stuarts brought bad luck to the Leslies of Glenkirk. Now, on the day of the king's proclamation, she found herself curtsying to a queen she had never known but who obviously knew her mother. It seemed odd to Autumn that her mother knew a queen so well; but then, everything had been different since they had left Scotland and England behind.

"Ah, Jasmime, *votre fille est trés charmante.* She is to be married soon, *non?*" The queen tipped Autumn's face up and gave her a kiss upon her cheek.

"We had affixed the date for August thirty-first, but then came Your Majesty's kind invitation," Jasmine said. "The wedding will now be held on the thirtieth of September, Your Majesty."

Henrietta Maria looked at Autumn. "Is he handsome, *ma petite?*"

"*Oui*, Your Majesty, he is *very* handsome," the girl replied with a blush.

"And what is this *very* handsome man's name?" the queen asked playfully.

"Jean Sebastian d'Oleron, Your Majesty. He is the Marquis d'Auriville," Autumn answered the queen.

"It is time, Madame la Reine," one of Queen Henrietta Maria's servants said. "The procession is forming now."

"Come," the queen said, rising. "You, your daughter, and your cousins will come with me. It will almost be like having members of my own court with me again." She sighed sadly.

The ceremony was to take place in the Parlement of Paris, and the hall was filled to overflowing. To the right, in the upper tiers of the building, Anne of Austria, Prince Gaston d'Orleans, the Prince de Conti, the marshalls of France, the high nobility, and the clergy were seated. Paris's troublemaking archbishop and two of the most powerful bishops in France, of Senlis and of Tarbes, were together looking pompous and quite smug, as if they alone were responsible for this event. To the left were seated other churchmen of rank, the papal nuncio, and the ambassadors of Portugal, Venice, Malta, and Holland, as well as the *conseillers de grand-chambre*, the presidents and the councilors of the Parisian Parlement, and other guests of rank.

In a wing to one side sat Queen Henrietta Marie of England; two of her sons, James, Duke of York, and Henry, Duke of Glocester; her little daughter, Princess Henriette Anne; la Grande Mademoiselle, the Duc d'Orleans's daughter; and many other duchesses and ladies of quality, including the widowed Duchess of Glenkirk and her party. Jasmine was frankly wide-eyed and realized what a true country mouse she really was. She had never before seen anything so magnificent.

Before her sat the young king on his *lit de justice*, which was, as

Autumn looked more closely, a pile of pillows. Around him in a strictly prescribed order was the Duc de Joyeuse, who was his grand chamberlain, and the Comte d'Harcourt. Monsieur de Saint-Brisson, the provost of Paris, in the company of the guards of the chamber knelt before Louis, hats off. The provost bore a chased silver mace. Chancellor Seguier knelt in his crimson gown and cloak. The master of ceremonies, who was called *le grand maître* of France, led the rest of the government officials, the *avocats generaux* and Monsieur Fouquet, the *procureur général*, into the hall to kneel before the king.

When all had entered, the young king arose and said, "Messieurs, I have come to my Parlement to tell you that, following the law of my state, I wish henceforth to take upon myself its government and administration. I trust that with God's grace, this will be with piety and justice. Monsieur the chancellor will explain my intentions in greater detail."*

The chancellor then spoke, and when he had finished Anne of Austria arose and, turning to the young king, said, "We are now in the ninth year since, according to the wishes of the late king my dead lord, I took charge of your education, and the government of your state. God has, by His goodness, blessed my work and kept you safe, you who are so dear and precious to me and to all your subjects. As the law of the kingdom presently calls you to govern this kingdom, I remit to you with great pleasure the power which was given to me for its government. I trust that God will give you grace and help you with the spirit of vigor and prudence and give you a happy reign."* She then knelt before the king, who kissed her.

Then, to everyone's surprise, the king spoke again, saying to his mother, "Madame, I thank you for the pains you have taken with my education and the administration of my kingdom. I beg you to continue to give me the benefits of your good counsel and desire that, after me, you should be the head of my Council."*

Then came everyone in the Parlement hall to pay homage to King Louis XIV, undisputed and now reigning king of France. There were other small speeches by various officials that day, and

*The actual speeches

three royal decisions were presented for registration. One involved blasphemers; a second reestablished the directive against dueling; the last proclaimed the Prince de Conde innocent of treason, although many knew he was guilty. On this day, however, the king was of a mind to be generous and offered an olive branch to Conde in the hope that he could be brought peacefully back into the royal fold.

The king now officially established, the celebrations began. Jasmine and her party had been invited to the Palais Royale as, it seemed, had everyone else in Paris. The king opened the fête by dancing with his mother. Prince James, the English Duke of York, led Autumn out onto the floor as his own mother was in mourning. Besides, he far preferred dancing with a beautiful girl. Autumn was thrilled, and grateful her *tantes* had taken the time to teach her the minuet, a dance that had become the fashion. *She was at court!* At long last she had taken her place in the kind of society her sisters had once enjoyed, and she was having a wonderful time.

"Why do you smile as if you have a secret, cousin?" James Stuart asked her as they finished the dance and he led her from the floor. "Not that it isn't a most delicious smile, mind you."

"We are not cousins," she replied.

"Your brother is my first cousin by virtue of his paternity. Therefore, I consider you my cousin as well, Lady Autumn," the prince returned with a grin.

"Are you flirting with me, my lord?" *He was!*

"Would you like me to cease, m'lady?" He again grinned engagingly, and Autumn suddenly realized they were in a remote alcove of the hall. His amber eyes were glittering speculatively at her.

"Yes," Autumn said firmly. "I should like you to stop, Jamie Stuart. I am betrothed to be married shortly. You will remember that the Leslies of Glenkirk are an honorable clan."

"You are very beautiful," he replied.

"So I have been told on many an occasion," Autumn responded.

"Why do you marry this Frenchman?" he asked her as he backed her into a corner of the alcove.

"Because I love him, and there was no one in Scotland, where I have spent most of my life, whom I loved. Have you ever been in love, my lord? It is an emotion that has no rhyme or reason, I fear. My eldest sister fell in love with a man who became another man. My second sister chose the *wrong* man and was forced for love of him to go to the New World, where they have built a wonderful life together. I came to France to escape the misery of what Cromwell has done to our homeland and found Sebastian. Is love not strange?"

He kissed her. James Stuart pulled Autumn into his arms and kissed her with all the passion in his eighteen-year-old soul. He felt her small but full breasts pressing against his jeweled doublet. His lust was engaged and he fondled her bosom.

Autumn pulled away and slapped the young man. "Oh, you Stuarts are all alike," she scolded him. "You think with your cock and not with your head! Shame on you, Jamie Stuart! Now ask my pardon, and we will remain friends." Autumn shook her skirts free of the embrace.

"Girls like it when I kiss them," he protested ingenuously.

Autumn laughed. "You are younger than me, and besides, you know well I am betrothed to the Marquis d'Auriville."

"Your mother was older than my uncle Henry," the prince said.

"By several years, I am told," Autumn agreed, "but I am not my mother, who when she fell in love with your uncle was a mature woman who had already outlived two husbands and had three children. I, on the other hand, am a virgin of noble family, affianced to a man I love whom I will wed at month's end. It is very dishonorable of you to make unwanted advances to me, Jamie Stuart. If there is one thing I know about the Stuarts, it is that they are not dishonorable men."

"We are related by blood, you know," he said, changing the subject as best he could. "The Leslies of Glenkirk have always intermarried down through the centuries with the Stuarts. Your grandfather, Lord Gordon, descends from James the Fifth of Scotland."

"Indeed?" Autumn said, not bothering to tell this prince that the Gordon of BrocCairn was her grandmother's husband but in no way related to her by blood. Then she smiled at him. "I am still awaiting your apology, *cousin.*"

"You have it," he said with a bow, "but I am not sorry I kissed you, Autumn Leslie. You are a most delicious armful."

They danced another minuet together, but as the dance ended, the Duke of York found himself skillfully replaced in the figure by the young king, who grinned mischievously at him.

"Noblesse oblige, sire," the prince said with a bow.

Louis nodded briefly but then turned his entire attention to Autumn as he led her from the floor and invited her to sit upon a stool by his throne. "I did not think to see you again, mademoiselle," he said. "How come you to my festive day?"

"My *maman* is a friend of your aunt, Queen Henrietta Maria. It was she who invited us, Your Majesty. It has all been very exciting, especially tonight! I have lived in the country all my life and have always hoped to come to court, although I always believed the court I would attend would be an English one."

"Where is your husband?" the king asked her.

"When the invitation came, we were forced to postpone the wedding, Your Majesty, but it will be celebrated at the end of this month, after I return home," Autumn explained, thinking as she did that the king, for all his youth, was a very handsome young man.

"Why did your marquis not accompany you?" Louis demanded, sounding a trifle affronted.

"He was not included in the queen's invitation, Your Majesty. Queen Henrietta Maria did not know I was betrothed. Besides, it is the harvest at Chermont. The grapes must be picked at just the right time if they are to be made into good wine. Only Sebastian and his winemaster can choose that exact moment, Your Majesty. Picked too soon, the grapes could make an inferior vintage. I should not like to send Your Majesty a *vin ordinaire* when we are capable of a superior vintage."

The king's brown eyes twinkled. "Mademoiselle, you are a clever girl and an excellent advocate for your marquis," Louis said. "I hope one day you will come to Versailles."

"You are really going to build it?"

"My uncle Gaston has already hired the finest model makers in all of France to come and live here with me while they do their work. Once I can see my dream, the architects will take over and we will begin," Louis said enthusiastically. "I am young yet, but by the time I am twenty-one, I shall have my dream well begun!"

"I shall look forward to it, Your Majesty," Autumn told him.

"And you and your husband shall come to see my creation," the king continued. "I want all the beautiful women in my kingdom about me, Lady Autumn."

She blushed prettily at the compliment. "It is sometimes difficult for me to realize how young you are, monseigneur," she told him. "You speak like a man grown, and yet you are just thirteen."

For a moment the kingly mask dropped, and she caught a brief glimpse of the boy. "I must be a man," he said low. "My struggle for what is mine by right is not yet over. If I show weakness for even a minute, they will be on me." Then, as quickly, the man reappeared.

"Oh, monseigneur," she said softly, sorrow tinting her voice. "I will pray for you and your good *maman.*"

"Pray for the cardinal as well, *ma belle.* I am surrounded by his enemies and will not be entirely safe until he returns."

"But he has been exiled," Autumn said.

"But I am now the king," Louis said firmly, his brown eyes serious. "Go back to your marquis, Autumn Leslie. Marry him, and live a peaceful life amid your vineyards. You are fortunate to have been given such a life. It is a blessing." Now the king held out his hand to the beautiful girl by his side. Autumn kissed it and, dismissed, she rose, curtsying deeply. Finding her party, they left the Palais Royale to return to Belle Fleurs and Archambault the next day.

Chapter

10

It was her wedding day. Autumn rose at first light as Lily still snored lightly in her trundle bed. Tiptoeing to the window, she looked out onto the lake. It was pink, reflecting the color of the clouds in the sky above. Narrow silver streamers of mist arose from the warmer water into the cool morning air. Everything was still and quiet. It was a magical time. The perfect beginning to a new and perfect life, she thought, smiling to herself as she did.

They had returned from Paris, and Sebastian's kisses made her realize how much they had missed one another. Monsieur Reynaud had appeared to make her wedding gown and trousseau, chortling and taking partial credit for her happiness because of his beautiful garments. Autumn did not tell him that Sebastian had seen her mostly in her riding clothes, and the simple gowns she already owned. The proud little tailor would have been hurt by such knowledge.

Autumn and her mother rode out one day to see Chermont. There was no time for them to make a proper visit, but Jasmine thought her daughter should have some idea of where she was to make her new home. Sebastian's chateau was like a fairy palace, with four pepperpot turrets at each corner of the building. It sat on a low rise just above the river, in a broad green meadow that was edged with green willows. Beyond the meadow the vineyards

stretched, their vines almost empty now of grapes, the leaves beginning to turn yellow about the edges.

Inside the chateau was exquisite. Unlike Belle Fleurs, with its
narrow and winding staircase, Chermont had a main staircase ramp
that ascended in the elegant Florentine fashion. It was obvious that
the chateau, while old, had been modernized. Most of the rooms
were paneled, decorated with paint. The ceilings were embellished
with gold and classical depictions. Glenkirk had been a fine castle
and Belle Fleurs was a comfortable home, but Chermont was
frankly the most beautiful house Autumn had ever seen.

"It is wonderful, monseigneur," she told the marquis, and he was
openly pleased that she was content.

"Would you like to see the Lady Chamber?" he asked her.

Autumn nodded, but then she said, "Mama too, please."

"Of course," he agreed, and led the two ladies up the beautiful,
broad marble staircase with its carved balustrades.

On the second floor of the chateau were the bedroom apartments.
Sebastian d'Oleron opened a door decorated with gold moldings
and ushered them inside. Autumn was stunned, but her mother
clapped her hands, delighted.

"Sebastian, *mon brave*, what a wonderful salon!" She turned to
her daughter. "Is it not marvelous, Autumn?"

The walls of the chamber were paneled, and each panel was
painted with a scene of romance. Venus with Adonis. Jupiter seduc-
ing Lyda. A maiden in flowing white robes being importuned by a
kneeling youth dressed in little but a small drape covering his most
private parts. There was Cupid shooting his arrows at a group of
fleeing maidens. Venus, again, this time with her husband, Vulcan,
god of the forge. Each panel told a small story of love. It was very
beautiful, and Autumn had never in her life seen anything like it.

"How charming!" she heard her mother exclaim. "Look at the
ceiling, *ma bébé*," Jasmine said. "How absolutely lovely!"

Autumn raised up her eyes and saw the ceiling was painted to resemble a morning sky, bright blue, its white clouds touched along
their edges with pink and gold. A flock of doves fluttered across the
firmament. Suddenly she began to cry, unable to help herself.

"What is the matter, *ma chérie?*" the marquis asked, surprised.

"I am not grand enough for such a beautiful place, Sebastian," Autumn sobbed. "I am a country lass and this is a palace."

He gathered her into his arms. "You are the perfect jewel in the crown of Chermont, *chérie,*" he told her. "Chermont is not a palace. It is your home. Chenonceaux was far grander."

"But it was supposed to be," Autumn said, her cheeks wet with the tears that refused to stop flowing. "It is a royal palace! Belle Fleurs is certainly not as grand, and neither is Archambault."

"Belle Fleurs is a country house," he explained, "and Archambault has never been modernized, *chérie*. My mother, who like the old queen came from Firenze, had a great flair for art. She oversaw the design of the public rooms at Chermont and had the marble staircase put in to replace an old twisting and winding one. These were her apartments, Autumn. Now they will be yours, and my mother would approve."

"Did Elise have these apartments?" Autumn asked, suddenly realizing she was jealous of Sebastian's first wife.

"Nay," he said quietly. "She never liked them, and said she believed my mother's ghost haunted the rooms. It was nonsense, of course, Autumn. If my mother would haunt any place in this chateau, it would be the nurseries where her grandchildren would live." He caressed her hair tenderly. "Shall we have many children, *ma petite?*"

"Perhaps," she sniffed, feeling just a little better.

"*Mon brave,*" Jasmine said quietly, "show us the rest of this wonderful apartment; and then I believe you should introduce Autumn to those who will serve her, eh?"

The bedchamber was all white and sky blue and gold. The wall panels were painted with floral motifs and the ceiling painting was an evening sky, all pink, lavender, and rosy gold tinting the clouds. Autumn's eyes widened at her first sight of the bed, but she said nothing. It was a very large bed, draped in a brocade with a cream background woven with gold, rose, and muted sage green threads. The bedposts were carved and gilded with vines and leaves.

"I hope you like your bedchamber," he said. "I had it redone for you. My mother's taste was a trifle more flamboyant. I did not think it would suit you, *chérie.*"

"It's beautiful," was all she could say, and it was. She had never seen furniture like this, all carved, painted, and gilded. It was like something out of a fairy tale. The fireplace opposite her bed was made of pink marble, the opening flanked by winged angels. There was a clock made of gilt upon the mantel. A large, carved armoire was set against another wall. Autumn walked across the room and saw the river beyond. She turned back to face him. "I cannot believe I am to live in this exquisite chamber, Sebastian. Just think! Our children shall be created here, and born here."

"My bedchamber is through here," he said, touching a molding on a wall panel.

"*Your bedchamber?*" Autum was very surprised. "Are we not to share this incredible bed, monseigneur?"

"We are," he agreed, "but certainly your parents had their own chambers at Glenkirk."

"Jemmie never used his," Jasmine replied softly.

"We cannot make children if you do not share my bed," Autumn said frankly. "What nonsense to think you need your own chamber."

"I will need it to store my clothing, Autumn," he responded with a twinkle in his silvery eyes. "If you are like other women, you will arrive at my house with enough gowns and other fripperies to clothe an entire convent school. Every bit of space in these chambers will be filled with your possessions quite soon. Am I not correct?"

"Monsieur Reynaud would not have it any other way," Autumn laughed. "I shall bring trunks and trunks and trunks to Chermont, Sebastian."

They returned to the main floor, and in the Great Hall the marquis introduced his bride-to-be to her servants. There was Lafite, the majordomo, and his wife, Madame Lafite, the housekeeper. There were eight housemaids; a man named Leon, whose only task was to polish all the silver and gold in the house; another named Pinabel, whose duty was to see that all the candelabras, lamps, and chandeliers were in proper working order. Candles could only be obtained from Pinabel, who kept a strict accounting of his stock. Caron was the chef, and he had half-a-dozen kitchen maids, a boy to scrub pots, and another who sharpened knives, in his charge. There were six footmen. The laundress was a large woman with thick arms and a ruddy complexion named Methina. She had two helpers.

"Will Madame la marquise require a maid to serve her? I have a well-trained niece, Orane, who could fill such a position."

"If Orane would be willing to serve in a secondary capacity to my serving woman, Lily, I would be glad to have her in my service, Madame Lafite," Autumn replied diplomatically.

"She will be more than happy to serve madame in that capacity," the housekeeper replied with a pleased smile. "She is quite good with her needle. Madame will certainly be satisfied." She curtsied.

"You have all made me feel so welcome," Autumn said. "I know I shall be very happy at Chermont. I already see I will be well taken care of by all of you."

Dismissed, the household staff departed. In their own hall afterwards Madame Lafite said, "We have all waited for monsieur le marquis to choose another wife. This marquise will do well for Chermont, I can already see it. She loves our master and is a well-brought-up young lady. Within the year we shall have a new generation for Chermont." Nodding, the servants raised their cups of wine to toast their master and his bride-to-be.

Autumn returned home with her mother, having met the outdoor staff before their departure. There had been Arno, the head groom, and his two undergrooms. The care and feeding of the horses was their duty. There were six stablemen who kept the stables clean and the animals fed. There was Henri, the coachman; Xarles, the gamekeeper and head huntsman, who had an assistant; and Yves, the kennelmaster, who also had an assistant. There was Florus, the head gardner, who had a staff of ten men under him. There was Marlon, the falconkeeper, and his assistant, who also kept the dovecote.

"I don't think I shall ever remember all the names," Autumn said to the marquis.

"You will in time," he replied with a smile. "These people are only those who serve the household. There are many others who work in the vineyards, and with the farm animals. We are self-sustaining here at Chermont. You will eventually have more to do than just be my beautiful wife and the mother of our children."

"I don't think I can do it," Autumn said as she and her mother rode home to Belle Fleurs late that afternoon. "I did not realize what was involved in marrying Sebastian."

"It would have been even more difficult with the Duc de Belfort, and little better with the Comte d'Auray," her mother said. "A woman must manage her household, knowing everything that goes on, learning to delegate authority to her servants but keeping an eye on all. You did very well with Madame Lafite, *ma bébé*. You might have said Lily was your serving woman, but instead you offered madame's niece a position, while not exactly what she hoped for, but a respectable position nonetheless. You will do fine, and I will be here to guide you, Autumn. I was not there for either of your sisters, but I will be here for you."

"What news from England, Mama?" Autumn asked.

"It is not good," Jasmine said. "I was not going to tell you until after the wedding, but you may as well know now. King Charles marched into England with a Scots army. Do I need to tell you how the English felt about that? Instead of getting the full support he needed from his countrymen, they recoiled in horror at the skirl of the pipes. All the English could see was an invading *Scots* army. That their own king was at its head meant little. The English have never really taken to the Stuarts. As much as they may dislike Master Cromwell they hate the Scots far more. It seems to be ingrained in their souls, this tribal hate for the Scots. What a pity the king did not consider the centuries of warfare before he came over the border in kilt and tam."

"What happened?" Autumn said.

"King Charles was defeated in early September at Worcester," her mother answered.

"Charlie?"

"I don't know. Henry sent me the news. He says there was no word that Charlie had been killed, but he has no idea where he may be, or even if he is alive," Jasmine responded, her voice suddenly hard.

"He's alive, Mama," Autumn said firmly.

"What makes you so certain? Henry writes that Worcester was terrible, and many were slain," Jasmine replied.

"Charlie is the not-so-royal Stuart, Mama. He isn't a Leslie. He is the Mughal's grandson. He has luck unlike poor Papa."

"You may very well be right," her mother said, and then she laughed. "Aye, you probably are right, Autumn. My son Charlie could charm even death out of taking him too soon. We will wait, and eventually we will hear what has happened."

Autumn's eye caught a movement at the lake's edge, and she was brought back to the reality of the morning. *Her wedding morning.* An antlered stag had come from the forest to drink. She watched him, fascinated. Then, as the beast lifted his handsome head, it seemed to look directly at her. Autumn laughed. The stag turned and leapt back into the forest.

"Yer awake." Lily's sleepy voice sounded from the trundle bed.

"Aye," Autumn answered her servant, "and you had best get up, lest Mama finds us lingering. My wedding is planned for ten, so we may have time for a feast and time to travel back to Chermont today. I will want a bath first, and I will need time for my hair to dry."

Lily clambered from her own bed and quickly pulled her clothes on before emptying the night jar out the window into the lake. Then she hurried off to arrange for hot water to be brought upstairs. Adali, however, had already anticipated Autumn's wishes, and the water was ready to be hauled from the kitchen to the bedchamber. Lily ran back up the stairs to pull the oak tub from its niche. Autumn climbed back into her bed and drew the curtains for modesty's sake as the young footmen hurried in with their buckets. When the last of them had gone, leaving several extra buckets of hot water, Autumn came from her bed again, drawing off her night garment as Lily poured a mixture of oil of apricot and oil of jasmine into the steaming water.

Autumn washed herself as she always did, but for her long and supple back, which Lily scrubbed. Then Lily proceeded to wash her mistress's hair, rinsing it first with vinegar and then clean water from the buckets. Vinegar removed excess soap and gave shine to dark hair. Autumn stood and wrapped her head in a towel as Lily rinsed her body with the remaining clean water. Then the bride stepped from the tub to be enfolded in a warm towel. The two girls squealed as the door to the bedchamber opened, but it was only the duchess.

"Good!" she approved. "You are awake and preparing. Father Bernard says you are excused from early mass because there will be a mass at your wedding. I will have Adali bring you something to eat."

"I don't think I can," Autumn admitted.

Her mother smiled. "You are nervous, but believe me, *ma fille*, it will be better if you eat. An egg poached in cream and marsala with some fresh bread?" she coaxed her daughter. "A cup of newly pressed cider with a stick of cinnamon?"

"You'll need your strength, m'lady," Lily chimed in, in an effort to help the duchess.

Autumn sighed. "Well," she considered, "I suppose I could eat a little something now."

"A wise decision," her mother agreed. "After the mass you may be too busy greeting your guests to eat at our little feast."

"When will Monsieur Reynaud want me to dress?" Autumn asked.

"I will come with him an hour before the ceremony," her mother said, and then hurried from the chamber.

Autumn sat in the windowseat of her bedchamber while Lily toweled and toweled her long hair until it was just damp. Then the maidservant brushed out the dark tresses, and Autumn sat back as Lily brushed the hair over the sill into the morning air to dry.

When Adali brought the two young women the meal, Autumn found she was more than able to eat. The chef had sent her favorite soft cheese in a small crock, and fresh pears, which she always enjoyed.

"You'll not fit into your gown," Lily chided as Autumn reached for another pear. "Put it back. My aunt will have my hide, and poor Monsieur Reynaud will have a fit right before us. 'Twould not be a particularly good omen, m'lady."

"I'm suddenly hungry," Autumn insisted.

" 'Tisn't food you crave," Lily said sharply.

"Shame!" Autumn scolded her maid, but Lily just laughed.

" 'Twas not the flavor of the pear you were just now contemplating as you licked your lips so laciviously, m'lady," Lily replied. "Come on now, and clean your face, hands, and teeth. Monsieur Reynaud will be here before we know it. You have to be decently clothed when he arrives clucking and crowing," the servant chuckled.

Now it was Autumn who laughed. The tailor's name in English might mean *fox*, but both young women thought of him more as a little bantam cock, strutting and preening.

Autumn had decided not to wear a chemise, but rather a waist-coat, which was like a man's half-shirt and fashioned of silk. It would not show above the neckline of her bodice, which was cut straight across. She also wore no *caleçons*, the drawers worn by French-women. She stepped into the twelve silk petticoats one by one, lifting them to sit down, so Lily might dress her hair into an elegant chignon at the nape of her neck. In Scotland her hair would have been left flowing to indicate her virginity, but the French did not hold with such customs any longer. Elegance above all was their rule. Carefully, Lily looped narrow strands of small pearls on either side of the chignon. Then she fastened fat pearl eardrops into Autumn's ears.

There was a cursory knock at the door. The duchess entered, with Monsieur Reynaud and his assistants in her wake. Jasmine nodded her approval at Lily's efforts. Then they all set about to get the bride into her wedding gown, which was a very rich cream in color, the underskirt and the bodice being silk, the overskirt looped to the back of velvet. The bodice was boned, and the sleeves tight to below the elbow. The waist of the gown was set *au naturel*, and where the overskirt encircled in back a large velvet bow decorated with pearls had been affixed. It was beautiful and fashionable in its simplicity.

Autumn stood, strangely quiet as they fussed and bustled about her. She suddenly felt as if she was in a dream. That wasn't really how she had imagined her wedding day. She had always thought she would be surrounded by her sister India and her brothers. Her father would escort her to the altar, where some faceless gentleman would be waiting for her. And afterwards in the Great Hall of Glenkirk Castle her family's piper would play for them, and her brothers would dance amid crossed swords for the entertainment of the bride, the groom, and their many guests. She would have been wed in Glenkirk Church amid the tombs of her ancestors, by a cleric who had known her since her infancy. It had been only a small dream, but so easily destroyed by Master Cromwell and his wicked Roundheads, who had dragged her country into civil war, caused her sire's death, and forced her mother to flee.

She should be grateful, Autumn suddenly considered. She had found her true love in Sebastian d'Oleron here in France. Life here was as it should be. While there might be bad men trying to control King Louis's thoughts and actions, they had been foiled, would be deterred. The boy king, she knew from their brief meetings, was determined and strong. No abusive parliament would lop off his head.

Her mother's small chateau had been here to shelter them. Her French family had welcomed them warmly and brought them into the society of the chèr region. They had introduced her to Sebastian. Today she would be married in the little chapel of Belle Fleurs, by a young priest who was thrilled to be performing the ceremony. She would be surrounded by her uncle and the two aunts, and by Adali, Rohana, Toramalli, Red Hugh, Fergus, and Lily. They were every bit as much her family as her siblings, and she was fortunate to have them. Suddenly she felt a hand on her shoulder and looked up to see her mother's face.

"I miss them too," Jasmine said softly.

"Oh, Mama, how did you know?" she asked aloud.

"Of all my children, Autumn, you have the most expressive face. You wear your heart on your sleeve, *ma petite*," Jasmine answered. "It isn't forever, you know. One day King Charles will sit upon his throne again, and you will see the others, except for Fortune, whom you do not remember. She always said once she crossed the sea to Mary's Land she would not come back again. She is the one I regret most."

"As intolerance has cost you Papa and your home," Autumn said wisely, "it cost you a daughter too, but I am here for you, Mama. I shall never leave you. Where I go, you must be. That is my promise to you on my wedding day."

Jasmine hugged her youngest child; then, taking her face in both her hands, kissed her cheeks. "And my promise to you is that only death shall separate us, *ma bébé.*"

"*Madame!* The mademoiselle's skirts! You will wrinkle them," Monsieur Reynaud fumed.

The women laughed as the duchess stepped back, and even the tailor smiled. Then Adali's head popped around the door.

"The guests and bridegroom await," he said.

"Will you and your assistants join us in the chapel, Monsieur Reynaud?" the duchess asked the tailor, who nodded, delighted. How envious his compatriots in Tours would be when he told them that not only had he fashioned Madame la marquise d'Auriville's wedding gown, he had been invited to remain to see her take her vows.

They all descended to the main floor of the chateau, where the little chapel was located. Autumn was left outside its door while her mother and the others entered. She could see Sebastian, so very elegant in his dark velvet suit and white lace, awaiting her at the altar rail. He was so handsome! Oh, if only Papa were here today to give her into his keeping, everything would be perfect. Then she jumped, startled, at the familiar voice by her ear.

"Will you take my arm, little sister?" Charles Frederick Stuart, the Duke of Lundy, said softly.

Autumn turned and looked up at her favorite brother. "*Charlie!*" she cried, and then promptly burst into tears.

Putting his arms about her, he said, "I arrived just at dawn this morning. Adali told me it was your wedding day. I decided to surprise you and Mama. For God's sake, Autumn, stop weeping or I shall regret I came."

"Oh, Charlie!" Autumn sobbed against his velvet doublet. "I have never been happier in my whole life to see anyone! We heard about Worcester. Mama was so worried. I told her you would have escaped. I knew you couldn't be dead. *I knew it!*"

He took his linen handkerchief from his doublet and gently wiped the tears from her face. "You knew more than I did, minx. I had one hell of a time escaping England, and there is no word on the king yet—although if he had been captured, Cromwell would be boasting on it. Still, no one knows where he is."

"Charlie!" Their mother's voice suddenly cut into their tender reunion. "Bring your sister forward immediately before the marquis cries off! There is a feast awaiting, not to mention a trip to Chermont."

Charlie grinned, then said to Autumn, "It's for love, isn't it? Remember what I told you?"

"It's for love," she reassured him. "You'll like him."

"Then I suppose I must give you away, minx," the Duke of Lundy told his little sister, and then he led her up the aisle of the chapel.

Jasmine couldn't help but think back to her own wedding day to James Leslie. She had married him in the chapel of her grandmother's house, Queen's Malvern. It had been the second time she had wed there, the first time being to Rowan Lindley. How long ago it had been. Now, her youngest child, Jemmie's only daughter, was being wed here at Belle Fleurs, where Autumn's great-grandparents had begun their long and happy married life. It was as if a circle was closing. She could almost sense Madame Skye here, approving.

The scented beeswax tapers in their gold candlesticks glittered. Sunlight poured through the stained-glass windows, throwing red and blue shadows on the gray stone floor. Young Père Bernard, in his white and gold garments, said the mass most beautifully. The bride's voice could be clearly heard as she spoke her vows. The groom stood tall, his own voice strong and sure. There was soft weeping: the two *tantes,* pleased with the outcome of their matchmaking; Jasmine, clutching her son's arm, suddenly missing James Leslie more than she ever had; Adali, Rohana, and Toramalli, happy for Autumn and astounded to find themselves here after all the years and their many wild adventures.

Afterwards, when they entered the chateau's hall, Autumn introduced her brother to her husband.

"I will admit I am relieved you are her kin," the marquis said. "When I saw my beloved Autumn clutching a strange man and weeping all over him, I thought I had lost her to another, an old love." He shook his brother-in-law's hand heartily.

"It was only by chance I arrived this day," the duke said.

"How could you not tell me he was here?" Jasmine demanded of Adali. "I almost fainted dead away when I heard his voice. I thought he was dead, and that I was imagining it!"

"Now, Mama, don't go scolding Adali. I am the one who decided to surprise you both." He chuckled. "I thought it a good jest."

"*A jest?*" his mother said angrily. "We had only gotten word of what happened at Worcester. All we knew was casualties, and the fact that the king was among the missing. Under the circumstances, I would have thought it far better to have announced yourself immediately instead of playing at boys' games, Charlie."

"I wasn't aware the news had penetrated so deep into the French countryside, Mama. I do apologize for frightening you."

"How long can you stay?" she demanded.

"My friend, Lord Carstairs, has remained behind in Paris, where we first went. Queen Henrietta Maria is beside herself with worry over her son. Carstairs will let me know when the king arrives. Then I must leave you, Mama. Cousin Charles needs all the help he can muster, especially now. I suspect he will shortly be on the Continent. He can't remain in England, and he hated Scotland."

"Where are my Stuart grandchildren?"

"With Patrick and his wife at Glenkirk," Charlie said. Then, seeing the look on his mother's face, he cried, "Oh, God! You didn't know? Mama, I am so sorry! I would have thought Patrick had written to you by now. His wife is the daughter of the Brodie of Killiecairn. Her dowry was Brae Castle and its lands. Her mother was a Gordon. Patrick wanted those lands for Glenkirk. He is very much drawing in and wants nothing to do with society."

"Is she *enceinte?*" Jasmine asked.

"Nay, although she wants bairns, she told me. She's a wee bit rough-spoken, but I like her, Mama."

"Let us see how long it will take your brother to inform me of this marriage," his mother said, and then, "God's boots! I am now the Dowager Duchess of Glenkirk! I do not know if I can forgive Patrick for that, although I did tell him to take a wife."

"So now we are all married, Mama," Autumn said. "You have certainly done your duty by us."

"Haven't I just," her mother replied dryly, and they all laughed.

The wedding feast was served to the assembled guests. Jasmine had invited all the servants both inside the chateau and out to join them. They sat at tables below the highboard, while those assigned to bring in the feast hurried back and forth before seating themselves. Père Bernard said the blessing. Then the Duke of Lundy raised a silver goblet and offered a toast to his youngest sibling.

"To Autumn Rose, the last of us, born to our mother when she believed she was past that time in her life. She has, I know, been a blessing and a joy to her parents. May she be one to her husband as well! And to Sebastian, her lord, who has not the faintest idea of what he has done in marrying this beautiful minx. Long life, prosperity, many healthy babies, and may every year you are together be a vintage year."

"*Salut! Salut!*" cried all the guests, raising their own silver goblets and pewter cups.

"Oh, Charlie," Autumn told her brother, "you have made this such a happy day for me. Thank God you are safe!"

Charles Frederick Stuart took his sister's hand in his and kissed it tenderly. "Thank God," he said in return, "that I was able to share this day with you and Sebastian. The others will be quite envious when they learn of it."

"You will stay with Mama? You will not go away too soon?" Her look was anxious.

Seeing that look, Sebastian felt a pang of jealousy. He had only an older sister he barely knew. He did not understand the closeness between siblings who loved one another.

"Family is everything," his mother-in-law said softly to him. "Now you are a part of us, *mon brave*. You will learn to love as we do each other, and so will your children." She patted his big hand. "Even though she was the last of my babies, Sebastian, and they all much older, we have always been together one way or another. Autumn is every bit as much a part of her brothers and sisters as they, who were so close in age, are. Charlie, however, was always her favorite. Stuarts have that rare sort of charm."

As if to prove her point, Charlie called to his mother's two Scots retainers. "Red Hugh, Fergus! Fetch the pipes, for I know you have them. What is a Scotsman wiout his pipes?" he said in his mother tongue. Then, excusing himself, he disappeared from the hall. When he returned he was clad in his kilt and carried two swords. Setting them on the floor of the hall, he nodded to Red Hugh and Fergus. They began to play, and Charles Frederick Stuart began to dance, moving gracefully among the crossed swords as he paid this familiar tribute to his sister.

The French in the hall watched with admiration as this tall, elegant man in his red plaid, with his dark curls and amber eyes, danced before them. They had never seen such a dance, but they recognized the passion in it. Autumn put her head against her husband's shoulder and wept softly. It was all so beautiful, she thought, so wonderful that Charlie was with them, and yet she wished the others could be too. She sighed deeply.

Sebastian dropped a kiss upon her ebony head. "It is quite wonderful," he said softly. "The perfect end to our wedding feast, but *chérie*, we must depart soon for Chermont. I would be home before dark. The river road is not easy to travel in the glooming."

For several days Autumn's possessions had been transferred from her mother's house to her husband's. A small baggage cart with the last of the bride's belongings would follow their coach, along with Lily and the young servant Marc, who would now become the marquise's personal courtier. Marc was intelligent, and Adali had thought it wise that Autumn have a male servant whose loyalty was to her alone. He had explained all of this to Marc before offering him the position.

"Serve the young marquise well, and first. You will not regret your loyalty to her. Madame's two women and I have served her from birth, even enduring a six months' voyage from our homeland to remain with her. Red Hugh and Fergus have come with her from

Scotland. This family places a great price upon loyalty, Marc. We have all become quite comfortable in her service. If, God forbid, she died tomorrow, none of us would lack for anything. Remember this should anyone, even monsieur le marquis, attempt to dissuade you from your duty toward the young marquise. Can you give her that kind of loyalty?"

"I can, Monsieur Adali," the young man said. "This offer you have made me is a blessing, for surely you have noticed I have a *tendre* for Mademoiselle Lily. I hope to wed her one day if madame le marquise will permit it and give us her blessing."

"Loyalty has its rewards," Adali replied meaningfully. "I am certain that once you are settled at Chermont and have proven your fidelity to your mistress, she would gladly give her consent. You will need it, however. Lily will not marry you without it. She is distant kin to her mistress through her uncles, my mistress's two Scotsmen, and has been raised by Fergus and his wife, Toramalli."

"I should never betray my mistress once I had pledged my allegiance," Marc said earnestly.

"Then it is settled," Adali said, satisfied, but afterwards he had spoken to Lily, explaining all to the girl's delight, and advising her to make certain no other lass caught Marc's eye. "I am certain you will know how to keep his devotion, my child," he told her. "Remember that there will be another maidservant to serve your mistress at Chermont. She is called Orane and is young, pretty, and pert. I do not know yet if she is ambitious, but be warned that if she is, she will want everything that is yours, including your swain. Her aunt is the housekeeper."

"I know how to protect myself and what is mine," Lily replied fiercely. "I am the stranger, and so they will all be watching to see if they can fault me. However, I shall be sweet and full of questions. I will be respectful but not servile. They will like me but quickly realize that they cannot replace me with one of their own. As for Marc, he will not stray, Adali. He is a good man and loves me truly."

Now, as he watched Autumn prepare to depart her mother's house, Adali prayed silently that he had been correct in his judgment, that Lily and Marc would continue to love and serve his mistress's child. He brought the pale blue velvet cloak trimmed in ermine and put it about Autumn's shoulders. Then, standing before her, he carefully fastened the scrolled silver frogs and drew up the hood, covering her hair. No words were necessary between the two. Autumn hugged him silently, and he acknowledged her with a faint smile and a nod of his white head.

"Come and see us in a few days' time," the marquis said to his new family.

Autumn hugged her mother and brother in their turn. Then she was helped into their coach by her husband. "I should far rather have ridden," she murmured to him as she settled herself. "I really don't like coaches. They are so confining."

He climbed in next to her, and the carriage door was firmly shut. "If," he said as their vehicle rumbled off, "we rode to Chermont, I should not have this private time with you, *chérie*, to make love."

"You want to make love in a coach?" Her face mirrored her surprise. "You cannot make love in a coach!"

"If one can make love lying before a fireplace, then why not in a coach?" he said, and his hand slipped beneath her cape to fondle her bosom. "Later," he told her, "when you have more experience, *ma petite*, I shall show you that a man and a woman can indeed make love almost anywhere. For now, however, I want to kiss and cuddle you."

"When we get home," she said, nestling against him, "can we go right to bed, monseigneur?"

"There will," he promised her, "be a supper placed in your salon, Madame la marquise. There will be wine. The fireplaces in your apartments will burn all night long, as will my ardor for you." He kissed her mouth slowly, tenderly. "We will make love, and I will begin to teach you passion," he continued. "We will eat when it pleases us, and rest from our desires when it pleases us. Have you any idea how much I want you, Autumn? How very much I need you?"

She turned herself into his arms, and her hand reached out to caress the very obvious bulge in his breeches. *"Oui,* Sebastian, I do," she murmured sweetly against his mouth. Her fingers slid up and down his length teasingly.

"You are the boldest virgin," he said with a sigh.

"Does it displease you?" she asked him.

"Non, ma chérie, it does not," he replied honestly.

"Then, *mon coeur,* we shall amuse ourselves all the way home, won't we?" Autumn told him, snuggling against him.

"I will undress you myself," he groaned through gritted teeth.

"You have expertise in maiding a lady?" she asked wickedly. "You cannot tear my wedding gown in your lust, Sebastian."

"I shall only tear your undergarments," he promised. "You are not wearing the *caleçons,* are you?"

"No," she murmured, kissing his earlobe. "Drawers are such a bother, monseigneur, are they not?"

He drew up her skirts and slid a hand beneath them to ascertain her veracity, pleased to find truth in her words. His fingers brushed her thighs above her gartered stockings. The skin was every bit as soft as the silk covering her legs. "Madame, you are, I fear, too tempting."

"You are too," she concurred. "Perhaps we would be better off if we ceased this delicious devilment and looked at the river."

"As Madame la marquise wishes," he agreed and, removing his hand from beneath her gown, he drew her skirts down.

"Madame la marquise doesn't wish it, but she is already so hungry for your passion she will turn to cinders before we get home unless you show a wee bit of restraint," Autumn said frankly.

"There will come a day," he promised, "when I shall set you upon my lance within the confines of this coach, and we shall ride together to its rhythm. For now, however, we shall view the river."

"And when we get home?" she pressed him.

"Ah, Madame la marquise, when we get home is a different matter entirely," he replied.

The countryside about them grew quieter as sunset approached and they came nearer to Chermont.

Chapter

 **11**

Everything was as he had promised. Lafite had greeted them when they arrived.

"Welcome home, Madame la marquise," he had said. "Lily and Marc will be settled immediately." He bowed.

"Merci," Autumn said softly. Her husband's hand was beneath her elbow as he gently but firmly led her up the broad staircase to their apartments.

Entering, the marquis said to the young girl who came forward to take Autumn's cloak, "You are dismissed, Orane. Go and greet Lily. She has your instructions for the morning."

Her large, dark eyes startled, Orane curtsied, and exited the salon, still clutching her new mistress's outer garment.

"Step back and let me look at you," the marquis said to his bride. "Ah, *chérie,* you are so beautiful. I do not believe I told you that today. Monsieur Reynaud's gown is exquisite."

Autumn felt a sudden heat warm her cheeks. "Remember," she cautioned him, "you promised not to tear it."

"I won't," he replied. "Are you hungry? Supper is laid upon the sideboard, even as I said it would be."

"No. I am not hungry . . . for food," she told him boldly.

"Turn around," he instructed her, and when she did he began to unlace her bodice. "Are the sleeves separate or attached?" he asked.

"Attached," she said and, feeling the bodice undone, pulled it off and laid it aside upon a chair. Her skirts, which had been fastened to the bodice with several tabs, now sagged over her petticoats.

The marquis carefuly studied this situation and then began to unbutton each petticoat in its turn until they were all loosened. Then, suddenly, he ripped the dainty silk waistcoat in half, drawing it off her and tossing the ruins aside. "I said I would not tear your gown, *ma petite,*" he explained, putting his hand about her narrow waist and lifting her from the muddle of her petticoats and skirts. Stepping back, he caught his breath, for she was certainly the loveliest girl he had ever looked upon.

She was naked but for her cream-colored silk stockings, which were embroidered with delicate golden butterflies and held up by pearl-encrusted gold silk garters. Her feet were encased in narrow, cream, silk-covered shoes with slender diamond-studded stilletto heels. She had delightful small, round breasts that he knew in time would mature into magnificence. Her hips were most pleasingly rounded, her limbs slim and shapely. Her belly was flat, and beneath it a forest of tightly bunched black curls caught his attention.

Shouldn't I be embarrassed? Autumn thought, as he viewed her nudity with open admiration? But she wasn't. Instead she pirouetted audaciously before him, striking a bold pose, one leg upon a settee, as she turned to look at him over her shoulder. "You are pleased, then?"

He could not keep his hand from reaching out to fondle an impudent buttock. "*Oui,* Madame la marquise, I am pleased," he responded.

"Then," she said, "it is my turn to disrobe you, monseigneur." Her fingers slipped the buttons from their buttonholes with surprising dexterity, and his doublet was quickly gone. Her hands now moved to his black velvet breeches, and to help her, he kicked off his shoes. She pulled at his breeches, surprised to see he was wearing short, white silk drawers beneath them. He stepped from the breeches and drawers.

"You are very good at this," he said.

"I've never done it before," she assured him, and then began to unlace his shirt. When the laces were undone she slipped her hands inside the garment and ran her palms over his smooth, warm flesh. Then she pushed the shirt off his shoulders, and it slid down his torso to the floor. Autumn now stepped back to observe him as he had her.

He was so beautiful, she thought, smiling to herself that she had used such a word to describe a man. But there simply was no other phrase that expressed it so well. Everything about him was long— his torso, his arms and legs, which she noted were very hairy, although his broad chest was smooth. His waist was narrow, his hips slim. Unable to restrain herself, Autumn reached out and caressed his manhood. It was, like the rest of him, long. She looked past his *lance d'amour* to his feet. They, too, were long and slender. Then it was true, she thought. Her brothers had not been teasing her: A man's feet indicated the size of his more manly part. Their eyes met, and she could see his were filled with laughter.

"What is so amusing, monseigneur?" she asked.

"I know what you are thinking, *chérie*, and I promise you that feet have nothing to do with it. 'Tis naught but an old wives's tale," he told her. Then he turned, saying as he did, "You have not examined all of me yet. I was once told my flanks are one of my best features."

"Whoever said it was not lying," Autumn agreed, giving his buttock a small smack of appreciation.

He laughed, and then said, "Sit down, Madame la marquise. I would remove your shoes and stockings now. The sight of you makes me eager to lay with you, to caress those adorable little breasts, to have your maidenhead so I may teach you what passion really is."

Autumn felt a quiver deep within her innards. Her legs were suddenly weak, and she sat almost gratefully upon a small blue velvet chair, her legs set primly together.

Her bridegroom knelt before her, running his big hands up her legs to her knees. Then, carefully, he removed each one of her shoes, setting them aside beneath the chair. Unfastening the first garter, he dropped it and slowly unrolled the silk stockings down her leg, kissing the shapely limb as it was revealed to him. Sliding the stocking off, he cradled her little foot between his two hands, fondling it gently, finally kissing it. He then removed the other stocking in the same seductive and sensuous manner. After he had kissed her second foot he leaned forward, kissed each of her knees, and gently spread them wide open to his sight.

She was already half-swooning with his attentions. Now she was unable to control the faint trembling that began to overcome her.

"Don't be afraid, Autumn," he told her. "I want to see your treasures." His two thumbs tenderly parted her nether lips to his view. His gaze was intense; his look almost pained. Finally, in a forced voice, he said, *"Mon Dieu, ma chérie,* but you are so perfect *there."* Leaning forward, he placed a kiss upon her flesh.

It was too much. Autumn crumpled forward, but Sebastian quickly caught her and held her close as he whispered soft and soothing words.

"There, my little virgin, 'tis all right. Did you not know that every part of a woman's body is meant to be adored?" He kissed the top of her dark head. "I cannot resist you, *chérie.* Did your mama not explain to you what is involved between a husband and a wife?"

"M . . . Mama explained," she managed to reply, and then, as the breath seemed to fill her body again, she continued, "and Charlie's wife told me more, but there is a difference between the words and the reality, monseigneur. Do it again! It was so very exciting!"

His laughter was low. "I can make it even better," he tempted her. "Do you want me to, *ma petite épouse?"*

"Oui!"

"Then do as I tell you, Autumn," he said as he sat her back upon the chair. "Put your pretty legs over my shoulders. Ah, that is right, *chérie.* Now I will pleasure you."

Fascinated, she watched his dark head push between her thighs. His thumbs opened her again. Then she felt it! His tongue was licking her sensitive flesh. She could feel the broad sweep of that wicked little organ teasing at her, caressing her intimately until she felt she was melting from the heat he engendered within her. Then his tongue found her little *bouton d'amour* and began to flick back and forth over it with relentless determination. Autumn gasped, surprised, as she felt a sudden tension growing within her. Unable to help herself, she moaned, but the sound, even in her own ears, was one of distinct pleasure. It was even better than the first time he had done this to her with his fingers. The pressure built and built, until it finally exploded with a force that rendered her giddy with the ensuing delight that filled her.

He felt her release and groaned with his own desire. His nostrils were filled with the scent of her, all sweet and pungent. His mouth was filled with the piquant taste of her. He slid his hands beneath her buttocks and pulled her down to the floor beneath him. His big body covered her. "I can't wait," he half-sobbed in her ear.

"Don't!" was all she said, and opened herself wide to him, feeling his hard length as it slid easily within her well prepared body. She gasped at the sharp sting of her lost maidenhead. Tears slipped down her cheeks, which he kissed away while whispering words of apology and love into her ear. She wrapped her limbs about his torso, enabling him a deeper passage, then gave herself up to the dizzying splendor that began to overcome her.

He plundered her sweetness, reveling within her tight, hot sheath. It welcomed him, opening to his advance, closing about him tightly to embrace him. Her soft little breasts gave way beneath his chest. Her silken thighs gripped him firmly as she would have gripped her mount. Now he began to piston her with a careful, measured cadence. He plunged and withdrew over and over again until he felt the storm rising within her. When he thought he could bear the tension no longer she cried out, and he released his love juices, flooding her body.

"Too sweet! Too sweet!" Autumn cried, her head thrashing back and forth. "Oh, I cannot bear it! *Mon Dieu! Mon Dieu!*" She shuddered violently, and then her body went limp.

He rolled onto his back and lay there a few moments until his ragged breathing began to slow and grow more even. Staggering to his feet, finally he picked his wife up in his arms, stumbled into her bedchamber, and lay her gently upon the bed. As he lifted her, he saw the blood upon the carpet that had been beneath them, the smears of crimson upon her milky thighs. Looking down, he could see his manhood bore traces of her innocence. Climbing into the bed, he cradled her in his arms, and Autumn sighed with contentment against him.

"*Je t'aime,*" she murmured, and then fell asleep.

"*Je t'aime aussi, ma chérie,*" he told her softly, and closed his eyes, but he did not sleep at first. Instead his mind went back to his wedding night with Elise. How coy and shy she had seemed. It had taken him almost a week to breach her, for she wept and demurred and sobbed that she was afraid. He had been just seventeen, and his father had always told him a gentleman never forced a lady. So he had played her waiting game, and when he had finally had her it had been a disappointment. And, he seemed to recall, there was no show of blood. He had not known then that there must be blood to prove virginity.

After that Elise could hardly seem to get enough of passion, yet she never seemed to be satisfied. He noticed suddenly that other men were beginning to look at him pityingly, especially men of his own station. Then one day his late mother's best friend, Madame St. Omer, had told him the rumors. He had investigated and learned them to be true. He had been angry at the older woman, but then Elise found herself *enceinte* and was unable to identify the sire of her babe. It had been providence that she had died trying to rid herself of the child. Now, he found, he owed Madame St. Omer a great debt for putting Autumn in his path. Sebastian d'Oleron believed in fate, and it was obvious to him now that Autumn Leslie was his destiny. Turning his head, he watched her in sleep and knew he would never love anyone more than he loved her.

When he awoke several hours later it was to find Autumn seated upon his chest, her back to him, bathing his male member. "Madame," he murmured sleepily, "what are you doing?"

"Washing it," she replied, not bothering to turn around. "I have been taught to bathe one's private parts after passion. It makes the next bout of Eros ever so much nicer, Mama says."

"And you are ready for another session of lovemaking with me then, Madame la marquise?" he asked her.

She swung about to face him, tossing the cloth in her hand into the basin by the bedside. "Aren't you, monseigneur?" she replied, leaning forward to brush her nipples over his chest before straightening up again, her odd-colored eyes twinkling at him.

Reaching up, he fondled both of her round little breasts. His silvery eyes narrowed speculatively. "So, madame," he said, "once is not enough for you?"

"My brothers are prodigious lovers, or so their wives claim. Mama says at least twice a night is good for one's health, Sebastian," she answered him seriously.

At first he wasn't certain if she was teasing him or not, but he erred on the side of caution. "Twice is pleasant, and I will admit that after several hours of rest I am contemplating the idea of coupling with you again, madame."

"Merely *contemplating*, monseigneur?" she murmured, wiggling her bottom provocatively against him as his thumbs teased her nipples.

With a swift motion he rolled her beneath him, his long, hard body pressing against her. "What I want, madame," he growled into her ear, "is to pinion you into the mattress and drive so deep inside you that I lose myself." His mouth found hers and he kissed her deeply, his lips conveying to her the intensity of his desire as they demanded an equal commitment from her.

Her head spun, but she kissed him back fiercely, and then with the pointed tip of her tongue she ran over his lips tauntingly. "I have wanted you inside me ever since we met," she admitted boldly. "You excited me that day in the forest. I was yet a child, and still I had the most erotic thoughts of you that I hid from everyone, even Mama, but I think she suspected. My brothers all warned me to marry only for love, but is this delicious lust really love, Sebastian?"

"It is part of it, *chérie*," he told her. "Do you know how jealous I was of your two other suitors?" He began to kiss her slowly again, his lips wandering over the soft flesh of her neck and shoulders. "The thought of either of those two popinjays touching you drove me mad!" His teeth sank into her shoulder, but then he licked where he had bitten her. "If you ever look at another man, I will kill you, Autumn!"

"I am not *her*," his bride said, refusing to even acknowledge Elise by name. "I want only you, *mon coeur*. Only you!"

He jumped suddenly from their bed. "We need wine to toast our love, *ma chérie!*" he cried, and hurried into the salon. Returning quickly, he brought with him a decanter and two silver goblets engraved with grape leaves and bunches of grapes. Filling the goblets, he handed her one and said, "To us! To Sebastian and Autumn d'Oleron and their love, which will last forever!" Then, entwining his arm in hers, they drank to seal the toast.

"Ummmm, this is delicious!" Autumn exclaimed as the pale golden wine slipped down her throat.

"It is even better tasting this way," he said, pouring a libation onto her torso and licking it up slowly. *"Merveilleux!"*

"I want to do it!" she told him and, laughing, he lay upon his back as she poured a stream of wine onto his torso and began to lick at it. "Oh, it is good this way!" she enthused, chasing after a thin stream of the wine as it rolled down his frame. She licked his body clean of the vintage, smacking her lips as she did so, but then a movement caught her eye and she drew back with a cry.

His manhood stood straight and tall before her. She had had no time to consider its size before, but now she was faced with the reality of it. Fascinated, she reached out and stroked the blue-veined pillar. It was as hard as marble. Her fingers drew his foreskin down as far as it would go, and she marveled at the shiny ruby head of the beast that had one shadowed eye. She could say nothing.

The marquis pushed her back upon the pillows. He kissed her lips and nuzzled her breasts, lapping at a rivulet of wine between them that had earlier escaped him, now licking her nipples until they stood frozen and hard beneath his tongue. He nudged her knees apart and slowly entered her body a second time. "You, Madame la marquise, are mine and mine alone," his deep voice rumbled in her ear. *"Mine!"* He thrust hard. *"Mine!"*

"And you are mine, *mon coeur*," Autumn told her husband, and she gave herself up to the pleasure that their bodies were engendering.

*   *   *

In the months that followed it was obvious that the Marquis and Marquise d'Auriville were a love match. Charlie Stuart remarked upon it to his mother, pleased that his sister had found happiness. The English king had finally escaped Cromwell's men to arrive in France. His adventures—hiding in an oak tree beneath the noses of the Roundheads and riding pillion disguised as a servant—were widely recounted. The main thing was that he was safe, to the relief of the many English nobles who had joined his mother in exile.

All of this information came via a letter to the not-so-royal Stuart from his friend, Lord Carstairs. Charlie knew he would have to join his royal cousin sooner or later, and open his purse to help support the king. The royal Stuart was quite impoverished upon his arrival in Rouen, where he had come ashore. At first he had been taken for a tramp. Even his old tutor, Dr. Earle, failed to recognize him, so gaunt and thin had the king grown in the six weeks since Worcester, while he had been on the run from Cromwell and his men. The young king was depressed, but despite all that had happened his spirit had not been broken. He tried hard, Lord Carstairs wrote, to be cheerful, but the situation was so grim that it kept returning to haunt him.

He could not speak of those who had aided him in those very long six weeks. Most were still in England. King Charles thought it a poor form of gratitude to endanger them. His friend, the Earl of Derby, who had been with him when he had escaped through the north gate at Worcester and had last been seen at Whiteladies, a safe house, had been caught and executed. Now the king found himself forced to accept the charity of his mother, who was accepting the charity of the archbishop, Gondi. It was a difficult situation. The French-born English queen was so poor that she made an account of what it cost to feed her son each time he ate at her table. By the time the French government had decided on what they could afford to give their own king's cousin, he owed it all to his mother, and found himself even poorer than she.

"At least our assets are available to us," the Duke of Lundy reminded his mother.

"Only because we are wise enough to do business with the Kiras and do not hold their faith againt them," Jasmine said sharply. "Your royal relations, Charlie, never considered the possibility that they might be driven from England. Why did not King Charles the First make provision for his wife and children when she fled? The queen has been gone from England several years now. Louis was not in control when she came, and he has still not gained a firm grip on France. He will, of course, but what will happen between now and then is a moot point. What is our king to do now? How will he regain his throne and his kingdom? He has left it all to Master Cromwell and his Roundheads."

"The people love him, Mama," the duke replied.

"Perhaps," she said, "but he did not understand them, else he would not have come down from the north at the head of a kilt-wearing, pipe-skirling army. It is to be hoped he knows better now," Jasmine concluded dryly.

Her son laughed and nodded. "He does. When royal Charles returns, it will be to England. He'll not go to Scotland again if he can avoid it. It was very bad, Mama. Bigots are the same the world over. Each time the king's forces met with some kind of defeat the Covenanters would blame the king because he did not accept their form of worship in his heart of hearts. Everything was God's judgment upon the king for his intransigence to their ways, but it was the Scots government that was intransigent. My cousin worked hard at compromise. I do not blame my brother Patrick for refusing to have any part in it all." The duke sighed. "He misses his father greatly."

"As do I," Jasmine reminded Charlie.

"Mama, I do beg your pardon," the duke said quickly and, taking her hands in his, kissed them.

She pulled away and caressed his cheek. "Oh, Charlie, I know you meant no harm. It is just that I am still angry at your father for getting himself killed. He had no right running off to Dunbar. I will never understand why his sense of duty and honor caused him to do such a foolish thing. I suppose he did not expect to be killed." She touched his cheek again. "Do not let yourself be killed," she warned him. Then she said, "If this conflict is not quickly resolved, I shall send for your children. They should not be raised in the wilds of Glenkirk by your brother and his rough-spoken wife. They will be totally unfit for proper society if we leave them there. Besides, they will really be safer in France. Master Cromwell has a long reach. If he should eventually learn where your children are hidden, he will come after them so he may use them against you. Bess's parents were cowed by me when her father came to demand the children's whereabouts, but I am no longer in England. The earl could now go to his Puritan friends for what he believes is justice. Having looked to Henry and found nothing, he may look to Patrick next. I think perhaps the sooner we bring the children to France the better."

"In the spring," Charlie said. "It is too late in the season for them to make a crossing from Scotland safely. Besides, Bess's father has no power now, and it will be awhile before he remembers my brother, the Duke of Glenkirk. And, Mama, let us not forget the weather in Scotland."

"I shall never forget the weather in Scotland," Jasmine said pithily.

"It is late autumn now, and winter will shortly set in at Glenkirk. You know it is impossible to reach it once the rains and snows start," Charlie recalled.

"I shall hope for a hard winter. Then, come the spring, I shall have my grandchildren with me," Jasmine said.

"You are just discovering how bored you are now that Autumn has wed her marquis," he teased her. "You want more children to raise."

"We had best go and see your sister before you leave for Paris," his mother remarked.

"I shall not go until after Twelfth Night," he promised. "I have sent the king a purse to tide him over and promised to join him in January," Charlie told his mother. "Until then I shall remain with you, Mama." He kissed her cheek. "I think this is the first time in all my life I have ever had you to myself."

"That," she told him with a small smile, "is something Henry Stuart would have said," and she patted his arm fondly.

"You loved him."

"I loved them all," Jasmine replied with a laugh. Then she grew more somber. "But they were all taken from me except for my Jemmie. We lived a long and good life together. I hope I will some day forgive him for leaving me when I begged him not to do so. Autumn needed him."

"You did well by my little sister," Charlie reminded her. "She is madly in love with her husband, and even more so since she has discovered the joys of the marriage bed," he chuckled.

"Do not be indelicate," his mother scolded him.

"And since when, Mama, did you find passion *indelicate?*" he asked her with a grin.

"What is indelicate?" Autumn demanded as she entered her mother's hall. *"Bonjour,* Mama, and Charlie. I have come to visit for two days."

"Where is Sebastian?" her mother said.

"Oh," Autumn said with a wave of her hand, " 'tis all very mysterious. Yesterday we had a visitor, a gentleman named Monsieur d'Albert. This morning Sebastian said he must go off with this fellow, and that I might come for two days to visit you if I wished. I think it had something to do with some new vine that has been propa . . . I don't remember the word my husband used, but you know how he is about his vineyards, Mama. Lily is opening up my bedchamber. Is that all right, Mama?"

"Of course, *ma petite,*" Jasmine replied, and then, "Do you know where Sebastian was going? Was it Tours, perhaps?"

"I have no idea," Autumn responded. "Why would he go to Tours?"

"You will remember his daughter and former mistress reside there," her mother reminded her.

Autumn laughed heartily. "Believe me, Mama, my husband has no need of another woman. I am, after all, your daughter. Nay, it really did have something to do with grapes, I am certain. Monsieur d'Albert had the look of an upper servant sent by his master."

"I was just gloating that I had never had Mama to myself before," Charlie said mischievously.

"Well, you shall have to share her, big brother," Autumn responded. "At least for the next two days. Will you be here for Christmas? You and Mama must come to Chermont!"

When Autumn returned home late in the afternoon several days later she discovered her husband, Monsieur d'Albert, and another quite distinguished gentleman, whom Sebastian introduced to her as Monsieur Robert Clary, a long-lost cousin who had been traveling for so long in the east, Sebastian had believed him dead.

"You are welcome to Chermont, Monsieur Clary," Autumn said.

"*Merci*, Madame la marquise," came the reply in a very cultured voice with just the faintest accent.

"Who is he really?" Autumn asked her husband as they lay abed that night.

He caressed a plump breast and kissed her mouth. "Who is who, *ma chérie?*" he replied.

Autumn pulled away from him. "I am not a fool, Sebastian," she said. "Monsieur Clary, if that is indeed his name, is no more your cousin than I am. His conversation at table tonight was too inciteful of current affairs for a man gone from France for twenty years. Who is he?"

"Autumn, there are some things you are simply going to have to trust me with, *ma petite*," he said, and reached for her again.

Autumn shoved him away angrily. "Do you really think me such a fool," she said, "that you cannot share this with me? I am your wife, not some pretty little plaything. My parents trusted one another with everything that touched their lives. If you cannot trust me in such a manner, then perhaps I have erred in marrying you, monseigneur."

"It is too dangerous," he said.

"If it is *that* dangerous, then I had certainly better know," she told him. "How can I help if I do not know what it is all about?"

She could see he was struggling to decide what to do. Finally, he said, "If I tell you, Autumn, you can tell no one, even your mother. A man's life is at stake, and not just his, but many others as well. Do you know how to keep a secret, *ma chérie?*"

"I do," she replied quietly.

"Our guest is Mazarin himself, Autumn."

"How are you involved with Mazarin?" she asked him, her voice calm, her mind clear, her emotions roiling.

"I have been one of his agents for several years. Here on the chèr I was little needed. D'Albert is his personal courier, although no one is aware of his identity or relationship to the cardinal."

"Why is he in France? I thought him in the duchy of Cologne." Autumn now sat up in their bed, drawing the coverlet over her bosom.

"The king has asked him back, although there are still many who oppose him and will therefore seek to prevent his ever reaching Louis. Then, too, there is the matter of the queen. Gaston d'Orleans and Gondi have kidnapped her from Paris and incarcerated her downriver at Chenonceaux. The king has been told that his mother desired to retire from public life. They are attempting to keep him busy with trifles so they may rule in his name, but Louis is too clever for them. D'Albert must return to Paris shortly to pass on the information of what has happened to Queen Anne. We must find a way to rescue the queen and restore her to her son's side. Mazarin is here because his enemies would never consider him to have such a refuge. His cousin, who is his double, is still in Cologne, and so d'Orleans, Conde, Gondi, and the others believe the cardinal is there. They know nothing of the cardinal's cousinly twin."

"This is a very danerous game you play," Autumn said. "How do you propose to extricate Queen Anne from Chenonceaux? She is certain to be very well guarded. And once you have her, how will you return her to Paris before her enemies can catch up with you?"

"We do not know yet. She is safe, Autumn, for her captors wish her no harm. They simply wanted to remove her influence from the king's sphere. Our escape plan must be flawless, for we will get no more than one chance, and once her captors are warned, they will certainly move her to a more secure environment."

"I know how to get her out," Autumn said, "and get her to Paris in safety. It is really quite simple."

Sebastian laughed. "*Ma petite*, it is most certainly not simple. These are dangerous men we deal with. They would as soon kill the queen's rescuers as smile upon them."

"Is the queen's residence at Chenonceaux supposed to be a secret?" she asked him.

He nodded.

"Then her captors would certainly not be expecting a stream of visitors, would they?" Autumn said. "So, if half the nobility in the district should appear at Chenonceaux on Martinsmas, armed with game, geese, and apples for the queen, we could hardly be denied entry. And, of course, the queen would have to be brought forth to render her neighbors her royal thanks and offer them her hospitality. Then, in the confusion of our departure, we could take the queen with us. It is simple."

Sebastian d'Oleron, Marquis d'Auriville, was astounded by his young wife's stratagem. It was simple. Very simple, but at the same time it was outrageously ingenious. "It might work," he said slowly, as if to himself. "It just might work!" Then, suddenly, he was filled with a new respect for his beautiful wife. He had never before considered her intelligence, although he knew she was quick-witted. This, however, was a scheme worthy of a seasoned politician. "I think," he said, "that I should be afraid of you, *ma chérie.*"

"Only," Autumn answered him, "if you are not able to sastisfy my insatiable desires." Then, without warning, she climbed atop him and began to tease his male member to a firm and upright stance. She mounted him boldly, leaning and arching back as he fondled her round little breasts. "Oh, monseigneur," she murmured, feeling his hard length filling her. "*Oh!*" She rocked back and forth, her body rising and falling like a tidal surge, her eyes half closed with her open delight. They found their pleasure simultaneously, and Autumn collapsed onto her husband's broad chest with a gusty sigh of delight. "That was nice," she whispered in his ear, licking at it provocatively. "Can we do it again?"

He laughed weakly. "After I have had some wine, you witch," he said, stroking her disheveled dark hair.

"I shall get it for you," she said, and climbed from their bed to pour them two goblets of the pale golden wine she loved. She handed him his and watched as he drank most of the goblet down Then, drizzling wine from her goblet onto his torso, she straddled him and began to lick up the liquid with broad laps of her facile tongue.

He watched her lazily, feeling the silkiness of the fleshy organ as it smoothed over his chest. *Lick. Lick. Lick.* She lapped the wine from his chest, paying particular attention to his nipples. Her tongue swept over his belly, moving in circular motions, around and around and around. He closed his eyes and let the sensuousness of the moment sweep over him. He could feel himself tingling and tightening as her wicked tongue roused him once again to passion. Rolling her over onto her back, he delved into the hot, marshy depths of her eager body, encasing himself to the hilt of his lance.

"Yessss," Autumn hissed as he filled her. *"Oh, yes!"*

"You are every man's dream," he told her through gritted teeth. "A wife who enjoys her husband's attentions and even seeks more of him." He began to move upon her with long, slow strokes of his manhood.

Autumn sighed deeply as her arms wrapped themselves about him. Her eyes were closed as she let the sensations of pure pleasure roll over her. She loved him and she loved his passion. Their lips met in a hot kiss. His mouth found her straining throat, and he licked at it with his tongue. She purred beneath him, and then together they sought for and found nirvana, crying out together in satisfaction.

"Beautiful. Clever, and insatiably lustful," he murmured to her as he rolled off her and gathered her into his embrace.

"I am as monseigneur would have me," she replied softly.

Then together they fell into a satisfied and restful sleep.

On the following day the marquis spoke with the cardinal, telling him, "My wife suspected you were not who we said you were. She is an astute young woman. I felt it necessary to tell her the truth. She is a woman who knows well how to keep a confidence, Your Grace."

"I understand," Jules Mazarin replied.

"She has," Sebastian continued, "come up with the most amazing design for freeing the queen." The marquis proceeded to outline his wife's scheme. He concluded by saying, "I believe it could work."

The cardinal was silent and thoughtful for a time, and then he said, "Bring Madame la marquise to me. I would speak with her."

Autumn came, and curtsied politely. Her gaze took in this powerful man in the dark clothing with his elegant face.

"Sit down, madame," he told her, and she sat down in a chair opposite him by the hall's fireplace. "Who would you ask to partake in this charade?"

"My relations, the de Savilles of Archambault, and other trusted neighbors, Your Grace. We are all loyal to King Louis. There is little love for the princes and Gondi here on the chèr."

"It cannot be known by the others that I am at Chermont, or even back in France," the cardinal said. "Tell me, Madame la marquise, how did you know that the queen was at Chenonceaux? We have sought to keep her retreat a private and quiet one."

"The servants knew, monsieur," Autumn replied, wide-eyed. "Do the servants not always know *everything?* One must be so very careful if a secret is to be kept, or lo, the entire neighborhood is made aware of it." She giggled, and then shrugged her shoulders.

The cardinal smiled and nodded. "Excellent, madame. You give the appearance of a charming but not particularly aware country noblewoman. I hope that, when this is all settled and the king secure, you and your husband will come to court. I could very much use a pair of eyes and ears as sharp as yours, Madame la marquise."

"*Merci*, Monsieur le cardinal," Autumn said, "but I think I prefer to remain in the country to have babies."

"An equally excellent occupation," he replied. "France will need educated young nobles to serve it in the years to come." He smiled briefly at her. "Your plan is a clever one, and I believe we will adopt it. How do you propose to disguise the queen?"

"It would be too difficult to make it a complicated guise," Autumn answered him. "A hooded cloak must do, and we will put the queen amid a group of other women of similar size similarly garbed. We shall rush out even as we have pushed and rushed in. Hopefully by the time they discover the queen is gone, it will be too late. They can and will mount a search, but we will secrete the queen here at Chermont for a brief time, and then send half a dozen different carriages on the road to Paris. Even if she is finally discovered, they cannot stop the queen of France from returning to her son's side. Not publicly. Not without causing an incident. We will make certain there are plenty of witnesses to attest to any attempt to force the queen back into captivity," Autumn finished.

"I was given to understand, Madame la marquise, that you were raised in the eastern Highlands of Scotland and had never been to court," the cardinal remarked.

"I was indeed, Your Grace," Autumn answered him.

"You are extremely clever for a simple country woman," he observed, peering sharply at her.

Autumn laughed. "Your Grace, if you but knew my bloodlines, you would understand. I descend from a race of very nimble-minded, intelligent, canny, and resourceful ladies. One was the mother of an Ottoman sultan, another a noble merchant queen respected and envied by good Queen Bess. My mother is the daughter of Akbar, who was Grande Mughal of India. The women in my family live by their own rules and thrive doing so." She laughed again. "No one would ever call us *simple*. One does not have to be raised at a royal court to show intellect, or to have the ability to handle difficult situations. I suspect it is better not to be raised at a royal court, where one's head is likely to be turned by flattery and one's ethics become confused."

The cardinal nodded slowly. "You are correct, Madame la marquise. A royal court, filled with men and women jockeying for position and for power, is always a dangerous place. It is not easy to raise a boy to be a good king, but his mother and I have done it. Gaston d'Orleans, poor deluded prince he is, and the others, must not be allowed to destroy what we have done. The king must be protected from those men who would corrupt him. His mother must be returned to his side. Assemble your petticoat army, Madame la marquise, but keep me informed of each step you take before you take it."

Autumn arose from her chair and curtsied to the cardinal. "I will, Your Grace, and may God favor our endeavors."

"He will," the cardinal assured her. "He will."

Autumn visited her relations, the de Savilles, the following day.

Then, over the next few days she went to the neighboring chateaux and spoke with their owners. She did not mention Cardinal Mazarin, but instead told her listeners that word of the queen's residence had come to her through her own servants, who had it from others who had been to Chenonceaux and trafficked with the servants there. The queen, she explained, had been taken secretly from her son's side, and he had been told she had retreated to the country to rest. Her informants, however, said that the queen was unhappy and fearful for her son, the king, because those who now surrounded him were wicked and self-serving.

"It is up to us to rescue the queen," Autumn told her listeners. "We must free her from her captivity, and help her to return to Paris! We must do this for our *bon Dieudonne*, King Louis! God will surely aid and protect our cause, for it is a right one! The king is young yet, and has been wise enough to solicit his mother's continued guidance. Evil men must not be allowed to corrupt him! For God, Louis, and France!" she cried dramatically, and her neighbors enthusiastically agreed.

"She was like a young Jeanne d'Arc," the marquis told the cardinal. "She was magnificent!"

"Your wife, I suspect, could be a dangerous woman in the proper circumstances," the cardinal remarked thoughtfully. "Has a date been set yet for the queen's rescue?"

"Autumn has said November eleventh, Martinmas, is still the best time, Your Grace. It is a holiday that countryfolk in particular celebrate with enthusiasm. We have learned that other than the musketeers who have accompanied the queen from Paris, all the servants are local folk, but one, who serves as the queen's chief serving woman, also came from Paris. She is undoubtedly in the employ of the prince. The musketeers believe they are serving the king," Sebastian finished. "Still, if told the truth, they might not believe it without certain proof, and what proof can we offer them?"

The cardinal smiled faintly at this observation. "Musketeers," he told the marquis, "are particularly hardheaded, as our relations with them in the past has proven. Do you know who the captain of this group is, *mon ami?*"

"Pierre d'Aumont," Sebastian said.

"Humph," the cardinal replied. "A particularly difficult individual, if I remember correctly."

"Do we have your permission then to proceed?" the marquis asked the cardinal. "Time grows short."

"We can but try," Jules Mazarin said with a deep sigh, "and God protect us all, particularly the queen."

Sebastian d'Oleron, Marquis d'Auriville, bowed low and left the chamber where the cardinal sat, now deep in thought. Despite his churchly title, Jules Mazarin, born Giulo Mazarini of Sicilian parents forty-nine years earlier, was not a priest, but rather a layman. He had been educated in Rome and in Spain by the Jesuits. While his education had made him devout, he had no desire to give up his carnal life. Still, his talents were appreciated by the Church. He had served in both the papal army and the papal diplomatic corps.

In 1634 he was made vice-legate to Avignon by the pope, and in less than a year, papal nuncio to the French court. His skills attracted the attention of Cardinal Richelieu. Recalled by the pope, Mazarin resigned from his service, quickly returned to France, became a naturalized French citizen and, on Richelieu's recommendation, entered the diplomatic service of King Louis XIII. He had served that king loyally, and with much distinction.

In 1641 the pope made Monsieur Mazarin a cardinal of the church despite his lack of holy orders. In the next year Richelieu picked Mazarin to succeed him as prime minister to the king. The queen was immediately attracted to him, and Mazarin to her, although both behaved with the utmost decorum. When Louis XIII died, Cardinal Mazarin became Anne of Austria's greatest champion and right hand. She trusted him utterly and adored him secretly.

The queen had not had an easy life. Her husband had disliked her, preferring his male companions, encouraged to believe his wife's loyalty lay with her native Spain rather than with her adopted France. She was thirty-seven years old before her son, called "the God-given," was born to her. Louis was followed two years later by his younger brother, known as le Petit Monsieur. Mazarin knew all of this, and offered Anne what her husband never had: gentleness, kindness, an ear that listened willingly, and love. While many considered his actions toward the queen self-serving, she knew better. She had spent her entire life in one royal court or another and understood the difference between what was real and what was false. She was far more intelligent than her detractors gave her credit for, which was why her son had now reached his majority.

But Louis was only thirteen. He needed his mother's counsel, and he was wise enough to know it. How long before the young king realized his mother had been taken from him? And how would he, yet a boy, be able to retaliate and free his parent? Nay, it was up to him, to Mazarin, the king's foster father, to bring Anne of Austria, safely back to Paris. And then he, already asked to return from exile, would return. When he did he would no longer be patient or give their enemies the benefit of the doubt. He would destroy them once and for all! He would make certain that nothing ever threatened Louis or his mother again. Even if it cost him his own life in the process.

Mazarin chuckled at his own thoughts. He was far too clever, he knew, to be done in by his enemies. He would live to see the king a grown man. Then he would engineer the marriage he and Anne had always wanted, with the Infanta of Spain. Nay. He would not die yet. There was too much work to be done.

Chapter

12

The guards at the gate at Chenonceaux saw the dust in the distance and wondered who was coming their way. Gradually the brownish mist began to clear, and they could observe fully a dozen or more carriages, and coaches approaching at a fast clip. The bridles of the horses jingled with tinkling bells. Outriders upon their mounts blew their trumpets lustily in the damp gray air of the midmorning.

"Send for Captain d'Aumont," the musketeer in charge said.

The captain arrived just as the first of the elegant vehicles arrived at the gate. The window to the carriage was lowered and a head popped out. It was a most beautiful lady wearing a crimson velvet cloak, its hood edged in ermine. The lady smiled a brilliant smile.

"Bonjour, Captain," she said gaily. "I am Madame la marquise d'Auriville. My neighbors and I have come to pay our respects to Her Majesty, Queen Anne."

"The queen?" Captain d'Aumont affected a puzzled countenance.

Autumn laughed merrily. "Now, Captain," she cajoled him, "this is not Paris. This is the country. There are no secrets here. We all know Her Majesty has come to Chenonceaux to relax and recover from a most busy year, culminating only two months ago in the official recognition of our good King Louis's majority. 'Tis Martinmas, Captain, and we have brought Her Majesty freshly slaughtered and dressed geese, a fine boar, and several stags that our husbands hunted. We have apples and pears from our orchards and wine from our vineyards. 'Tis a day we countryfolk celebrate, and we would share our bounty with the queen. Now do be a dear man and allow us in, *s'il vous plait.*" She smiled at him once again. "Some of us have had to travel several hours to reach Chenonceaux. Surely you would not have us go home dissatisfied."

As she leaned farther from her coach to plead with him, her cape opened slightly, and he could see the creamy flesh beneath. "Madame la marquise," he began, "the queen's residence is supposed to be a quiet and most private visit. We have orders specifically from the king that his mother rest in the peaceful environs of this chateau."

"But Captain, the queen has been here for several weeks. Certainly by now she is ready for a visit from her neighbors. Please! We all came, our husbands and children and entire families, last spring when she was here with the king and the Prince d'Orleans. We are only a little group of ladies. If you are afraid of us, we will leave our coaches outside the gates and walk, but you will have to carry our gifts, I fear. They are too heavy for mere women."

He sighed. "I must ask the queen if she would like her privacy disturbed, Madame la marquise. If she says, *oui*, then you and your coaches may enter Chenonceaux."

"Will you go yourself and ask her, Captain? If you just send one of your men, some upper servant may prove too overprotective and refuse us. The queen will not even know we are here," Autumn said astutely.

Now it was his turn to smile. "You are a clever pretty puss, Madame la marquise," the captain replied boldly, "but I will go myself." He turned away, chuckling. He was a country man himself, having been born and raised in Poitou. These women who had come calling would most likely never see Paris or the court. If it had been up to him, he would have allowed them in immediately. They were harmless little country ladies eager to reach out to their king's mother.

Entering the queen's apartments, he found the king's mother sitting before a tapestry frame, a needle in her hand. He bowed politely, waiting for permission to speak. It came. "Majesty, at our gates this very minute is a covey of local noblewomen who have brought you gifts this Martinmas. It is difficult to keep secrets in the country," he said, almost apologetically. "These ladies beg permission to enter your presence and offer their gifts to you. They have, I have been told, brought geese, boar, venison, pears, apples, and wine." He bowed again.

Before the queen might speak, Madame de Laurent, who had accompanied her from Paris, said brusquely, "Send them away!"

"*Non!*" the queen responded firmly. "I am bored, and it would be rude to send these ladies away when they have come bearing such lovely tribute. It would also seem odd. Ask them in, Captain d'Aumont, and you, Madame de Laurent, will see to providing refreshments for my guests. Wine and biscuits will do nicely." The queen stood and stuck her tapestry needle into the frame. "Show them into the salon overlooking the river, Captain."

He bowed smartly. "As Your Majesty commands," he said, but he noted that Madame de Laurent appeared most irritated. Surely she was as bored as her mistress, he thought, hurrying off to give the good news to the beautiful Marquise d'Auriville.

The white and gold salon overlooking the chèr was a floor below the gallery where the young king had walked with Autumn the previous spring. The women crowded in, chattering and laughing. The queen arrived, and they all curtsied low. Autumn's heart was hammering with her nervousness. If they failed, what would happen to them all? she wondered for the first time, not having previously considered failure.

"There, the watchdog," her aunt, Madame St. Omer, said low. "We will have to separate her from the queen if we are to succeed, but there is time, *ma chèr* Autumn. There is time."

Each of the women was introduced, and the queen delighted them by remembering small bits of information about each one's visit the previous April. All the while by Queen Anne's side Madame de Laurent lurked so obviously that finally the queen turned to the woman and said irritably, "Leave me at once, madame! You shadow me as if I were some criminal. Return to my apartments and see it is prepared for evening. I will call you when I need you. Do not darken my presence until then."

"But the king . . . ," Madame de Laurent began, only to be cut short.

"Leave me! We both know your orders come from my brother-in-law and not my son," the queen hissed angrily. "Go, or by God's good grace, I will have you thrown in the dungeons. As long as I make no move to leave Chenonceaux, madame, the musketeers obey me."

Two red spots had appeared on Madame de Laurent's cheeks. She curtsied and backed from the queen's presence, clearly angry but unable to give vent to her ire.

"Your Majesty," Autumn murmured to the queen softly when the woman had gone, "do not allow your face to betray us, but we have come to your rescue. We have been sent by your confidante. My aunt, Madame de Belfort, has worn two cloaks. She is divesting herself of one now amid the crowd of women. Please put it on, but leave the hood off for the moment so your face may be seen by all. Captain d'Aumont said we would be allowed but a short visit. When he comes to say we must depart, we shall all raise our hoods up and hurry out, laughing. You will be put in the midst of us all, and you must be silent. If God is on our side, we shall effect your release from Chenonceaux and help you to reach Paris."

"And if He is not on our side, Madame la marquise?" the queen asked Autumn in an equally soft voice.

Autumn shrugged. "I do not know, but I do not think it will be pleasant, Your Majesty. Still, it is worth our efforts. The king needs you, Madame la reine. Those surrounding him now are wicked."

The queen felt a garment being set upon her shoulders. Glancing down, she saw it was, but coincidence, the same deep purple of her gown. Reaching up, she drew the halves together and fastened the silver frogs. "*Merci,*" she murmured to the unseen hands that helped her.

They ate wine and biscuits, and then Captain d'Aumont was standing in the door, advising them that their visit with Her Majesty was over and they must all leave.

"You will see my guests to their carriages and safely through the gates of the chateau, Captain," the queen said in a loud voice. "I shall retire to my apartments. Tell the chef that I should like one of those lovely geese roasted for my supper when you return."

"Yes, Your Majesty," the captain replied, and then with a wave of his hands he said, "Come, mesdames."

With a twinkle in her eye, Queen Anne raised the hood of her cape and pulled it up. It was edged in a dark mink, the further to obscure her features. Then, surrounded by her guests, she hurried out amid the chattering and giggling women. She could scarcely believe what was happening, but she followed along and quickly found herself hustled into a carriage with Madame de Belfort and Madame St. Omer. The vehicle started up and moved from the chateau's courtyard, followed by the rest of the convoy.

Autumn, however, lingered, thanking Captain d'Aumont girlishly. "It was so sweet of you to intercede for us, Captain. How rested and pretty the queen looks. We shall come again during the twelve days of Noël. I hope to see you if the queen is still here," she flirted, fluttering her thick, dark eyelashes at him. Then she offered him her hand, smiling seductively.

He kissed the elegant little gloved hand. The glove was perfumed, and her scent was intoxicating. "Madame la marquise," he murmured. "I shall certainly look forward to your return." Then he helped her into her coach, his hand lingering a tiny bit too long upon her arm before he closed the door.

Autumn lowered the window and leaned out. "*Adieu*, Captain," she said softly and blew him a kiss.

He watched her carriage depart, wondering what kind of a man her husband was. Probably some stiff old country gentleman. Madame la marquise was looking to play, he was certain. When she returned to Chenonceaux they would have to find some opportunity in which to indulge her playfulness. This posting was proving to be far more interesting than he had anticipated, Captain d'Aumont considered to himself.

Several miles from Chenonceaux, two carriages stopped along the river road. A muffled figure emerged from the first vehicle, and it quickly departed. It climbed into the second coach, where Autumn was seated. The seat facing the driver was pulled forward.

"I regret you must secret yourself behind my seat, Your Majesty," said Autumn. "There is the chance your absence may be quickly discovered. I suspect my coach will be the first sought, because I am the one who insisted upon entry into Chenonceaux. The journey is not long."

Queen Anne did not argue with the younger woman. She was surprisingly agile for a lady of middle years and fitted herself into the orifice with little difficulty.

"I shall not close it, Your Majesty, unless I am advised we are being followed. I hope you are not discomfitted by small spaces."

"I have no idea, having never been put into one. No. Once, when I was a little girl in Spain, I hid from my old *duenna* in a cabinet used for linens. I thought it rather cozy, surrounded by all those sweet-smelling sheets. I had quite forgotten about my adventure until now. Tell me, why is Jules at your chateau, madame?"

"The king has asked him to return, but of course, there are those who oppose the king's will. My husband has been one of the cardinal's agents for several years, I was only recently informed. The cardinal has a cousin, a man who is his twin in features. He displays himself boldly in Cologne, and so your enemies believe the cardinal is yet there. They have no idea he is already in France. He awaits you eagerly, Your Majesty."

"I have missed him so very much these past months," the queen said, almost to herself. "I was not certain when I should ever see him again; and then, when I was kidnapped from Paris, I truly feared, not just for Jules, but for my beloved sons as well."

"Madame, we are being pursued," the coachman called down to Autumn. "Shall I evade them, or pretend I do not notice?"

"Maintain your current speed, Henri," she called back. Then she said to the queen, "Majesty, I am sorry, but I must close up the seat. Be as silent as a mouse, I beg you." Autumn smiled encouragingly at the queen, who nodded as the back of the seat was raised and fastened with its tiny concealed latches. Then Autumn returned to the seat facing forward, slumping into a corner as she pretended to doze. She could hear the thunder of hoofbeats coming up behind them.

"Stop the coach!" an authoritative voice called out, and the vehicle drew to a slow halt. Almost immediately the door to the carriage was pulled open.

Autumn feigned a scream of fright; and then, seeing Captain d'Autmont, cried, "What do you mean by stopping my coach, Captain?" Then her voice grew almost seductive in its tone. "You are *really* quite naughty, monsieur, chasing after me. What shall I say to my husband when the coachman tells him? Shoo! Go away this instant!" Her lips pouted temptingly, and she shook a finger at him in reproach.

"As much as I should like to say it is Madame la marquise who brings me out this night, I cannot lie to such a beautiful woman." The light from her carriage lantern touched the tips of his mustache, making it glisten. He was quite attractive, Autumn thought.

"Then why have you stopped me?" she asked.

"The queen is missing from Chenonceaux, madame," he replied.

"*What!* Surely you have made a mistake, monsieur. Why would the queen be gone from Chenonceaux? Who has said it? How can you be absolutely certain? But if it is so, a search must be mounted immediately! The queen might be in grave danger, Captain!" Autumn replied.

"I went to the queen's apartments after I had carried out her instructions to see you and the other ladies off, and to speak to her chef regarding the goose for her dinner. When I arrived at Her Majesty's door, Madame de Laurent told me the queen was not there. A search was made at once of the rooms in which Her Majesty lives. She was nowhere to be found, I regret to say. A search has indeed been mounted, Madame la marquise. It will not be concluded until Her Majesty is safely returned to Chenonceaux. Her kidnappers will be dealt with harshly, I can assure you," he finished.

"As well they should be, Captain," Autumn agreed with him in firm tones. "But that still does not answer my original question. Why have you stopped my carriage? Surely you don't think I took the queen away? As you can see, I travel quite alone. Besides, did you not help me into this vehicle yourself? I was the last to leave our little fête. Why on earth would anyone steal Queen Anne?"

"Step from the coach, Madame la marquise. I must satisfy myself that it is indeed empty of anyone but yourself," he said, and offered her his hand so she might step down.

"This is quite outrageous," Autumn protested as he lifted her out. Her anger was just enough to convince him of her outrage, but not enough to engender his suspicions. She had no fear that the captain would discover the queen's hiding place. Both the hinges and the fasteners holding the back seat closed were too well concealed.

Captain d'Aumont climbed into her carriage, poking about it, but all appeared to be quite in order, and after a few very long minutes he climbed out again. "I ask your pardon, Madame la marquise," he said, "but you will understand it was necessary."

"Indeed, Captain," she replied dryly as he helped her back into her coach and firmly shut the door behind her. "Drive on, Henri," Autumn called to her coachman, allowing the musketeer to believe she was piqued at him, as any normal, innocent woman would have been.

"*Oui*, madame!" Henri called down and whipped the horses up again.

"Your Majesty must remain where she is for now," Autumn said softly. "I cannot be certain they have gone away entirely. Do not reply, madame. Just stay silent. We are not far from Chermont, I promise." Then, suddenly, she had a new thought. She called to her coachman, "Henri, only one woman will exit the carriage when we arrive home. Do not be surprised. Afterwards you will drive the coach into the stables."

"*Oui*, madame," came the impassive reply. The coachman understood his mistress quite well. The fewer people in on this dangerous secret, the better chance they had of keeping it, and of helping their good queen.

The marquis was awaiting his wife in the chateau's courtyard. He helped the hooded lady from the carriage, and it then moved on into the stables. When the doors had been closed and bolted, Autumn arose from her seat and was helped out by Henri. She nodded at him, and then without a word slipped from the stables, running quickly across the the darkened courtyard and into the chateau through a small side door that opened into a narrow hallway with a small staircase. Hurrying up the stairs, she exited into the broad corridor of the bedroom floor and ran to her apartments.

"You're back!" Lily greeted her eagerly.

"Where is Orane?" Autumn demanded.

"I sent her to the kitchens to have her supper. She knows nothing, nor will she," Lily answered.

"We were stopped along the road, but I had her hidden by then. Where is my husband?"

"He took her to him," Lily replied.

The door to the salon opened, and Sebastian entered. "Well done, Madame la marquise," he said with a broad smile. "You would, it seems, have a talent for intrigue. They want to see you. Come!" He held out his hand to her.

Cardinal Mazarin and Queen Anne were awaiting them in a tower of the chateau. Jules Mazarn had his arm about the queen, and she was smiling up at him, but her eyes were tear-filled with her relief. They turned as the marquis and his wife entered the room.

"Ahh," the cardinal said, "here is our brave heroine. My dear marquise, you did very well indeed. The queen tells me that your demeanor was quite clever, and you now have a musketeer captain enthralled."

"Captain d'Aumont is too clever, I believe, to be enthralled. He simply couldn't figure out whether I had the queen or not, or if there was a plot or not. All he knew for certain was that the queen was missing, and she had gone missing after her guests left. Since my coach was the last to depart Chenonceaux, he caught up with it first."

"We are so grateful to you," Queen Anne said. "Jules has told me that the plot was devised by you, and that you went to all your neighbors and enlisted them in our cause. Bless you, my dear marquise, but now, how do I manage to return to Paris?"

"We must hide you for the next few days, Your Majesty," Autumn replied. "They will be searching every coach and cart on the Paris road after they have searched every chateau in the region. Neither of you are safe here, but there is one place I am certain you will be safe, although even it may be searched. My mother lives just past Archambault in a small chateau called Belle Fleurs. It has always been a refuge to my family and is quite off the beaten track. It is just possible Captain d'Aumont will not know of it, but even if he does, Mama will make certain that neither you nor the cardinal will be found. We must, however, go tonight, before your enemies mount a great search. My mother is expecting us. As soon as the servants are in bed we will leave. We have entrusted this secret to only a few people. It is much better that way, and even they do not know that the cardinal is the cardinal," she finished with a small smile.

"Such a clever madame," Jules Mazarin said, "and she would remain in the country. 'Tis a great waste."

"Now, Jules," the queen replied, "I am not certain she hasn't chosen a better course than any of us. Her life will be tranquil. Ours has been chaotic, to say the least."

"Ah, but she was not born infanta of Spain, my dear, nor will she ever become queen of France. You were and are all those things," the cardinal reminded his beloved. "You have done your duty, and you have performed well. Your life has brought you two fine sons."

"And it brought me you," the queen quickly added meaningfully.

He took her hand in his and kissed it, nodding. "Despite it all, my dear, we have been happy, and Louis is at last king in his own right, but he yet needs us, so you must return to Paris."

"What of you?" she cried.

"Louis has asked me to return, but it is not quite safe for me to do so. I will arrange to meet him well outside of Paris, probably in January at Poitiers. By the time we return to Paris we shall have things well in hand. The country can no longer take all this fighting. The princes of the blood and their allies must be brought to heel once and for all. Paris must be quieted. I think a cardinal's hat for

Gondi will accomplish that. I have already written to the pope from Cologne. He has promised that when I have regained my authority and our king is firmly enthroned, he will grant my request. Then, my dear Anne, we will set about to defang these noble snakes who surround us. Louis's power *must* be absolute!"

The queen turned to Autumn. "How do we reach your mother? Will not a coach at midnight attract attention?"

"We will ride, and the horses' hooves will be muffled, Your Majesty," Autumn said. "My husband and I will accompany you ourselves. I will have my serving woman, Lily, bring you some supper, Your Majesty, and then I would suggest you rest until I come for you." Autumn curtsied.

"This is a new side of you, *chérie*, that I certainly never expected," Sebastian said to her as they returned to their own apartments.

"I thought by now," she teased him, "that you had seen every side of me, *mon coeur*. If you have missed something, it is not from want of trying." She spun about and kissed him quickly upon the lips.

He laughed. "Behave yourself, Madame la marquise," he told her with mock sternness. "We have not yet come to the end of our day."

"When did that ever stop us?" Autumn said mischievously.

He chuckled. "Tonight it will. I would feel the cardinal was peeping over our shoulder the whole time. Let us get them settled and then, madame, we will play together."

"He loves her," Autumn observed, "and she loves him. They behave like an old married couple. I remember my parents interacting in that way. It is rather sad, and yet very touching."

"It is rumored that they are married, and have been for several years; but, of course, there is no proof of it. Such proof of a morganatic marriage between Anne of Austria and Jules Mazarin would be a disaster."

"Why?" Autumn asked him.

"The queen was wed to King Louis the Thirteenth for twenty-three years before her first son was born," he explained. "There would be those who claimed Louis was Mazarin's son, and not the legal and legitimate offspring of King Louis the Thirteenth."

"That's ridiculous," Autumn replied. "The queen hardly knew Mazarin then, for his station was not high enough to allow them daily contact. Besides, the king looks like the portrait of his father I have seen at Chenonceaux."

"That is true, and the queen is a virtuous woman, but, *ma petite*, you are wise enough to know there are those who would not care about that if a lie would gain them greater power," Sebastian said.

"I am glad we live a simple life," Autumn responded.

"And yet the cardinal believes that a royal court would be a proper venue for your talents, Autumn," her husband said. "Would you like to visit Louis's court?"

"Perhaps one day, when our children are grown," she admitted. "By then Louis should have his palace at Versailles built. That would be interesting, *mon coeur*. Oh, Lily, there you are," she said to her serving woman. "Go to the kitchens and bring a tray to the queen and Monsieur Jules in the north tower. Say the tray is for us if you are asked. Marc may help you. Hurry!"

"Yes, madame," Lily said, and hurried out.

"Marc will go with us tonight," Autumn said. "He will carry the lantern that will guide us. It will be slow going, but we cannot be certain whether Captain d'Aumont is out searching. We must attract no attention on our way to Belle Fleurs."

"I don't want you to go," he finally said to her.

"*What?*" Autumn was outraged.

"The fewer horses, the less difficulty, Autumn," Sebastian told her. "Besides, if your musketeer should come to Chermont tonight, you can hold him off. If he sees you, he will be satisfied, but if Lily insists you cannot be disturbed, his suspicions will be aroused. I will take our guests to your mother's. You know I am right, *chérie.*"

Autumn sighed. He was right, but this whole adventure had been such fun, she was loath to have it end. Still, she would not endanger Queen Anne or the cardinal. King Louis's reign depended on the queen returning safely to Paris and the cardinal meeting the king in January. She nodded, albeit reluctantly. "I shall take a leisurely bath and be awaiting your return in our bed, *mon coeur,*" she told him.

He pulled her into his arms and kissed her hard. "Madame, you would tempt the very angels with your words. I shall return to your side as quickly as I possibly can."

When the hour came for the queen and the cardinal to depart Chermont, the marquis offered his wife's farewells and God speeds, explaining why she would not accompany them. The cardinal agreed.

"Captain d'Aumont is like a rat terrier when he is seeking something. It is best that your wife remain here."

Lafite had made certain their passage through the house was unobstructed and empty of servants. Marc awaited them in the stables with the horses. Their journey would take several hours, as they must go slowly through a black woods with Marc leading them, the dark light of his lantern falling only on the ground at his feet. It was a tedious trip, with few night sounds, the muffled hooves of the horses barely audible. By the time they reached Belle Fleurs it was obvious that Captain d'Aumont had erred on the side of caution and did not intend to conduct his hunt for his missing prisoner until the morning.

Exiting the forest, they came to the edge of the low garden wall and the marquis dismounted, helping the queen, who was now quite exhausted, from her mount. With his own key he opened the gate into the chateau's gardens and led his two companions through them, entering the house by means of a small hidden door, almost entirely covered over with ivy. Adali was awaiting them. He bowed first to Queen Anne and then to the cardinal.

"My mistress bids you welcome. If you will follow me, I shall take you to your chambers."

"How can we thank you?" the queen said, taking Sebastian's hands in hers. "With such loyal friends as we have found here on the chèr, Louis's reign is secure."

The marquis kissed the queen's hands. "It has, Madame la reine, been our pleasure to serve you."

"You will hear from me," the cardinal said, before turning away to follow the queen and Adali.

"Of that I have no doubt, Your Grace," the marquis replied with a wry smile. Then, letting himself out through the same door through which he had entered, he rejoined Marc and the horses. Together they returned to Chermont, arriving just before dawn.

Autumn greeted her husband sleepily, holding out her arms to him as he entered their bed. "The sky is lightening," she murmured.

"It is dawn," he responded, nuzzling her round little breasts.

"Ummmm," she encouraged him.

He opened her nightrail and licked between the shadowed valley of her breasts. Then his dark head moved to kiss a nipple, his mouth opening to close again over the sentient nub of scented flesh.

Her fingers entwined in his soft hair. "Ohh, that's nice," she told him, enjoying the sensation of his mouth tugging upon her flesh. His head moved to her other nipple, and she sighed with her pleasure.

He pushed her garment up to to her waist and covered her body with his. Autumn's hand smoothed down his long back as he entered her. She was no longer embarrassed by her eager response to him and welcomed him readily, her body wet and hot as he pistoned her slowly at first, and then with increasing vigor. Her legs wrapped about him. She made little sounds of passion and utter delight as together they exploded into a fury of utter satisfaction. Collapsing into each other's arms, they fell into a contented sleep, but they did not sleep long, for a pounding came upon their bedchamber door, and it burst open suddenly.

Sebastian d'Oleron sat up, half-awake and utterly startled to find his bedchamber filled with musketeers. "What the hell . . ." he began. By his side, his wife clutched the bedclothes to her half-naked body, eyes wide with her shock.

"I told them you were sleeping, monseigneur," Lafite, the major-domo said angrily. "I said I should fetch you, as this man insisted he must see you and Madame la marquise." His look marked Captain d'Aumont. "But he would not allow it. He demanded I take him to you."

"It is all right, Lafite. Captain d'Aumont comes on the king's business. Is that not right, Captain? However, I should ask that you remove your men from my bedchamber. Lafite will take them to the kitchens for some wine and food. Then, if you will await me in the salon, I shall be happy to speak with you." He stepped naked from the bed, his demeanor assured and cool. "You have frightened my wife, and I do not appreciate the lustful looks your men are directing at her." He slid his arms into the fur-lined velvet robe Lafite wrapped him in, and then moved toward the door to the salon. "Come, messieurs," he said to them, and they followed him.

When the salon had emptied of all but the marquis and the captain, Sebastian said, "I assume this unseemly invasion of my home is in regard to the queen's disappearance. Has she been found yet? I told my wife she had probably wandered into an unused portion of the chateau. Chenonceaux is a large place, after all."

"She has not been found, monseigneur," Captain d'Aumont replied.

"Ah, so you have come to search my house, then," the marquis remarked with a small, amused smile. "You have my permission, Captain." He poured them both a goblet of wine, handing one to his visitor.

Captain d'Aumont took the silver vessel and raising it, then said, "To the king!"

"The king!" the marquis agreed, lifting his goblet in return.

"I should search your house with or without permission, monseigneur for, as you noted, I am on the king's business. His mother, placed in my care, is missing. The king will be very distressed."

"I have it on the best authority that the king is already upset, Captain, for he does not even know where his mother is," Sebastian said to the soldier.

"But my orders came from the king! They had his seal." The musketeer looked discomfitted. "Certainly the king knows his mother's whereabouts. Why wouldn't he?"

"Perhaps it is because the same men who have kept France at war with itself since this Louis succeeded his father wish it. Only the queen and the cardinal kept the boy safe from those orders. You are no fool, Captain d'Aumont. You know how power corrupts. The king is still a boy, despite his responsibilities. Did I not hear it said that he asked his mother to be his right hand when he was crowned?

My wife was there and told me this. Ask yourself why this faithful and devoted woman would have left her son at this critical juncture in his life? I do not think I should look to the families of the chèr for some plot or other. I should look to those who seek to gain power and wealth for themselves by means of a young boy king. It is to their advantage that his mother disappear, certainly not to the people of this region. We are grape growers and makers of wine. Politics does not interest us, nor do we involve ourselves in the power struggles of the Seine valley."

Now the captain looked confused, but then he stubbornly said, "I must search your house and the chateau of every family who came to Chenonceaux yesterday. I should not be doing my duty otherwise."

"Suit yourself, Captain, but you will understand if I wish to rejoin my wife." He put down his goblet and with a smile turned, reentering his bedchamber. Closing the door behind him, he waited until he heard the door to the salon open and close. Then, looking out, he satisfied himself that the musketeer had left their apartments. He could see the questions in Autumn's eyes. He put his finger to his lips in a cautionary gesture. Then he climbed into bed with her and, enfolding her in his arms, kissed her a long, sweet kiss, one hand going to fondle her breast.

Autumn slapped the hand away. "I cannot!" she whispered at him. "Not while those men are in our house, Sebastian!"

Kissing her hand, he laughed, then nodded his assent.

In early January there came from Paris a king's messenger bearing a gift for the Marquis and Marquise d'Auriville. It was a large silver and gold gilt salt cellar engraved with both the king's crest and the crest of d'Auriville. With it came a small parchment with but three words scribbled upon it: *Our thanks. Louis.* By mid-February word had come that the king had welcomed Cardinal Mazarin in Poiters in late January. The cardinal had arrived at the head of an army of twenty-five hundred men, fifteen hundred of whom were foot and a thousand cavalry.

The cardinal immediately began to consolidate his power, acting in the king's best interest to jail his enemies, soothe egos, and strengthen France internally. Those who had fought Jules Mazarin so hard were finally forced to realize that he could not be beaten. He would do whatever was necessary to make Louis XIV a strong and good king. Any who attempted to stand in his way would be disposed of without hesitation.

Spring came, and the vineyards were green again. The summer passed, and with autumn came a bountiful harvest and a good vintage. When the next year came Autumn, to her delight, found she was with child. After an initial bout of sickness she began to bloom, spending the summer months in her gardens, sewing on tiny garments with her mother and the two *tantes* from Archambault. She laughed when her parent commented that she had become as swollen as her husband's grapes.

"I love the feel of new life within me, Mama," she said. "I am going to have lots and lots of children!"

On the second wedding anniversary of the Marquis and Marquise d'Auriville, September 30, 1653, Autumn was delivered in an exceedingly easy birth of a daughter.

"We'll have a boy next year," she told her delighted husband, who wasn't in the least bit disappointed to have fathered this dainty, dark-haired child. "We shall call her Madeline Marie."

"Why?" he asked, curious.

"Because the last two queens France gave Scotland were called Madeline and Marie. La petite Madeline was the king's daughter, but she died, unable to take our Scots' winters. Marie was Marie de Guise, the mother of our Queen Mary, mother of James Stuart. She was also for a time, France's queen. So I should like our daughter to be called Madeline Marie," Autumn finished.

"Mademoiselle Madeline d'Oleron," he said softly. "I like it."

The baby was baptized by Père Bernard, Madame de Belfort and Madame St. Omer standing as her godmothers. Autumn's choice of her daughter's godfather came as a surprise to everyone.

"I want Adali," she said firmly. "He is as good a Christian as any, and I have known him my whole life. Madeline could not have a better godfather."

And so the old gentleman stood proudly in the church at Chermont while Madeline was baptized. He prayed silently that he would live long enough to see this baby grown, but that, he knew, would be a miracle. Still, miracles did happen, although in this day and age they were rare.

Madeline's first birthday came, and she had grown into a plump baby with dark curls and smoky blue eyes. She walked, and was a most determined child. By her second birthday she was chattering and running. Both of her parents adored her, and everyone who knew her loved her, for Madeline was by nature a very sweet child, despite her resolute nature. It was true she wanted what she wanted when she wanted it, but Madeline never held a grudge, even when denied her heart's desire of the moment.

Autumn was once again with child. The baby was to be born in the spring. Several days after her daughter's birthday, a worker came running in from the vineyards, shouting for Madame la marquise. Behind him Lafite could see a party of workers carrying something, and as they grew closer his heart sank. His mistress ran from the house, and her sudden screams of grief broke his heart.

The vineyard workers carrying Sebastian d'Oleron upon a board passed him as they entered the house. White-faced, Autumn hurried along with them, her hand upon her husband's hand comforting him.

"Send for my mother," she cried to Lafite, "and for a doctor if there is one nearby. Upstairs," she told the workers, running ahead to show them.

They set the marquis on his bed. Lily and little Orane both burst into tears when they saw their master.

Autumn glared at them both. "Your weeping isn't going to help," she snapped at them. "Help me undress my husband. Marc, fetch your master's nightshirt from his valet." She bent over her husband. "There, *mon coeur*, it will be all right. Where does it hurt?" Weakly he pointed to his chest. Orane brought a small cup of wine, and Autumn helped her husband to sit enough to sip the liquid, which he did slowly.

Together the three women managed to get him out of his clothing and into his nightshirt, then beneath the coverlet.

Sebastian clutched Autumn's hand. "I . . . am . . . dying," he managed to say to her. The words surprised him even as he said them, but he knew they were true. "A . . . priest," he gasped to her.

"I'll go," Marc said quickly, before Autumn could either protest or give him the order. Marc didn't like to admit it, even to himself, but he knew his master was correct: He was dying. He ran from the room to seek out Lafite. Finding him, he said, "The marquis wants the priest. Where is he?"

"The church at Archambault," Lafite said.

The young courier ran to the stables and, taking a horse, rode off at a gallop toward Archambault. In the village church he found Père Hugo. "Our master, the Marquis d'Auriville, is dying, good Father. He begs you come to him at once. Take my horse. I must go and speak with the comte, and he will see me back." Then he ran from the church and up the hill to the chateau to find the Comte de Saville and his sisters. When he had told them what little he knew, the comte ordered a carriage for his siblings and then hurried off to the stables with Marc to fetch themselves horses. They rode with all haste back to Chermont.

"Is he still alive?" the comte demanded of Lafite as he and Marc entered the house. "Where is my niece?"

"He yet lives. The priest is with him, and madame," Lafite replied. "Madame la duchesse has been sent for, monseigneur."

"Do you know what happened?" the comte asked.

"The vineyard foreman said the marquis was in the fields with them as he so often is at the harvest. Suddenly he clutched at his left arm. A spasm crossed his features. He gave a great cry and then fell to the ground. He could not arise, and so they brought him home."

"Send Madame Jasmine upstairs as soon as she arrives," the comte ordered the majordomo.

In the darkened bedchamber, lit only by two candelabra, the Marquis d'Auriville lay quietly, Père Hugo by his side murmuring his prayers. Autumn sat on the other side of her husband, her face stony, her eyes anguished. The Comte de Saville could see his niece was struggling very hard not to break into tears. In her lap she held her two-year-old daughter. Madeline was strangely silent, as if she sensed that this was a most terrible and momentous occasion. The Comte de Saville put a comforting hand on his niece's shoulder.

Autumn looked up at him and smiled weakly. Then she shook her head. "I don't understand," she said softly. "This should not be happening, *Oncle*. How can this be?"

"I do not know, Autumn," he told her honestly, seating himself as he spoke in a chair that Lily pushed behind him.

They sat in silence as the marquis's breathing became more and more labored. Autumn was trembling visibly as she watched her husband's life fading before her very eyes. It was like a bad dream, and she kept pinching her arm in hopes that she would awaken. *They were so happy. They had Madeline, and had only just discovered that there would be another child in the late spring. He couldn't die! He couldn't! There was too much reason for him to live.* She started as she felt a cold hand take hers.

"*Ma chérie,*" he said. His voice was stronger than it had been.

Words failed her as she looked into his beloved face.

He smiled gently at her and squeezed her hand with what little strength he had left. "*Je t'aime, et notre* Madeline *aussi,*" he told her. "*Je t'aime.*" Then his eyes glazed over, and with a great sigh the life flew out of him.

Autumn's hand went to her mouth to stifle her cry of anguish. The priest stood and made the sign of the cross over the dead man, closing his eyes afterwards. Orane, with unusual foresight, took Madeline from her mother's lap and hurried from the bedchamber with the sleepy child. Only when the door had closed behind her did Autumn begin to weep with great, sobbing gulps of sorrow while Lily and the comte stood by, unable to help her.

"He died shriven and in God's good grace," Père Hugo said in an effort to comfort the grieving woman.

Autumn looked at the priest. "He died too young and suddenly, without warning. What kind of a God does that, *mon père?* Answer me that? What kind of a God takes a young man from his family without warning and in the prime of his life?"

"I cannot answer that, Madame la marquise, but I know that whatever God does has a reason, even if we do not see it or understand it," the priest replied.

"Tell that to my fatherless children," Autumn said bitterly.

"You will love again one day, Madame la marquise," the priest said.

"You dare say that to me *now? Get out! Get out!* I will never love again. Never!"

Part Three

MADAME LA MARQUISE
1656–1662

Chapter ❧ 13 ❧

"**Y**ou cannot hide yourself here forever," Jasmine said to her daughter. "Sebastian has been dead a year now. You must go home to chèrmont, Autumn. Madeline should be raised in her own home, not her grandmother's house."

"If I were dead, would you not raise her, Mama?" the grieving widow said to her parent.

"Yes, I would, but at Chermont, not Belle Fleurs," Jasmine replied firmly.

"You could not live at Glenkirk after Papa died," Autumn returned.

"I had lived at Glenkirk for over thirty years, Autumn. All my Leslie children but you were born there. But if my children had been young when your father died, I should have remained there. They were Leslies, and entitled to be raised on their own lands. Sebastian's family have lived at Chermont for more centuries than I can count. Madeline is the last of them. Should she not be raised on her own lands too?"

"I can still see them bringing him home from the vineyards on that board. I see him lying in our bed gasping with every breath. *I see him dying there.*" She began to weep as she had almost every day since her husband had expired.

Jesu! Jasmine thought irritably. *She is making a vocation out of her mourning. I did not think Autumn so fragile, but between Jemmie's death, Sebastian's death, and the loss of her baby, it has been too much for her. Was I this heartbroken when Jamal died, and I lost our child? I cannot remember, it has been so long. But she will weep herself into the grave if I do not do something about it.* Jasmine took a deep breath, then said, "You are going back to Chermont tomorrow, Autumn. If your bedchamber distresses you, then close it up and choose another chamber. God only knows Chermont has enough of them. I will go with you, and remain a time until you have acclimated yourself once more."

"*I cannot!*" Autumn wailed.

"God's boots, I have listened to you whine and moan for over a year now! I will have no more of it, *ma fille!* Do you think your tears will change anything? Do you think they will bring Sebastian back to you? Do you think that looking down from heaven he is happy with your behavior, and how you have ignored his daughter in your self-pitying humor? You are not the first young woman to lose a husband after so short a time, nor are you the first woman to lose an expected child. My grandmother mourned six husbands, yet after each loss she survived to live and love again. So will you, Autumn. I am not asking that you forget Sebastian or the happiness you had with him, but it is over. You must get on with your life!"

"How can you possibly understand?" Autumn said tragically.

Jasmine slapped her daughter hard. "How dare you!" she cried.

Stunned, Autumn's hand went to her cheek. "*Mama!*" she said.

"Do you think my life began with your father?" Jasmine demanded. "I lost two husbands to murder before I married James Leslie. I lost a child in the womb, and another just when she had learned to say, '*Mama.*' That baby had a smile so sweet it broke the heart each time she exhibited it. You were born to me when I believed I was past having babies. You have been a joy to me, and to your father, may God assoil his good soul; but because your siblings were grown you have been raised as a single child might have been. You have known nothing of real sorrow until now. This is real life, Autumn, not some romantic fairy tale. You must take the bitter with the sweet. If you cannot, then perhaps it is better that you pine away and orphan your daughter entirely."

"Mama!" Autumn was shocked by her mother's harsh words.

"Do not *mama* me, *ma fille*. Go and tell Lily, Orane, and Marie to start packing. We leave on the morrow."

Looking at her mother's face, Autumn realized that there was no argument she could make that would change Jasmine's mind. She curtsied to her parent and departed the room.

"About time you told her the truth of the matter," the duchess's old serving woman, Toramalli, said pithily. "We have all spoiled her rotten in our delight at having another bairn again, my lady. These young women today are nothing like we were in our youth. They seem to lack the strength of character we had."

Jasmine laughed. "She is young yet. I think she will be all right if we stop cossetting her as we always have done. Now, we must pack if we are to go to Chermont with Autumn. Rohana will come with me. You, Toramalli, and the others can remain behind. There is no necessity for us all to be uprooted, and I intend staying less than a month. Just long enough to get her settled once again."

"You'll not travel even so short a distance without Red Hugh," Toramalli said firmly. "Two women all alone in a chateau without realiable protection? The master wouldn't have it, and neither will we, my princess. I'll not trust these Frenchies to look after your safety."

"Will there ever come a time when you do not consider my well-being, dearest Toramalli?" Jasmine said with a smile.

"We were born to serve you, my lady," Toramalli said, "and so we will, my sister, Adali, and I, until the day we die."

The servants at Chermont almost wept with joy as they welcomed Autumn and little Madeline back. It was seeing them that made Autumn realize how selfish she had been in her grief. Lafite and the others had known Sebastian since he was born. They surely had felt his loss almost as deeply as she had, and then she had taken the very future of Chermont, Sebastian's daughter, away from them, leaving them doubly bereft. Jasmine saw the change in her daughter at once and was greatly relieved.

They were just settled when Lafite came to say that Michel Dupont, the master of the vineyard, wished to speak with her.

"I know nothing of the vineyards," Autumn voiced the thought aloud.

"Michel is a good man and can be trusted," Lafite said boldly. "If you wish to learn, he will be pleased to teach Madame la marquise. And certainly la petite mademoiselle must learn her heritage. The Duponts have been at Chermont for over a thousand years, madame."

"He may enter," Autumn said.

Michel Dupont was a tall man with a robust build. His face was tanned and lined, attesting to his many hours out in the sunshine. His nut-brown hair was peppered with silver, and the blue eyes that briefly met hers were kind. He bowed, cap in hand, and waited for Autumn to give him permission to speak.

"Is the harvest going well, Michel Dupont?" she said, attempting a show of interest.

"Very well, Madame la marquise," he answered with a small smile.

"The vintage will be good?"

"It will be very good," came the reply.

There was a long silence. Then Autumn said, "I know nothing of the vineyards, but I know I must learn, and when she is old enough, so must mademoiselle. Will you teach us, Michel Dupont?"

"Gladly, Madame la marquise," he said with another small smile.

"Why did you wish to see me?" she inquired.

"The harvest is bounteous, Madame la marquise. We have more grapes than we can use this year. Archambault wishes to purchase what we cannot use. I would have your permission before I agree."

"Our winery is small, then?" Autumn's interest was now engaged.

Michel Dupont nodded. "We often cannot use all we grow," he admitted to her. "Monsieur le marquis was thinking of enlarging the winery, but then . . ." He broke off suddenly, looking down at his well-worn boots as he attempted to avoid the unpleasant subject of his master's demise.

"Are there plans?" Autumn asked him softly.

"*Oui*, Madame la marquise, there are."

"If my husband thought it advisable to have a bigger winery, then we must have one," Autumn said slowly. "Sell what we cannot use to my cousins at Archambault. Then we must begin digging the foundation for the new winery before the frost hardens the ground. That way the men can work during the winter months, and our winery will be ready for next year's crop. If we do not have enough laborers, then we shall hire more. There must be men who will be glad of winter employment hereabouts. I do not know a great deal about vineyards, Michel Dupont, but I do know about business and its affairs. We must expand to be profitable."

A delighted grin split the vineyard master's face. He bowed to Autumn. "It shall be as Madame la marquise orders. I shall keep you fully informed."

"Then, if there is nothing more, Michel Dupont, you may go," Autumn said, smoothing the deep violet silk of her gown, well pleased with herself. She felt she had done well.

"One thing, a small thing, Madame la marquise. Would you not ride through the vineyards before the harvest is in with la petite mademoiselle upon your saddle? The people would be very encouraged," he finished meaningfully. "They have mourned too, if I dare to say it."

Tears sprang to her eyes. *God*, Autumn thought, *I really have been selfish*. She blinked the tears back, but one escaped, pearling down her cheek so that she brushed it quickly away. "I will come tomorrow, Michel Dupont," she replied to his humble request.

He bowed again. *"Merci,* Madame la marquise," he said, and backed from the room.

Autumn rose and went to the windows. The vineyards were a tired yellow-green in the hazy early October sunshine. *Oh, Sebastian,* she thought to herself. *How I loved you, but Mama is right. You are gone from me, and nothing is going to bring you back. I have to get on with my life, not just for my sake, but for Madeline's as well.* She closed her eyes for a brief moment and felt the tears pricking at them again. Opening them she let the salty drops roll down her cheeks. *Adieu, mon coeur. The time has come to let you go. Adieu!* Then she turned away from the windows. Strangely, her heart felt lighter.

Jasmine noticed the change in her daughter almost immediately. She said nothing. The plans were found for the new winery, and the preparations began to build the addition. Autumn had been back at Chermont a week when a visitor arrived one morning. It was her old suitor, the Comte de Montroi. Amusing as ever, his blue eyes twinkling, he greeted Autumn with a smile and a jest, and almost immediately Autumn was laughing.

"Guy Claude, you have not changed, I see," she said with a small chuckle. "What brings you to Chermont?"

"I am the bearer of an invitation, *ma belle,*" he replied. "The king has just arrived at Chambord to hunt, and he wishes you to join him. *Chérie*, how did you manage to catch the eye of the monarch from this backwater?" The comte accepted a silver goblet of wine that a servant offered.

"I cannot imagine I have caught his eye," Autumn said. "I met him several years ago. He was a child, but very bold."

"He is still bold where the ladies are concerned," the comte told her, "but he is no longer a child. He is eighteen, and a man full grown. The women throw themselves at him. The queen mother labors night and day with the cardinal to marry him off. Not that that will keep his eye from roving, *ma chère* Autumn. He has the blood of Henri the Fourth and Françoise the First in him. It is hot blood." He sipped his wine. "Excellent vintage," he pronounced. "Is it yours or Archambault's?"

"Ours," she said.

"I was sorry to hear of your loss," he said to her.

"We have survived," she responded dryly.

"When shall I tell the king to expect you?" the comte asked.

"Say to His Majesty that I would be excused as I yet mourn my husband. I thank him for his kind invitation and for remembering me, but I should be poor company."

The comte's blue eyes grew troubled. "I do not think you should refuse the king, Autumn," he said to her.

"I do not think the king should invade my mourning," she replied.

"The marquis has been dead a year now, hasn't he?" the comte responded. "I believe a year is a respectable time of mourning for one's husband. The king will certainly think so, Autumn."

"The king may think what he wants. I will not go to Chambord, Guy Claude. It is unthinkable!"

"I shall deliver your message, *chérie,*" the Comte de Montroi said reluctantly. "The king will not be happy, however."

"I cannot imagine the refusal of a country widow should matter much to him," Autumn said with a laugh. "His invitation was a polite one and nothing more. I'm certain such invitations have gone to others in the region. My absence will hardly be noted or spoken about."

The Comte de Montroi departed, troubled. Louis might only have met Autumn once, but she had obviously made a deep impression upon him. All he had spoken about on their journey from Paris was the beautiful widow of Chermont. He remembered every nuance of her features. Her odd eyes. The scent she wore, which the king recalled as being fresh and wholesome. Louis, the comte realized, wanted more than to render his personal condolences to Madame la marquise. He wanted Autumn in his bed, and she, innocent as she remained, hadn't the faintest idea with regard to the king's intentions. He already knew what the king's reaction to her refusal would be. Louis would not be pleased at all.

And he was not. "She said she would not come?" the king asked, quite astonished. Women did not refuse King Louis.

"She thanks Your Majesty but says she is still in mourning for her husband. She was surprised you remembered her," the comte said.

"How does she look, Guy Claude?" the king demanded.

"More beautiful, if that is possible, sire," the comte told the monarch honestly. "Her skin is like white silk, and those gemstone eyes are as fascinating as ever."

"What was she wearing?" came the query.

"Her gown was of midnight blue silk. It was plain, without any ornamentation, however," the comte recounted. "Her hair is still long, and she wears it in a chignon as she ever did."

Louis sighed deeply. "I can imagine I still smell her scent," he said softly. "Honeysuckle and woodbine. So English. No Frenchwoman would wear something so simple, yet the memory of it haunts me."

"I am sorry, Your Majesty," the comte said.

"Do not be. We will ride to Chermont tomorrow and pursuade the reluctant widow that she cannot refuse her king when he calls," Louis said with a smile. "I want her, Montroi, and I shall have her. Did you not court her once? Did you kiss her? Fondle her pretty breasts?"

"Alas, Your Majesty, Autumn never took my suit seriously, and I never took liberties with her. It would have been unthinkable. She was a virgin of good reputation and good family. Besides, no one had a chance with her once her eye lit on Sebastian d'Oleron," the comte explained. Best the king not consider him even a distant rival, Guy Claude thought wisely to himself. "Autumn and I became friends only. She says I make her laugh. No woman ever gravely considers a man who makes her laugh, I believe," he concluded with an impudent grin.

The king chuckled. "Perhaps, but perhaps not, Montroi," he said thoughtfully. "You will come with me tomorrow." It was an order, not a question, and the Comte de Montroi bowed servilely in agreement.

"As Your Majesty wishes," he said.

"We shall have to teach Madame la marquise the same nature of obedience as you exhibit, my dear comte," the king replied. Then his brown eyes grew thoughtful. "Is she fire or ice?" he wondered aloud. "I attempted to seduce her just before I became king in fact. She set me down quite firmly. I have never been able to forget that fire, and yet now she is so cold."

"Her heart is broken, Your Majesty," the comte offered.

"Then I shall have to mend it," Louis said with a small smile.

"Knowing women as I do, Your Majesty," the comte said, "and I base my knowledge upon my years, of course, I think Autumn will resist you and be angry that you have approached her."

"I shall win her over, Montroi. I shall coax those fires she has banked so neatly into a conflagration of passion," the king said confidently. "Madame la marquise shall be mine!"

Guy Claude d'Auray battled with his conscience over the king's words. Should he send a message to Autumn warning her of the visitor she would have the following day? In the end he decided that discretion was advised. He had become an intimate of the young king, and Louis trusted him. It didn't matter whether Autumn was advised of the king's coming or not. What Louis wanted he would have. Autumn might dispute the king's lust, but in the end she would yield to it, and she would probably enjoy it. Louis, at eighteen, already had a reputation as a great lover.

They left at first light for Chermont, several hours' ride across the countryside from Chambord. The day was sunny and there was only the slightest breeze. In the vineyards through which they passed the grapes were being harvested, and the air was redolent with their lush fragrance. Louis was in a particulary good mood as he anticipated meeting again with Autumn. She might have changed little, but he had changed a great deal. Madame la marquise was in for a great surprise.

"*The king?*" Autumn jumped to her feet, growing pale. She swayed and grasped the back of the settee to keep from falling. "Mama?"

"Show His Majesty in, Lafite," Jasmine said calmly.

"At once, Madame la duchese," the majordomo said, and hurried from the salon.

Autumn's hand went automatically to her hair to smooth it. She shook her skirts to remove any unseemly folds they might have. "What can this mean, Mama?" she whispered.

"I think you know what it means," Jasmine replied. "Keep your temper, *ma fille*. Remember, this young man is the king."

The salon's door opened and Louis entered. Autumn's eyes widened with surprise. Then she curtsied deeply, holding her position until the king raised her up. "Welcome to Chermont, Your Majesty," she said, her voice breathless with her nervousness.

"*Merci*, Madame la marquise," Louis replied. He had not released her hand. Then he turned to the comte. "You did not lie, Montroi. Madame la marquise is as beautiful as ever; more so, I think." He tucked Autumn's hand into his arm and then smiled at Jasmine. "I can easily see, Madame la duchese, where your daughter gets such loveliness."

"I thank Your Majesty for his gallant speech," Jasmine replied, curtsying in return. "My daughter forgets her manners, sire. Please, will you have some wine?" She smiled and nodded to the attending footman.

The king drew Autumn over to the settee and sat, drawing her down with him to sit by his side. He accepted a goblet, but before she might take one, Louis put his goblet to Autumn's lips, encouraging her to sip. Then, after she had, he drank himself. He behaved as if no one else was in the salon. "It pleases me to see you again, *ma bijou*," he told her in a soft, caressing voice.

The Comte de Montroi took the Duchess of Glenkirk's arm and quickly escorted her from the salon, signaling the footman to follow.

Autumn heard the doors click shut and, panic-stricken, realized her mother and the others were gone. She attempted to rise from her place at the king's side, but he would not permit it.

"Why are you afraid of me?" Louis demanded. "I only want to love you, *ma bijou*."

"How dare you speak to me in such a manner?" Autumn said, but the king put two fingers over her lips to still her protests.

"I am your king, madame. You owe me perfect obedience," he told her. Then his knuckles grazed her cheek. "Montroi is right. You have skin like white silk." He tipped her chin up with his hand and brushed her lips very lightly.

Autumn recoiled, her eyes widening with her surprise. "You were a bold boy," she said. "I see little has changed."

"Except now," he replied, "I am a man full grown, madame. I wanted you as a boy, and now I am a man, nothing has changed. I yet desire you, *ma bijou*."

"I am not your jewel," Autumn snapped.

Louis laughed. "Do you presume to resist your king, madame? I have always enjoyed a challenge far more than an easy conquest."

" 'Tis you who presume," Autumn responded angrily. "I am a respectable widow, Your Majesty. I am not some Paris whore you may buy with a few coins or paste jewels! I am not some alleged lady of the court who seeks to gain your favor! I refused your invitation. Now you dare to come into my home and solicit me."

"You are plainspoken, Madame la marquise. I shall be equally plainspoken. I am the king. You and your daughter are my subjects. You owe me your obedience, and I will have it. Do you understand me, Madame la marquise? You will yield yourself to my will!"

Autumn burst into tears, and the king knew he had won. A woman without a good defense always resorted to tears. He put his arms about her and caressed her dark head. "There, *ma bijou*, I will not be unkind. I adore you. You have been in my thoughts since that afternoon at Chenonceaux those five years back. I have longed to kiss your lips and cuddle your delicious form against my body. I have dreamed many a night of having you beneath me, of entering your body slowly, slowly, of making you weep with our combined pleasure. Do not resist me, Autumn. Let me love you the way you were meant to be loved."

"How can you make me betray my husband?" Autumn sobbed.

"You cannot betray a dead man, *ma bijou*," he murmured softly against the side of her head, kissing her ear tenderly. His tongue began to gently explore the whorl of that ear, and she shuddered. "You are not a nun," the king said softly. His hand began to fondle her breasts through the silk of her gown.

"Please, no!" Autumn gasped.

In response, he caught her chin between his thumb and his forefinger and kissed her. His fleshy mouth pressed passionately upon hers, coaxing from her, to her great astonishment, a reply. Her lips softened, yielded, parted to exchange breaths with the king. His tongue found hers, and she shuddered again as the two digits intertwined and brushed against one another alluringly. Autumn halfswooned, falling back against the king's velvet-clad arm with a soft cry.

Louis groaned aloud. Time, it would seem, had not dimmed his great desire for this beautiful woman. He could feel his manhood, tight and hard, pressing against the fabric of his breeches with an urgency he could barely contain. He could have taken her then and there. She would have been powerless to prevent him from doing so, but he did not. He had planned his seduction of her ever since he had learned of the untimely death of Sebastian d'Oleron. When he first possessed Autumn it would be amid flowers and candlelight. He would lay her back against the pillows of his bed and caress her until she begged for his favor. He would not lift her skirts here in her salon and take her on an ancient, creaking settee.

Leaning forward, he tenderly kissed her lips again. Then her closed eyelids, saying as he did, "It will be all right, *ma bijou*. You shall come back to Chambord with me, and we shall enjoy a sweet idyll, you and I. Open your eyes now, *chérie*."

Autumn obeyed, and Louis was startled as always by the emerald and turquoise of her two eyes. Her demeanor was serious. "You would make me your whore, Your Majesty. Can I say nothing that will dissuade you from this course, sire? And when you have satisfied your passion for me, then what? Who will have me to wife? If indeed I ever wanted to wed again, which I do not."

"There is no shame, *ma bijou*, in being a king's mistress," Louis said in matter-of-fact tones. "The women who are, are usually the most desirable and greatly sought after as wives, particularly if they have been wise and kept their king's friendship after their mutual passions waned, Autumn."

"You comfort me," she replied dryly, sitting up, and he laughed.

"We shall ride back to Chambord this very afternoon," Louis said decisively.

"No," she replied. "I shall come tomorrow, properly, with my carriage and my maids and a wardrobe. Who is with you?"

"But a few gentlemen friends," he answered.

"There are no other women?" She was surprised.

"We have come to hunt, *ma bijou*." he said.

Autumn shook her head. "And now that you have captured your prey, sire, she will sit at your highboard and hold court over your gentlemen, I think. You are fortunate I am used to my father's hall, where only my mother and I held sway." Then, suddenly, she said, "Mama must come with me to give the appearance of propriety, Your Majesty. If you would take me to your bed, at least allow me the illusion of decorum and dignity. People may think what they choose, but if Mama is with us, they cannot say for certain that I have entered your bed."

"This is important to you, *ma bijou?*" he asked.

"*Oui*, Your Majesty, it is," she replied quietly.

"Then your mama shall come to Chambord," he decided. "Now, give me a kiss to thank me, mouth open, so I may salute your naughty little tongue with my own. Oh, the things I shall teach you, *ma bijou!* Things your good husband, I am certain, did not think proper knowledge for a respectable French wife. You will be an excellent student, I have not a doubt. You are filled with fire, Autumn. I shall very much enjoy warming myself by that fire." They kissed, and then the king leapt up with a smile. "I have changed, haven't I?" he said.

"You were still a boy the last time I saw you," Autumn replied. "Aye, you have changed, Your Majesty. You are a handsome man now, but I am still seven years your senior."

"Remember the story I told you of Diane de Poitiers, who first possessed Chenonceaux?" he demanded.

Now it was Autumn who smiled. "*Oui*, Your Majesty, I remember," she responded. "So, I am to be your Diane, eh?"

"You will not be unhappy, *ma bijou*," he promised her. Then he swept her a graceful bow and left the room.

Autumn sighed, shaking her head in amazement at what the past minutes had wrought. Louis had indeed changed. He was a man of medium height and build. His long hair, which he wore clubbed back, was jet black. His eyes were a warm amber brown. He had a face that was more long than round, and an aquiline nose, beneath which lay his lush mouth. He was so completely different than Sebastian had been. The door to the salon opened and her mother reentered.

"What has happened?" Jasmine demanded.

"Are they gone?" Autumn countered.

"Aye, the king smiling broadly as he went." She sat down and patted the settee by her side. "Tell me."

"He wants me for his mistress," Autumn said frankly. "I have said we will come to Chambord, but what am I to do, Mama?"

"You have no choice, *ma fille*," Jasmine replied. "If you claim the citizenship of your native land, Autumn, then you reside in France at the king's pleasure. If you have become French by virtue of your marriage to Sebastian, then you must obey your king."

Autumn bit her lip. "We could go to . . ."

"We cannot go home until Cromwell's forces are driven out and King Charles restored to his throne," Jasmine said quietly. "We could go to Holland or to Rome, I suppose, but what of Madeline? She is the heiress of Chermont. Will you risk her legacy over this matter? You are no virgin protecting your maidenhead, *ma fille*. You are a woman, and sometimes we women make choices we would prefer not to make."

"Was that how it was with you and Prince Henry, Mama?" Autumn asked astutely.

Jasmine nodded. "While I found him attractive and very exciting," she said, "I was outraged by the knowledge of what he wanted from me. I can still remember my stepfather, the Earl of BrocCairn, saying to my mother that a handsome, charming young man wished to make love to me, and I would have to yield myself to the inevitable. He scolded me quite roundly for my prudishness, for as he wisely pointed out, I was not being asked to give up my life or my wealth. Still, I would have run back to Cadby but that Alex locked me in my chamber," Jasmine chuckled with the remembrance. "Oh, I was angry with him. I threw a vase of flowers—roses I think—at him in my fury. Then Prince Henry came, and before I knew it I was won over by his charm. Your brother, Charlie, has that same Stuart charm," Jasmine concluded with a smile.

"Did you love him, Mama?" Autumn asked.

"Yes, but I never told him. You see, *ma fille*, even though I was the daughter of a great monarch, my birth was deemed irregular by English standards, although it was certainly not in India. Henry was in love with me, but he would never be allowed to marry me. If I had admitted my love to him, he would have never married a proper princess, but in the end it didn't matter. He died suddenly shortly after Charlie was born, and his little brother became England's next king. A most unfortunate king. King Louis has been more forward than my prince was so long ago, but he is a king, Autumn. This position you find yourself in is not of your making, but it is up to you how you will solve the problem."

"What would you do, Mama, if you were in my place?" Autumn asked her mother seriously. "Would you yield yourself to this man?"

"Yes," Jasmine replied as seriously. "It is but a temporary situation, Autumn. The queen and the cardinal seek to marry Louis off and gain legitimate heirs for France as soon as possible. There are already two candidates for the king's hand: the Spanish princess, Maria-Theresa, and the Savoyard princess, Marguerite. Any mistress the king may have when he marries will disappear from his life. No amour should embarrass his queen, whoever she is. My cousins also tell me that the cardinal's niece, Marie Mancini, has also caught the king's eye in Paris. This king will not enslave you, Autumn; but he will provide you with a momentary and delightful diversion. You have never known any man but Sebastian, may God assoil his good soul. You now have the opportunity to see what another man is like before you fall in love and remarry one day, which you will, *ma fille*, no matter what you may think now. You will love again," her mother concluded.

"Mama, I am surprised at you," Autumn said. "I should have never thought to hear such advice coming from your lips."

Jasmine laughed heartily. "Why is it," she said, "that all children believe their parents have had no life before their birth? I was forty-one when you were born, Autumn. I had lived a long and adventurous life even before you were a glint in my eye. Life, since your birth, I will admit, has been quiet, even staid, but these past years cannot take away from who I am, and I am who I am because of the life I lived before you were born. All you have ever known is that you were born at Maguire's Ford in Ulster. Were you aware that you came early into life? That several hours before your birth I stood off a mob of angry men bent on murder and destruction?"

"You never told me this," Autumn said, surprised by the revelation.

"It wasn't necessary that you know," her mother replied. "I tell you now because I want you to understand that life is not always predictable, Autumn. It twists and turns like any road. Until now you have walked a fairly straight path, *ma fille*. King Louis is a steep curve that you must negotiate carefully, but you are my daughter, and I know you will do well." Jasmine leaned forward and kissed Autumn's cheek. "And when your time with Louis is over, *ma fille*, bow gracefully out while keeping the king's friendship. That is the clever and wise thing to do."

The young woman sighed. "I will tell Lily and Orane to pack for our visit to Chambord, Mama," she said, resigned. "Madeline will be safe here at Chermont for these few days."

"She will," Jasmine agreed, knowing, but not saying aloud, that it was unlikely her daughter would return for less than several weeks if the king was pleased. This was something Autumn would come to face herself after she had been with Louis. Ah, the older woman thought, to be young again, and have a virile lover! Then she smiled. How Jemmie would laugh at her thoughts. But perhaps not. James Leslie's notions of honor were strongly fixed. They had gotten him killed. Their daughter was very much like her father, but she must see that she became more flexible like herself, Jasmine considered. Especially if she was to survive in this man's world.

Before they departed the following morning, they were visited by Madame de Belfort and Madame St. Omer. Both Jasmine and Autumn were surprised to see the two ladies, but the forthright Madame St. Omer spoke up, dispelling their curiosity.

"We have heard that the king was here yesterday, *mes cousines*. What is it all about? Did he come to pay his condolences? How kind of him. Queen Anne and the cardinal raised a good man."

Autumn began to laugh. "How do the servants do it?" she asked aloud. "I know there is no keeping secrets from them, but how did the news travel from Chermont to Archambault so quickly, and in time for you to arrive here so early in the morning, *tantes?*"

Her query gave Madame St. Omer pause; but then, shaking her head, she said, "I have no idea, *ma petite*. All I can tell you is that last evening I learned of the king's visit from my own maidservant. It is true, isn't it?" Her eyes shifted to the trunks in the foyer. "Where are you going?" she demanded to know.

"The king has invited Autumn and me to join him at Chambord," Jasmine replied.

"*Mon Dieu!*" Madame de Belfort exclaimed, her blue eyes wide with surprise, and then sudden understanding.

"As long as Jasmine is there, there can be speculation, but no one can say for certain what is going on," Madame St. Omer said thoughtfully. "You will, of course, deny any and everything, *ma petite,*" she advised her niece. "Will you return to Paris with him?"

"Why would I go to Paris?" Autumn asked.

"If you are to become the king's mistress . . ." her aunt began.

"The king has offered me nothing more than a 'sweet idyll.'" Autumn responded, "and I want nothing more than that, *tantes*. Moreover, I most certainly do not want to go to Paris. My home is here, and my place is with my daughter. There will be nothing more."

"We shall see," Madame St. Omer said. "The rumor is that he is a splendid lover, *ma petite*. I shall want a full report when you return from Chambord, eh?" she chuckled.

"Oh, sister, how can you be so indelicate?" Madame de Belfort twittered, her cheeks red with embarrassment over her elder's frankness.

"Well, sister, don't you want to know if the rumors are true?" Madame St. Omer said bluntly.

"If the king becomes my lover, Aunt, I can hardly fault his prowess, can I?" Autumn said with a small smile.

"Not publicly," her aunt agreed, "but privately I shall expect to know *everything, ma petite!*"

Autumn and her mother bid the aunts *adieu* and departed for the journey to Chambord, which would take them most of the day. Chambord, Autumn had been told, was the royal hunting lodge, and while Louis used it each fall, it had been given by his father Louis XIII to the current Louis's uncle, Gaston d'Orleans, who would not be in residence now. The king, while polite to his uncle, would never forget how that relation had made his childhood difficult and schemed to overthrow his mother's authority, and especially how he had managed to have Cardinal Mazarin exiled for a time, endangering them all.

Late in the afternoon, the marquise's carriage approached the chateau. Autumn and her mother could only gape with amazement at the sight before their eyes, for the king's hunting lodge of Chambord was the largest and most lavish chateau in the whole of the Loire Valley. The building and its great forest were girded by over twenty miles of perimeter walls. The great roof of the chateau, which seemed to stretch forever, was filled from one end to the other with turrets and dormers, windows and spires, lanterns, balconies, and chimneys.

"It is almost oriental in appearance," Jasmine noted. "I am reminded of the palaces of my youth."

"It is too big," Autumn pronounced. "We shall never find our way about it. I thought Chenonceaux was large, but this chateau is huge. I am already sorry that I agreed to come."

"There was no choice," her mother reminded her.

Autumn just stared ahead at the great white stone building with its blue slate roof. There were four towers at each edge of the chateau, and at its midsection she could see more towers rising. She sighed and shook her head. To go to court as an observer was one thing, but to be part and parcel of such an elite grouping was another. And who would be there? There were no women, the king had told her. What would that make her appear to be? Her reputation was going to be in tatters by the time all of this was over and done with, despite her mother's presence. And what if Louis did want her to go to Paris? She would not go. She simply would not go!

The moat surrounding Chambord had been diverted from a nearby stream. The carriage crossed over it and rumbled onward, finally stopping at the main entrance of the chateau. Immediately liveried servants came running to open the coach's door, lower the steps, and help the two women out. A more senior member of their number stepped forward and bowed very politely to them.

"Madame la marquise, Madame la duchese, the king bids you welcome to Chambord. If you will follow me, I will escort you to your apartments. His Majesty is still out hunting but should return quite soon." He bowed again and, turning, walked quickly back into the chateau.

They followed even as Lily, Orane, and Rohana scrambled from the carriage, following their mistresses, as behind them the footmen unloaded the luggage from the coach and then led the vehicle away to the stables.

Autumn tried hard not to goggle at the magnificence of her surroundings, but it wasn't easy. The upper servant led them through the foyer and up a flight of wide marble stairs into the central keep of the building and down a corridor. Before them was an incredible staircase with twin helical flights that made it impossible for those ascending to see those descending. "*Mon Dieu!*" the half-whispered words escaped her before she could restrain them.

"It is amazing, isn't it?" the servant said quietly. "All who first come to Chambord are astounded by it. Ah, here we are."

He turned and gave them a small smile. "You will both be staying in the king's apartments. You, Madame la marquise, here." He flung open a door. "And you, Madame la duchese, but a little ways down the corridor, here. The trunks will be brought up, and your serving women may share the cabinet next to your chambers, mesdames. You will find chateau serving women at your command, and a footman will come to escort you to the evening meal. I shall tell the king when he returns of your arrival." He bowed again most politely.

"I will want a bath," Autumn suddenly found her voice.

"I will see to it, Madame la marquise," he told her and then, turning, he was swiftly gone.

"I have not seen such grandeur since my father's palaces," Jasmine said. "It is all quite overwhelming, but exquisite."

"It is too much," Autumn said to her mother.

"Ah, my little Scots daughter, who thought nothing was finer than Glenkirk and Queen's Malvern," Jasmine teased. "These French kings have a great flair for style. I think it comes from the Italian blood in them."

"Where do you think the king's bedchamber is?" Autumn wondered.

"Quite near to yours, I suspect," her mother said. "He will certainly want to come and go without being observed by anyone, *ma fille.*"

"Oh, Mama, I am afraid," Autumn admitted suddenly.

Jasmine shrugged. "He is only a man, *ma petite*. There is no mystery, and you are no virgin."

"But I have never known any man but my husband!" Autumn was pale.

"Sebastian is dead, and now you will know another man," her mother replied in practical tones. "Do not be a fool, *chérie*. Since you must do this, do it with goodwill and endear yourself to the king. It will be the better for you, for Madeline, and for Chermont when he finally tires of you and you are no longer in his life."

"I wonder if I shall ever be as sanguine as you, Mama," Autumn said.

The older woman laughed. "Perhaps one day, *ma fille*," Jasmine replied.

Chapter

14

Autumn and her mother were escorted to the king's *salle à manger* by a liveried footman. Within the dining room were eight gentlemen. Louis came forward and kissed the ladies' hands, introducing them immediately afterwards to the others in the room. None were noblemen of particularly high rank, which Autumn found interesting. As their manner was informal, the beautiful marquise assumed the king preferred it that way. Her mother was seated at the foot of the dining table, the king leading Jasmine there personally, while the Comte de Montroi placed Autumn on the king's right at the table's head.

As the servants began serving their first course, the king took Autumn's hand in his and kissed it once again, this time turning it over and embracing the palm. She flushed prettily, surprised at his public action, pulling the hand from his light grip.

"Sire," she chided him softly. "You are not being very discreet."

"How can I be when all I want to do is kiss your pretty lips?" Louis replied, his brown eyes twinkling.

Autumn laughed and shook her head at him. "Eat your soup, monseigneur," she advised, and dipped her own spoon into her bowl, sipping delicately, her gaze modestly lowered.

The king chuckled. "You make it most difficult for me, *ma bijou*, but later tonight I shall make it most difficult for you."

Again Autumn's cheeks colored, but then she boldly looked up at the king and responded. "Perhaps, sire, I shall make it quite arduous for you in return." Then she was shocked at her own words, which seemed challenging in her own ears, but she had somehow sensed that she must not allow herself to be this man's victim. If he would have her in his bed, then they would play the game as equals. *Where on earth had that idea come from?* she wondered to herself. She almost sounded like her own mother.

But Louis smiled, not in the least offended by her speech, turning his attention to his meal now.

Autumn heaved a silent sigh of relief, but her appetite was scant despite the delicious dishes offered by the well-trained servants. Looking about her, she was enchanted by the dining room. It was beautiful, with much gilt, exquisite carvings, and wood panels covered in silk. There was a huge marble fireplace flanked by lifesize knights in full armour, their swords before them, pointed down. The heavy bronze andirons in the fireplace were large and held enormous logs that crackled merrily as they burned. The shorter walls were hung with large woven silk tapestries, the longer walls with great paintings. The floors were black-and-white marble, but beneath the sizable oak dining table was a beautiful Turkey carpet.

Autumn remarked on it, and immediately the king said, "One day we shall make such exquisite carpets here in France, and we shall make silk as well. I do not wish France to be overly dependent upon foreigners for rare and unique things. We shall make our own porcelain too. I vow it, *chérie!* When I complete my palace at Versailles it shall be filled with all manner of wonderful things, and many of them will have been made here in France!"

"Then you have begun your new palace," she replied.

"Ah, yes," he said. "You will come and see it one day." It was a statement, not a request.

The evening ended early for, as the king announced, they would hunt at dawn. The king's companions looked archly at one another, all thinking their master was far more interested in the hunt he would conduct that night than the one scheduled for the dawn.

"Not that I blame him," the sieur de Belleville said to his companions. "What a rare beauty. Such skin! And those bewitching eyes. One blue and one green." He sighed. "Why is it that kings always have nothing but the best?"

"You defame Madame la marquise," Montroi said quickly. "If you do not cease, I shall be obliged, law or no law, to challenge you, de Belleville." Because of the affection in which he held Autumn, Guy Claude felt obliged to defend her honor. She was not some loose woman of the court.

"Come now, *mon ami,*" de Belleville reasoned, "we all know why Madame la marquise is here at Chambord, though how the king ferreted out such a beauty in the midst of the wilds is beyond my ken."

"Having lived most of your life in Normandy," Montroi replied, "you cannot know it, but five years ago, madame and her deceased husband did the king and his mother a great service. As you are aware, the king never forgets a kindness."

"Or a great beauty," Baron Chaizefleurs chortled knowingly.

"For God's sake, monsieurs, her mother chaperones her!" Montroi said angrily.

"I think, Montroi, that you are still in love with her," de Belleville insinuated slyly.

"I was never in love with her," Guy Claude said bluntly.

"But you courted her!"

The Comte de Montroi laughed. "Come now, de Belleville, do not be so naive. Who would not, given the opportunity, have courted her? She is beautiful. She is wealthy. She was a virgin of impeccable lineage. I would have been a fool not to have tried for such a prize. I am not in love with her now, or ever, but we are friends, and I will not have her reputation so quickly compromised by a group of ignorant fools who know nothing of Madame la marquise or her peerless reputation."

"Then I must apologize, *mon ami,*" de Belleville said, ending the discussion quite peacefully. He bowed to the Comte de Montroi.

"Your apology is accepted," Guy Claude said, satisfied that he had protected Autumn's reputation as best he could. He did not for a moment believe his companions thought any differently now than they had several minutes before, but at least they would not discuss the matter too easily or too publicly.

Autumn had bid her mother good night, saying nothing that would reveal her nervousness, although Jasmine certainly knew. Both Lily and Orane had come with her. They helped their mistress to disrobe, and Orane brushed out Autumn's long dark hair with firm but gentle strokes, while Lily fetched a clean, soft silk chemise for her lady to wear to bed. Autumn dismissed them, having washed her hands, her face, and her teeth, rinsing her mouth with violet water. She was not yet ready to get into bed, and she wondered how soon it would be before the king visited her.

She stood by a window looking out over the wide lawn of the chateau. The moonlight dappled the greens, and she saw several deer grazing. It was a sight she had not seen since she had last visited Queen's Malvern. She sighed deeply, affected by the beauty of it, which almost hurt her heart. How far she had come since those days of her innocence. Her ears picked up a faint sound behind her. She did not even start when the king's voice said to her, "It is lovely."

"*Oui*, it is," she agreed.

He reached about to undo the pale blue ribbons that held her silk chemise closed. Deftly they were loosened until the king was able to slide the garment back off her shoulders, letting it slip to the floor with an almost silent hiss. Autumn stood naked, but strangely she found she wasn't afraid, and she had certainly thought she would be.

"Tonight," the king told her, "I shall leave you to sleep in peace. It has been a long day, I know, but you will allow me the favor of your loveliness for just a few more moments. My appetite is already well whetted, but I know you need your rest after a tiring journey from Chermont."

"Your Majesty is kind," Autumn replied, relieved to be able to postpone the inevitable.

The king chuckled. "Your manners, *ma bijou*, are exquisite, even as everything about you is exquisite; but I believe it is permitted for lovers to call one another by their Christian names, no matter if one of them is a king. You will address me as Louis when we are in private, although I will admit it would be fascinating to hear you cry out, 'Oh, Your Majesty!' in your passion."

"Then perhaps I shall one day," Autumn answered him boldly.

Again the king laughed softly. His hands cupped her two round breasts, lifting them slightly to his gaze from over her shoulder. "They are lovely," he said almost regretfully, brushing the nipples with his thumbs as he released them. He wrapped an arm about her waist, drawing her back against the silk of his nightshirt. The fingers of his hand pressing lightly, splayed out across the soft round of her belly. Then the fingers of his other hand sought out her nether lips, pushing between them, with unerring instinct finding her *bouton d'amour*. A single and very skillful finger began to stroke at the sensitive nub of sentient flesh.

Autumn drew her breath in sharply. *This* was totally unexpected. It was a too suggestive and intimate invasion of her person. Worse, to her total shock, she could feel herself being aroused. How could, that be? How could this virtual stranger, *this king*, kindle and bestir her desires? Was that not a husband's privilege? And then she realized as a jolt of feeling startled her, that perhaps these sensual skills were not just the province of a husband. What a fool she had been!

"You are growing wet for me," Louis murmured approvingly in her ear. His breath was hot and moist. His fingers teased and played with her.

Autumn's head fell back against his shoulder. She closed her eyes, her breathing ragged, as the pleasure began to build up within her nether regions.

"You like it, don't you?" the king said softly.

"*Oui*," she heard herself answer and, as if to emphasize her point, her bottom began to rotate against his groin.

He purred with his delight but then said, "*Non, ma bijou.* If you continue such naughtiness I shall regret my promise to leave you in peace tonight." He could feel her little *bouton d'amour* swollen and throbbing beneath his fingers. With his thumb and his forefinger he pinched it hard, smiling to himself as she cried out, and her love juices soaked his fingers and hand. "Ah, is that not nice, *chérie?*" he whispered to her. He began to suck each of his fingers and, giving her his hand, he commanded her to lick it so she might taste her own juices. Then he turned her about to face him, and Autumn half collapsed against him.

The king gathered her up in his arms and walked across the room to lay her in her bed, bending to kiss her ripe lips. "Tomorrow," he told her, "you will grow wet with the memory of these last few minutes each time I look at you, *ma bijou*. You do not wear *caleçons*, do you?"

Wordlessly, Autumn shook her head.

"Good," the king said meaningfully. Then, with a smile, he turned and left her bedchamber.

She lay stunned by his words, weak with the quick pleasure he had given her, amazed by her own wanton response to his lust. She hadn't known. How could she have known? Why hadn't her mother explained these things to her? Were they even explainable? And what other surprises awaited her in Louis's arms? To her great amazement, she fell asleep amid the jumble of her very confused thoughts.

Jasmine asked no questions in the morning when they met to hunt. Autumn's face was an expressionless mask that offered no informaton at all. Madame la duchesse thought her daughter very beautiful in her forest green riding costume with a wide-brimmed chapeau atop her head, its soft white plumes brushing her cheek. The gentlemen were most complimentary of the ladies as they were helped to mount their horses. Louis looked directly at Autumn with a knowing smile. He noted the faint blush staining her cheeks and chuckled wickedly. They began to walk from the courtyard, the dogs and the beaters dashing ahead as the king's head huntsman trumpeted his horn.

The sun was not quite yet above the horizon, but the heavens above them were a bright blue. To the east the sky was a wonderful mixture of muted gold, deep orange, and creamy lavender. The earth was warm but the air cool. A light haze hung over the fields.

"It is like riding through fine lace," Autumn remarked as she kicked her horse into a canter. She had not ridden like this since

Sebastian's death, she thought quietly to herself, but it felt wonderful to be astride again, the wind in her face. It was a rare freedom, and yet she really wasn't free at all.

"You ride well, madame," the king remarked as he drew his own mount up by her side. "You learned young?"

"My father took me up on his horse before I could walk," she told him with a small smile, avoiding his gaze. "I was given my own pony when I was three."

Ahead of them the beaters flushed out a buck deer and the dogs dashed madly after the beast, who immediately made for the thick forest where, to their disappointment, they lost it. Their next prey, a large boar, was not so fortunate and was quickly killed. The creature was lashed by its feet to a carrying pole and sent back to Chambord to be prepared for dinner that evening.

When the noon hour came they stopped in a sunny clearing where the royal servants had already set up a picnic for the hunters. There were roasted capons and ducks; a large country ham; a wheel of nutty-flavored cheese and another of soft Brie; fresh bread wrapped in linen serviettes that was still faintly warm; a basket of apples and pears; and, finally, several decanters of fine wine. They ate heartily, and then were up again to hunt, leaving the servants behind them to return to Chambord with what little remained of their open-air feast.

Jasmine particularly enjoyed the hunt, as she had not been on one in several years. She rode enthusiastically and gained the open admiration of her companions, who found it difficult to believe this beautiful woman was in her sixth decade, or so she claimed. Consequently, none of them but the sharp-eyed Montroi noticed that the king and Autumn were among the missing. As the comte knew his master was well acquainted with the forest about Chambord, he did not worry. Obviously the king had had enough of the sporting life today and had seduction in mind for an afternoon's entertainment. Guy Claude rode on with the hunt.

"Where are we going?" Autumn asked the king when he leaned over and took her horse's bridle in his gloved hand to direct it away from the others.

"There is a charming glade up ahead I thought you might enjoy seeing," he answered her. "I know the way back to the chateau when it is time for us to return, *ma bijou.*" His warm brown eyes gazed directly at her, and then he chuckled at the look upon her face. "You are wet for me, *n'est-ce pas?*" he teased her. "I told you that you would be when I looked at you today."

"You are very wicked, Louis," she gently scolded him.

"You must trust me, Autumn," he said. "I will never hurt you, *ma bijou.* Women are meant to be loved and cherished, not harmed."

"Your words are most charming," she replied, amazed that he could exert such control over her. "I suppose I must trust you, for it would seem I have no other choice."

He grinned boyishly at her. "*Non, ma bijou,* you do not," he agreed cheerfully.

Suddenly the forest about them opened slightly to reveal a small grassy clearing edged with a narrow brook on one side. The brook formed a little pool of dark water that tumbled over a small waterfall before going on its way again. They stopped and dismounted, allowing their horses to graze freely. The king spread out his cloak and invited Autumn to sit by his side.

"It is lovely," she said as she joined him. "I would not have imagined such a delightful place in the midst of this thick forest. How did you ever find it?"

"I have visited here since I was a boy," he told her. "Chambord was a royal residence. My father gave it to my uncle, in hopes that the renovations he wished to make to the chateau would keep him down in the country and out of trouble in Paris. It will revert back to me upon his death. Unfortunately, my uncle Gaston found very competent artisans and workmen, not to mention an excellent foreman to oversee it all for him. Then he trotted back to Paris and enmeshed himself in all manner of political duplicity, intrigue, and schemes. I shall never forgive him for presuming to exile Mazarin, or the troubles he caused my mother after my father's death. I might have died at his hands had it not been for Mama and Papa Jules." The king stopped and flushed. Then he said gravely to Autumn, "You did not hear me address the cardinal in that manner, *ma bijou.* I will admit that, to my shame, I forgot myself for a moment with you. You are very easy to be with, *chérie.*"

"I heard nothing I should not have, Louis," Autumn reassured him.

Reaching out, he cupped her face in his hand. "You really are quite beautiful, *ma bijou.* I thought so the first day I saw you. I was quite heartbroken at the set-down you gave me," he told her. Then, leaning forward, he kissed her softly, murmuring with pleasure as her lips softened beneath his and she kissed him back, easily engaging his lust for her. Pushing her back, he looked into her eyes again.

Once more Autumn flushed, feeling the dampness welling up between her legs. He smiled knowingly, pulling his gloves off and slipping a hand beneath her skirts to caress the inside of her thigh.

"Lift your skirts up for me," he said. "I want to see the treasures you hide beneath them. Ah," he sighed as the material raised revealed her slender legs encased in their knitted green stockings, held up by gold ribbon garters garnished with tiny cream-colored rosettes. Above the garters her thighs gleamed almost translucently, and at their junction a mound of dark, tightly bunched curls caught his eye. Her nether lips were slightly puffy and swollen. He could see in the dark curls the silver pearling of her juices.

The king groaned as if in genuine pain. "I promised myself," he told her aloud, "that when I first took you it would be in a candlelit and flower-filled room. But alas! I cannot wait, *ma bijou.* Open yourself to me, my beautiful Autumn. I must have you now!"

"What if the hunt returns this way?" she said nervously, but she knew from the look in his eye that there would be no deterring him.

"They will not come this way again today," the king said, and before she might protest further he quickly mounted her, freeing his manhood from his garments as he did so. He placed its tip at the mouth of her love channel and, leaning forward, kissed her again, but this time with genuine passion.

Autumn could feel the hot flesh actually throbbing against her. Her own body ached in response. Deliberately she spread herself even wider for him, wrapping her arms about him and crying out softly as he thrust himself forward and filled her. She was ashamed of her response, but she could not help it. How long had it been since she had enjoyed the attentions of a virile man who wanted her? No matter how she rationalized it, she was no better than a common whore, but she didn't care any longer. She wanted him. She wanted his dark and furious lust for her. She wrapped her legs about him, encouraging him onward, and was quickly rewarded as his love juices flooded her. To her surprise her own hunger peaked almost immediately with his.

"*Oh, Your Majesty!*" she murmured.

"*Oh, Madam, la marquise,*" he replied. "How delicious and how hot-blooded you are, much to my delight. Your passion is even more than I had dared to hope."

"I have ruined my chapeau," she told him, sighing at the two broken plumes.

"You shall have another, a dozen!" he promised, and then he leapt up, restoring his clothing to a more respectable state. "Come, *ma bijou,* we must leave this secret place of our first passion and return to the hunt, but tonight, madame, you shall come to my bed and we will continue this delight. I could take you again this minute, and I will, if you do not lower your skirts, you charming and bewitching beauty!" He bent and pulled the fabric down, covering her nakedness. Then he pulled her to her feet, and she swayed for a moment, quite dizzy.

"Wait but a moment," she pleaded with him. "I am faint with your vigorous attentions, Louis." She leaned against him, her head pressed against his shoulder, her eyes closed.

He put his arms about her and stood quietly, holding her, until at last she raised her head up and smiled at him. "You are divine, *ma bijou,*" he told her. Then he helped her mount her horse.

They caught up with the hunt just as a stag was being taken back to Chambord to be butchered and hung in the royal larder for a future meal. Several of the hunters had game birds slung across their saddles. The sun was dipping lower on the horizon. The air had become chill. It was decided to return to the chateau.

"I want a hot bath," Autumn told her servants when she entered her bedchamber, flinging her gloves aside carelessly.

"What will madame wear tonight?" Lily asked her mistress.

"The garnet velvet," Autumn replied. "God's mercy, I am frozen to the bone! Build the fire up, Orane."

"Making love in the open air on an October afternoon will do that," Jasmine remarked, walking into her daughter's chamber.

"And how was I to prevent it, Mama?" the younger woman replied. "He is the king, and for the moment I am his favored one." She kicked the last of her petticoats aside and sat down so Orane might remove her boots. Then she climbed into the bed to await the footmen who would fill her tub.

Jasmine climbed in next to her daughter and Lily drew the bed curtains to allow mother and daughter their privacy, as well as shield them from the water bearers. "Is he a good lover?" Jasmine asked her daughter.

"I am not experienced enough in such knowledge that I can say, Mama," Autumn primly answered her parent.

"Compared to your deceased husband, then?" Jasmine persisted.

"They are different," Autumn noted, not bothering to elucidate further on the matter.

"How many times have you made love?"

"Once. This afternoon, Mama, and yes, I enjoyed it. I had forgotten how pleasant it is, but why did you not tell me that a woman can feel passion without being in love with the man? I was quite surprised to learn it, I can assure you. Such erudition makes me feel like a common whore. It is a difficult emotion to contain. I believed that enjoying passion was only possible with a man you loved. To learn otherwise, to find I can actually savor the king's embraces . . ."

"It is frightening at first, *ma fille*, I will grant you," Jasmine agreed. "When your father and I first made love, it was simply to gain pleasure and comfort from each other. Your Aunt Sybilla thought she was to be his wife. I had no interest in James Leslie, other than as a convenient lover of the moment."

"*Mama!*" Autumn was astounded.

"Do not look so shocked," her mother said, half-laughing. "It is true. I hardly felt like a whore afterwards, nor should you. You didn't seek the king out and enchant him by your wicked wiles with an eye toward personal gain. Rather he has sought you out and demanded you for his own—temporarily, I will grant you, for he must wed a Catholic princess sooner than later. Now, answer me this, *ma fille:* Why did the king not make love to you last night? I am certain they all thought he would."

"He said he thought I should be tired from our journey, and he wanted me to be well rested for today's hunt," Autumn answered.

"He is a more dangerous man than I anticipated," Jasmine mused, "and he is so young yet. Cardinal Mazarin has taught him very well, indeed. He will not be a Henry Stuart, falling in love with you. Do not, I advise you, Autumn, fall in love with him. This king will break your heart, I fear, if you do."

"I could not fall in love with him," Autumn said. "While he is a charming man, I know he could not wed me, Mama. I suppose you are right when you say I will marry again one day. I had not thought it, but now I understand I may love again one day. Making love with the king has made me realize I like making love with a man, but I have not the temperament to be a mistress forever. I must have my own man, my own children, my own home, and live a country life. Louis cannot give me that."

"The right man will appear at the right time," Jasmine said. "Until then, Autumn, please the king, gain his favor, and when he tires of you, which he will, retain his friendship by sending him off with a kiss, a smile, and a blessing on his reign. Such elegant manners will delight him, for like his mother he appreciates a nicety of behavior. You will also gain the queen's and the cardinal's friendship by doing so."

"You should have been a general, Mama, for you certainly know how to plan a campaign," Autumn teased her mother.

"I take after my Mughal ancestors, great warriors all from Tamurlane and Chingis Khan to my great-grandfather, Babur, to my grandfather, Humayun, and my father, Akbar. Once my father said that I should have been a boy, and had I been he would have named me his successor. My mother hushed him, and he never said it again."

"Do you ever wish you had remained in India?" Autumn asked.

"Never! My fate was here in the Western world, with Rowan Lindley and James Leslie," came the positive reply. Then Jasmine changed the subject entirely. "What will you wear this evening?"

By the time the two women had thoroughly discussed the advantages of the garnet velvet gown and the rubies she would wear with it, Autumn's bath was ready. Lily opened the curtains, and they climbed from the bed. Kissing her daughter on the cheek, Jasmine returned to her own chamber, which was located at the far end of the corridor. Orane helped her mistress finish disrobing, and then Autumn entered her tub, settling happily into the water even as the king entered the room through a little door in the silk-paneled wall. The two young maidservants cried out, surprised, but remembered their manners enough to curtsey.

"Shall I put a screen about the tub, madame?" Lily said boldly.

"I think not," Autumn replied. "I believe the king has come to watch me bathe. Is that not so, sire? Bring His Majesty a comfortable chair, Orane. Lily, some wine for the king, please."

"I love your fragrance," the king said, seating himself and accepting the goblet of wine from Lily. "Honeysuckle and woodbine, is it not? It radiates innocence, *ma bijou*, and is most exciting."

"You have a good nose, sire. I quite like your violet scent," she replied.

"It reminds me of the countryside in spring," he said almost wistfully. "When I am in Paris I wear sandalwood or ambergris, which are more suitable to the surroundings there." He drained the goblet and handed it back to Lily. Then he stood, knelt, and took the soft flannel cloth from the tub's side. Soaping it, he began to wash her back. "Send your women away," he said softly. "I want to make love to you, Autumn. I can barely contain myself after this afternoon!"

"No," she heard herself saying. "Remember that you promised me you would be discreet. I cannot be ready for the evening meal if you distract me now, Louis. Restrain yourself. Anticipation but whets the appetite, monseigneur. Remain while I finish bathing and I shall let you see me naked in the light." She brushed his lips with hers.

"I am not used to having anyone deny me, *ma bijou*," he said.

Autumn smiled sweetly. "I am not some Parisian whore brought in to amuse Your Majesty, nor am I a highborn court whore eager to advance herself and her family by pleasing Your Majesty. I do not refuse you. I ask that you wait until after our meal so whatever may be thought of me, nothing can be proved of me. If Your Majesty does not choose to keep his word, I shall depart within the hour for Chermont with my mother."

His visage darkened, but then he laughed. "You are a vixen," he told her. "And you shall pay for your behavior, madame, I promise you."

"I am Your Majesty's most obedient servant," she replied blandly. "Do not be in such a hurry to celebrate passion, sire. There is time for us, is there not?"

He nodded, then said, "I want to see you naked *now!*"

"But a moment more and I shall be properly washed," she told him. And when she was, she stood and stepped down the tub's steps to the carpet. Her two women gasped, shocked, and did not know what to do. Autumn slowly pirouetted about once, saying as she did, "Lily, my towel, please."

The king took the warmed towel from the serving woman and slowly wrapped it about Autumn, kissing her wet shoulder as he did. "I want you naked in your bed tonight," he said softly. Then he turned abruptly and left her.

Autumn laughed to herself. So that was the way to handle a man. It was like making a donkey move forward with a carrot on a stick, she giggled. But she must be careful, for she could but drive him only so far. "Come," she called to her serving women. "I must be ready sooner than later."

"He's a bold one," Lily remarked in English.

"He is the king," Autumn replied in the same tongue, and then, "Speak French, Lily, or you will make poor Orane overly curious."

"I am teaching Orane to speak our language, my lady, for the day when we return to Scotland. We'll get to go back one day."

"There is nothing for us there, Lily. Do you miss it?"

"Sometimes," the serving girl replied, "but Marc makes it easier for me. He is so kind."

"Do you wish to wed him?" Autumn asked. "You have kept company for several years now. I will permit it if it is what you both want."

Lily nodded eagerly, and then she and Orane hugged one another.

"I must get dressed," Autumn reminded her servants. "What a pair of lazy wenches you two are," she teased them.

Quickly, Lily and Orane returned to their duties. They dried Autumn and began bringing her garments. A chemise and a dozen petticoats, stockings of pure, soft silk, a garnet velvet skirt, and finally the matching bodice, with its horizontal neckline cut across her bare shoulders. The sleeves of her bodice were slit up the front from wrist to elbow and trimmed with gold ribbons. Square ruby broaches were fastened at either side of her neckline. She wore a necklace of pink pearls that matched the fat pearls in her ears. Autumn's hair was affixed in a simple chignon, and on her feet she wore gold silk shoes with ruby-studded heels.

"No wonder the king is in love with you," Orane said when they had finished and stepped back to examine their handiwork.

Autumn did not bother to disabuse the romantic Orane with the truth. The king did not love her, nor did she love him. They had an arrangement to enjoy a sweet idyll together. Instead she said, "It is the two of you who keep me at my best. Thank you." She accepted the painted fan Lily handed her and departed her bedchamber for the *salle à manger,* where the king would be awaiting her.

Tonight the king's companions paid no especial attention to her, except to admire her gown. To Autumn's surprise her mother was not in the dining room. She looked about anxiously, and Montroi came to her side.

"Madame la duchesse has asked to be excused tonight. She sent word that the day's hunt was more strenuous than she had anticipated," the comte told Autumn.

"It has been several years since she last spent a day such as this one," Autumn admitted. "I shall go and see her after the meal."

The boar they had killed early in the morning was now brought to table, well roasted and with a bright red apple in his mouth. The royal carver sliced the beast with agility and skill, placing the first two pieces upon a gold plate for the king. Then he proceeded to serve the rest of the guests. There was a rabbit stew smelling of leek and rosemary in a wined gravy. There was a flaky-crusted pie filled with tiny ortolons in a cream and dill sauce. There were artichokes in white wine, braised celery, hearty breads, sweet butter, and cheeses.

"I love country foods!" Baron Chaizefleurs said, smacking his lips and downing his second goblet of rich red wine. "In Paris it is all so delicate and saucy and overly rich. I am always filled with the bloat, but not here in the country. How fortunate you are, Madame la marquise, to live in this rural paradise."

"I am indeed fortunate, monsieur," Autumn agreed. "May I suggest that you eat less food in Paris and take a bit more exercise, but if that does not help you, then I would suggest peppermint tea to cure you of your complaint. It is quite excellent for getting out the wind."

"Peppermint tea! My mama often prescribed it for my papa. I had forgotten. *Merci*, madame, for reminding me."

Autumn smiled and nodded at the baron. His complaint obviously came about because he ate too much in Paris and moved far too little. Here at Chambord the meals were simple affairs, and they spent most of their time out-of-doors. The king preferred it that way, for he disliked the city greatly. That was why he was building his palace at Versailles. It would be near enough to Paris, but also far enough away.

After the meal was over they were entertained by a group of local villagers who danced for them and played upon their simple instruments, the pipe, the drum, the tambourine, and the whistle. When the entertainment had ceased, the king announced that they should all seek their beds as the hunt would begin again early, and he expected to see them all ready to ride. Autumn hurried off to see her mother while the others scattered to their own chambers.

Jasmine was ensconced in a large bed surrounded by plump pillows when her daughter entered the room. "Are you all right?" Autumn asked anxiously and sat by her mother's side on the bed.

"I am fine," came the reply. "Just astounded to find I am not as young as I used to be," Jasmine chuckled. "There was a time when I could hunt all day and dance the night away. Obviously those days are past for me now. I even intend staying a-bed in the morning. Did I miss anything, *ma fille?*"

"Nothing," Autumn responded. "Just a group of men bragging about things that I certainly didn't see happen today. Some villagers came and entertained after the meal, and the baron complained about having the bloat all the time in Paris."

Jasmine chuckled again, and patted her daughter's hand. "You had best go now, Autumn. The king will be awaiting you impatiently, I am quite certain. Good night, *ma fille*. I will see you tomorrow."

Autumn arose from the bed and, bending, kissed her mother tenderly. "Good night, Mama," she said. "Sleep well." Then she left the duchess's bedchamber and hurried down the corridor to her own room. Lily and Orane were waiting to prepare her for bed. Her gown, her petticoats, and her jewelry were removed, along with her stockings and shoes. She used the chamber pot, then bathed herself in a basin of warm scented water and scrubbed her teeth. She sat naked as Orane brushed her hair, but when Lily offered her a clean silk chemise she waved her away.

"No nightgarment?" Lily looked askance, and Orane was hard put to keep from giggling.

"The king has ordered it," Autumn told her women, "and I am here at the king's invitation, after all. Neither of you will speak of this. Whatever anyone may believe, only the king and I can determine what goes on between us. We both prefer to keep it that way. Do you both understand me? Discretion is most important in this matter."

"*Oui,* madame," both servants replied together, and they curtsied.

"Good. Now you are both dismissed until the morning," Autumn said quietly.

"Duke Jemmie would not approve of this," Lily burst out, and then blushed that she had voiced her thoughts aloud.

"Nay, he would not, Lily," Autumn agreed, "but if he had heeded my mother and not gone to Dunbar, he should not have died and we would be safe in Scotland. He didn't heed Mama. Now he lies in his tomb at Glenkirk and we are, for good or bad, here. We will make the best of it, eh? I am told being a king's mistress is different than being just an ordinary man's mistress, although for the life of me I cannot fathom why. Fornication is fornication."

"Oh, but madame, to lie with King Louis is indeed a great honor!" Orane said suddenly. "I wish it were me he favored!"

"Your auntie hears you talking like that, Orane, and she'll take a hazel switch to you," Lily said. "That kind of behavior is not tolerated among the likes of us."

"Go to bed, you two," Autumn told them. She was close to laughter. Lily was so typically Scots and Orane so very French. It was rare they agreed on anything, but they served her well. She waved them off, and with a final curtsey the two girls left the bedchamber.

Realizing she was chilled, Autumn climbed into her bed beneath the warm down comforter. There was a bevy of goosedown pillows behind her back, so she was half seated. The bed was almost as comfortable as her own. The fire crackled in the hearth opposite the bed, and the few candles that Lily had left burning cast a golden glow about the chamber.

She heard the click of the lock on the small hidden door, and it swung open with a protesting little creak. The king stepped through into the bedchamber. He was quite as naked as she, and for the first time she was able to observe him. He was of medium height with sturdy limbs. His dark curls, pulled back earlier, now hung loosely about his shoulders. He really did have wonderful hair. Her gaze swept briefly to his manhood. It hung relaxed and was relatively long and thick in its repose. She quickly turned her eyes back to him as he came to the bedside and took her hand to kiss it.

"*Bonsoir, ma bijou,*" he said.

"*Bonsoir,* Louis," she replied, flinging the comforter back so he might enter the bed.

Joining her, he immediately yanked her into his arms and began kissing her most passionately, murmuring in her ear between kisses,

"I want you right now, Autumn! I have waited all evening to slack my hunger for you!" Flinging back the coverlet, he literally dove between her legs, pulling them apart and pushing his dark head between her thighs. His fingers opened her nether lips and he began at once to tongue her most sensitive parts quite vigorously.

Autumn gave a little shriek of surprise, but so skillful was his tongue that she felt herself being aroused in spite of herself. It was outrageous! It was scandalous and uncivilized, not to mention very, very wicked, but she couldn't help herself. She cried out almost immediately with undisguised pleasure. Encouraged, Louis ceased his loveplay and mounted her, his love lance quite engorged and ready to do battle with her. He thrust fiercely into her over and over again until she was sobbing with open delight. Then, with a loud cry, his passions burst, filling her with his juices.

He withdrew from her with a sigh of deep satisfaction. "Ahhh, *ma bijou*, that was marvelous! We shall repeat it again shortly when I have caught my breath. Will you bring me a goblet of wine, *chérie?*"

Autumn arose from the bed on slightly shaky legs. Slowly, she walked across the chamber to where the wine decanter sat with two silver goblets. She poured them both a draught, but then, seeing the cloths and basin, she picked them up instead, and returned to bathe his manhood, having first bathed herself. He watched her, fascinated, but remained silent until she had returned a second time with the wine.

"I've never had my lover attend me so tenderly," he said. Then he drank deeply.

"It is a custom of my mother's land," she told him.

"It is charming, *chérie*. Now come back to bed. I am eager for you again." He pulled her down and caressed her breasts. "Lovely," he said. "They are simply lovely. Women's breasts are quite distinct in their differences," he told her. "I fancy myself an expert."

Autumn laughed; and then, surprising him, she climbed atop the king. "Are you indeed, Louis?" she teased, taking her breasts in her two hands and lifting them up so he might admire them further.

"Be careful, *chérie*," he warned her, wagging his dark eyebrows at her in what he hoped was a dangerous manner.

In response Autum took the wine goblet from his hand. Sliding her body down his thighs, she poured several drops of the ruby liquid upon his chest and belly and began to lick it up, her facile tongue sliding over his taut skin. "Ummm," she said. "You are most delicious, Louis. Slide yourself down farther and let me tease you even more." When he had, she moved up again, now leaning over him and taunting his lips with just the tips of her nipples, rubbing them over his sensuous mouth until he reached up and, grasping a breast, began to suckle hard upon it, his teeth grazing the delicate flesh and sending a shiver rippling down her spine. Releasing her breast, he reached out with both hands and, lifting her, impaled her upon his manhood. Autumn rode him quite expertly, the walls of her love sheath closing and releasing him until he was moaning with total pleasure. Unable to control himself, he poured his juices into her again, shouting a cry of utter delight as he did so.

"Ah, witch," he told her afterwards, "your husband taught you well. I have never had such satisfaction from even the most skilled whores in Paris, *ma bijou*. You must come back with me when I return."

"No," she said. "I am a country girl, Louis. You promised me a sweet idyll, and we shall have it for as long as you are at Chambord. When you leave, however, I shall go back to Chermont, to my child and to my vineyards. If when October comes again, and you return to Chambord, I shall be at your disposal for as long as you desire me, monseigneur."

"You are hard," he replied, reaching up and stroking her hair.

"I am a realist, Your Majesty. I choose to keep my reputation intact and not have all of France pointing at me and saying, 'There goes Madame la marquise d'Auriville, the king's whore.' I am older than you are, Louis, and I believe, for all your sophistication, that I am a bit wiser. Trust me in this, and let us be friends."

"Very well, *ma bijou*," he agreed, although there was a reluctant tone in his voice. Still, he thought, she was a clever young woman to prefer his friendship to his false vows of love. How often Mazarin had told him that the Marquise d'Auriville would make an excellent courtier. He was beginning to understand what the cardinal had seen in this woman. He looked at her, saying, "Fetch the cloths, *chérie*, for I will soon want to play with you again."

Autumn was shocked. "Louis! You are the most insatiable man I have ever known! How can you be so damned randy after the two bouts *d'amour* we have just completed?"

"You have only known two men in your life, *ma bijou*," he began, "but in answer to your query, I am only eighteen. They say that men my age are the most passionate. I, however, intend remaining this way forever and ever. *Sacrebleu*, your lips are tempting, *chérie*. Kiss me!"

With a laugh Autumn bent and complied, preparing herself for a very long night. She must remember to ask her mother in the morning if men the king's age were indeed the randiest, or whether he had just been teasing her. By dawn, however, she had learned the answer to the question herself, and the hunt departed without her.

Chapter ⚜ 15 ⚜

"Oh, God!" Autumn wretched into the basin Lily was holding, her face pale and beaded with perspiration.

"It was to be expected," her mother remarked sanguinely.

"*What* was to be expected?" Autumn demanded. She backed away from the bowl. Her head hurt and her belly wouldn't stop roiling.

"God's blood, Autumn, you have had one child! Don't you realize you are expecting another?" Jasmine said, exasperated.

"I can't be!" Autumn wailed.

"Of course you can," Jasmine replied, her patience strained. "There was but one night the king was not in your bed while we were at Chambord. We were there six weeks, *ma fille*. Did you once while we were with him break your link with the moon?"

Autumn shook her head wearily. She was suddenly exhausted. Her belly was at last quieting. She wanted nothing more than to lie down in her bed and sleep forever.

"When was the last time your monthly courses were upon you?" her mother asked.

"Just before we went to Chambord," came the dull reply.

Jasmine's brow furrowed, and she calculated mentally. "The child," she announced, "will be born sometime between mid-July and mid-August."

"Oh, God!" Autumn suddenly began to weep. "What am I to do, Mama? Now everybody will know! I am ruined! And what of Madeline? She will be ruined too!"

"Heiresses are seldom ruined at the age of three," Jasmine said dryly. "There is no shame in bearing a royal bastard, Autumn, and you know I speak from experience. You must write the king at once. He must be informed, as he will wish to provide for his child."

"Write to Louis? And what am I to say to him, Mama? He cannot marry me. This is not England, nor Louis a Henry Stuart."

"No, it is not England, but the French kings are no less liberal in the matter of their offspring, legitimate or otherwise, than are the English. Tomorrow is Twelfth Night, and the Comte de Montroi is still at his chateau. He can carry your message to the king. That way Louis will get it without the interference of court bureaucrats. It will remain more private that way."

"*Private?*" Autumn almost shrieked the word. "By summer I shall be as fat as a sow about to litter, and you think the matter will remain private, Mama? Hardly!"

"You are so unsophisticated," her mother noted, irritated. "This is what comes of raising you entirely at Glenkirk and not taking you to court, as I did your sisters. I did what was convenient for me and for your father, not what was right for you. Now we see the result of my selfishness and lack of foresight." Jasmine sighed deeply. Then, shaking herself, she addressed her daughter patiently. "If you were with child by a person unknown, it would be a different matter, although ladies of our station have managed to overcome such difficulties. However, you are with child by King Louis. No matter that you thought your liaison with him could be kept private; it was not private, although society in this region is too polite to speak openly of it. When your condition begins to show it will be realized the king is your child's father. Guy Claude will help to confirm that suspicion on the part of our neighbors. More important, *ma fille*, the king will recognize the child as his own. He could hardly have demurred, having seduced the respectable widow of Chermont openly at Chambord for six weeks last October and November. Have Marc ride over to Montroi's chateau and bring him back. Tell Guy Claude the truth, and have him take your message to Louis. It is really quite a simple matter, Autumn," Jasmine concluded.

"Is it really, Mama?" her daughter said, tears beginning to flow again.

"*Oui,*" Jasmine replied, and she put her arms about her daughter comfortingly. "It is a most simple matter, *ma bébé.*"

The king stared down at the small scrap of parchment with its four words. *Je suis enceinte,* he read. It was signed, *Bijou.* There was nothing more. Four little words. Simple, but momentous. He felt a thrill of pleasure for a brief moment. Was it a son or a daughter? He was genuinely pleased by the news the Comte de Montroi had brought him.

"Do you know what is in this letter?" he asked the older man.

"*Oui,* Your Majesty," came the reply.

"How is she?" Louis inquired.

"More beautiful than ever. Her condition becomes her," was the answer. "Healthy," he quickly added.

"You will take a reply back to Chermont, Guy Claude, and then I would have you remain at home until you bring me word of the child's birth. You will confirm the identity of its paternity to quell any gossip that may ensue. If the truth is known, there is little that can be chattered about."

The Comte de Montroi nodded and bowed to the king. Louis knew little about the vagaries of country life. There would be much gossip over Madame la marquise's condition, but no one but a fool would dare to shun her or condemn the king's mistress for her condition.

"She has chosen names, Your Majesty," the comte said, "and would appreciate your approval. She would like the child baptized shortly after its birth. For a son she suggests James Louis, after her late father and Your Majesty. If she bears a daughter, she would call her Marguerite Louise. It would seem that Henri the Fourth first queen was the godmother of Autumn's grandmother on her mother's side. She believes that under the circumstances such a name would be suitable, coupled with the feminine version of Your Majesty's name."

"Quite suitable," the king agreed. "I did not know this piece of Madame la marquise's history. So, our families have been connected before, have they? What a shame she is not royal, Montroi. She would have made me a very excellent queen."

"Indeed, Your Majesty," the comte agreed, bowing once again. "Does Your Majesty have a message he wishes me to convey to Madame la marquise? A kind word on your part would be most encouraging."

"Call in one of my secretaries," the king ordered, and when the man came with his writing tools the king dictated a letter to Autumn. He assured her of his friendship and devotion to her. He expressed his delight that she was to bear his child and approved her choices of names. The child's surname would be de La Bois, he informed his mistress. The income from the dairies at Chambord and Chenonceaux would be the child's, paid quarterly and beginning immediately. The Comte de Montroi would be his personal liaison between himself and Madame la marquise. He would speak for the king on Autumn's behalf, and that of her children. He ended his missive by suggesting she find a good wet nurse, for he expected her at Chambord next October when he came again to hunt. Chambord, he informed her, would not be half as enjoyable without his *bijou.*

"Oh, Mama!" Autumn exclaimed happily when she read the king's message. "You were correct! I am so happy!"

"Surely she does not love him," the Comte de Montroi murmured, horrified, to Jasmine.

"*Non, non!*" Jasmine reassured him. "Like all women in her condition, her emotions run riot. She had convinced herself while you were gone that the king would dismiss their passion and therefore their child. His generosity restores her confidence." She patted his arm. "Poor Guy Claude. Denied the pleasures of court and forced to play nursemaid to the king's *chére amie.* I am glad for my daughter but weep for you."

"If the truth be known, Madame la duchese," Montroi admitted, "I prefer being here to being at court. Paris is a sinkhole for poor courtiers like me, seeking an heiress wife. The city is expensive and dirty. The people still agitate just for their own amusement. *Non*, madame, I am content for the excuse to remain on the Cher. Madame St. Omer says she has found me a suitable wife. I shall take her advice and marry the girl."

"Who is she?" Jasmine asked, curious.

"The only daughter of a most well-to-do wine merchant," he replied. "She has no siblings and is therefore her papa's heiress. Her mama was a distant relation of the St. Omers. She is not of the nobility, but her bloodlines are good and her prospects are excellent. She has been convent-bred and will be quite acceptable. My family may be noble, but it is hardly a great or powerful family. We have very little but our chateau and lands. Her name is Cecile Bougette."

"When will you wed her?" the duchess asked him.

"Not until next year," Montroi replied. "I have my duty to Autumn and the king to consider first, madame."

"If you will take my advice, you will wed her after the king's sojourn at Chambord, Guy Claude. You do not want to lose such a prize," Jasmine told him wisely. "Set the date now, *mon ami*."

"Perhaps you are correct," he considered.

"Bring her to Belle Fleurs to see me," Jasmine said. "It isn't proper for her to meet Autumn yet, under the circumstances. You do not want to offend her papa, but you do want him to feel you have honored his daughter by introducing her to your friends."

"Madame, how can I thank you?" Montroi said, taking up the older woman's hands and kissing them.

"Why is he thanking you?" Autumn demanded, and her mother explained. Autumn nodded. "You are so good to me, Guy Claude. When I am not considered such a scandalous woman, you will bring your bride to visit me here at Chermont. I apologize that you must delay your wedding."

"I still have a few more wild oats to sow," he chuckled with a smile. "Why are you women always in such a hurry to marry a man off?"

"Because without us," Jasmine told him, "you get into such difficulties." And she laughed.

"We get into them with you as well," he quickly replied. "In Paris they speak of nothing but marrying the king off. The Spanish infanta, Maria-Theresa, is the favorite, of course, being the queen's niece; but there is talk of Marguerite of Savoy. She and the king get on quite well and genuinely like each other. Of course, right now the king is involved. . . ." He stopped and flushed.

"Tell me," Autumn said eagerly. "You do not hurt my feelings. Neither the king nor I ever expressed any feelings of love. Is it the cardinal's niece, Marie Mancini? He spoke of her quite often."

"*Oui!*" Guy Claude replied. "It is the Mancini, and they say the cardinal is very angry with his young relation. He has warned her off, but the king will not have it, and so the affair goes on."

"She is foolish," Jasmine said. "He cannot wed her no matter what happens. She should have the good manners to step aside."

"She will not until the king sends her away, I fear. I think she believes he will defy the world for her and marry her in the end," the comte told them.

"But he will not," Autumn said quietly. "The king is in his own way honorable, but his duty comes before everything else. Mazarin taught him well, and he will not disappoint the cardinal or his mother. He will marry the girl they choose for him, and he will do his duty by her and by France. The Mancini girl is in for a great disappointment, I fear. I know the king well now, so I can say it."

"They will marry her off to someone powerful and important eventually. The cardinal will give her a magnificent dowry. All the attention and the right husband will assuage her anger over losing the game. She is a vain and over-proud girl. She doesn't really love the king. She loves the idea of being queen and lording it over all those who scorn her because her birth is not noble," Guy Claude noted.

"Does the king love her?" Autumn asked.

"He thinks he does, but it is the idea of love that fascinates him. He has, as you well know, a roving eye. He will marry, sire an heir, and then grow bored with his queen, whoever she may be. The court is filled with beautiful and willing women," he said. "There will be even more beautiful creatures come to court when there is a queen there."

"I am surprised the king bothered with me at all," Autumn said honestly, her hands going to her belly, where she sensed the faintest flutter of life.

"You attracted the king when he was a young boy," the comte told her. "He never forgot you. Possessing you did not dim the attraction, and you have been kind to him. He will always be your friend, Autumn, and he will not ignore the child you share."

"But will his queen, whoever she is, not be offended?" Autumn wondered. "A vindictive woman makes a bad enemy."

"Your liaison with the king had begun before any betrothal or marriage. It will remain discreet, and if you are discreet, then the queen will not be publicly humiliated if it continues. The king hunts each October and November at Chambord. Until he tells you otherwise, Autumn, your presence will be required. There may come a day when he brings another friend with him, or even his queen, but until then you are at his command, *chérie.*"

I cannot, Autumn thought to herself, *have a baby a year with this man. I shall have to take Mama's potion in future. Why I did not think of that, why she did not think of it, before we went to Chambord I cannot imagine, but come next October I will remember. Still, it will be nice for Madeline to have a little brother or sister with whom she can play. I missed not having my siblings at Glenkirk, for only Patrick was there when I was growing up. He was older and not in the least interested in a little sister. These two children will only be four years apart.*

The winter was mild and the new winery was being built. It was finished by spring, when the men went back into the vineyards to prune, to cultivate, and to tie the vines. News was slow to reach the Cher, but it did come eventually. Autumn was furious to learn that in order to gain use of the English navy, Cardinal Mazarin had publicly come out in support of Cromwell.

"Will it ever end?" she demanded angrily of no one in particular. "How is King Charles to be restored if France will not support him? Charles Stuart is King Louis's first cousin! Queen Henrietta Maria is

Louis's aunt! His mother is Spanish. Why are we fighting with Spain? I do not understand this at all."

"God only knows," Jasmine replied. "Politics grows more confusing each day. Here the cardinal and the queen want a marriage with Spain, yet they quarrel over territory. But Mazarin is running France. The king confirmed his authority years ago. Part of the problem, I believe, is that the Prince de Conde, the king's old enemy, offered his services to Spain and is commanding their forces."

"Marshal de Turenne will beat him when it comes to doing battle," Autumn predicted. "Louis spoke of how clever a strategist de Turenne was, and that he trusted him implicitly."

The summer came, and with it a surprising visit from the Duke of Lundy. Jasmine wept at the sight of her second son, hugging him happily. They had not seen Charlie Stuart since Autumn's wedding day, almost six years earlier. He was leaner than they had ever known him to be, and he looked exhausted.

"What has happened to you?" Jasmine cried.

He grinned his old familiar grin and kissed her cheek. " 'Tis life on the run, madame. That, and the fact that both my English and my French funds are now held back from me. The Kiras don't dare to disobey, although they have when they could loan me funds against my own wealth." He turned to his sister. "I was sorry to learn of Sebastian's death." Then his eyes took in her belly, and he cocked an inquiring eyebrow. "Little sister?" he said.

"I was called to Chambord last October when the king came to hunt," Autumn began, but she got no further.

"Ah," her brother said, and then, "He knows?"

"Aye, and is happy," Autumn replied. "The income from the dairies at both Chenonceaux and Chambord are the child's, to be paid quarterly. The names are chosen and the surname is to be, by royal order, de La Bois. He will officially recognize the baby when it is born," Autumn told her brother. "I seem to be following in Mama's footsteps, except that she loved your father, while Louis and I are merely friends."

"You are asking me to remain and be the baby's godfather, aren't you, Autumn?" Charlie said.

"Of course you will remain!" she replied. "I think Mama will agree that you need to be fed up, for you are woefully thin, Charlie. Where is King Charles now?"

"Here, there, wherever he can gain a welcome. There is a rumor that Cromwell isn't well. His son, Richard, is a fool and will not be able to hold England. Though Mazarin has signed a treaty with England for aid, King Louis supports his cousin. It is thought that when Cromwell dies, which is certain to be sooner than later if our information is correct, General Monck will support the king's return. It seems to be a matter of waiting now." He kissed his sister's cheek and patted her distended belly. "If you don't mind, little sister, I should just as soon await my cousin's restoration here, where I can eat regular meals and sleep in a dry bed, as wait with the king, who does not always have these advantages nowadays." He looked very tired. Both Autumn and her mother realized he had been traveling for some days in order to get to them. "Will you have me, Autumn? I cannot go home to England, and Scotland is also closed to me."

"Of course you can remain, Charlie!" Autumn told her elder brother. "My hospitality can hardly repay the happy days I had at Queen's Malvern so long ago. What news of your home? Of your children?"

"The children are safe with Patrick. Sabrina and Frederick will be practically grown and my wee Willie half-grown. I have not seen them since I left Scotland. Queen's Malvern stands empty. Becket writes me when he can get a letter out of England. It will need restoration, but I have the funds and will rebuild it when we can return."

"You will have to if you want to find a wife," Jasmine told her son frankly. "And you must remarry, Charlie."

"I know," he agreed, "but right now all I want to do is eat, Mama. I smell beef cooking, do I not?"

Autumn struggled to her feet. "Come, the *salle à manger* is this way, big brother."

"Are you staying here?" Charlie asked his mother as he seated himself at the foot of the table.

"Aye," Jasmine replied. "Autumn's time is quite near now. I

wanted to be with her. You must meet your niece, Madeline, after the meal. She is a delightful child who looks just like her papa."

"How old is she?" Charlie inquired, helping himself to a large slab of beef from the silver platter the servant offered.

"She will be four at the end of September," Autumn said. Then, "Keep monsieur le duc's goblet and plate filled," she instructed her servants. She turned to her mother. "We must get Monsieur Reynaud to come from Nantes, Mama. Charlie's wardrobe leaves much to be desired, and I doubt, brother, what little you carry is any better."

"It isn't," he admitted between bites of food.

"The king isn't going to be restored this year, I will wager," Autumn said. "So, brother, you will come to Chambord in October with us. Louis is a delightful host, as you will see, but you will need a decent wardrobe. Mama, could the Kiras in Nantes release some of Charlie's funds for him?"

Jasmine shook her head. "I would not even ask," she told her daughter. "The Kiras have served us faithfully for more years than I have on this earth. If Cromwell will not allow Charlie to draw on his English funds, and Mazarin, by virtue of his treaty with Cromwell, has stopped the flow of his French funds, we cannot attmept to circumvent these orders and endanger the Kiras. My funds are available, and I shall make note of every penny you spend, Charlie. When your funds are released to you once again you will repay me. Agreed?"

"Agreed, madame," Charlie replied, raising his goblet to his mother in salute.

"It is so nice to have a man in the house again," Autumn said happily. "I had not realized until now how important a man's presence is."

The summer deepened, and a month after Charlie's arrival at his sister's home, Autumn gave birth to a second daughter on the twenty-fifth of July. Marguerite Louise de La Bois was a plump, good-natured infant, with her father's dark black curls and dark blue eyes that Autumn suspected would one day be the amber of her sire's. There was a great deal of a to-do made over the king's daughter, much to her older sister's irritation.

"She isn't half as interesting as you are, *ma petite chou*," Charlie Stuart said, picking up his niece and walking off into the gardens with her to show her the empty bird's nest he had found.

"I am a big girl," Madeline said. "Baby Margot smells, *Oncle*." She giggled. "I do not pee my nappies. I do not wear nappies anymore," she announced triumphantly, pulling her skirts up to show him.

Charlie burst out laughing. "Madeline," he advised her, "a lady does not show a gentleman her treasures unless he is her husband." He pulled the little one's skirts down and pointed. "Look, *ma petite*, here is the bird's nest I told you about."

Autumn could not resist nursing her new baby for a month. Then Margot, as the baby was quickly nicknamed, was given to her wet nurse, the wife of one of the vineyard workers who had weaned her own baby in preparation for her duties. Her name was Giselle, and having borne four sons she doted on this wee girl who was the king's daughter. It was soon obvious that Giselle would not only wet nurse Margot but care for her as well. Marie, Madeline's nursemaid, was happy not to have the extra work of a baby as her little mistress was very active now and required much supervision. The only free time Marie seemed to have was when her little mistress was with the priest, learning her letters, or sleeping.

The king surprised them on the fifth of October, arrriving with the Comte de Montroi to see his daughter. Seeing the Duke of Lundy, he raised a quizzical eyebrow.

"May I introduce my brother, Charles Frederick Stuart, the Duke of Lundy, Your Majesty. He is known in the family as the not-so-royal Stuart. He is visiting with us and stood as Margot's godfather, along with Guy Claude. I hope Your Majesty approves."

The king held out his hand and Charlie quickly took it and kissed it. "You are most welcome in France, cousin," Louis said, "for we are cousins by virtue of your paternity."

"I am honored that Your Majesty would acknowledge it," the duke said, and he bowed again. Their kinship was quite distant, he knew.

"You will join us at Chambord," the king told Charlie. "Your mother and sister are coming in two days' time, are you not, *ma bijou?*"

"We are," Autumn said, curtsying prettily to the king.

"You have given me a beautiful daughter," the king told her.

"She looks like you, sire," Autumn replied with a smile.

"Then Mademoiselle de La Bois should grow up to be quite a beauty. I shall choose a husband for her at the proper time, madame," the king said. "Do you plan to raise her yourself?"

"Of course! It is not the custom of the women in my family to foster out their children to others. Where I go, my daughters will go. They shall grow up here at Chermont, sire."

The king smiled approvingly. He took his daughter from the arms of Giselle and walked about the salon with the infant for a few moments. Margot, usually quite vocal, was silent in her father's arms. Finally the king kissed the baby's little head and handed her back to her nursemaid. "She has charm and knows how to listen," he announced. "Those two qualities are most valuable in a woman." Then he turned away from his daughter and said, "In two days' time, madame." He kissed Autumn's hand and then Jasmine's, bowing to Charlie before he departed.

When the king had gone the Duke of Lundy said to his sister, "You have done well, sister. Will you have more children by him, or do you plan to remarry?"

"I do not know if I will remarry, but I suppose I might one day if I can find love again. For I shall not, Charlie, wed for any other reason, just as you taught me. I loved Sebastian. His death still pains me greatly, but I have survived. As for giving the king more children, I believe that would be ill advised. He will marry soon and does not need a bevy of illegimate offspring annoying his queen who, if the rumor is correct, will be the Spanish infanta. The Spanish are not as open-minded about royal bastards as are the French and the English."

They went to Chambord to join the king and his party, and once again Autumn was placed in the bedchamber next to the king. More sure of herself this year, she greeted the gentlemen with charm and assurance. She was congratulated on the birth of her daughter and

much admired by all for her sparkling personality, and wit. The king
had not lost any of his desire for her.

"I cannot believe a year has passed since we last made love," he
told her as they lay abed. The fingers of one hand caressed her
breasts, moving down her belly to tease at her Venus *mont*.

"You are as passionate as ever, Louis," Autumn told him, and
then, leaning over, she kissed his mouth.

"There has been no one since our last sweet idyll?" he said.

"Of course not!" she said indignantly.

"You were, of course, full with my daughter," he remarked. "Will
you give me another child, Autumn, *ma bijou?*" he asked.

"It will be as God wills, monseigneur," she replied piously. The
king, she knew, was very devout. It would hardly do to tell him that
she would not give him any more bastards. She sighed softly.

"You are sad, *ma bijou*. Why?" he demanded.

"I imagine this will be our last idyll, Louis, as you must marry
soon. I will admit to enjoying your company," she told him, turning
his thoughts from children to himself.

"It is unlikely I will bring my queen to Chambord," he said. "A
man must have a place for himself alone where he may play. I shall
always look forward to having you join me when I come, *ma bijou*. I
may not, however, be able to come every year."

"And perhaps you will prefer another companion," Autumn said
wickedly. "I am told Mademoiselle Mancini is quite in your favor."

"When I am in Paris, *oui*," he admitted. "Are you jealous?"

"Perhaps," she answered him, and thought, *God's blood, I have become such a coquette. I am not in the least bit jealous. The king may be my
lover, but I am not in love with him. Why should I care about Marie
Mancini? God help me but I say these words to flatter him.*

His fingers slipped between her nether lips and, finding her *bouton d'amour*, began to play with it. "You need not be jealous of the
Mancini, *ma bijou*," he murmured against her ear, his tongue teasing
at the interior of it. "She is nowhere near as beautiful as you are, and
her passions are not nearly as great as are yours."

"Then, why," Autumn demanded of him, "is she said to be your
mistress, Louis?"

"Because she is," he replied. His fingers moved with determiniation. "Her uncle thinks to keep me amused with his niece while he and my mother negotiate a princess bride for me. They feel Marie is a harmless diversion, and that a man of my years needs a mistress to keep him out of trouble." He swung himself over her and, seating himself upon her hips, began to fondle her round breasts. "*Sacrebleu, ma bijou*, these are the most delightful little love apples you have for me to play with, *chérie.*"

Autumn shifted her weight slightly. She hadn't realized until now how much she had missed his passion. She wanted him inside her. She liked the feel of his weight upon her, and his lance thrusting and thrusting until she was mindless with the pleasure he could provide. She whimpered softly and slipping, her arms about his neck, drew him down so that their lips were just barely brushing. "Make love to me, Louis. I have longed for you so!" And that was true. She had longed for his touch, his hot desire.

The king pushed himself slowly into his mistress, smiling at her long, audible release of breath. "Ah, *ma bijou*," he murmured, "I have missed you also!"

"I hope you are as enthusiastic this year as you were last, Louis, *ma chèr,*" she daringly told him, "for I am quite randy, I fear!"

The king laughed aloud at this admission. "I am, I believe, even more enthusiastic, *ma bijou*," he told her. And then he proceeded to show her exactly what he meant, much to Autumn's delight.

The king returned to Paris in early November. "Until next year," he told Autumn, kissing her lips a final time before he rode off, and she smiled up at him, nodding.

The Comte de Montroi had been released from the king's service so he might marry and look after his own holding. His wedding day was set for December 1 and, bidding Autumn and her companions farewell, he hurried off home to prepare for the arrival of his bride.

"Bring her to Archambault at Christmas," Jasmine said. "The de Savilles will welcome you both, and we will be there."

"I will," Guy Claude said. Then he looked at Autumn and said, "You will not change your mind, *chérie*, and marry me?"

She shook her head with a small smile. "You are so damned gallant, Guy Claude. I thank you, but no. I am not yet ready to settle down again, and it will take someone very special to fill the hole in my heart that Sebastian left, I fear. May we remain friends?"

He kissed both of her hands. "Always, *chérie.*" he promised. Then he was gone.

The winter set in again with its gray days and bursts of snow. At Christmas they went to Archambault to celebrate with the family. Phillipe de Saville was as gallant as ever and welcomed them warmly. Madame de Belfort and Madame St. Omer were delighted to see Charlie again. He flattered and teased the two ladies, giving them a most enjoyable time. The Comte de Montroi arrived with his bride, and the new comtesse was immediately drawn into their little group. She was a pretty young woman with a sweet smile, and she obviously adored her bridegroom.

"Treat her well, Montroi," Madame St. Omer said sternly. "She is, I am certain, far better than a rascal like you deserves. I like you, madame la comtesse. You are always welcome to Archambault."

The winter passed slowly. A letter arrived from Glenkirk from Patrick, who was unaware that his brother was with their mother. Charlie's children were well, and growing quickly. He was worried about his brother's daughter, Sabrina, approaching her seventeenth birthday. She was, Patrick wrote, as wild as any colt. Frederick, now fourteen, and William, who had just had his tenth birthday, were far more manageable.

"Patrick must send the girl to me," Jasmine said. "She faces the same difficulty that Autumn faced at that age. There is no fit society with whom she may associate. I cannot have my granddaughter growing up like that, Charlie. She is your daughter, a duke's daughter."

"*A Stuart,*" he reminded his mother. "It would be too dangerous to get her out of either England or Scotland now. Just a little more time and the king will certainly be restored. Then I shall reclaim my children and my home. You will come back to Queen's Malvern, Mama, and teach Brie all she needs to know about being a proper lady. She has time, and her dowry will gain her any man she wants," Charlie said.

"That, my son, could be the very problem you want to avoid," his mother warned. "If the king is not restored within the year, you must arrange for Sabrina to come to France."

Spring came, and the vines began to show signs of life once more. Shortly before Margot's first birthday, word came of a great battle, called the Battle of the Dunes, that had been fought near Dunkirk, between the French army and their Cromwellian allies against the Spanish and their allies the English royalists, led by Prince James, the Duke of York. On the fourteenth of June the French, under Marshal de Turenne, defeated the Spanish, led by the renegade French Prince de Conde.

A peace was signed. The French gained Roussillon, Artois, and several isolated strongholds along their northern border with the Spanish Netherlands. The Treaty of the Pyrenees also called for a marriage between King Louis and the Spanish infanta, Maria-Theresa. Cromwell had been promised Dunkirk, but he died on September 3 of that year, and the promise was not kept.

Almost immediately upon Cromwell's death, King Louis publicly declared for his cousin, King Charles II, and supported General Monck, who sought the king's return. Richard Cromwell had neither his father's magnetism nor the strength of character to hold together the anti-Royalists. It would require some months of negotiation, but King Charles was going home to England, and almost immediately his supporters, who had been scattered, began returning to his side for that glorious day when they would return to their native land with him. But not quite yet.

In his excitement King Charles proposed marriage to Princess Henrietta Catherine, sister of his brother-in-law, the Prince of Orange. When by November it was observed that Charles's prospects were not quite realized—and possibly might not be unless the negotiations proceeded better—the betrothal was forgotten. Henrietta Catherine married John George of Anhalt-Dessau. The king was regretful, but he moved on with his life. Like all of Europe he observed the almost supernatural calm that seemed to blanket England after Cromwell's death. But then came the reality that Richard Cromwell, or Tumbledown Dick, as he became known, could not manage the government.

His supporters wanted Charles II to return, but the time was not yet right. There was dissension among the Royalists over everything. Scandal broke when it was discovered that Sir Richard Willys, one of the founders of the Sealed Knot Society, a Royalist organization operating secretly within England during the Cromwell years, had been a double agent. That he had managed to get away with his duplicity for so long was both amazing and frightening. The timing of this revelation was bad, and it delayed the king's return. A small Royalist force led by Sir George Booth attempted a rising at harvest time. It was quickly put down, and hopes for the king's restoration were brought low, though not entirely extinguished.

Charlie had left Chermont to rejoin the king. He returned at Christmas to tell his mother and sister what was happening. There was only one man in all of England whom the king trusted to aid him in his restoration. This, Charlie told them, was General George Monck. Monck was a professional soldier who belonged more properly to the generation of King Charles I. He had governed the Cromwellian forces in Scotland, and ruled fairly. He was a man who believed in order and efficiency.

Monck had not profitted from the confiscation of either Royalist or church lands during the Cromwell years. He had taken no part in the death of King Charles I, neither signing the arrest warrant, sitting in judgment, nor condemning the king to death. This was very important to King Charles II, who had no forgiveness in his heart for his father's murderers. If England was not to find itself enmeshed in another civil war, General Monck decided, the monarchy would need to be restored. His brother, a clergyman in Cornwall, acting as his intermediary, set about to make it so.

"I will remain with you until spring," Charlie informed his sister. "The king was so discouraged this October that he considered seeking his fortunes in Spain. We have now convinced him otherwise, and he will wait for General Monck to make his move." He looked at his sister. "Did you see *your* king this year, little sister?"

"Of course," Autumn laughed. "He came in October but was very sad. The cardinal and the queen have separated him finally from his little friend, Marie Mancini. Marie, it seemed, thought she might circumvent her uncle's wishes and trap the king into marriage. He was really quite fond of her, for she is clever, intelligent, and witty, I am told. I have heard it said, even from Louis, however, that her features are quite common and coarse. Like a tavern wench, it is said."

"The king's wedding is set for next summer," Charlie noted.

"I know," Autumn replied. "Louis says that Mama and I are to come. I do not know, though, if it would be proper under the circumstances."

"If you receive an invitation, you will have to go," her brother responded. "You cannot refuse a royal command."

"I think the cardinal and Queen Anne will oversee the guest list, and it is unlikely we shall be invited," Jasmine said to her children. "It is also a moot point as to when we shall see King Louis again, now that he is to be married. He will certainly not come to Chambord next year, but a few months after his marriage. What I look forward to is the possibility of going home. Of seeing India and Henry and their families. We have been away so long."

"What of Patrick?" Autumn asked her mother. "And Glenkirk?"

"I want to see all my children," Jasmine said, "but I do not know if I can go back to Glenkirk."

They were not, as the Duchess of Glenkirk anticipated, invited to the king's wedding to the Spanish infanta. The English king, Charles II, was restored to his throne on the thirtieth of May in the year 1660. Charlie had returned to his cousin's side and was already in England. He wanted his mother and sister to return as well. Autumn wisely waited until the harvest, and then departed Chermont, her children and servants in tow.

"When will you return, Madame la marquise?" Lafite asked his mistress. "When will the petite mademoiselle return?"

"I will be back," Autumn promised him, "and so will my daughters, Lafite. They are, after all, French, and is not Mademoiselle d'Oleron mistress of this estate? And Mademoiselle de La Bois, King Louis's own child? We will return."

He bowed to her. "We will anxiously await your coming, Madame la marquise," Lafite said gravely.

Chapter ✦ 16 ✦

Autumn stared from the hillsides at her brother's home, Queen's, Malvern. It looked deserted and forlorn. It was all overgrown. The wing that had been set afire by the Roundheads those years back was a burnt ruin. Autumn's horse shifted beneath her and, reaching out, she touched her brother's hand.

"God's blood, Charlie, is it habitable? It looks absolutely wretched. I'm glad we left Mama and the children in Worcester."

"If it isn't, little sister, it soon will be," her brother assured her. "Thank God I don't have to petition the king for the monies to restore Queen's Malvern. Poor Charles, who is poor enough himself, is being beseiged by those returning supporters and those who remained here in England faithful to him. He says I am the only one among his friends and family who have not asked him for something," the Duke of Lundy chuckled. "I think my task will be far easier than his." He kicked his stallion into a walk. "Come on, Autumn, let's go down and see what we can see of my home."

They rode down the hill to the house, dismounted, and tethered their horses to a bush. Charlie drew forth a large key from his pocket and, putting it into the old iron lock set in his front door, turned it. To his surprise, it operated quite smoothly.

"Someone has been keeping the lock in order," he said almost to himself as the door swung open, and they stepped into the hallway.

To their surprise the house was clean; the floors, bare of their carpets, swept clean, the wood polished. As they moved from room to room, they found the furniture swathed, the windows covered by their heavy draperies through which just enough light penetrated to allow them to move freely. The duke drew a drape aside, and sunlight filled the room. "Queen's Malvern has been cared for," he noted aloud to his sister.

"And why would it not be, sir?" a voice behind them said. As they turned, the man fell to his knees before Charlie and caught up his hand to kiss it. "Welcome home, my lord duke," Becket said. There were tears in his eyes that overflowed, falling upon the threadbare black fabric of his garment.

Charles Frederick Stuart, Duke of Lundy, bent down and raised up the man before him. Their eyes met, and Charlie said two words to the faithful servant: *"Thank you!"* Then he gave Becket his hand to shake and clapped him on the back. "How have you managed to keep the house in such incredible condition, Becket? Did not the Roundheads give it over to one of their people?"

"They did, your lordship. Some self-important little lordling with overpious ways called Dunstan. Oh, how delighted they were to be here, but determined to put their own stamp upon the house. The first thing they did was remove the portraits of Lord and Lady de Marisco that hang in the family hall. Lady Dunstan said to me that she had heard he was a pirate, and she no better than a common . . . well, you know what she said, my lord. Well, sir, it was right after that that things started happening. Doors would open and close before you, and no one there. The portraits of Lord and Lady Dunstan that replaced those of your great-grandparents kept falling from the wall, no matter how hard we tacked 'em up. Once the fireplaces all began to smoke, and yet none of them had a fire in 'em. The servants the Dunstans brought with 'em began to swear that they had seen a dark-haired woman with startlingly bright blue-green eyes walking the halls of the house. What really sent those interlopers scampering, however, happened on Twelfth Night, my lord, and as I seen it myself I can honestly attest to it. Lord Dunstan suggested they toast Protector Cromwell. Well, my lord, before you could say

God Bless, both Lord and Lady Dunstan's goblets rose straight off
the table and poured themselves out over their heads!"

Autumn burst out laughing.

Becket grinned and continued his tale. "Well, my lord, after a
moment of shocked silence, Lady Dunstan jumped up and told her
husband she wouldn't spend another night in this house. It was obviously haunted by demons, and they could have the place for all
she cared. It was too old-fashioned and drafty to suit her, she said.
Then their portraits fell from the wall again with a horrible bang,
and she ran shrieking from the hall. Her maid packed the essentials
and she was gone from Queen's Malvern within the hour. By the following day they were both gone, bag and baggage, I'm happy to say.
After that no one came here. My wife and I closed the place up, and
we've kept it ready for your lordship's return. As soon as the Dunstans were gone, I rehung the portraits that belonged in the family
hall. They ain't ever fallen," he finished.

"How soon can the house be ready for occupancy, Becket?" the
duke asked him.

"By tomorrow, your lordship," replied the majordomo. "I'll call
the servants back, them that aren't too old to work, and I'll replace
the rest with their relations. We've all been waiting for you to come
home, my lord. Are we to expect your children?"

"No, not yet. Just myself, my mother and sister, and Lady
Autumn's two little girls, Becket. They are in Worcester, but we
shall ride back today and return tomorrow. Get the gardeners working on all that growth outside, and tell those too elderly to return to
their places that there will be cottages and pensions for all. I do not
forget those who have served my family so well in good times and
bad," the duke told Becket. He turned to his sister. "Come,
Autumn."

"Your ladyship . . . ," the majordomo said.

"Yes, Becket?"

"I never welcomed you home, your ladyship, but I do most
heartily," the majordomo said. "Will your husband be joining you?"

"Thank you, Becket, and in answer to your question, no. I am a
widow. I am now Madame la Marquise d'Auriville."

"Very good, your ladyship," Becket replied, and he bowed to her.

"One more thing, Becket," the duke said. "The Dunstans—have they ever been back since they departed? The king has promised that no one will be dispossessed, and I should hate to have the house fall out of the family's hands."

"They were killed, my lord, leaving Worcester. Their coach horses were startled by something and bolted from the inn yard before their driver was on the box. It overturned several miles down the road. They had no children to mourn their passing, and as no one knew from whence they had originally come, they were buried in the cathedral graveyard. Their serving people disappeared with their possessions, and the church took what was in the coach and Lady Dunstan's jewelry to pay for their graves and coffins."

Charlie nodded, pleased that he should not have to annoy his cousin the king in an effort to retrieve his family's home. "We will return tomorrow, Becket," he said. Then he and his sister departed the house to ride back to Worcester town.

They returned the next day, the two coaches and the baggage carts rumbling down the hill to Queen's Malvern. The doors of the house were flung open and a troop of young footmen in the duke's livery hurried out to open the coach doors, put down the steps, and help the occupants out. Becket hurried forward to welcome them, but his warmest welcome now was for Adali, the duchess's major-domo. He helped the elderly gentleman from the carriage, smiling and chattering.

"Do I have my old room, Becket?" Autumn asked him.

"Yes, your ladyship, and your wee ones are next to you. There is a connecting door," Becket answered. "The duchess will be in her old suite. Everything will be as it once was," he concluded happily.

"I miss my pony," Madeline complained.

"You shall have another," her uncle promised.

"Speak English," her grandmother said sharply. "You are in England now, my child. And you, also, Margot."

"I want to go home," Madeline whined as they entered the house. "I don't like England. I want to go to Chermont."

Autumn stopped, and then she picked up her eldest daughter

and set her on a chair so that they were eye to eye. "You will go home to Chermont, Maddie, but not now. I am a Scot, and our king has now been restored to his throne. Uncle Charlie is the king's cousin. You should be honored to be here in this house. We are going to remain in England for a time. Most of my family is here. Perhaps we shall even go up to Scotland, and you and Margot can see the castle where I was raised. I have told you this before. I shall not tell you again. You have Marie with you, and Margot has Giselle. Do not upset your little sister, Maddie. You know she copies everything you do, and if you make yourself unhappy, she will be unhappy. And that would make me unhappy. You may speak French in your chambers, but all other times you will speak English. Is that understood?"

"Yes, Mama," Madeline said as her mother set her on the floor once again. "Will I get to see your king?"

"Perhaps if you are very good," Autumn answered. Then she turned to her daughters' nursemaids. "I expect you both to enforce my will," she said. "And you will not encourage the girls to complaints or comparisons between England and France. Is that understood?"

"Yes, madame," the two nursemainds chorused, curtseying.

They settled into Queen's Malvern, although Charlie had to go off to court to stand by their king. Back in England, Autumn realized that for all her wealth she had nothing here. She had no home of her own. She had no title other than her French one.

Henry and his family came to welcome them home, and Autumn was astounded to see how old her brother had gotten. He was now over fifty, and three of his five children were grown. Her nephew, Henry, was already married, as was her niece, Anne. Then it occurred to Autumn that she, the baby of her siblings, would be twenty-nine on her next birthday, which was only a few months away.

She had thought she had gotten over missing Sebastian. Perhaps it had just been easier in France, at Chermont, at Chambord one month a year with Louis. For the first time since her husband's death almost five years earlier, Autumn began to consider the possibility of remarriage. But who would have her? she wondered. She wasn't her mother, with a James Leslie madly in love with her and pursuing her to the ends of the earth to make her his wife. She was the widow of a foreign nobleman who had a bastard child by the French king. What was she to do?

She could spend several months visiting with her family, but she had no place of her own in England or Scotland. She could return to France, but Chermont belonged to her daughter. Maddie was almost seven now. Before she knew it, Autumn thought, her daughter would be of marriagable age. Chermont had no dower house. Was her fate to be to remain in her daughter's chateau, barely tolerated, but with nowhere else to go? And would King Louis, despite his marriage, insist on having his sweet idyll with her every October and November? Would that be her only chance at passion? And what if he no longer wanted that sweet idyll? Contemplating her future, Autumn found it very bleak. She might as well be dead. Who would miss her?

Charlie, returning in mid-October from court, noticed the change in his little sister and asked his mother what was wrong.

"I haven't the faintest idea," Jasmine admitted to him. "I have asked her, but she says I am imagining it. That there is nothing wrong at all, but there is. Perhaps you can find out what is troubling Autumn. I will admit I feel quite helpless."

The Duke of Lundy invited his sister to walk with him. They found themselves in the family burial ground, where the graves of the family and their faithful servants were located. Charlie sat down on a marble bench that was set between his great-grandparents, Skye O'Malley and her husband, Adam de Marisco. He patted the space by his side, and Autumn joined him. They sat silently for several minutes.

Then Charlie said, "You may deny it, but both Mother and I know there is something wrong, Autumn. What is it?"

"I have nothing," Autumn told him, her voice tinged with sadness. "No home. No life. *Nothing.*" She sighed despairingly. "Chermont is Maddie's, not mine. I don't even know if I want to go back to France, although my daughters must eventually. Everyone has a home but me, Charlie. I am truly alone."

Charlie didn't know whether to laugh or weep at this revelation. While he understood the depression his sister was suffering now, she was in reality a fortunate woman. When Sebastian had died, she had suddenly had the entire responsibility for Chermont thrust upon her, not to mention her orphaned daughter. And then came the French king, who determined to be her lover, and their child. There had been no time for Autumn to mourn or come to terms with herself over her husband's death five years ago.

Despite the fact that her mother had been there to comfort and aid her, it had all been, Charlie could now see, too much for his youngest sister. While their sister India had been headstrong and adventurous and their sister Fortune practical and determined, Autumn had not had enough experience with life to find herself. But he could easily tell that she was a survivor. Back in her own land she was heavy-hearted and filled with melancholy. Remaining here at Queen's Malvern would not help her to rise above her doldrums.

"You are coming to court with me," Charlie announced.

"*What?*" She certainly couldn't have heard him right.

"You are coming back to court with me," the duke repeated.

"But the children . . . ," Autumn protested

"Have Mama, Marie, Giselle, and a houseful of servants to look after them, spoil them, and dote upon them, little sister. You need gaiety and a change of scene. There is no better place to find it than at Cousin Charlie's court. And, Madame la marquise, you have never been to court. You are facing your twenty-ninth birthday, and you have never been to court!"

"There hasn't been a court," Autumn reasoned.

"But there is one now," he replied and, leaping up from the bench, he pulled her to her feet. Taking her hands in his, he danced them about. "I have just celebrated by forty-eighth birthday, little sister, and I remember the courts of my grandfather, King James, and my uncle, King Charles the First. There was laughter and music and masques and dancing, Autumn. Everyone wore marvelous clothing, and all was light and gaiety. Then those joyless damned Puritans came with Master Cromwell and it was gone. Well, now it is back again, little sister. I shall take you there, and introduce you to the king and the most important of the courtiers. Perhaps you'll even find a new husband, eh?" Charlie teased her, and then he collapsed upon the bench, puffing with his exertions.

Autumn fell into his lap, laughing. She hadn't laughed in so long, and it felt so good. "I should like to go to court, Charlie. I always wanted to see it just once, although I truly believe I am a country mouse at heart. I'm not like her," and Autumn pointed to the grave of Lady de Marisco.

"No one," Charlie said softly, "is like her."

"Do you remember her?" Autumn asked. "You must. How old were you when she died?"

"Thirteen," he said. "She would approve of your going to court, Autumn. Our great-grandmother wasn't a woman to stand still. She was always moving forward, seeking new adventures, peeping around corners to see what tomorrow would bring." He chuckled.

"When are we going?" Autumn demanded of him

"How long will it take your maids to pack up your lavish French wardrobe?" he asked her with a smile.

"I have no idea," Autumn replied. "I don't know what I will need for court. And where will we stay in London?"

"I have apartments at Whitehall," Charlie said. "You may stay there or, if you prefer, at Mama's house, Greenwood."

"I think I should prefer to stay there rather than at the palace," Autumn told him shyly. She stood up. "Come on, big brother. Let's ask Mama what I will need to go to court, and how long it will take us to pack it."

Jasmine was delighted that her son had managed to draw Autumn from her miseries. When she learned what it was that had been distressing her daughter she absolutely agreed with her son's solution to the problem. Her two ancient maidservants, Toramalli and Rohana, advised that Lady Autumn was going to court, went immediately to teach Lily and Orane how they must pack and what they must take. Jasmine had Adali bring her jewel cases to her bedchamber and, with Autumn by her side began to sort through her fabulous jewels for items her daughter might wear.

"Oh, let me borrow the rubies!" Autumn begged. "I have always loved your rubies, Mama."

"Kali's Tears, the necklace and the earbobs," her mother said. "They are called Kali's Tears, and you may have them, my darling. I have given emeralds to Fortune, although in the new world she lives in I doubt she has any use for emeralds. India has been given sapphires. I had magnificent sapphires, didn't I, Adali?"

"Indeed, my princess," the old man agreed, "you still do."

"But nothing like the Stars of Kashmir," the duchess said. She picked up a scarlet velvet bag and handed it to Autumn. "Your rubies, my darling. Enjoy them. I have always enjoyed my jewels. Now, what else?" She began pouring through the cases while Autumn watched.

After a week's time, Autumn was packed and ready to depart for London with her brother. Her daughters had adjusted quite well to their new surroundings. They weren't in the least distressed that their mother was leaving them—particularly as their grandmother had promised that without her they would have a most marvelous time.

They reached London after several days traveling, and in that they were fortunate. The weather had been pleasant and the roads dry. Had it been otherwise, the coach would have had a terrible time. As their vehicle drew up before the gates of Jasmine's London house, Greenwood, a gatekeeper stepped forth and bowed.

"I was not told anyone was expected," he said politely.

"I am the Dowager Duchess of Glenkirk's son, the Duke of Lundy, and inside the carriage is my sister, the Marquise d'Auriville. My sister will be staying here while she is visiting at court," Charlie said, and then he waited for the gates to be opened.

The gatekeeper looked very uncomfortable. "I'm sorry, your grace, but Greenwood was confiscated by the Protectorate. It is now the property of the Duke of Garwood, who is currently in residence."

"God's blood," Charlie swore softly.

The coach window was lowered and Autumn leaned out. "What is the problem?" she asked her brother.

"Greenwood was confiscated by Cromwell," Charlie said. "We

were never told." He thought for a moment, and then said to the gatekeeper. "Does the Earl of Lynmouth still have possession of Lynmouth House next door, do you know?"

"Oh, yes, your grace, and he is there, I know, for he and the duke are good friends. They ride together almost every morning."

"It's all right, Autumn. We'll go there. The Southwoods are cousins and will gladly put us up." He tossed a coin to the gate-keeper and thanked him for his courtesy.

"Have I ever met them?" Autumn asked her brother as the carriage slowly made its way next door to Lynmouth House. He shook his head in the negative.

"Duke of Lundy to see the Earl of Lynmouth," the coachman said to the gatekeeper at Lynmouth House, and the gates were opened by the keeper and his son.

The carriage moved through, the horses trotting down the gravel drive and finally pulling up before a great house. Immediately servants in pristine livery were pouring out of the mansion. As the duke dismounted, they helped Autumn from her vehicle. She shook out her skirts and then followed her brother up the marble steps and into the building. The house's majordomo hurried forward, exuding an air of importance. He bowed to Charles Frederick Stuart, immediately recognizing him as a person of quality.

"My lord?" he said in questioning tones.

"I am the Duke of Lundy," Charlie replied quietly. "I should like to see the Earl of Lynmouth."

"His lordship is resting for tonight's masque at Whitehall, your grace. I have been given orders not to disturb him," the servant said.

"I have not made myself clear," Charlie responded in the softest of tones. So soft, the majordomo had to lean forward to hear him. "I am Charles Frederick Stuart, the king's beloved first cousin, known as the not-so-royal Stuart. This lady is my youngest sister, Madame la Marquise d'Auriville. We have been traveling for several days and have arrived to learn my mother's home next door was confiscated by Cromwell's lot." Charlie's voice was rising as he spoke. "I should like to see my cousin, the Earl of Lynmouth." He glowered. "What is your name, my man?"

"Betts, your grace," the majordomo said nervously.

"I should like to see my cousin, the Earl of Lynmouth, Betts. *Now!*" the duke shouted.

"Yes, your grace, at once," Betts said, backing away and almost falling over his own feet. "Allow me to show you into the earl's library, where you may wait while I fetch his lordship." Betts hurried ahead of them, flinging open a door and ushering them into a book-lined room. There was a fire burning in the fireplace, and the major-domo gestured to a silver tray holding a decanter and some crystal goblets. "Shall I pour, your grace?" he asked the duke.

"I believe I can manage, Betts," Charlie said, his tone gentler now. He even smiled at the servant.

"I will fetch his lordship immediately," Betts promised them as he backed from the room."

"I never saw you like that, Charlie," Autumn told her brother.

"Upper servants tend to be overprotective of their masters," Charlie said. "Do not ever allow one to speak to you disrespect-fully." He poured out two small goblets of wine and handed his sister one. "London servants, particularly those employed by the king, have a tendency to be disdainful, even overbearing. Never permit it, little sister."

She nodded, and they sat down together upon a settee to await the Earl of Lynmouth. "Who are these cousins?" she asked her brother.

"They descend from our great-grandmother, Madame Skye's third son by her husband Geoffrey Southwood, the Earl of Lynmouth. That son was our great-uncle Robin. I don't know who the current earl is, but we are related. Uncle Robin died the year before the old king. His eldest son, also a Geoffrey, died fighting for the king at Nasby in sixteen forty-five. I know he had a son, and that son had sons."

The door to the library opened, and a handsome young man with golden hair and lime-green eyes hurried in, his expression curious. "I am John Southwood, the Earl of Lynmouth," he said. "You wished to see me? Betts said you were my cousins."

"I am Charles Frederick Stuart, the Duke of Lundy, my lord. Our great-grandmother was married to . . ." He stopped to set it all out in his head and then said, "Our great-grandmother was the second wife of Geoffrey Southwood, the Earl of Lynmouth."

"Impossible!" John Southwood said. "My grandmother's name is Penelope, and my grandfather had no second wife."

"Not *that* Geoffrey Southwood," Charlie told him. "This one was called '*the Angel Earl*,' and he lived in the time of the great Elizabeth."

"God bless me," the earl replied. "That Geoffrey Southwood was my great-great-grandfather!" Then he went on to enlighten them. "My great-grandparents were Robin Southwood, and his wife Angel. My grandfather was their eldest son, also a Geoffrey, who married his cousin, Penelope Blakeley. Their eldest son was Robert, my father, and my mother was Lady Daphne Rogers. My father and my eldest brother, Geoffrey, died at Worcester. I was seventeen at the time, and before I might join the fray, my mother hauled me home to Lynmouth, where we sat quietly, not involving ourselves in politics, and waited for the king to be restored. Now, explain again to me how we are related, your grace."

"My great-grandmother was Skye O'Malley. My grandmother is her youngest daughter, Velvet, the Countess of BrocCairn. My mother, Jasmine, was her daughter, and my father was Prince Henry Stuart. The lady with me is my youngest sister, the Marquise d'Auriville, born Lady Autumn Leslie. She is the Duke of Glenkirk's daughter. He was my mother's last husband, who died at Dunbar, also fighting for the king."

The young earl nodded, and then he said with a smile, "How may I be of service to you, cousins?"

"Greenwood, which was my mother's house, seems to have been confiscated during the Protectorate. My sister has just returned from France. She is a widow, and I thought I might bring her to court. But now she has no place in which to lay her pretty head. I was hoping you would allow her to stay here at Lynmouth House, my lord. My apartments at Whitehall aren't large enough for both of us."

"You have apartments at Whitehall?" The earl was impressed.

"The privilege of being the king's first cousin," Charlie answered him, waving his hand in a blasé fashion. "I always have quarters where the king has quarters." He smiled at John Southwood. "Now, about my sister . . . ?"

"Of course you may stay with me, Cousin Autumn," the earl said. 'Sblood! When he told all his friends he would be the envy of the whole damned world. He peered at the lady in question and caught his breath sharply. She was absolutely beautiful, although she was looking a trifle pale. Reaching out, he yanked the bellpull hard. Betts was there immediately. He'd probably been peeping through the keyhole.

"Yes, my lord?" Betts said smoothly.

"Have the Rose apartment opened immediately for her ladyship, Betts." He turned to Autumn. "You have servants with you?"

"My two maids, Lily and Orane," Autumn answered softly. "Thank you so much, Cousin John. I am a stranger to you, and yet you are willing to open your home to me. How kind."

"Would you like to come to Whitehall tonight with me?" he asked her. "They're performing a masque to cheer the king. His mistress, Lady Palmer, is expecting a child and has retired from court for the present. Not that she won't be back. She will. Ambitious wench, Barbara Palmer. Was born a Villiers, you know."

"Will you excuse me?" Autumn said. "We have been traveling for several days and I am exhausted. I want nothing more than a hot bath, a light supper, and my bed."

"I will see to it at once, your ladyship," Betts said and withdrew from the library.

"I'll go with you," Charlie said. "I want to let the king know I'm back and speak to him about Greenwood."

"Won't do you any good," the earl said. "He promised not to take back property reassigned during the Protectorate. He ain't made any exceptions to date," John Southwood informed them.

"But Greenwood wasn't a crown property ever," Autumn said. "Madame Skye bought it years ago when she returned from Algiers. Mama is going to be furious about its loss."

"Cromwell gave away the properties of people he believed disloyal to his regime," the earl said.

"How could Mama be disloyal? She took no sides and left the country," Autumn replied.

"Mama didn't openly support Cromwell, and she was the mother of Henry Stuart's only son," Charlie said wisely. "I will speak to the king, but I suspect Greenwood is gone for good. Mama doesn't need it anyway, and the family has other houses in London at which to stay on the rare occasions we come to town."

"That isn't the point!" Autumn said angrily. "The king should at least compensate Mama for her loss. Remember, my father died at Dunbar for the Royal Stuarts. And who is this Duke of Garwood who was loyal to Cromwell and yet is allowed to retain stolen property?"

"He was a double agent for the king during the wars, and afterwards," the Earl of Southwood said to her. "They say it was he who exposed the traitors in the Sealed Knot Society."

"He was the one?" Charlie exclaimed. "I should like to shake his hand for ferreting out that dastard, Sir Richard Willys. How did he manage it? It had to be dangerous work."

"He took the identity of his dead cousin, a boy raised with him from the time his parents—the mother was the previous duke's sister—were lost at sea on their way back from Ireland. The two cousins were inseparable growing up and looked very much alike. The young gentleman died of a fever just as the war began. Everything was so confused then. Records weren't kept or lost. Somewhere along the way the duke was able to take the identity of his dead cousin. It was given out that the duke himself had fled England with the Stuarts. His servants were incredibly loyal, and so the secret has been kept these past nine years. The king has publicly praised the duke's loyalty and bravery."

"It still doesn't alter the fact that Greenwood is my mother's house, given to her by Madame Skye," Autumn said stubbornly.

"Sweeting, you are upset," Charlie said gently. "You are tired and not seeing things clearly. You have no idea how terrible it was for the king these last years. He is a man who does not forget friendship or loyalty, Autumn."

The door to the library opened. Lily hurried in, curtsying. "I've

come to take you upstairs, my lady. The bath is being filled, and the
cook says she will send you up a nice supper when we're ready."

"Go along, and get some rest, little sister," Charlie said, and he
kissed her on the forehead.

Autumn sighed. Then she curtsied to the Earl of Southwood.
"Again, cousin, I thank you for your hospitality," she told him.

"Call me Johnnie," he told her. "Everyone does." And he smiled.
"Don't let old Betts bully you either. He responds to arrogance, for
some reason, so don't be too kind to him."

Autumn giggled and then, in Lily's company, departed the library.

When the door had closed behind them Charlie said, "Shall we
go to Whitehall now, Johnnie? While my immediate family likes to
call me 'the not-so-royal Stuart,' my friends call me Charlie."

The two men went off together, the young earl giving orders that
Autumn's coach and horses be stabled, and that her servants be well
taken care of, else he be annoyed.

"It shall be as you ordered, my lord," Betts answered his master,
bowing servilely. "Shall I prepare an apartment for his grace?"

"His grace has apartments at Whitehall," the earl replied loftily,
and almost laughed at the look of awe on his majordomo's face. But
he managed to retain his composure long enough for him and Charlie
to mount their horses and ride off.

"You don't have a barge?" the duke asked his cousin, curious, for
the house was located directly on the river.

"Too expensive to keep one anymore," Johnnie said. "I prefer to
ride, anyway, and there are always werrymen available."

Autumn watched them go from the window in her day room. It
would have been fun, she thought, to go to court, but she would not
have been at her best tonight How her older brother managed to be
so full of energy amazed her. She supposed it was the life he had
led, going to court from his earliest childhood. He hardly seemed to
need any sleep, she noticed. Autumn turned away from the window
and entered her bedchamber, which overlooked the river. She recalled the stories she had been told of how her mother had arrived
by barge from her ship when she had first come from India. She

tried to imagine Jasmine coming up the showy lawns of the house next door and into Madame Skye's arms. There was so much history in Greenwood. She had to get it back!

At Whitehall the Duke of Lundy went immediately to pay his respects to his cousin the king, kneeling before Charles II and kissing his outstretched hand. "I'll go and make myself presentable shortly, Your Majesty, but I wanted to come to you first."

"Get up, Charlie," the king said. "Every time you kneel before me I remember who your father was, and that had he been wed to your mother, I should be kneeling to you," chuckled Charles Stuart. "You remember George Villiers, and this is Gabriel Bainbridge, the Duke of Garwood. I know you haven't met, but I think you should. He has been waiting for you to return to court so he might speak with you."

The Duke of Lundy rose. "About Mama's house, Greenwood?" he said. "I should warn you, sir, that I have brought my widowed sister up to London with me, and Autumn is very put out about Greenwood's loss."

"You've brought your sister to court?" the king said, sounding quite interested. "Is she as beautiful as the other ladies in your family, Charlie? Where is she?"

"Sheltering at Cousin Johnnie's house next door, and quite annoyed, Your Majesty," the Duke of Lundy said with a small smile. "She was tired, and we have been traveling several days from Queen's Malvern."

"A widow, you say?" the king questioned him.

"Aye. Mama took her to her chateau in France right after Bess was killed. She married a French nobleman who died suddenly five years ago, leaving Autumn with a small daughter. When Your Majesty was restored to his rightful place my mother and sister returned to England. She has been pining of late, and I thought that perhaps a visit to court might amuse her. She has never been there, as there was no court when she was finally old enough to come."

"That's right," the king recalled. "Your mother surprised your father with a final child shortly after I was born, and they raised her in that Highland lair of theirs, Glenkirk, didn't they?"

"I am amazed Your Majesty remembers such minutiae," Charlie said.

"When she is rested bring her to court, Charlie. But now you and Gabriel must talk. It is important that you do," the king told his cousin. "Go and find a quiet place now, remembering that you are a member of my family and in my presence."

What a strange thing to have said, Charlie thought as he and the Duke of Garwood sought a quiet alcove where they might speak. When they had found one, the two men stood awkwardly for a moment, and then Gabriel Bainbridge began to speak.

"I do not know, my lord, how much you know of me," he said.

"I know you were a double agent for His Majesty," Charlie replied, "and that you are responsible for exposing Sir Richard Willys. I would shake your hand, sir!" Charlie held out his own.

"You may feel differently when you hear what I have to say, my lord. I shall wait until then to offer you my hand," the Duke of Garwood told Charlie seriously. "You are aware that I impersonated my deceased cousin?"

"I am," Charlie responded. "Your servants are to be commended for keeping the secret, my lord."

Gabriel Bainbridge smiled faintly. "They are good people," he said quietly. "Without their cooperation I should not have been able to pull it off at all." He was a handsome man with dark blond hair and very deep blue eyes. The Duke of Lundy estimated his age at close to forty.

"Your wife must be proud," he said.

"I have never married," Gabriel Bainbridge answered him. "By the time I was ready to consider it, we were at war and all the young ladies had fled or were spouting Puritan nonsense."

"I understand," Charlie replied. "My sister left England for the same reason. Mama said there was no decent society where one might introduce a young lady to young gentlemen."

"We are getting off the subject," the Duke of Garwood said. "I must unburden myself to you, my lord, and I must ask your forgiveness."

"We have never met," Charlie retorted.

"The identity I took during the wars and the Protectorate was that of my cousin, Sir Simon Bates," Gabriel Bainbridge said, and his body tightened, as if he was expecting Charlie Stuart to deliver him a great blow. He wouldn't have blamed him if he had.

"God's blood!" the Duke of Lundy swore softly. He was stunned by the revelation, and wondered how long the king had known it. For a moment he was actually at a loss for words. This man had led the men who killed his Bess.

"It should never have happened," Gabriel Bainbridge said. "If I had entered the house first, it wouldn't have."

"Why didn't you?" Charlie asked him softly. *"Why didn't you?"*

"I don't know," the Duke of Garwood said brokenly. "I was sent to take livestock, any horses I could find, and foodstuffs, for the troops. The men with me that day were not my own, most of whom were down with a flux of the bowels. I was given a troop of ill-disciplined scum, criminals and layabouts for the most part. Because I couldn't trust them, because I couldn't delegate authority to any of them, I had to reconnoiter myself. I was inspecting your stables and barns when I heard the shot. The troopers with me weren't supposed to enter the house. When I had finished my scouting I had intended to tell whomever was there that I was taking supplies in the name of the Commonwealth. Then I was to give them a chit to be redeemed later, when peace had been restored."

"Sir Simon Bates's reputation was horrific," Charlie said. "It is said he slaughtered the family of a Sir Gerald Crofts in Oxford."

"There was no Sir Gerald Crofts, and Simon Bates's reputation was manufactured by Cromwell's people to instill fear into the hearts of any who heard he was coming their way," Gabriel Bainbridge explained. "They did that with a dozen or so more of us. That way when the people in the district where we were sent to make a reconnaissance heard we were coming, they were more than likely to cooperate with us. I will admit it was a clever tactic."

"Aye," Charlie agreed quietly.

"Your wife shouldn't have died, nor your servant, my lord. If that young girl had not killed the trooper who shot them herself, I surely would have. Jesu, she was brave!"

"My sister, Autumn," Charlie said.

"Yes! Yes! That was her name, Lady Autumn Leslie," the Duke of Garwood anwswered. Then his excitement faded and he grew serious once again. "My lord, I beg you to forgive me," he said. "I know my sorrow and guilt cannot bring back your duchess, but if I could go back and give my life in place of hers, I would! It should not have happened!" And his eyes were filled with tears that began to flow down his handsome face. He knelt suddenly before Charlie, his head bowed.

The Duke of Lundy thought he had put the sorrow of his wife's violent death behind him. He found now, faced with the man who was in part responsible for Bess's demise, he wasn't certain. He looked down at Gabriel Bainbridge and sighed. Damn Cromwell and his pocky Roundheads, his little sister's favorite curse in those days came to his mind almost immediately. He sighed again. Bess was gone, and nothing was going to bring her back. This man kneeling before him wasn't responsible for Oliver Cromwell and his ilk. He wasn't responsible for the two civil wars or the years of the Protectorate. He wasn't responsible for King Charles I's murder. He had helped the Stuarts in his own way, risking his life in a dangerous game. Had he been caught, he would have been hanged or beheaded. But he hadn't been caught, and he had exposed those who would have kept Charles II from returning and reclaiming his rightful place on England's throne. He knew what Bess would have said and done in this instance. She had been a sensible, loving woman with a kind heart.

"I forgive you, Gabriel Bainbridge," Charlie Stuart said quietly, and he raised the man to his feet again. "Now, sir, shake my hand."

"Thank you, my lord," his companion said, taking the outstretched hand in a firm grip. Their eyes met, and the Duke of Garwood saw the genuine pardon in the Duke of Lundy's eyes. "Thank you," he repeated.

"When you met Autumn," Charlie said, "did you look like you do now, Gabriel Bainbridge?"

"Nay. My hair was cropped in Roundhead fashion, and my garments plain. I looked quite severe, I have been told."

"Then let us not mention your deception to my sister," Charlie said quietly. "Autumn will be quite aggravated to meet the man who now possesses Greenwood, but if she learns that you were Sir Simon Bates, there will be no living with her, I fear. I shall speak to my cousin the king about this as well. Come now, and let us reassure him that there is no bad blood between us. I know it was difficult for those of you in England these past years, but I can assure you that the king suffered far worse than any of us. I would not distress him."

"Agreed," the Duke of Garwood said, "and I also agree to your suggestion regarding your sister. She was hot-tempered then. I don't expect she has changed, has she?"

Charles Frederick Stuart laughed aloud as they crossed the room back to the king. "Autumn is no less hot-tempered today than she was when you met her. Best you begin any acquaintance with her anew. It is unlikely she will ever have to know of your past."

"It is settled, then?" the king said as they approached him.

"It is settled," Charlie reassured him.

"Excellent! Now, cousin, bring your sister to court tomorrow so we may personally welcome her home to England," the king said, and there was a definite gleam of interest in his amber eyes.

God's blood, Charlie thought to himself. *What mischief have I done in bringing Autumn to court?* But then he remembered that his sister was about to celebrate her twenty-ninth birthday. She was an experienced woman who had had a husband, and a royal lover. Autumn could certainly take care of herself. And she would have to.

Chapter

17

Whitehall was the king's favorite palace. It had begun its existence as the inn of the Archbishop of York, an unimpressive and rather dreary two-story building of no particular distinction located in the district of Westminster. Then Henry VIII's Archbishop of York, Thomas Wolsey, renovated his London residence into a magnificent palace, enlarging it, decorating, and adorning it until it was the envy of even the king. Wolsey, created a cardinal, then failed his king in the matter of Henry's divorce from his first queen, Catherine of Aragon. The king's own London house, Westminster Palace, had burned to the ground several years earlier. Wolsey, in a desperate effort to save himself and his career, offered the king York Palace, which was promptly rechristened Whitehall.

Wolsey's original palace was situated between the river Thames and the street that ran to Charing Cross, and thence to Westminster itself. Henry VIII wanted a larger palace, which required more land, but even he couldn't close off a public thoroughfare. Nonetheless he purchased twenty-four acres across the road from the original palace, demolished the structures standing on his new land, and began to build. The palace ended up being a hodgepodge of connecting galleries, halls, and courts that, while an architectural nightmare on the exterior, was quite beautiful inside. Whitehall also rambled and straggled through a maze of inner courts and hidden recesses that were never seen by the court, for this was where the legion of servants necessary to make court life tolerable lived and worked.

Because the street divided the palace there was no unity to it at all. Still Whitehall had all the amenities a king could want. It had gardens, a tiltyard, tennis courts, a cockpit, a ballhouse, where featherball was played, and an area set aside for playing bowls. The palace had three gateways. On the riverside of the road the turretted Palace, or Whitehall Gate, kept the public from straying into the Great Court. The King Street Gate and the Holbein Gate were constructed astride the street, in order to give the court access to the parkside of Whitehall, which was referred to as the "cockpit." The King Street Gate stood at the southwestern end of the palace and opened into King Street. The Holbein Gate was opposite the king's Banqueting House.

Before he had been murdered, Charles I had commissioned John Webb, the son-in-law of Indigo Jones, to draw up plans for the rebuilding of Whitehall. It was a project never realized by the unfortunate king, and his son had not the funds for it, although he lavished borrowed moneys upon his ill-built home. Still, the beauty of its interior more than made up for the ugliness of the exterior, with carved stonework, lavish gilt moldings, painted ceilings, great works of art, magnificent tapestries, and beautiful furniture.

Autumn's coach was admitted to the Great Court. She descended from it in the company of her brother. She shook her skirts out nervously, and as her hood fell back she patted her hair. "How do I look?" she demanded of Charlie.

"Even more beautiful than when we left the house," he told her with a grin. "For God's sake, Autumn, he's only a man."

"Kings are not mere men," she advised him sagely. "Kings have unlimited power. It is that power that makes them different from people like you and me, Charlie."

"I keep thinking of you as my baby sister," he said slowly, shaking his auburn head, "but you are very clever, Autumn, and mayhap too wise."

"I have known one king, brother," she reminded him.

"And now you are to know another. Be warned, however, that this king likes beautiful women and thinks nothing of compromising them to his own advantage. Do not be swayed by his charm, which is great."

"His cousin, Louis, likes beautiful women too, and has charm," Autumn replied. "I'm not the innocent I was when Louis first bedded me."

"Surely you aren't expecting to . . ." Charlie began, not certain he wasn't just a little shocked, not ready to believe she would dare . . .

"The king has a mistress who is very much in his favor, and he likes it that way, I am told," Autumn replied with a small smile.

"What mischief are you planning?" he demanded of her.

Autumn laughed. "If a small flirtation can regain Greenwood for us, where is the harm, Charlie?"

"Don't even consider it!" he almost shouted at her. "I am taking you back to Lynmouth House right now, Autumn! No woman as beautiful as you are can expect to have a *small* flirtation with King Charles and gain by it. My cousin is one of the most carnal men I have ever known. Engage his interest and you will have a tiger by the tail!"

Autumn's gem-colored eyes twinkled at him. "What fun," she teased him wickedly. "I am in the mood for some sport, big brother."

Charles Frederick Stuart, Duke of Lundy, grew red in the face, at a complete loss for words. He wasn't certain if she was jesting with him or not, and that frightened him. It suddenly dawned on him that while he might have known Autumn, the girl, he really didn't know the woman she had become.

Seeing his distress, Autumn stopped in her passage and took her brother's hands in hers. "Oh, Charlie, I didn't mean to upset you."

His voice returned. "We'll go to my apartments so you may remove your cloak and see to your hair," he said, suddenly calm. His little sister was a grown woman, and very unlike his other two sisters. He couldn't control her even if he tried. He led her down several corridors until finally he stopped before a door and, opening it, ushered her inside.

Immediately his valet came forward to take Autumn's enveloping cape and gloves from her. Then he led her to a basin of scented water. Autumn washed her hands and face quickly, pinching her cheeks to bring more color into them. She did not paint her face with white lead, flour, or rice, as some women did. Her hair lay smooth, her chignon neat, several fetching curls on either side of her head.

"I'm ready," she said at last.

"And you will behave yourself?" he queried her.

Autumn laughed. "I'll not disgrace you," she said to his relief, until he realized that she had not answerd his question at all.

With a deep sigh Charlie gave his sister his arm and escorted her back through the winding corridors to the king's audience chamber, where he was receiving at that particular hour. His heart sank when he saw Charles Stuart's immediate interest as they entered the room. Leading his sister up to the throne, the Duke of Lundy bowed to his cousin, the king. "Your Majesty, I have the honor to present to you my youngest sister, Autumn, Madame la Marquise d'Auriville." Then he steadied her as she swept the king an elegant curtsey.

The king's eyes dipped swiftly to the deep cleavage between Autumn's small but perfect breasts. He smiled toothily and, rising, took Autumn's hand from Charlie. "Madame," he said, "I am delighted to meet you at long last. I regret there has been no court for you to attend until now." His dark brown eyes looked deeply into hers.

Autumn felt a distinct tingle of excitement. "Your Majesty's warm welcome makes up for my years of waiting," she said almost breathlessly. The king was a very attractive man. He was not handsome in a classical sense, but he was certainly comely in a magnetic way. He didn't look like a Stuart, but rather like his French mother, with his dark eyes and curls. His face was saturnine, with a slight hook to his nose. He had a very well-turned leg, and he reminded her of King Louis. She told him so, and he smiled again.

"You know my cousin Louis?" he said. "I had heard, Madame la marquise, that you were a simple country matron. How do you compare my court with my cousin's?"

"I have never been to the French court, Your Majesty," Autumn answered him honestly. "King Louis has the habit of coming each October to Chambord to hunt. My mother and I have joined his party for several years now. Chambord is a bit overwhelming for a hunting lodge, however."

"How long did you know Louis?" the king asked her, suddenly intrigued. He had not been aware that women joined the king's yearly sojourn to the chateau of Chambord.

"I met your cousin when he was thirteen, Your Majesty, just before my marriage to Sebastian d'Oleron. He was a bold boy, and I found it necessary to put him in his place, I fear. He never forgot me for it," she explained, and then she smiled mischievously.

King Charles laughed, genuinely amused. "Nay, madame, I don't imagine he could forget you. When were you first invited to Chambord?"

"The year after my husband died," Autumn said quietly.

"Ah," the king said, beginning to think he understood.

A servant came to their side, offering wine. The king took a goblet and handed it to Autumn. Then he took one for himself.

"Charlie tells me you have a daughter. Let's us walk the room, madame. There are too many ears that listen when one remains still. How old is your little girl?"

"I have two daughters, Your Majesty," Autumn said. "Mademoiselle Madeline d'Oleron, the heiress to Chermont, my husband's estate, has just turned seven. My younger daughter, Mademoiselle Marguerite Louise de La Bois, is now two, Your Majesty."

"Ah," the king responded. *He did understand!* "Your younger daughter is my cousin's child?"

"Yes, Your Majesty. King Louis promptly acknowledged her and gave her an income of her own. He says he will choose a husband for her one day, when she is old enough, but I think Margot will choose her own husband, like her female antecedents before her."

"Your brother did not mention Mademoiselle de La Bois," the king said softly. "Why is that, I wonder?"

"I think Charlie seeks to protect my reputation. He and Mama say I must marry again, although I cannot see a need for it," Autumn replied to the king. "I also think my brother believes you mean to seduce me, Your Majesty."

Charles Stuart laughed heartily, and then he looked directly at Autumn. "My cousin, the not-so-royal Stuart, knows me well, Madame la marquise. I most certainly mean to seduce you. You are far too delicious for me to resist."

"But I understand Your Majesty has a mistress of whom he is deeply fond," Autumn boldly responded. "I yielded to King Louis because I had no other choice, and I had my child to protect. Surely Your Majesty would not coerce me in a similar manner. I don't even know you. I am no whore to be casually tumbled and then as casually deserted."

"Barbara is with child and has withdrawn from the court, madame. She is unlikely to return for some months. Would you allow your king to languish alone? I cannot believe you that cruel."

"And I cannot believe you are as bold as King Louis," Autumn told him audaciously, her heart hammering. She had not expected the king to be quite so brazen in his approach to her, although she had certainly considered a flirtation with him. She had told Charlie as much. He would surely blame her for this.

They had stopped walking at the far end of the audience chamber, and the king gently pushed Autumn into an alcove, pressing himself against her as he backed her into the wall. "I like your gown," he said. "Garnet becomes you with your mahogany curls." Then the king gently fingered one, bringing it to his lips to kiss. "Your rubies are quite magnificent," he said, touching them. His fingers brushed across the swell of her bosom. "And your skin is wonderfully soft, madame."

Autumn was having difficulty drawing a breath, but she finally managed to do so. "Your Majesty, you must not hurry me into a decision," she pleaded prettily. "I must speak with my brother first."

"The decision is not yours to make, madame, but mine, and I have made it. You really are a dreadful little fraud, Autumn. I love you already for it. Charlie will certainly assure you that you must obey your king, my beauty. You know it to be so."

"He will also rail at me, and insist I have seduced you instead of the other way around," Autumn replied, a piqued tone to her voice.

The king chuckled. "I will assure him the seduction is all mine, Madame la marquise." He caught her chin between a thumb and a forefinger. "We are about to begin a delicious idyll, m'dear."

Now Autumn laughed. "That is what Louis called our relationship. He always said I was his sweet idyll, his jewel."

"And you shall be my Autumn idyll," the king said, smiling at his own play on words. Then he quickly kissed her lips before they began their walk back down the long chamber to his throne, where he left her with Charlie. "We owe you a great debt, cousin," he said, "for bringing your beautiful sister to court. She is going to stay for some time, and we shall enjoy her company."

"What have you done?" the Duke of Lundy hissed as they withdrew from the king's immediate presence.

"Why do you assume I have done anything?" Autumn demanded.

"Because I know the king, and he has that *look* on his face," Charlie said. "I didn't bring you to court to play the whore!"

"I should slap you for that remark were you not my own dear brother," Autumn said angrily. "The king wishes to seduce me, and he will because he is the king. That much I learned with King Louis. Is it possible for a woman to refuse a king, Charlie? Have you ever heard of it being done? If, however, I am to be seduced by a royal lover again, at least I shall gain something for myself this time. It can hardly do my reputation any good to be publicly acknowledged as the king's new friend, which means it is unlikely I shall be able to find myself a husband now. I am not so great a fool as to believe that Lady Castlemaine will not come back to court and to the king's arms once her confinement is over and done with and she has regained her strength. Well, brother, I shall make good use of the time allotted me. When Barbara Palmer returns I shall have an English title and a house of my own, I promise you!"

"And a full belly, I've not a doubt," her brother said bitterly.

"So much the better," Autumn told him. "I shall not be easily forgotten then, Charlie, and my child will profit too."

"How have you become so hard?" the Duke of Lundy asked his sister. "What has happened to you, Autumn?"

"Oh, Charlie, I am not our great-grandmother, who could joust with a queen and make her own great fortune. I am not Mama, who is clever with her business investments. I am more like my grandmother Gordon, who while brave of heart was forced by life to accept what was offered her and not go out to get what she really wanted. I would have been happy to remain Sebastian's wife forever. To bear him a child each year. To live the simple life of a chateau owner on the Cher. It was not, however, to be. Widowed, I was forced to become King Louis's mistress for several weeks each year. I was a convenience, like Chambord itself. While Louis is fond of me, he has no heart, even as this English king has no heart.

"You say you know your cousin. If that is so, then why did you bring me to court? No one need tell me I am beautiful, brother. I see it in my own mirror. And you have yourself said that King Charles enjoys beautiful women. Surely you knew he would seek to seduce me. And that being the case, why are you angry at me for accepting the inevitable? I could not refuse King Louis. I cannot refuse King Charles."

"I wasn't aware that Barbara had withdrawn from the court," Charlie said despairingly. "Oh, I knew she must, and soon, but I did not realize she was already gone, and the king on the prowl once more, or I should have never brought you. He seems to be a man who cannot do without a woman, I fear. I just hate that the woman is my own baby sister."

"Who will be twenty-nine in three weeks' time," Autumn reminded him, now amused.

"Mama is going to be furious," Charlie said.

"We will distract her by seeking a wife for you instead," Autumn told her brother.

"I don't need a wife," he groused. "Oh, I know I tell Mama that I do, but I don't. Besides, I have two sons for Lundy."

"Two sons you haven't seen in several years, who are growing up wild savages at Glenkirk," Autumn replied. "You should really bring them down from Scotland before the winter sets in, and Sabrina too."

A crafty look came into Charlie's eyes. "You're right!" he said. "You, my clever little sister, are absolutely right! We will distract Mama from your situation by giving her my trio of brats to civilize! I'll wait a few days to see you settled here at court. Then, if you will release me, sister, I'll ride for Scotland without further delay. When I appear again on my own doorstep at Queen's Malvern, I shall have my brood with me. Mama will have little time to ask questions that I don't really want to answer. That, dear sister, will eventually be your problem, not mine."

"Agreed," Autumn said cheerfully.

"Come and meet some of the people you should know," Charlie said, and led her off to introduce her to George Villiers, the second Duke of Buckingham, and Gabriel Bainbridge, the Duke of Garwood.

"My parents were friends of your father," Autumn told Buckingham. "They called your father Steenie, didn't they?"

"I never knew my father," George Villiers said. "He was killed when I was an infant, and my mother ripening with my brother."

"How sad," Autumn told him. "I am so glad I knew my father!"

"You were indeed most fortunate, Madame la marquise," the Duke of Buckingham said.

They returned to Charlie's apartment to collect her cloak, then descended to the Great Court, where the coach waited. Autumn turned to enter her carriage when a soberly dressed gentleman came up to them. "Madame la marquise," he said, "I am William Chiffinch, His Majesty's servant. I have been sent to fetch you to the king. If you will follow me, please?"

Autumn's face darkened with her anger. "Sir," she said in steely tones, "you may tell His Majesty that I am not some common whore to be *fetched* from the streets. I make my residence at the Earl of Lynmouth's house on the Strand. If His Majesty wishes to see me, he will come there whenever it pleases him." Then, without another word, she climbed into her coach. "Charlie, are you coming, or will you remain here at Whitehall?"

Wordless, the Duke of Lundy waved his sister off, not knowing whether to laugh or not as her vehicle moved out of the Great Court into the street beyond the Whitehall Gate.

It was Buckingham who broke the tension. "Well, damn me! If your sister don't beat all, Charlie," he said. "A woman who will have the king her way. I can't wait to tell my cousin Barbara. If he goes, she'll be absolutely furious, though even Barbara is not dense enough to believe the king will remain celibate until her return. But she's never been as bold as your sister. Still, there is nothing she can do right now, for her big belly impedes her. Aha! Ha! Ha! Ha!" he chortled.

"You don't think the king will be insulted?" Charlie said.

"Hell no!" Buckingham replied. "He'll be as intrigued as can be by this woman who refused to follow Mr. Chiffinch meekly to the royal bed. Eh, Mr. Chiffinch?" the duke said with a good-natured poke at the servant's chest.

"It is not for me to say, your grace," William Chiffinch replied, but there was indeed a faint hint of a smile at the corners of his mouth.

"Well, go and tell your master, Chiffinch," Buckingham told him. "I'd give a gold piece to hear what the king says when you do, but I don't suppose you'd let us go with you, Chiffinch, would you?"

"I'm afraid not, Your Grace," the servant said quietly, and then he withdrew, bowing to them before he went.

"Come on," Buckingham said, "let's go and play some cards, gentlemen."

As they moved off, Gabriel Bainbridge, who had been silent, said angrily to the Duke of Lundy, "How can you allow this, Charlie?"

"How can I prevent it?" was his answer. "Autumn isn't a child, my lord. She's a grown woman with children, and her own wealth."

The Duke of Garwood sighed. "I wanted to get to know her," he said, almost forlornly.

"You will have your chance," Charlie said. "When Madame Barbara returns to court she will see my sister gone from it. Autumn is but a diversion. The king and Lady Barbara have grown up together, suffered exile together. They have far more in common than my sister does with the king. Besides, His Majesty will shortly have to choose a queen. Then, my friend, there will be no time for anyone or anything else."

"You speak so casually of your sister's dishonor," the Duke of Garwood said.

"There is no dishonor in being a king's mistress," Charlie told him, "or so the women in my family have always been assured. You recall my sister as that brave, foolish girl who shot your trooper, Gabriel. She is no longer that girl. She is a woman who has loved, borne her husband a child, suffered his death, and enjoyed the favors of King Louis, who sought her out a year after Sebastian died. Her second daughter is Louis's child. Autumn is a grown and mature woman."

"Your sister was correct when she said she was no common whore," the Duke of Garwood replied, suddenly angry. "She is a courtesan of the first rank, my lord, and you no better than her pimp!"

"I shall not demand satisfaction for those remarks, my lord, because I can see you have an unrequited *tendre* for my sister. You are disappointed and choleric, but I will excuse you this time. I have been in love myself."

"I am not in love!" the Duke of Garwood protested.

Charles Frederick Stuart smiled knowingly, grinning at the duke. "Your time will come, sir," he said, "but be advised that neither I nor my brothers will allow you to treat Autumn with contempt or disgrace her. You do understand that, sir, don't you?"

"You need not fear, Your Grace, for I shall have nothing further to do with the wench at all," Gabriel Bainbridge replied stiffly.

"It will be your loss, sir," Charlie said, wondering what his sister would think of all this; but then, he didn't intend telling her. Autumn would have her hands full soon enough. If she really believed being King Louis's discreet mistress each October had thoroughly prepared her to be Charles Stuart's temporary and most public mistress, she would soon find out she was greatly mistaken.

Autumn's thoughts as she returned to Lynmouth House were quite clear. She was through being a helpless plaything for men. If the King of England wanted to bed her, then she would make certain that she was in control of the situation at all times. *And* she would get more out of the relationship than a baby this time. *Sebastian, why did you leave me?* her heart cried out, as it had so many times since the day he died. *And why is it all so damned hard? Perhaps I should return to France,* she considered, but she knew that that would not be the answer.

She hurried into the house, telling Betts as she came, "We may be having a rather important visitor this evening. I want the bath filled immediately!"

"But, madame . . . ," he began.

Autumn cut him short. "This is not a matter for discussion, Betts, nor am I soliciting your advice. Do as I say immediately!" She half-ran up the stairs to her apartments, where Lily and Orane were dozing as they waited for her. "Awaken!" she told them. "We will be having an important visitor shortly."

A footman ran into the house. "Where shall we set the tub, m'lady?" he asked her.

"Before the fire in the day room," she instructed.

"But you had a bath before you went out this evening," Lily protested to her mistress.

"Come, help me disrobe, both of you," Autumn said, not bothering to explain further. "Quickly! Make certain the water is good and hot," she called to the footmen before disappearing into her bedchamber.

Off came her bodice and gown, her petticoats and her chemise. When Orane knelt to remove her stockings and slippers Autumn stopped her with a shake of her head. Orane's eyes grew wide at the implications. Lily, wiser, took a cream-colored silk chamber robe, and wrapped it about her mistress. She touched her mistress's ruby necklace.

"No," Autumn said.

"Does madame wish her hair brushed tonight?" Orane inquired.

"Yes," was all Autumn replied, and she sat down upon a small chair.

Orane pulled the pins from her mistress's long mahogany-colored hair and began to brush it with smooth strokes.

"See to the bath, Lily," Autumn said. "Put some sandalwood oil in the water, and get out a cake of the soap."

"Yes, m'lady," Lily replied, returning to the day room, where the footmen had just finished. She poured a generous dollop of oil into the great oak tub. Then she laid out the soap and towels, which she placed on a heating rack by the edge of the fire. She hurried to light several candles and then returned to the bedchamber, where she adjusted the lighting to a more subtle glow. A knock upon the outer door sent her scurrying to answer it. Opening the door, the maidservant gaped, and then gasped with her surprise. She had never seen King Charles before, but she sensed immediately who he was. She curtsied deeply even as Autumn came from the bedchamber with Orane by her side.

"Make your curtsey," Autumn whispered to Orane. "Then be gone."

Lily had recovered enough to take the gentleman's hat, gloves, and cape. Then she looked nervously to her mistress.

"Put His Majesty's things on the chair, Lily, where he may easily retrieve them when he departs," Autumn said quietly. "I will see you both in the morning. Good night."

The two young women backed from the day room, closing the door firmly behind them.

"Are you hungry?" Autumn asked him. "I see Betts has put a tray on the sideboard, along with some wine. I am happy to say that every member of this family has a good stock of our French relations' wine."

"Give me some wine, madame," he told her.

Hiding a smile, Autumn went to the sideboard and poured the king a large silver goblet of rich, fragrant red wine. Turning, she handed it to him, then poured herself some of the potent liquid.

The king drank and then, slamming the goblet down forcefully, he said, "You are the boldest damn woman I have ever met, Autumn. I was not particularly pleased when Mr. Chiffinch returned with your reply to my most generous invitation."

"And yet," Autumn said bravely, "here you are, Charles Stuart."

"Yes, here I am," he answered her.

"Have you come to scold me and then leave?" she taunted.

"No, my dear, I have come to fuck you," he responded, half-angrily.

"Not before you have had a bath," she told him.

"*What?!*"

"You men will play in mud puddles as boys, or swim naked in an icy sea, but suggest a bath and you go all to pieces," Autumn said as she briskly removed his short jacket first and put it aside. Then her slim fingers nimbly undid his shirt, pulling it off. Next came his belt, and then Autumn pushed the king into a chair so she could yank his boots and stockings off. When this was done she ordered him up, but he pulled her into his lap, his big hand sliding quickly beneath her robe to fondle a breast. She struggled up, laughing.

"Oh, no, sire, not until you have been properly washed." She jerked his breeches and drawers down. "Step out of them," she ordered sternly. When he had she led him to the great oak tub. "Get in. Do you know how to bathe yourself, or shall I do it for you?"

"As tempting as the thought of you washing me like a babe is, madame, I shall do it myself to save time," the king told her.

"Your buttocks are most shapely," she remarked.

He laughed and slid beneath the water. "You're a proper hussy," he told her. He had decided to be amused by all of this. After all, had Mr. Chiffinch brought her to his bed as he did so many women, it might have proved uninteresting in the sameness. His first thought, however, when his servant had delivered her reply to his invitation, was to either ignore her from then on or drag her back by force, if necessary. Then it occurred to him that her saucy proposal was an adventure. He had had enough of adventures these eleven years past, but erotic adventures were far different than the hazardous ventures he had previously experienced. He chuckled as he scrubbed himself thoroughly. "When did you last bathe, madame?" he asked her.

"Earlier this evening," she replied. "Come out of the tub now, Charles Stuart. I shall dry you off. It would not do to have you catch cold in my care. I don't want to be accused of treason." Then she threw aside her chamber robe and picked up a towel from the drying rack, where it had been warming.

Exiting the tub, the king's dark eyes widened in appreciation. "Madame, you are, I can see, a proper minx," he murmured. She was naked but for her red striped silk stockings, her ruby-studded shoes, and the rubies she wore about her neck and in her ears. Her stockings were held up by golden garters that fastened with small golden cupids. Her breasts were absolutely exquisite, and far surpassed the promise he had anticipated. She had a slender waist, and her belly was just faintly rounded. Her torso long, her legs short. He reached out for her, but Autumn eluded him.

"Nay, sir, not until you are properly tended to," she told him as she began to rub him briskly. He was quickly dry, and his skin tingled. Seating him, she knelt to dry his feet, doing each toe carefully. When she had finished she put the towel aside and, slipping between his legs, took his manhood in the warm cave of her mouth and began to suckle upon it.

The king gasped, surprised, but then he closed his eyes, almost purring as she ministered to his love lance, which was growing hard and throbbing with his excitement. He thought surely she meant to drink his juices, but again she startled him by releasing him from her mouth and climbing upon his thighs to sheath him in her welcoming body. "Jesu!" he exclaimed as she rode him to completion.

Feeling his hot, boiling tribute, Autumn sat back, her arms about the king's neck. "There," she said with a satisfied sigh. "We have taken the edge off your lust, sire, and may now spend the next several hours enjoying ourselves." She dismounted him and, taking the wash rag from where he had left it, she cleansed herself first, and then him.

The breath was finally coming back into his body. "Is that a French custom? The washing afterwards?"

"No," she said. "I taught Louis. It is a custom of my mother's homeland. She taught me, and my sisters. Come on, Charles Stuart, I'm cold and want to get into bed now." She walked into the bedchamber and climbed into the bed, flipping the coverlet back in invitation. "Unless, of course, you are satisfied and wish to leave."

"*No!*" he said, and then, "I believe it will take some time for you to properly satisfy me, Autumn." He climbed into the bed next to her. "Come here, you delightfully wicked bitch. I want to play with your tempting little breasts. Such exquisite fruits, my darling. They are so perfectly round, so soft." His dark head dipped, his mouth enclosing itself over a nipple. "Mmmmm, so delicious," he pronounced.

Autumn lay back amid the pillows and closed her eyes, enjoying his attentions. She now had the upper hand over this lustful king who was so much like his first cousin, King Louis of France. There was, however, a difference. Louis had been yet a boy; Charles was very much a man. She had a trunkful of surprises that would keep this king enthralled, and desiring more. For now she would caress his ego so that even while she ruled him, he would think he was in total command of their passion.

Autumn emptied her mind of all thoughts now, allowing herself to receive the pleasure he was so skilled at giving his lovers. His mouth was strong and tugged upon her nipples in turn. She could feel the excitement beginning to build within her nether regions. His mouth was suddenly upon hers, his dark mustache tickling her slightly. Her lips softened beneath his, allowing his tongue to enter in, where it danced and parried with her tongue until she was hot with desire.

Now his lips were moving down her torso, slowly, very slowly. His tongue licked at her belly. "You are delicious," he groaned, repeating himself.

"I want more," she teased him softly, writhing beneath him.

Immediately his head moved lower and lower, until he was positioned between her soft thighs. His teeth nipped her provocatively, then he kissed the tender flesh hungrily.

"Much more!" she goaded him, pressing her mount into his face.

He complied, pulling her nether lips apart and expertly arousing her *bouton d'amour* until she was sobbing and shuddering her pleasure. Only then did the king mount her and push slowly into her hot, wet love channel until he was fully sheathed. "Now, you naughty little bitch, I am going to fuck you until you are begging me for mercy!" he growled at her.

"*Yes!*" Autumn told him in a breathless voice. "*Yes!*" And when he began to move upon her, thrusting and withdrawing, thrusting and withdrawing, she realized that this man astride her was indeed an expert in the arts of love. Every bit of his reputation was more than well deserved. He pushed her legs back, driving into her so deeply that she could swear he had entered her very womb. "Ahhhh!" she cried, and he laughed. "More!" she begged him, and he complied. Her love passage seemed to widen as he grew harder and thicker within her. "Oh, yes, sire! Yes! Yes! *Yes!*" She shuddered violently.

"Ah, little bitch! What pleasure you give me! Ah!" the king cried out as he reached his peak and loosed his love juices.

Autumn was half fainting with the delight he had offered her. It had been so long since she had been with a man. Was she fated to go through life like this? Her head spun slowly until finally she could feel her heartbeat returning to normal. The king lay sprawled across her body, panting. Finally regaining control of herself, Autumn pushed him off her. "You are too heavy for me, Charles Stuart. Recover upon your back like a large sea turtle. I will wash us so we may be ready for our next bout of Eros."

"Madame, how many times do you expect me to service you tonight?" he demanded, half-jesting, half-serious.

"Your cousin manages to tire even me, five or six times in a night," Autumn told him sweetly. Once he had passed twenty, however, Louis began to flag in his enthusiasm, although Autumn would have never said it aloud to anyone. He was, after all, the father of one of her daughters.

"I am older by eight years than my French cousin," the king protested. "Have mercy, madame."

"If you are through then, Your Majesty, I must tell you that I prefer to sleep alone, don't you?" Autumn said in dulcet tones.

"I am not yet through," he said. "I simply need a small rest, and perhaps some wine as a restorative, madame."

"At once, Your Majesty," Autumn said, springing from the bed and moving across the room. But by the time she had poured the wine and returned with it, the king was asleep, snoring softly. With a smile Autumn set the goblet on the bedside table. Then she bathed their private parts. The king would indeed have her again before he left, if for no other reason than his pride.

The evening, Autumn considered, had gone very well indeed. She had captured his interest, and no other woman would be able to do that while Barbara Palmer grew fatter and fatter with the king's child. It was due, Autumn knew, in February. *I shall have at least six or seven months with the king,* Autumn thought to herself. *It is time for me to gain an English title and a home of my own.*

The king slept several hours. When he awoke he awakened Autumn so that he might take his pleasure of her again. When he had finished he arose and, going out into the day room, dressed himself. He returned, fully clothed, to kiss her a final time. "I expect you at court later today. And tonight we shall try my bed, my darling."

"Perhaps," Autumn told him, pretending exhaustion, her eyes closing.

"I think I shall have to spank you into obedience," the king muttered low, but loud enough so she might hear.

Autumn's eyes opened lazily. "Do not be ridiculous, Charles Stuart. You know as well as I do that no woman has ever pleasured you as I did last night. Even Lady Barbara, for all she holds a place in your heart, if indeed you even have a heart. But if it pleases you that I join you in your bed tonight, then I will do it this once." Then Autumn rolled over and smiled to herself as she heard the door close behind him. She was in complete control of this situation. She intended to remain in control. She wasn't going to allow any king to take advantage of her again. This time she would gain what she wanted! Autumn slept.

Betts, told by his master the earl to wait up until the king had departed, escorted His Majesty down the dew-damp lawns to the quai, where the royal barge was waiting.

"Good night, Your Majesty," Betts said.

"Good night, Betts," the king responded and, stepping into his barge, gave the order to return to Whitehall.

Betts was astounded that the king should know his name. He hurried back up the lawns to lock up the house for the night. The tall clock in the hall struck three hours after midnight. Betts yawned. He would have quite a tale to tell his wife on the morrow.

The Duke of Lundy arrived shortly after the noon hour and hurried up the staircase to his sister's apartments. Autumn was sitting up in her bed, a lacy shawl covering her naked breasts. She was sipping from a saucer of green tea and munching upon a thick slice of freshly baked bread, lavishly buttered and topped with a slice of Cheddar cheese.

"You look like the cat who swallowed the canary," Charlie said, pulling up a chair by the bed. He accepted the goblet of wine that Lily offered him, smiling at the maidservant in thanks. "So he came."

"He came," she said, savoring the cheese on her bread, her tongue snagging on an errant crumb.

"Do you think you held his interest?" Charlie queried her. God's blood, he was indeed sounding like the pimp Garwood had accused him of being. Still, he had to know. It would have been dreadful if the king bedded Autumn once and then ignored her.

"I indeed held his interest, Charlie. No woman has ever taken the initiative with the king. Lucy Walters was his sweet victim and ended up drinking herself to death in Paris, poor wretch. And while Barbara Palmer uses him to her own advantage as I do, she has not my experience with kingly lovers." Autumn laughed. "He adored my arrogance. I treated him as an almost equal and he loved it! I was, however, wise enough to allow my own passions to run riot, thus giving him the impression he was in full control. He says tonight I must sleep in his bed. I have said perhaps, but I shall not. I shall go to court today and leave early with the headache." She laughed again. "He will be very disappointed. He will worry. He will even grow angry, for I have truly engaged his lust and he wants more of me."

"Do not outsmart yourself, Autumn," her brother warned her.

"I won't, Charlie. I may play the sick card once. Best I use it to my advantage. Denied my presence, he will only desire it," Autumn told him, smiling.

"How did my little sister become so cynical?" he said.

"I must play the hand fate has given me, Charlie. I played it badly in France. I will not make that same mistake here in England and once more be a royal casualty. I refuse to be this king's convenient prey, brother. I should disgrace all my female relatives and antecedents if I were."

"I think you have grown older than Mama," he said quietly.

"Speaking of Mama," she replied, "when are you leaving for Scotland, Charlie? If Mama hears of my situation before you can bring her grandchildren to distract her, she will come pell-mell to London and spoil everything."

"I'll leave in a few days. I want to be certain your situation is as you think it is. Then I will go," he told her.

"Help me pick out a gown to wear to court today," Autumn said. "I think black velvet with diamonds. What say you?"

"That my cousin Charles will need all of God's help to survive you, Autumn," Charlie laughed. "I never thought I should feel sorry for the king again, as he has been returned to his rightful place, but by God, sister, I do!"

"Don't be so damned dramatic, Charlie," Autumn said, and yanked upon the bellpull to summon her servants.

There were very few secrets at the court of King Charles II. Within several days it was known that the beautiful widowed Marquise d'Auriville was the king's new mistress. Ambitious and unimportant courtiers sought her favor. Autumn was charming but noncommittal. Certain men eyed her speculatively, particularly as it was known the Marquise d'Auriville was a wealthy woman in her own right. Autumn ignored the gentlemen, her full attention being given to the king. There were women, jealous the king had not chosen them for his new companion, who made spiteful remarks in her presence, but Autumn just laughed at them. She was more than well aware that when Barbara Palmer had her child and recovered from its birth, she would return to court and into the king's affections.

After Charlie had departed for Scotland her two gallants were the Duke of Buckingham and the Duke of Garwood. Buckingham was quick-witted and humorous. Garwood glowered a great deal, speaking little, but when he did, his words were often harsh when directed at her. His attitude irritated her, but she knew she would not have to put up with it after she gained her own title and departed the court. So she teased George Villiers and sparred with Gabriel Bainbridge, much to the king's amusement and that of the court.

There was something about the duke of Garwood that tugged at the back of her mind. Some memory she could not quite pull up. Yet she knew that she had never met Gabriel Bainbridge before. He had certainly never been in Scotland at Glenkirk, and he had not been to Queen's Malvern. What was it about him that seem familiar, and yet was not? Autumn shrugged, and pushed the troubling thought away. She needed to concentrate upon her goals of a house, and an English title; for when the time came that Barbara Palmer returned to court, Autumn knew she must step gracefully aside, and yield her place in the king's bed back to the woman who had already born his child.

Henry Lindley, Marquess of Westleigh, was visited in December by a neighbor on his way home from London. The neighbor could hardly wait to unburden himself of the latest gossip concerning the marquis's sister who, it was being said, pleased the king better than any woman he had ever had, knowing certain erotic secrets she had learned from King Louis of France, her former lover. The neighbor did not remain long before he was on his way again.

"I am going to London," Henry Lindley told his wife, Rosamund.

Rosamund had listened to their neighbor's scurrilous scandalmongering. "I think you must, my dear," she said worriedly. "Do you think your mama knows what is being said about Autumn? And where is Charlie in all of this? Should he not be guarding his sister's reputation?"

"Being the king's blood, I fear, Charlie's authority is overruled by his kingly cousin, but I do not want our sister taken advantage of by the king. Mama has told me how French Louis forced her to his bed. Now for our king to attempt the same coercion is outrageous. I doubt Mama knows, or she would have been over to Cadby as quick as a wink in a temper. I must go up to London before she learns of Autumn's latest behavior and takes it upon herself to correct it."

The Marquess of Westleigh took to the road the following morning with several of his own men riding with him. He arrived in London several days later, and before even seeking lodgings for himself and his men, went directly to Whitehall and his brother's apartments. Charlie, however, was not there.

"He has gone up to Scotland to fetch his children, my lord," the under valet said politely. "He means to bring them home to Queen's Malvern for the dowager duchess to help him raise."

"Do you know where my sister is currently residing?" the marquis demanded of the man.

"Yes, my lord. She is in residence at Lynmouth House on the Strand. She will be there now, for she does not come to court this early in the day," the under valet answered nervously, suddenly suspecting why the Marquess of Westleigh was here at Whitehall.

"Thank you," Henry Lindley said and hurried off once again. He rode with his men to Lynmouth House, wondering why Autumn was not at Greenwood. Lynmouth belonged to cousins he had met long ago. Well, at least Autumn was not ensconced at Whitehall like a strumpet.

The gates to Lynmouth opened for him when he identified himself. Reaching the house, Henry dismounted, tossing his reins to a stable lad. Entering the dwelling, he was met by a pompous servant who offered a scanty bow.

"I am the Marquess of Westleigh, come to see my sister, the Marquise d'Auriville. Where is she?"

"Her ladyship is not receiving as she has not yet risen," the servant said.

"I did not ask you whether she was awake," Henry said in even tones, "I asked you where she is. I will not ask again." His face was dark with his anger, his manner quite threatening.

Betts bowed again, but he stood his ground to a certain degree. "I will go and tell her ladyship that you are here," he said.

"You will take me to her immediately," the Marquess of Westleigh said, grasping the servant by the arm and pushing him up the wide staircase.

Finally cowed, Betts complied, leading Henry Lindley to his sister's apartments. He knocked upon a wide door. Then, with a third bow he scurried off before it could be answered.

Lily opened the door and quickly curtsied. By the grim look on the Marquess of Westleigh's face, she knew very well why he was here. "M'lord," she said, and then she stepped back.

"Where is she?" he demanded.

"Her bedchamber, my lord," Lily quavered.

"Awake?" His handsome face was angry.

Lily nodded.

The Marquess of Westleigh moved past her and, opening the door to Autumn's bedchamber, stepped into the room. "Good morning, or perhaps I should say good afternoon, sister," he said.

"Lower your voice, Henry," Autumn replied, her eyes closed, a cloth across her forehead. "I have the headache and my temples are throbbing."

Her assured manner took him aback somewhat, but he pressed onward. "Is it true?" he said. "And do not fence words with me, Autumn."

"If you are asking me if I am the king's current mistress, Henry, then the answer is yes, and again I plead with you to moderate your tone. I must be at court soon. If I have to go with the headache, I shall not be a happy woman."

"Jesu!" he swore and sat down, his hand running through his faded gold hair. "Have you no shame, Autumn?"

"Why? Someone had to take Barbara Palmer's place while she has her little royal bastard. Why not me?"

"Because you are too good for such a life, sister," Henry said desperately. "Barbara Palmer is not a duke's daughter. You are!"

"Barbara Palmer has an English title and a home of her own, Henry. I have neither. I am, to be absolutely correct, the *Dowager* Marquise d'Auriville. The title of marquise actually belongs to Madeline, although she is far too young to use it. Chermont does not belong to me; it is my daughter's home. I have nothing. When Barbara Palmer comes back to court in the spring the king will dismiss me. When he does he will be generous, as he is wont to be. I will have an English title of my own and a house that I may call my own," Autumn told her brother in a hard voice. "Oh, I know I could buy my own house, but I cannot buy an English title for myself other than by bartering my honor to the royal stallion. When men compromise their honor for gain of one kind or another, there is little fuss, Henry. Why is it women must be so damned different? Well, I choose not to be."

He was astounded. "You have grown cynical," he said.

"Charlie accuses me of the same thing," she said quietly, "but what else is there for me to do?"

"You could remarry," Henry said.

"I will remarry only for love," she told him, "but I doubt that love, the wonderful kind of love I had for Sebastian, comes more than once in a lifetime. Nay, Henry, I shall be content with my new English title and my own home. I shall live quietly, spending most of the year in England and the summer in France. I cannot deny Maddie her heritage. As for Margot, she will one day be able to choose between France and England. It will be her decision, although Louis says he will find her a husband. I think now he is wed he will conveniently forget, but that is all right. I can take care of my own."

Henry Lindley shook his head despairingly. "What has happened to you, Autumn?" he asked her. "Where is the sweet girl I knew?"

"Long gone, Henry," she told him. "So long gone I can scarce remember her myself. I think I began to grow up the day Bess was murdered. Nothing has ever been the same since then for me." She took the cloth from her head and handed it to Orane.

"I cannot persuade you to give up this life and come home with me?" he asked her.

Autumn laughed, genuinely amused. "Dearest brother Henry, you are indeed very provincial. Charles Stuart's mistress does not leave him. She is dismissed when it pleases the king, and not a moment before." She reached out and patted his arm. "I am quite happy, Henry. I cannot be harmed, as my heart is not involved. Kings have no hearts, you see. It is better not to love them."

Her words brought tears to his eyes, and he turned away. How unhappy she must be underneath it all, he thought intuitively. Yet in a strange way she was very brave, and he admired her for it. It was not the life he or her father would have envisaged for Autumn, but like all the women in his family, she was a survivor. He could not help but be proud of her for it. "Mother doesn't know," he said.

"I don't want her to know until it is all over. Then she cannot worry me over it. I am far too old to be fretted about, Henry. That's why I sent Charlie up to Glenkirk to fetch his children back. Mama will have her hands very full with those three. I understand that Sabrina is quite a wood's colt and will need a great deal of polishing. If they expect to marry her well, she will have to mend her wild ways. Mama is just the person to help her, and it will keep her so busy she will forget about me entirely. With my two and Charlie's three, there will be a house full of children again, and that is just what Mama always liked, Henry, eh?" Autumn smiled at him, and Henry Lindley realized she was the most beautiful of all his sisters.

"You don't have an apartment at Whitehall?" he queried.

"Nay, I don't want one," Autumn told him. "Charles has grumbled at me about it, but I prefer being here with Cousin Johnnie."

"Why not Greenwood, and who is Cousin Johnnie?"

"Greenwood was confiscated during the Protectorate, and the king promised as part of his restoration pact that he would not take back the properties that had been reassigned. As for Johnnie, he is the current Earl of Lynmouth, our cousin. He's a charming fellow who is almost the mirror image of Madame Skye's husband, Geoffrey Southwood. I adore him! Where are you staying, and for how long?" she asked.

He shrugged. "I'll go back to Cadby if there is nothing I can do for you," he said. "God forbid Mama discovers I'm missing and begins to ask questions. You know Rosamund cannot keep a secret or lie particularly well. Mama would have the gossip ferretted out of her in a thrice and be down here to London, raising all manner of hell."

"With poor old Adali, Rhohana, and Toramalli creaking after her," Autumn chuckled.

"Don't forget Red Hugh and his brother," Henry laughed.

"Stay here tonight, Henry. Johnnie won't mind. Then you can come to court with me and meet the king. It would be the politic thing to do. Mama would agree with me."

"Very well," he agreed. "I suppose Cousin Johnnie can put up my men. I didn't want to travel alone. There are just four of them."

"Of course," Autumn said. Then she yanked on the bellpull by her bed. Lily and Orane answered her, and their mistress began giving instructions. Betts was to be informed that the Marquis of Westleigh and his men would be remaining overnight. The earl was to come and meet his cousin. Her bath was to be readied immediately. "I'll want the violet velvet, to be worn with the diamonds and amethysts," she concluded. "Henry, go into the day room. I want to get out of bed, and I am quite naked beneath the coverlet." Then she laughed again as her brother, cheeks red, departed hurriedly from her bedchamber.

Although John Southwood was young enough to be Henry's own son, the two men took to each other immediately. Johnnie was very admiring of Autumn, and confided to Henry that he worried about her and would watch over her as if she were his own sister. Henry found himself relieved to know that Autumn was in safe hands. After two hours, during which time the two gentlemen changed their own clothing, Autumn was ready to go.

"Magnificent, ain't she?" Johnnie Southwood said with a grin. "I'm certain poor old Lady Barbara is gnashing her teeth over the many descriptions of your beauty and your wardrobe she is being sent by all her dearest friends at the court."

Autumn's gown was beautiful and very stylish. The bodice was decorated, as were the sleeves, with pale lavender and silver striped ribbons. The neckline was cut quite deeply in a very low scoop, allowing her breasts to swell invitingly above a narrow edging of silver lace. The full, ribbon-decorated sleeves had wide silver lace cuffs. Her rich violet velvet skirts fell over her many petticoats. She wore a necklace of amethysts and diamonds and matching earbobs. Her hair was styled as usual in a chignon, with two tempting curls falling over her left shoulder. A cloth-of-silver and violet velvet cloak trimmed in mink followed the lines of her skirts. Her purple leather gloves were scented, and she carried a small ermine muff inside of which were a fan and a fine lawn handkerchief. Unseen beneath her skirts were silver-and-violet-striped stockings held up by silver garters with small silver roses, in the center of which were tiny amethysts. Her shoes were violet leather, the heels studded with pearls.

"I haven't seen garments like these since I was a boy at court," Henry Lindley said almost wistfully. "You are beautiful, Autumn."

When they reached Whitehall Henry was amazed to see the number of people who approached his sister. She was charming, amusing, and kind to all. She greeted each by name. How did she remember them all? he wondered.

The Duke of Buckingham came up to be introduced. "I remember your father quite well," Henry said. "He was a good friend to both my mother and my stepfather."

"I am happy to hear it, given the manner in which he died," George Villiers said.

"Horrible! Horrible!" Henry Lindley agreed, remembering the first duke's assassination.

"Have you come to court to stay?" the Duke of Buckingham asked the Marquess of Westleigh.

"Nay, I am just up for the day to see Autumn," Henry replied.

"Ah," chuckled George Villiers knowingly, "some gossip reached you down in the country, did it?"

Henry nodded. "But now that I see how well Autumn is getting on, I can go home and not worry."

"She's hard as a fine diamond where the king is concerned," the duke said. "She knows better than to fall in love."

"I see that now," Henry agreed. "I had to make certain. We don't want Mama to know, of course, until it is over and done with."

"Your mother loved Henry Stuart, didn't she?" the duke said.

"Yes," Henry answered without going into further detail.

The king entered the audience chamber, and there was much bowing and curtseying. Charles Stuart immediately raised Autumn up and kissed her hand, his dark eyes devouring her. "You have outdone yourself tonight, madame." Then he lowered his voice. "What kind of stockings and garters do you wear?" he queried her lecherously.

"I fear Your Majesty shall have to wait to learn those small secets," Autumn told him with a wicked grin, "but Your Majesty will be well pleased, I promise you. Or perhaps not. I dress to please myself alone, sire." She smiled a brilliant smile at him.

"Where is Garwood?" the king asked of no one in particular.

"Probably sulking darkly in some remote corner," Autumn replied quickly. "He does not, I fear, like me."

"He likes you," the king assured her with a twinkle. "I believe he would like to bed you, my dear, but that I outrank him and got to you first. Do you mind, Autumn?"

"You have more to offer me," Autumn replied boldly, laughing up into the king's saturnine face.

"I shall not pursue *that* further, darling," Charles said chuckling. "Who is this new face who comes with you and Johnnie?"

"My eldest brother, Henry Lindley, Marquess of Westleigh, Your Majesty. He came up to London, having heard some rather wicked gossip, to ascertain if I was all right. 'Twas sweet of him, wasn't it?"

"Aye, it was," the king agreed. "I have a little sister in Paris of whom I am quite fond, my lord. For her sake I promise you I shall treat Lady Autumn with kindness."

"She has already assured me of it, sire," Henry replied quickly.

"Has she?" The king raised an eyebrow. "Are you softening toward me then, darling?" he teased Autumn.

" 'Oddsfish, Your Majesty, no!" she cried, using his favorite oath. "I am far too wise to fall in love again."

The king laughed. "Come and walk with me, madame," he said, and they moved off arm in arm.

"He keeps his promises," George Villiers said to Henry Lindley. "I know. We were raised together from infancy."

Henry Lindley departed the following day for his seat at Cadby. When he arrived he was relieved to learn that his mother had not come to visit. He told his wife of his trip, of how he had found his sister, of meeting the king, and their brief conversation.

"How was the king dressed?" Rosamund asked him.

"There was a great deal of ribbon and lace, along with very rich fabrics. His shoes had red rosettes upon them, and he carried a silver staff with a great knob of ivory atop it. I was quite the country mouse, m'dear."

"So Charlie is bringing his children home," Rosamund said. "Autumn is clever to think of distracting your mama with three more grandchildren. They will need all her care, growing up as they have at Glenkirk. Especially Sabrina, poor girl. As soon as they come we must go over to Queen's Malvern and welcome them home. Do you think they will remember us, Henry?"

"Brie and Freddie will, but I think wee Willy will not," her husband replied, strangely relieved to be home and absolved of Autumn. *I don't have to think about it again,* Henry decided. *My sister is all right, and Charlie will be back at court sooner than later. Besides, both the Duke of Buckingham and our cousin of Lynmouth assure me that no harm will be done to Autumn.*

Charlie arrived from Scotland with his three children in tow the week before Christmas. Jasmine was thrilled. At nineteen, Lady Sabrina Stuart was a great beauty. Unfortunately she had absolutely no idea how to speak proper English anymore. Her Scots accent was thicker than any Jasmine could remember. Her temper was quick, and she could swear better than any man. Madeline and Margot were terrified of her and began to weep if she looked their way. Sabrina mocked them for crybabies. Her brothers were, to Jasmine's surprise, a trifle more civilized and mannerly.

" 'Tis a mighty task you've given me, Charlie," his mother said. "Your sons I can manage, but your daughter . . ." Jasmine sighed.

"I have to go back to court," Charlie said, almost apologetically.

"Of course," she agreed. "While you have assured me that the young Earl of Lynmouth is watching over Autumn, I will be easier knowing you are with her. I hear from her but infrequently, and there is no mention of a possible new husband, although I will say she does seem over her doldrums."

"I'll remain with you for Christmas, but I must be back for Twelfth Night at Whitehall," Charlie replied, avoiding the issue of his sister as best he could.

"I am sorry about Greenwood, though," Jasmine said. "I would have preferred Autumn had her own house."

"Nay, Mama, I think it better she resides with a male relation," he quickly said, "and you will remember I have apartments at Whitehall."

"Of course," Jasmine agreed. "You are absolutely correct, Charlie. We have Autumn's reputation to consider, don't we?"

"Indeed," the Duke of Lundy agreed. "Indeed, Mama."

Charles Frederick Stuart arrived back at Whitehall on the fourth of January. He learned to his shock that the king had appointed Autumn as the Lord of Misrule for the holiday season. She had obviously been quite successful in her duties, as the court was rollicking and filled with laughing people. Her favorite target for jests seemed to be the Duke of Garwood. His apparent lack of a sense of humor made for great hilarity among the courtiers; especially the day she imposed a penalty upon him that required the proud gentleman to walk backwards all day, which meant each time he bowed, his shapely posterior was stuck into the face of whoever he must greet. It was cause for much laughter. Gabriel Bainbridge finally lost his temper and stormed from court for the next two days.

Autumn welcomed her brother gaily, hugging him and giving him a kiss upon the cheek. "You are back! How are the bairns, and how is Mama?"

"I may not have retrieved Sabrina in time," he told her, "and Mama wonders why she hears so infrequently from you," he answered.

"I am busy," she told him airily.

"And the king is still pleased?"

Autumn smiled archly. "Of course," she said.

"Has Lady Barbara had her child yet?"

"Not until February," Autumn responded. "The coronation is scheduled for April twenty-third. I expect La Palmer will be back in time for that, even if it kills her, which, of course, means I must give over."

"Have you asked him for your title?" Charlie wondered.

"Not yet. The proper time has not yet presented itself, but it will. It must be soon, or I am lost." Autumn sounded worried for the first time since she had begun her deliberate campaign.

That night, however, she joined the king in his own bed, much to his pleasure. A young serving woman had helped her from her gown and undergarments and been dismissed. The king, in a dark-patterned chamber robe, watched as she paraded about in a pair of white silk stockings with green ivy climbing up them. Her garters were creamy white silk with large rosettes fastening them. In the center of each flower was a single small emerald. Her white silk shoes had large green enamel buckles upon them, and heels studded with emeralds and pearls.

"I never grow tired of seeing you thus," the king said. "Come here to me now, my darling," and when she complied with his request his hands fastened about her delightfully rounded buttocks to draw her near. He pushed his face into the tightly bunched dark curls covering her Venus *mont*. He inhaled her fragrance, breathing deeply. The innocence of woodbine and honeysuckle combined with her divine sensuality aroused him as no aphrodisiac ever had. His facile tongue wormed its way between her nether lips and he licked at her sweet flesh. "Delicious," he said in muffled tones, his tongue finding the treasure it sought and moving rapidly now.

"Oh, yes, you devil!" Autumn encouraged him, her hands upon his silk-covered shoulders to steady herself. She squirmed in his grasp as he began to achieve the desired effect.

The king's voice growled a command. "Open my robe, my adorable little bitch," he said thickly.

Autumn hurried to do his bidding, moving carefully so as not to dislodge his wicked tongue. She felt his naked shoulders beneath her hands now and caressed them fervently. Then she looked down and saw his lance, engorged and ready. Without hesitation Autumn pulled away from her lover a brief moment and then, sitting upon his lap, encased him within her hot sheath. "There, darling," she purred at him. "Isn't that nice?" She moved subtly upon him while his hands fondled her buttocks. "Does His Majesty want a little kiss?" she teased him, brushing her lips across his lightly.

In response the king arose from the chair where he had been seated. His manhood still firmly within her, he carried her across the room to his bed and lay her back upon its edge. Then he began to pump her hard, moving at first with slow and majestic strokes of his weapon until Autumn was whimpering, her eyes tightly shut, her beautiful face a mask of lustful pleasure. The king increased his strokes faster and faster until she was half-screaming with delight and, unable to help himself, he exploded within her, his juices so copious that she could not take them all.

Autumn sighed and kissed him deeply. "You are, Charles Stuart," she told him, "a far better lover than your cousin Louis!" And she kissed him again.

They made love once more that night, and then Autumn arose and dressed, waiting for Mr. Chiffinch to come and lead her back through the maze of passages out through a secret entrance to the street, where her carriage was waiting.

As they waited the king said from his bed, "You must have a gift from me, Autumn, when our time together is done. What will you have of me, darling? You have been so kind, but in a few months' time Barbara will want to come back, and I would have her."

Autumn pretended to consider his request. Then she said softly, "I have wealth enough, Charles Stuart, and I have been loved by a wonderful man. I have two daughters, but there is one thing I do not have. I want to remain in England, but alas, I have no English title or a home of my own. Would you give me those two things in exchange for our time together? The title need not be great, nor the house large, but I would have something of my own, Charles Stuart. I am the daughter of a duke. I have two brothers who are dukes, one who is a marquess, and two who are barons, but nothing of my own. Give me that and I shall be forever grateful to you."

"You will have both a title and a house when our time comes to an end, Autumn. It is a small thing you ask of me. I can certainly afford to be generous to a woman who has been more than generous with me," the king told her, smiling. "Come and give me a kiss good night now, for I hear Chiffinch approaching."

Autumn came to the bed and kissed him sweetly. "Thank you, Charles Stuart," she said, and she meant it.

For the first time since he had known her the king believed he had been given a glimpse of the real Autumn. Not the beautiful courtesan who gave him such great pleasure, but the woman herself. The duke's daughter. The widow of an honorable man. It almost made him uncomfortable to have been privy to the truth. He called to his dogs to come and join him in the bed and, comforted by their presence, he fell asleep.

Her heart soaring, Autumn followed Mr. Chiffinch through winding corridors and down a flight of narrow steps. At the bottom the king's personal servant carefully unlocked the small door and, opening it, stepped out into the dark alleyway where Autumn's coach was waiting for her. He helped her in, and as he closed the door, Chiffinch said, "Good night, my lady." The carriage moved out of the street slowly, only picking up speed as it escaped the confines of the narrow way and entered the high road. *I can hardly wait to tell Charlie*, Autumn thought.

The next afternoon, in her brother's apartments at Whitehall, Autumn said quietly, "The king has promised me a title and a home when Lady Barbara comes back to court. It will be wonderful!" She turned her gaze on George Villiers. "Will he really keep his promise, my lord?"

Villiers nodded. "Aye. He values loyalty, as you know. You have been loyal and kind to him in Barbara's absence. Not only that, you have always been quite clear that you would step graciously aside when Barbara returns. If he says he will give you a title and a home, then he will."

"I am glad," Autumn replied, "for I am with child. But I wanted him to do it for me. Now I shall tell him my news without being fearful."

"Well, damn me," Buckingham said with a grin. "The man fathers brats like a tomcat. History repeats itself, eh, Charlie?"

The Duke of Lundy had grown pale. "Yes," was all he said, but afterwards, when he was alone with Autumn, he berated her. "You did it deliberately so that no matter what you would get what you wanted, Autumn. I cannot believe you could be that callous!"

"Yes, I had to be sure," she admitted, "but I like children, Charlie. I shall enjoy having one more before I retire from court and take up residence in my new home as Lady Whoever. Mayhap the

king will give his child a title too. I feel completely different this
time, Charlie. I have a son from the king. I know it!"

"Tell him tonight," her brother said. "Tell him, or I will!"

"I will tell him," Autumn promised. "Do you think he'll be
happy?"

"Why not?" her brother said sourly. "He likes children too, and
your condition will but once again prove his virility."

And the king was delighted by Autumn's news. "When is the
child due, do you think?" he asked her.

"Late August," Autumn said. "I shall, with Your Majesty's permission, withdraw from court when you order me."

"Barbara's little girl, Anne, was born just two weeks ago. She has
said she will not return until the coronation. She is a good mother, I
believe. When I know the day she means to return, I shall ask you to
depart the day before. That way I do not distress either Barbara or
you by the other's presence."

"I will give you a son," Autumn said.

"Will you?" He was amused. "I like all children, lads or lasses, my
darling girl. I shall be delighted with whatever comes." Then he
kissed her, and his hands moved to fondle her breasts. "I can feel
these little fruits already ripening," he purred and bent to salute
them. "What pleasure you have given me, Autumn, for all your
saucy and impudent ways," he chuckled.

"You should not like me meek and mild," she assured him, and
he agreed that he wouldn't.

The king could hardly wait to mention to his immediate circle of
courtiers that his beautiful mistress, the Marquise d'Auriville, was
expecting his child. He was congratulated all around as if he, himself, had performed some miracle. Autumn didn't know whether to
laugh or be angry. She decided to find amusement in her situation,
which was indeed the wiser course.

February passed, and then March. Lady Barbara sent word that
she would be returning to Whitehall on the twentieth of April, three
days before the coronation. Autumn prepared to depart from Whitehall on the eighteenth.

She was beginning to feel uncomfortable with her condition and wanted nothing more than to return to the country to await the birth of the child in August. She was concerned, for the king had not yet told her what her title would be, or where her house was located. She knew if the Duke of Buckingham said the king's word was good, it would be good, but still she worried. Three days before she was to depart she sat by the king's side while he diced with several of his friends. His luck had not been running well that evening, and dicing was not a game where men might cheat to allow the king to win. The Duke of Garwood's luck, however, was running very well. Now only he and the king played.

The king tossed the ivories and the last of his coins vanished. " 'Oddsfish!" he swore softly. Then he brightened. "Will you dice with me a final time, double or nothing, Gabriel? If I lose, you may choose your own forfeit—within reason, of course." He grinned at his friend.

"I know Your Majesty for an honorable man," the Duke of Garwood said. "I agree to your terms." He handed the dice to the king.

Charles offered them to Autumn. "Give them a kiss for luck, darling," he said to her with another grin.

With a smile, Autumn kissed the dice. "I'm not certain how fortunate my kiss will be," she warned him.

Rolling the dice enthusiastically in his palm, the king threw them. When they came to a halt he grinned. " 'Tis a hard point to beat, Gabriel," he told the Duke of Garwood.

The duke nodded in agreement and tossed the ivories onto the table carelessly. There was a gasp from the other gentlemen who stood round the table watching. The duke's toss had beaten the king's.

"Well, damn me," the king said softly. Then he looked up at his gaming partner. "You've beaten me fairly, Gabriel," he said good-naturedly. "What will you have off me?"

"Your whore," the Duke of Garwood said quietly.

"What?" The king decided that he hadn't heard aright.

About the table his other companions were open-mouthed. Autumn was white with shock.

"I would have your whore, sire," the Duke of Garwood drawled. "You are quite finished with her, aren't you?"

The king nodded, still stunned by the request. But his facile mind was beginning to contemplate the possibilities.

Autumn jumped up. "How dare you, my lord? How dare you! I am not some street trull to be passed about from man to man!"

"You may have her," the king said, "but under certain conditions. You are aware she is with child? *My child*. I will acknowledge it when it is born, and provide for it with a title of its own."

"*Charles Stuart!*" Autumn's voice was a shriek. "You cannot give me away as if I were a possession! Your promised me a title and my own home when I left you. You are a man of your word!"

"Madame," the duke cautioned Autumn, "your tongue is sharper than my sword. This is the king to whom you speak."

Your tongue is sharper than my sword. The seven words slammed into her memory like a cannon burst. She gasped, disbelieving. *It was he!* Despite his dark fashionable curls, and his rich garb, she suddenly saw Sir Simon Bates in his severe dark suit, with his cropped head. Sir Simon Bates who had killed Charlie's wife and servant.

"This man is not who he says he is. He is a murderer, and a traitor!" Autumn told the king. "Will you give me to such a man?"

"He is exactly who he says he is. Gabriel Bainbridge, the duke of Garwood," the king said quietly to her. She had remembered.

"He is Sir Simon Bates, who murdered my brother's wife!" Autumn cried dispairingly.

"He is Gabriel Bainbridge, who took his deceased cousin's identity during the war in order to spy for me, and for my cause. The reputation attributed to him was manufactured in order that he seem fanatically loyal to Cromwell's cause," the king told the distraught young woman who now clutched at his velvet sleeve. "He did not kill Bess Stuart, or her servant. It was the trooper who disobeyed orders while he was elsewhere with the rest of his men. You know that is the truth, my darling, and you must face it. We have all lost love ones in Cromwell's quest for power. They will not come back to us, Autumn. I never break my promises to a beautiful woman," he cajoled her gently.

Autumn bit her lip to keep her tears from flowing before them. This Charles Stuart was every bit as good at winning over the ladies as was his uncle, and namesake, her brother. "I could learn to hate you, sire," she told him with a touch of her old arrogance.

"You shall have a title and a home, madame," the king told her with a smile. "If Gabriel Bainbridge wants you, he must marry you. That will make you the Duchess of Garwood. His home, while in the north, is lovely, I am told by those who have visited it."

"No!" Autumn said stubbornly.

"Will you accept my terms, Gabriel? Will you marry this delightful vixen, make her your duchess, and take her from court for me?" the king asked his friend.

"I will, sire," the Duke of Garwood said.

"Then it is settled," the king agreed. "My debt to you both is met, eh?"

"It is not settled!" Autumn shouted. "I will never marry this man. I loved my late husband. I will only marry for love!"

"That," the king said, "is a charming but most childish notion, darling. Marriages are a blend of wealth and power, first and foremost. The Duke of Garwood is your equal in rank, Autumn. He has a fine home, and you will enjoy being its mistress."

"He will not wed me when he learns the conditions my family place on the betrothals of its females, sire; and I will marry no man unless those conditions are met," Autumn said firmly.

"He may discuss that matter with your brothers, madame. I have kept my word to you both. You, Garwood, may indeed have my whore. And you, Madame la marquise, have been given a title and a house."

Suddenly Autumn burst out laughing, to everyone's surprise. What else was she to do? She had been outflanked by her royal lover quite neatly. She could not appear a poor sport about it. She must accept the king's will, and be remembered kindly "You are, sir, despite your French mama, a true Stuart. The Leslies of Glenkirk never do well in your service," she said.

"What do you mean?" he asked her, amused by her words.

"My mother tells the story of when your grandfather, King James,

raised my father's earldom to a dukedom. King James said it was a
fine present for my parents because it cost him naught. He said the
Leslies had the castle and the lands already," Autumn explained to
them.

The king and his companions laughed heartily at the anecdote.

Then the king said, "So you will take the Duke of Garwood for a
husband then, Autumn?"

"If he agrees to my family's terms, Your Majesty, I think I have
no other choice but to marry him if I am to have my title and my
house," she said. She was not happy, but Autumn was intelligent
enough to know it was wiser to keep the king for a friend rather
than an enemy. If Garwood would not agree—and she suspected he
was too proud—then the fault lay not with her. She would buy her
own house, and to hell with her English title. "And, sire, one more
boon, I beg. I would prefer not to wed anyone until after my child
is born."

"I think that reasonable," Garbriel Bainbridge said.

"Do you indeed, my lord?" Autumn snapped.

The king grinned. He had always liked Autumn's independent
streak, but he would not have enjoyed such an attitude in a wife. He
wondered if the Duke of Garwood would enjoy it, but he had asked
for Autumn and been given her. The royal debt was quite satisfied.

"You may escort Madame la marquise back to Lynmouth House,"
the king told the duke. Then he took Autumn's two hands in his
own. "I believe this is *adieu*, darling," he told her. "You have been a
delight, and I thank you for your generous nature. You shall always
have Charles Stuart's friendship, Madame la marquise. Send me
word when the child is born. Remember, you have promised me a
son. What shall you name him?" The king's amber eyes were twinkling.

"*Louis,*" Autumn said wickedly.

The king burst out laughing. He laughed so hard that tears rolled
down his cheeks. When he finally was able to gain control over himself again, he raised her hands to his lips and kissed them, saying, "I
agree, madame." Then he turned to the duke. "Take her home,

Gabriel, before I change my mind. I will admit to you all that I have never had so much fun with a mistress as I have with Madame la marquise."

The duke offered his arm to Autumn. She gravely accepted it, and they turned to leave the card room. "I have a barge," Gabriel Bainbridge said. "It might be easier for you, madame."

"Then send a servant to tell my coach to return to Lynmouth House, my lord," she answered him.

He nodded, and spoke with one of the footmen, who hurried off to do his bidding.

They walked down together to the royal quai, where the duke's barge was called for and was rowed to the landing. He helped her down into the craft, joining her and seating her within the enclosed cabin, which had lisle glass windows. There were heated bricks beneath the padded leather seat and a fox lap robe.

"Was this barge part of the house when you received it?" she asked him.

"It was," he answered her.

"Then it belonged to my great-grandmother," Autumn said. "Greenwood was her home, and she gave it to my mother. The Protectorate had no right to give it away."

"Well, madame," he told her, "when you are my wife it will belong to you, and that, I suspect, will solve the problem."

Autumn grew silent again as the barge was rowed upriver from Whitehall to the strand. It was the time between the tides and the water was calm. The vessel glided along smoothly. Finally she said, "You will not agree to my family's terms, you know."

"Are you certain?" he replied.

"Yes!" she said, and her tone was smug.

"Do not be," he told her. "I have wanted you since that first day, Autumn, when you were yet a girl, demanding justice for the deaths of your sister-in-law, and her servant. I will still want you. I am a man who always gets what he wants."

"We shall see, my lord," Autumn said, but his admission had startled her. She would have never expected such an acknowledgment from him. He had never given her the slightest indication that he had anything but contempt for her. "I don't love you," she told him.

"That will come, Autumn, as we learn more about one another," he assured her.

She grew silent then. She had never before met a man like Gabriel Bainbridge, Duke of Garwood. Suddenly her life had taken a new turn. She had absolutely no idea where it was going to take her this time. She wasn't certain she liked surprises, but then, what choice did she have now? But he wouldn't accept her family's terms. Or would he?

Chapter
⚜ 19 ⚜

When the Duke of Garwood escorted Autumn back to Lynmouth House they found her brother Charlie and Cousin Johnnie already there. The two men, older and younger, but both with similar expressions upon their faces, stood together silently.

"Go to your apartment," Charles Frederick Stuart said to his sister. His tone was so severe that she obeyed him without question, much to his surprise. He had fully expected Autumn to aruge with him, but instead she curtsied to the three men and hurried up the stairs.

"We'll go into the library to speak," John Southwood said, and led the way. "Tray's on the table, my lords. Help yourselves," he told them, pouring himself a good measure of whiskey. He was going to need it, he suspected.

His cousin and their guest followed suit, and then, at their host's invitation, they sat by the fire, which hissed and crackled as it burned brightly. Outside it had begun to rain, the droplets pelting fiercely against the lead-paned windows of the library.

"I was not there at that moment," the Duke of Lundy began, "but I am told by George Villiers that you referred to my sister as a whore. Is that so, my lord?" His amber eyes stared directly at Gabriel Bainbridge.

"It is so," the Duke of Garwood said.

"Yet you are willing to marry her," Charlie continued.

"I am." Gabriel Bainbridge's own blue eyes did not waver from Charlie's darker gaze.

"Why?" Charlie demanded.

"I am not certain myself," came the candid reply. "All I can tell you is that from that first day I saw her I could not forget her. She haunts my dreams, if that makes any sense."

"You love her, as I once told you," the Duke of Lundy replied.

"How can I, given her moral character?" came the answer.

"You poor fool," Charlie told him. "You love her, but you cannot admit it to yourself because she has lain with the king. She was no virgin, and my royal cousin was not the first king with whom she lay. Her younger daughter, my niece Margot, is King Louis's daughter."

"Then how indeed can I love such a woman?" the Duke of Garwood cried, genuinely distressed.

"Listen to me, my lord. I shall tell you things that my proud sister will never admit to you, but if you and she are to have any chance at happiness, I must speak. You will never, however, say I did. Autumn was my mother's last child, born when Mama thought she was past such things as having babies. There were nine of us, although only eight grew to adulthood. Five of us were full-grown when Autumn was born. The two who were half-grown lived in Ireland, where they had adjoining estates. Of all our siblings, only Patrick Leslie, the eldest of James Leslie's sons, remained at Glenkirk, but he was already a man when our sister entered this world. Autumn has been raised as an only child would be, cossetted and spoiled by us all.

"Then came the war. James Leslie died at Dunbar. Autumn was at Queen's Malvern when it happened. Mama arrived at Glenkirk to take Autumn to her chateau in France. There was nothing left for them in England. It was there that my sister met her husband, Sebastian d'Oleron. They were wildly in love and they married. They had a daughter, Madeline, but when Maddie was just two her father died suddenly. My sister was absolutely devastated. Could scarcely rise from her bed on some days. She barely ate and worse, she ignored her child.

"Finally she began to escape from her deep doldrums, taking an interest in Chermont's vineyards and her child once more. But a year after Sebastian died, King Louis came to hunt at Chambord. He remembered Autumn from his boyhood, when he had lusted after her and she had put him firmly down for his presumption. He sent for her to come to Chambord. He did not ask whether she wanted to become his mistress. He was Louis, King of France, and she was his subject. She feared for her daughter if she did not obey. Louis was kind to her and acknowledged their child, Margot. Then at last our own king was restored, and Autumn came home."

"Into Charles Stuart's most eager arms," the Duke of Garwood said scathingly. He could forgive her Louis of France, but knowing his own king had made love to her would be harder. Still he wanted Autumn.

"Indeed she did," Charlie admitted frankly. "She saw an opportunity and she took it. My sister is a wealthy woman, but she would prefer not to live in France. Here, however, she has no title of her own any longer. Nor did she have a home of her own. She deliberately sought to fill Barbara Palmer's place in the king's bed until that lady returned from her maternal holiday. Autumn's no innocent, but an experienced female. A woman of the streets who spreads her legs for a ha'penny might be called a whore, but a well-born lady of the court who does the same for a king is not. No one dared to call my mother a whore, my lord. *Would you?*"

The Duke of Lundy watched as the realization spread over Gabriel Bainbridge's handsome face.

"No, Your Grace, I would not!" he quickly said. "It is said, though, that your mother loved your father deeply. Autumn certainly did not love King Charles."

"My mother did love Prince Henry," Charlie said with a small smile. He knew from family tales that his father had helped to birth him, but he had never known him, for Henry Stuart had died shortly after his birth. "As for Autumn, she would tell you herself that she did not love the king, but she does respect his power. She is honest to a fault."

"I am not used to such a woman," the Duke of Garwood admitted.

"If you really want to marry my sister, my lord, you must accept her as she is, and not as you would like her to be. She will not change. The women in our family are unique in their independent spirit. Is that not so, Johnnie?" the duke queried his cousin.

Johnnie Southwood grinned. "My great-great-grandmother was known to command a pirate fleet and fought with old Queen Bess. My great-grandmother, known as Angel, served that queen. My grandmother, Penelope, fought off pirates who invaded our estate in Devon. She was with child at the time. My own mother, Daphne, held our home and kept it safe from Cromwell's men. I could tell you about my Aunt MaryAnne, but it would take half the night, I fear. And this, my lord, is but one small branch of the family. We have several branches in Ireland and Scotland, as well as England. All are descendants of Skye O'Malley and her husbands. She had six of them, you know."

"At once?" the Duke of Garwood said nervously.

"One at a time," Charlie assured him before Johnnie could tease the man and frighten him off. The Duke of Lundy had long since decided that Gabriel Bainbridge would make a perfect husband for his sister, and he intended to see it happen. "Mam; that is what we called her. She was my great-grandmother, outlived them all. My home was her home, and my title came to me from her late husband, courtesy of my grandfather, King James, who elevated my great-grandfather's earldom to a dukedom.

"Now, sir, if you would have Autumn to wife there are several matters we must clear up. First, I would have your apology. Do I?"

"Aye, you do," the Duke of Garwood replied honestly. "I spoke in anger. No one can make me angrier than your sister, my lord. What other conditions do you have for me to fulfill?"

"It is the custom of the women in our family, all of whom possess their own wealth, to keep that wealth. Their betrothed husbands are given a dower portion, and some of my female cousins have even preferred allowing their mates to manage their monies, but most do not. We seem to have sired a race of women who are clever with their funds. Autumn, as I suspect you already know, is one of them.

This conversation will go no further if you cannot meet such a condition."

"It is indeed unusual," the Duke of Garwood said slowly. Then he chuckled. "Now I know why Autumn thought I would cry off when I heard it. I imagine many men would."

"Would you?" Charlie asked him.

"Nay, I wouldn't," came the honest reply.

Charlie grinned. "Nor has any man in our family history. Our ladies seem to be that fascinating to their swains," he chuckled.

"And your other conditions, my lord?"

"There is only one. You cannot wed with my sister until you have gotten to know one another better. I know it is the custom for marriages to be made for dynastic, financial, and other practical reasons, but that is the other thing about the women in our family. They marry for love." He shrugged. "I do not know what is to be done with such females, who would manage their own wealth and insist on loving their husbands."

"The king . . . ," Gabriel Bainbridge began, but Charlie put him off.

"I know my cousin said you could have Autumn, but be assured he will change his mind if I ask him to do so, my lord. I believe, however, that you are the right man for my sister. Only give her the time to come to that conclusion. Let her have her bairn, and we shall see. I believe in love at first sight, Gabriel, but I do not think Autumn does."

"The king dismissed her quite publicly this afternoon," the Duke of Garwood told Charlie. "I should advise she leave London before the coronation. What think you, sir?"

"I agree," the Duke of Lundy said. "I would like you to escort her home, if the king will permit your absence from his triumph."

"I'll go with them," the young Earl of Lynmouth said. "I'll not be missed, and I should like to meet your mother. My great-grandfather always spoke of how beautiful she was. My brother and I loved the tale of how she came to England and was presented to the family."

"Aye," Charlie said, "I think it would be an excellent idea if you escorted Autumn back to mama at Queen's Malvern. If I cannot join you immediately, you will be a buffer between them until my sister's temper cools and she becomes more reasonable. She will need to concentrate all her effort on calming Mama, once our mama learns of her condition and who the father of her expected child is. I will come as soon as the king is crowned and he releases me. Lady Barbara has never really liked me, or she is jealous of anyone she believes takes the king's attention from her. I will be happy to avoid the rough side of her wicked tongue this summer. By the time I return to court, she will be secure in her position as *maîtress en titre* once more. Autumn is of far better birth than Lady Barbara, and this is the first time the king has sired a child on a woman of such noble birth. Lady Barbara will not be happy."

"She will be far more unhappy when the king weds, which he is bound to do next year," Johnnie said. "It is to be the Portuguese infanta, they say. Her dowry will take him out of debt. The French have no princesses right now, and the Protestant Northern kingdoms have no dowries large enough to outstrip the Portuguese."

"For a man who claims not to spend a great deal of time at court, Johnnie, you know more gossip," the Duke of Lundy chuckled. Then he turned to the Duke of Garwood. "Then we are agreed, my lord?"

"We are agreed," Gabriel Bainbridge replied.

So King Charles II was crowned on April 23, 1661 in Westminster Abbey. The ceremony and the banquets that followed were colorful and lavish. Barbara Palmer, newly returned to court and restored to her lover's bed, was prominent, her rich chestnut curls shining and her bright blue eyes flashing her triumph. The king had reassured her that he adored her above all women, and her friends had assured her that she was far more beautiful than Madame la Marquise d'Auriville. That her friends lied made no difference, for Madame la marquise had been dismissed from court and was unlikely to ever return. Barbara Palmer would never have the chance for comparison, nor the opportunity to learn of her friends' deception.

The coach carrying Autumn back to Queen's Malvern traveled at a leisurely pace, but Autumn preferred riding despite the objections of her cousin and the Duke of Garwood. Lily and Orane sat within the vehicle while Lily's husband, Marc, rode with the others. Halfway through each day Johnnie would ride ahead to the inn where they would be staying for the night to make certain everything was in perfect order for his cousin and her party. The day before they reached Queen's Malvern Charlie caught up with them. At his jealous mistress's urging the king had released the Duke of Lundy until Martinsmas.

Secretly relieved, Autumn greeted her brother warmly. She had not wanted to face her mother alone. Until this very moment she hadn't really considered how angry Jasmine was going to be with her for her deliberate actions, but Autumn had not a doubt that her mother would like Gabriel Bainbridge. But there was going to be no quick wedding, if indeed there was a wedding at all. The king had tricked her, although Autumn didn't believe his actions were calculated. He had simply taken a convenient path that allowed him to satisfy in one stroke both his honor and his promise. Autumn smiled to herself. It was really quite deliciously clever of Charles, and she was not in the least angry. If she decided that she could abolutely not marry the Duke of Garwood, she was certain for her child's sake that the king would give her her own title.

They at last reached Queen's Malvern. Gabriel Bainbridge lifted Autumn down from her horse, setting her gently on her feet. "You must be happy to be home," he said softly.

"This isn't my home," she answered him. "It is Charlie's home. I have no home."

"You are very stubborn, aren't you?" he remarked.

"I am," she agreed. "Where is your home?"

"To the north, in Durham," he answered her. "It is a large house built of brick, very much like this one."

"It's not a castle?" Autumn sounded disappointed.

He choked back his laughter at the look on her face. "Nay, Autumn, it's not a castle. I have a title, a fine house, and a goodly estate that supports a deer park and herds of cattle, but that is all I have. Did you really want a castle?"

"I grew up in a castle, and Chermont is a castle," she said, but before she might continue her mother's voice rang out.

"God's blood! I let you go to court and you return with a belly, Autumn! One of these gentlemen had better be your future husband. Come into the house, all of you. Charlie, you had best have an explanation for returning your sister from court in this condition." She whirled about and stamped away.

"That is Mama," Autumn said sweetly. "Daughter of an emperor, wife of a prince, a marquis, and a duke. Mistress of another prince."

They followed Jasmine into the house, and into the family hall. The servants scurried about taking cloaks and passing out wine and sugar wafers. Suddenly the hall was full of children. Madeline and Margot ran to their mother, shrieking their delight as she bent awkwardly to hug and kiss them. Charlie's sons hurried forward, their young faces wreathed in smiles.

"*Maman! Maman!*" the little girls cried.

"Papa!" Frederick and William greeted their father.

A slender young girl entered the hall, and Johnnie Southwood's mouth fell open in unabashed admiration. "Papa," Lady Sabrina Stuart said, going to Charlie and kissing him on the cheek. "Welcoom hame . . . home, Papa." She spoke slowly, carefully, and under her grandmother's approving eye. "I'm glad yer finally back. We've missed ye, eh, laddies?"

"My bairns," Jasmine said to the older children, "now that you have greeted your parent, take the wee ones from the hall. We have business to discuss." She smiled at her little French granddaughters. "Mama will come to you soon, *mes enfants*. Go with your cousins until you are called back. Sabrina, take them to the kitchens. Cook will give you all a treat."

Sabrina took the little girls by the hand and led them off, followed by her two brothers. Maddie and Margot no longer feared their big cousin.

"Who is she?"

"More important, who are you? Have you never seen a pretty lass before? Why do you look so damned familiar?" Jasmine demanded.

"I am John Southwood, Your Grace, the Earl of Lynmouth," Johnnie said, remembering his manners and bowing to Jasmine gallantly.

"God's blood, sir, you look like my uncle Robin," Jasmine told him.

"He was my great-grandfather, madame," Johnnie told her.

Jasmine sat down heavily. "God's blood, I am an old woman!" she said. "My uncle died the year before the king was murdered. But what of his son and his grandson?" she asked the Earl of Lynmouth.

"My grandfather died at Naseby, my father and my eldest brother at Worcester. I was just seventeen then. My mother kept me penned up at Lynmouth and out of mischief until the king was restored."

"A very wise woman. What of your grandmother? Your father married one of my uncle Padraic's daughters," Jasmine recalled.

"My grandmother, Penelope, and my mama share the dower house at Lynmouth and pray that I will marry sooner than later," Johnnie told her with a chuckle.

"And today for the first time you are considering it," Jasmine said. "My granddaughter is very lovely, isn't she? How clever of you, Charlie, to bring home a possible suitor for Brie. I'm smoothing her rough Highland edges very nicely. She is a quick study." Now she looked at the other young man unfamliar to her. He was very handsome, and in an odd way reminded her of her second husband, Rowan Lindley but then realized it was only his dark blond hair.

"May I present Gabriel Bainbridge, the Duke of Garwood, Mama," Charlie said formally. "The king wants him to marry Autumn."

"Why? Because he put a baby in her belly?" Jasmine snapped.

"The king put the bairn in my belly, Mama," Autumn said sweetly.

"*What?*" Jasmine's hand went to her heart. She sat down heavily.

"Did Mam act this way when Prince Henry gave you a chld?" Autumn asked her mother. "How interesting that history is repeating itself. Do you not think so, Mama?"

Jasmine was stunned by her daughter's words. They were cold. Still she recalled how loving and welcoming her grandmother had been when she learned that Jasmine was expecting Prince Henry's son. "Do you love the king?" she asked her daughter.

"Nay," Autumn said quietly.

"Then how could you want his child?" Jasmine asked.

Autumn explained her reasoning to her mother, who was visibly distressed and shocked by it.

"I did not raise you to be so heartless," she said quietly. "I loved Henry Stuart, and his son was a blessing, a joy to me, particularly given that Hal died two months after Charlie was born. But your behavior is reprehensible, Autumn. You have been deliberately calculating, and I do not understand it. How can you love a child not created of love?"

"Margot was not created of love, Mama, and I love her," Autumn answered fiercely, defending herself.

"Margot was different," Jasmine replied.

"Why? Because I was King Louis's victim and, given the choice, would never have graced his bed? Does that make my child more lovable than the one lying now beneath my heart, Mama? Does the fact that Louis forced himself on me and conceived a daughter make her better than the baby I willingly conceived with King Charles? I am not like you, Mama. I cannot easily give up one love and love another man. I loved Sebastian. I shall always love him. No other shall ever take his place in my heart, Mama."

"That is not the point," Jasmine said, but Autumn was very angry now.

"Are you jealous of me, Mama? After all, you had but a Stuart prince for a lover. I have had not only a Stuart king but a Bourbon king in my bed. And I have given each of them children, or soon will."

"Madame!" the Duke of Garwood roared. "You will not speak that way to your mother. She deserves your respect."

Autumn jumped up. "Who are you, my lord, to tell me what to do? You may go to the devil!" Then she threw her wine goblet at him and ran from the hall.

Gabriel Bainbridge ducked the silver goblet as it crashed to the floor, spilling its contents. "Well," he said dryly, "she does have a temper, doesn't she? But a mighty poor aim."

Jasmine had begun to cry, and Charlie knelt by her chair, his arms about her comfortingly. "She has never been the same since Sebastian died," Jasmine said despairingly. "There has been nothing that pleases her, and then to be taken by that lustful king. It has all been too much for her, I fear."

"She is a spoilt brat," Charlie said. "She had this image in her mind of living happily ever after. Life doesn't always work that way, Mama. You know it. My older sisters know it. What is the matter with Autumn that she does not understand it?"

Jasmine looked at the Duke of Garwood. "Do you really want to marry her? Even after having seen this display of her temper?"

"Tell your mother how I first met Autumn, Charlie," Gabriel Bainbridge said to the Duke of Lundy. Charlie complied. When he had finished, Garwood continued, "From that day I have held her in my heart, madame. Is that love? I do not know, but I want to find out, and if indeed it is love, I shall teach her to love me as well. I do not want to wipe away the memories she has of Sebastian d'Oleron; I want to make new memories with her that we may share together into the twilight of our years. Her temper does not deter me. I am told that women who are breeding are prone to vagaries of disposition. Our journey has been long, and certainly tedious. Autumn needs her rest and the love of her family to regain her composure."

Jasmine looked closely at the Duke of Garwood. "Has my son explained the terms by which you may marry my daughter, sir?"

"He has, madame."

"Forgive me, but I must ask. Are you in debt?" Jasmine said.

"Nay, madame, I am not," he told her. "I am not a rich man, but neither am I a poor one. My title comes from the reign of the third Richard. My home is very much like Queen's Malvern: comfortable, but not elegant. My income derives from my cattle. My herds are large. I have never been married before. My parents are deceased, and I have no siblings. I follow England's church, my health is good, and I have all my teeth."

Jasmine burst out laughing. "You have humor too," she said. "I like that, my lord. Well, welcome to Queen's Malvern. You are welcome to remain as long as you can bear us all. We are, I warn you, a noisy household."

"May I remain as long as I like, cousin?" the young Earl of Lynmouth asked her.

"If you are going to attempt to court my granddaughter, sir, I suspect that you must. Aye, you too are welcome."

The days were lengthening, and it was obvious that spring would arrive sooner than later. Green shoots were beginning to puncture the earth, and after a time the hillsides were bright with yellow daffodils. John Southwood courted Lady Sabrina Stuart beneath the careful eye of both her father and her grandmother. It was plain to anyone with eyes that they were a match. While they both descended from Skye O'Malley, their kinship was not so close as to forbid a marriage. The Earl of Lynmouth thought that Sabrina's Scots accent, which was now much softer than when she had arrived in England four months earlier, charming. And to Jasmine's surprise her granddaughter knew everything a young woman should know about running a house. There was no impediment to the marriage, which was scheduled to be celebrated on the second day of May.

Autumn had quieted and drawn into herself after her initial explosion of anger. Jasmine had struggled to remember how kind and supportive her grandmother had been to her when she found herself in the very same situation. The breach between mother and daughter, always so close, was healed, although Autumn could not understand her mother's approval of Gabriel Bainbridge. "He has not Sebastian's charm," she said, "and he isn't anywhere near as handsome, Mama."

"That," Jasmine replied with perfect logic, "is because he isn't Sebastian d'Oleron. He is a completely different man. Stop looking at him as Sebastian. Stop comparing him to Sebastian. See him for who he is. He is a good man, Autumn."

"Good men are boring, Mama," was Autumn's response.

Jasmine laughed. "Not always, poppet."

So Autumn began to try to see Gabriel Bainbridge for who he was and not whom she wished him to be. What was the matter with her anyway? Her husband would be dead six years in October. Suddenly she wished she was not quite so full with her child. How could a man court a woman who looked like a cow about to calf? She mockingly told him this.

"I raise cattle," he said with a twinkle in his blue eyes. "I find breeding cows quite beautiful, madame."

"I will not foster out my children," she said seriously.

"Why would you?" he asked her. "Garwood Hall is a house meant for children, madame. Yours and ours."

"I will be thirty in October," she said. "I know not how many more years I have left to breed."

"I will be forty-one in August," he countered. "If we are diligent, Autumn, I think we can manage a few children before we are too old and gray." The blue eyes twinkled at her.

"You are making fun of me," she said.

He nodded in agreement. "I am," he said. "You will get used to it in time, Autumn."

"Perhaps I don't want to," she responded, not certain she liked this teasing.

He grinned. "You would be a wicked termagant if you were not so adorable, madame."

"I am not a termagant!" she cried. "How dare you, sir?"

"A vixen, then," he told her. "A delicious little vixen."

Autumn ran her hands over her extended belly. "Hardly little, my lord," she teased him back, "and likely to get bigger, I vow."

He laughed at her sally, and then she laughed too.

Watching them, Jasmine had a faint glimmer of hope. How she would love it if Autumn could fall in love with the Duke of Garwood. If Autumn were remarried and settled with her children, her world would be complete. Nay, not quite complete. The servants who had been with her her entire life were fading away before her eyes. Adali was close to ninety, and she had never before heard of anyone living to that age. Rohana and Toramalli, her twin serving maids, were over eighty. They had been ten years old when she was born, and she would soon be seventy-one. What would she do when she lost them all?

Adali, back in England again, spent his days sitting in the sun by a window. Becket took care of Queen's Malvern, so there was nothing left for him to do. Both Rohana and Toramalli were having difficulty in walking of late. Their knees, they complained, would not function properly, and they shuffled as they walked. Toramalli's hands had grown quite gnarled. Her husband, Fergus, wasn't much better. He and Red Hugh sat all day and played at chess, which Adali had taught them. *We are a household of old men and women*, Jasmine thought.

Lady Sabrina Stuart was married to the Earl of Lynmouth on the second of May. The day was sunny and mild with no wind. The bride wore an antique cream-colored silk wedding gown that had belonged to one of her female antecedents, although no one knew whom. It had been found in the attics, carefully preserved in a trunk. Her unbound hair was crowned with a wreath of daisies. Her handsome bridegroom wore sky-blue velvet and seemed to have a waterfall of lace flowing from his cuffs. A banquet was set up on the lawns after the religious ceremony in the family's ancient chapel.

The Marquess of Westleigh and his wife had come for the event with all their children, spouses, and grandchildren. Nearby neighbors had been asked. Pits had been dug to roast the beef, which was packed in rock salt. There were country hams and ducks roasted with a stuffing of raisins and apples swimming in plum sauce. There was salmon sent down from the streams at Glenkirk, broiled and set upon silver platters of green cress; golden-crusted pies filled with pieces of goose; rabbit stew in red wine; spring lamb chops; and a large turkey stuffed with cherries, plums, and saffroned rice. There were bowls of new peas and tiny beets, artichokes in white wine, and asparagus in a dilled cream sauce. There were wheels of sharp Cheddar, smaller wheels of soft French brie, freshly baked loaves of bread, and crocks of sweet butter. A cake with a spun-sugar couple atop it, surrounded by tiny, fresh strawberries concluded the meal. The wines came from Archambault and Chermont. The beer flowed freely from its kegs, as did the cider.

They danced country dances, reels, and in a straight line, weaving in and out. They played at bowls upon the lawns and shot arrows at butts set up for the purpose. They sang. Then, finally, the bride and groom were chased up the stairs of the house, giggling and laughing, to be undressed and put to bed. It had been a wonderful day for them all, they agreed afterwards, sitting about the fire in the family hall, the bridal couple well occupied, the children abed.

In the middle of the night Rohana came and woke her mistress. "It is time," she said meaningfully, and Jasmine rose, drawing her chamber robe about her to follow her serving woman to Adali's chamber.

Entering, she saw Toramalli waiting. Jasmine sat by her ancient servant's bedside and took his hand. The old man's breathing was shallow and growing fainter by the minute. Afraid he would think she hadn't come, Jasmine spoke softly to him. "Adali."

The brown eyes opened and, seeing her, he smiled. "I have stayed as long as I could, my princess. I will be waiting for you with the master, who says I must go now," the old man said with great effort and his last bit of strength. Adali's eyes closed again. He died just as the sun rose on the morning of the third of May.

Jasmine said nothing to her family, instead seeing her granddaughter, who looked extremely happy, off with her new husband. Only after they had gone did she announce to the household that Adali had died. His grave was dug and he was buried in the family's private burial grounds. He had served his mistress faithfully for some seventy years. Jasmine wept, inconsolable at his loss and at the knowledge that sooner than later she would lose the others as well.

Several days later Red Hugh came to her to say he wanted to go home to Glenkirk. She knew why. "Remain there," she told him. "I am past the day when I need you to watch over me. Our adventuring is long done, I fear."

"Ye were always getting into trouble when I wasna there, my lady," he reminded. " 'Twas a mercy, and no thanks to me ye weren't killed half a dozen times." He kissed her still elegant hands.

"Take a letter to Patrick for me," she said, and he nodded. She asked her other manservant, Fergus More-Leslie, if he would go home to Glenkirk, but Fergus surprised her by declining.

"I'll stay wi ye, m'lady. Don't make no difference to me where I die. When I'm dead, I'm dead. Besides, that old woman of mine would nae leave her sister, nae would I. We'll stay wi ye till God calls us, I vow."

"You are behaving as if you're going to die, Mama, and you are frightening me," Autumn said.

"Well, I'm not," her mother said firmly, "but Adali's passing has made me realize what I have refused to see. None of us are young anymore, and those who have served me are entitled to some peace on earth before they must be put into it. They will not go, however."

"Where would they go, Mama?" Autumn said. "They love you and have been with you your whole life. They will die in your service."

"I suppose I should get someone to help Rohana and Toramalli," Jasmine considered. "We tried before, but no one ever seems to work out or suit them."

"I think they have always been jealous of anyone else serving you, Mama, but now they may be more amenable to having a helper."

Spring faded away into summer. Gabriel Bainbridge made several brief trips to Durham to his estate to be certain that everything was running smoothly there. He also, unbeknownst to Autumn, arranged to have his house ready to receive his bride and her children. July passed, and then August came with terrible thunderstorms that flattened the fields of grain just before the harvest and knocked apples and pears from the trees in the orchards. The grains were quickly gathered before rot or mildew could set in, but the damaged fruit could only be pressed immediately into cider that had to be sweetened with precious sugar as the fruits had not been fully ripe.

Autumn went into labor on the twentieth of August. She had had little warning and few pains, but suddenly she could feel the pressure between her legs and knew that this birth was different from the others. Her waters broke, soaking her skirts, as she screamed for help. Then came the pains—hard, racking pains that ripped through her as if she were being carved up for butchering. Gabriel Bainbridge refused to leave her, standing at her head, wiping her moist brow as she cried and swore in her travail. Finally, after several hours, the baby was born. It was a perfectly formed little boy and he was quite dead, the cord wrapped about his neck so tightly that he was blue.

"Why isn't it crying?" Autumn demanded. "Mama, is it a laddie? I did promise the king a laddie. Why isn't he crying?"

There was no help for it. Jasmine showed Autumn the child just born, and her daughter began to wail a cry of such terrible anguish that Jasmine began to weep too. "It's God's will," she sobbed, as if to explain the terrible tragedy. Then she began unwrapping the cord from about the little boy's neck.

"God again!" Autumn cried out. "The same God who stole my husband from me and my first son! Now this wee laddie! I hate this God who would do such a terrible thing to me and to my child! What harm did that innocent little baby do, Mama? What harm?" Then she began to wail and cry once more.

Rohana pressed a goblet of wine to Autumn's lips. "Drink, my lady. It has the juice of the poppy in it. You must sleep to escape the pain."

Autumn gulped the liquid offered. "I hope I never wake up," she said bitterly. "I hope I never awaken again!"

"Do not say such a thing," the Duke of Garwood begged her. "What of Madeline and little Margot, Autumn? Think of your daughters."

"Mama will raise them," she replied sleepily.

"What of us?" he demanded.

"You will find another wife," Autumn said. Her eyes were closing. "One better than me. Kinder."

"But I love you," he told her.

"That's nice," Autumn said as she slid into unconsciousness. He loved her. Someone loved her again, she thought muzzily as she seemed to fade away into nothingness.

Chapter

20

She didn't want to wake up. *She didn't!* But consciousness forced itself upon her. Autumn opened her eyes to see her mother sitting by her bedside. She felt empty. So very empty, and looking down at her belly, the awful reality slammed back into her with such force that it almost took her breath away. "He's dead, isn't he?" she half-whispered.

"Baptized and buried," Jasmine said quietly, "How do you feel, my darling child?"

"How long have I been asleep?" Autumn ignored her mother's question. She felt awful. Absolutely awful. How else was she supposed to feel after carrying a child to full term only to have it born dead?

"You have been unconscious for two-and-a-half days," her mother answered her. Jasmine stood up and, going to the sideboard, poured a small goblet of wine for Autumn.

Autumn accepted the liquid, drinking it down quickly, for she was thirsty. "I have to write to the king," she said.

"It is already done," Jasmine said.

"Thank you," Autumn replied. "I would not have known what to say to him. I promised him a son and I have failed. This is the second son I have lost, Mama. What is the matter with me?"

"There is nothing the matter with you," Jasmine reassured her daughter. "You lost Sebastian's son because of the shock you suffered at your husband's sudden and unexpected death. This poor wee bairn had the bad luck to get entangled with his cord. He strangled even before he was born. I would not make you sad, my darling, but he was a perfect child, all fat little arms and legs and a beautiful face. 'Tis a terrible tragedy, Autumn, but it was not your fault. These awful things happen." She paused, and then she said, "I sent Charlie directly to the king to tell him personally, and he took my note to His Majesty. Your sorrow will be a private one, Autumn."

"Where did you put him, Mama?" the grieving woman asked.

"Next to your great-grandmother," Jasmine said quietly. "He will be safe there."

"I want to see him," Autumn begged.

"In a few days, my daughter, when you have regained a small bit of your strength," Jasmine told her. "For now you need rest and nourishment, Autumn. Let me look after you."

"It would seem I have no choice," Autumn replied bitterly.

She ate what they put before her. She drank the hot possets and healing draughts they brought to her. She slept, but she did not cry. It seemed to Autumn that her heart had turned to stone in her chest. Several days after her son had been born and died her daughters came to keep her company. Madeline and Margot both now spoke accentless English, although they were made to converse daily in their native French tongue.

Madeline, who would shortly be eight, said, "We saw our little brother before they put him in the ground, Mama. He was a very pretty child. I'm sorry he did not live to play with us. Are you sorry he died?" She climbed up into the bed with her mother as Margot clambered onto the other side of Autumn.

"Are you sorry, Mama?" Margot parroted her elder sister.

"Yes, I am sorry," Autumn said.

"Poor little Louis," Madeline said, shaking her head sadly.

"Poor Louis," Margot reprised.

"He is to have his own stone marker," Madeline told her mother with an air of self-importance. "Grandma says it will read: Louis

Charles Stuart, born and died August twentieth, sixteen hundred and sixty-one. And there is to be angel carved on it."

"Angel. Angel. Angel," Margot sing-songed.

"Oh, be quiet, Maggot! I am telling Mama," Maddie said irritably.

"Do not call your sister 'Maggot,'" Autumn scolded her elder daughter, although she was forced to push back a giggle. Maddie was obviously quite clever. "She is Marquerite Louise or Margot."

"She is a botheration, Mama," Maddie said. "She is always following me about. She is too little to be any fun."

"You are sisters," Autumn told them. "You must love one another and protect one another. You only have each other, *mes filles*. Go now, and let Mama rest again."

"Papa says we are to all have a beautiful home of our own soon," Maddie announced to her mother as she and her sister climbed off Autumn's bed. "We are to have our own ponies. He says he is the luckiest man alive to have three beautiful ladies to bring to Garwood Hall." She giggled. "It is so nice to have a papa at last, isn't it, Margot?"

Margot nodded enthusiastically. "I want a black pony," she said.

Then the two little girls departed Autumn's bedchamber hand in hand, leaving their shocked mother to ponder what her children had just said. *Papa* was obviously Gabriel Bainbridge. How dared he take it upon himself to tell her daughters to address him in such a manner? She had not said she would marry him. *She wouldn't marry him!* She didn't need his title and she didn't need his house. She would build her own house, and to hell with an English title. She was still Madame la Marquise d'Auriville.

On the first of September Autumn felt strong enough to get up and get dressed. Then, with Lily and Orane supporting her, she left the house and walked slowly to the family burial ground. When she had finally reached the site she sat down upon the marble bench saying, "Leave me," to her two serving women.

"And how do you propose to get back?" Lily demanded irritably. "You couldn't have got here at all if it weren't for me and Orane, m'lady."

"I want to be alone," Autumn said. "Go! Come back later if you must, but leave me in peace for now."

The two women hurried away, Lily muttering beneath her breath about how some people were so stubborn and never learned.

Autumn sat quietly, the warm September sun on her back. The tiny mound next to her great-grandmother's grave was already grassed over. The marker, of course, was not yet ready. Two sons, she thought, both born dead. In her belly one day and gone the next. She had not been to either funeral. Nay, she lay prostrate, desperately trying to escape the pain of it all while her sons were buried by others. Sebastian's hadn't even had a name, although she always thought of him as Michel when he crept into her consciousness.

But Louis—her little Louis she had carried until he was due to be born. To lose him so easily at that point was incomprehensible to her. How could such a terrible thing have happened? Was God punishing her? Why had he not punished Mama, and Charlie been born dead too? Or was it, as her mother was so fond of saying, fate? Plain, ordinary fate that had taken a hand in her sons' deaths. Why could she not successfully birth lads? Her daughters were both hale and hearty enough.

She did not hear him, and so Gabriel Bainbridge stood quietly by a tree watching Autumn. Except at the moment of the child's birth, when she had realized its fate, she had not cried. Was she so heartless then? he wondered. She had made no secret of the fact she had deliberately set out to fill Barbara Palmer's place in her absence. She had been pleased to be having the king's child. Now that child was lost to her. Had it only been a means to an end for her? Was she that callous, that coldhearted?

Then he heard the noise. A tiny noise at first, and then, as if a dam had broken her sobs poured forth in a sorrowful stream of weeping. There was such anguish and genuine pain in the sound that it reached out to him and touched his heart. So she was not the unfeeling bitch he had thought her to be. It was then Gabriel Bainbridge realized that Autumn was a far more complicated woman than he had anticipated. He debated going to her and comforting her, but she had come here to mourn in private. She was not ready to share her grief with anyone yet, let alone him. The Duke of Garwood slipped quietly away without Autumn ever having known he was there.

She came into the hall that evening to join them at their meal. "Sir," she said to him, and he heard the irritation in her voice, "who gave you leave to tell my daughters that they might call you *papa?*"

"I did," her mother quickly spoke up. "It is best the girls begin accepting Gabriel as their father right now."

"I have not said I would marry him," Autumn replied. "If I decide I do not want to be the Duchess of Garwood, it will confuse my babies entirely. Particularly if I do eventually remarry. It was not your place, Mama, to give the girls such permission."

"You are being obdurate," Jasmine said.

"I am my own mistress, Mama," was the swift reply.

"I will only marry a woman who loves me," the duke said quietly.

"And I will only wed a man who loves me," Autumn told him.

"But I do love you," Gabriel Bainbridge told her. "Do you not recall the day that Louis was born, when I told you so?"

"I do not remember any such thing," Autumn replied quickly, but she had as soon as he had mentioned it, and her blush told him so.

"Well, madame, I do love you, although why I do I cannot tell. You are difficult and shrewish, as well as being charming and beautiful. You puzzle me, and yet I love you," he finished with a shrug.

"*Shrewish? Difficult?* You have not had a great deal of experience courting a woman, my lord, have you?" Autumn snapped.

"But you have had a great deal of experience at being courted, madame. I must rely upon you to teach me what it is that will please you so you will keep a civil tongue in your head," he replied blandly, his blue eyes twinkling wickedly.

Autumn flushed angrily, but then she said, "A gentleman never points out a lady's faults of character, my lord. Not if he wishes to please her, of course." She smiled sweetly, but the smile had no warmth to it at all.

He bowed to her. "I shall remember, madame. I hope you will

enlighten me further on the subject of courting a lady. May I seat you at the highboard now?" He offered her his arm.

Charlie, back from court, caught his mother's eye and swallowed back a chuckle. Jasmine, he could see, was also hard-pressed not to laugh. It would appear that Autumn had at last met her match in Gabriel Bainbridge, Duke of Garwood. Unlike Sebastian d'Oleron, the duke, while in love, was not so bowled over by Autumn that he would entirely allow her her lead. There was going to be quite a battle between the two as to who would wear the breeches in their family, Charlie thought, amused. And even he was not certain on whom he would put his money.

September passed, and October came. Autumn had recovered from her son's birth and was now ready to ride again. Lafite, who could write, had sent word that the harvest at Chermont had been a good one. When, he wondered, were Madame la marquis and *les deux petite* mademoiselles coming home? Autumn did not have the heart to tell him that in all likelihood she was not coming back to France. She silently vowed, however, to send her daughters there next spring. Perhaps Mama would go with them, and then bring them back after the harvest. She knew that would please the people of Chermont. It was Madeline's inheritance, and one day she must return to live there.

The Duke of Garwood was beginning to become familiar to Autumn. They continued to spar verbally, but his words were never cruel. He merely sought to exert his mastery over her, and Autumn was not certain she was willing to allow him that right. Sebastian d'Oleron, she now realized, while loving her had considered her a possession to be treasured and guarded. Had she been older, Autumn considered, as she now was, she would not have allowed him that prerogative, but rather she would have taught him that she was an independent creature.

She remembered how surprised he had been when she had devised the plan to free Queen Anne from Chenonceaux, and Cardinal Mazarin had approved it. She recalled how amazed he had seemed when it had all worked and the queen was returned safely to Paris.

Prior to that she knew he had not believed a woman capable of being so clever. But the cardinal had appreciated her cleverness and had said so. He had even wished aloud that she would come to court. Autumn crossed herself. Cardinal Mazarin had died several months back, and King Louis, in a surprising move, had announced he would now personally run his own kingdom, down to the everyday details that had previously been the cardinal's province. Louis was clever and had learned well.

Her mind flitted back to the duke. Gabriel Bainbridge, she recognized, was every bit as stubborn as she was. He had to understand, however, that she was not a pretty toy that he might own. He must comprehend that she was a woman with an intellect she enjoyed using. But how was she to convince him? She finally went to her mother for advice. God only knew Jasmine had until the end managed her father, a man very much like the Duke of Garwood. Her mother would know what to do.

"Tell him," Jasmine said simply.

"Tell him *what?*" Autumn said, confused.

"Tell him that if you are to wed him, he must accept you as an equal partner in the marriage. Gabriel is not a fool. He appreciates you already, although, like you, he is stubborn. He will not admit it until you give him an equal advantage," Jasmine advised. "Stop fighting with the man and speak plainly to him."

Autumn decided to take her mother's advice. She simply didn't know what else to do. Charlie would soon be returning to court with his two sons in tow, and the king was going to ask if she and the duke were married. If they were not, she knew Charles would damn well want to know why they were not.

Her opportunity came that same evening, when she suddenly found herself alone with Gabriel in the family hall. The meal was over, and everyone else had conveniently disappeared.

Autumn swallowed hard and said, "Don't you want to kiss me, my lord? You say you want to wed me, and the look in your eyes says you certainly want to bed me, but you have yet to share any intimacies with me." She blushed, much to her surprise, at her own boldness.

He was sprawled in a chair before the fire and, looking up at her standing there, he said, "Come here to me, Autumn."

Was she a dog to be called to her master's side? Autumn opened her mouth to spit out a rude reply, but then closed it and plunked herself into his lap, surprising him. "I am here, my lord. Now what?"

He smiled a slow smile at her. "Is this a change of heart, then, madame?"

"Do you really want to marry me?" she asked him frankly.

"Yes," came the immediate reply. The blue eyes questioned her silently. "I have said I love you, Autumn. I have never, ever spoken those words to any woman. If I say them, I mean them."

"Then why don't you kiss me?" she demanded.

Without delay his lips met hers in a long and slow kiss that actually left her breathless for a moment. "Is that satisfactory, madame?"

The kiss had sent a tingle down her spine. Her nipples had half-hardened. "It will do for a start, my lord," she murmured, brushing his big, sensuous mouth with her full lips. "Is that satisfactory, sir?"

"Quite," he agreed. "What is it you want of me?" he calmly questioned her.

"There is a final condition to our marriage," she said. "Whatever the law may say, I am not and shall never be your possession, Gabriel. I am a clever woman. I say it with all modesty, although I know men do not like to hear such words from a woman's mouth. I know the land is yours to administer, and Garwood Hall will be mine to govern. There will, however, be certain decisions that *we* should make together. Will you listen to my opinions on such matters? And if my judgment is the better, accept it, not allowing your pride to overrule your common sense? I will promise you to do the same. I know it will not be easy, my lord, but if you can agree to this, then we will set a wedding date this very night. I know if you give me your word I can accept it, for you are an honorable man."

He thought a long moment. Then he said to her, "I am a jealous man, Autumn. There is something I must know. I understand that you loved your first husband, but are you truly a virtuous woman? I know what King Louis did, and that you did not go willingly to him. I even understand, although it was not easy at first, why you pursued

King Charles to briefly become his mistress. But will you be true to me, and me alone? I could not bear it if you used your body for gain again, Autumn."

Her first instinct was to be deeply offended, but then she realized that he had every right to ask such a question of her. "When I marry you, Gabriel Bainbridge," she assured him quietly, "I shall be true to you, and you alone. There will be no other who comes between us, if you can truly put my past behind you as I mean to do."

"I can!" he assured her. Then he kissed her once again. This time Autumn melted into his arms, her lips softening beneath his hungry mouth, her arms about him, her fingers threading themselves through his dark blond hair. "I love you!" he whispered hotly in her ear.

"And I will try to love you," she promised him, "but whatever happens I will respect you and be true to you, Gabriel."

"God, Autumn, how I want you!" he groaned, his big hand fondling her sweet, round breast.

She sighed with undisguised pleasure at his touch, but then she said, "Not yet, Gabriel. Please let us wait a bit longer."

Now he sighed, for his male member was throbbing as if he were a boy with his first woman. He reluctantly said, "It will be in your own time, my love. Will that please you?"

"Yes," she answered him, knowing the sacrifice he was making for her. Perhaps he really did love her, Autumn considered, a tiny plume of happiness beginning to take root in her heart. Was it possible that she could love and be loved again? Maybe she wasn't being punished after all.

They set their wedding date for the first of December. When told, Jasmine protested that there was not enough time, but Autumn was most adamant, and Gabriel supported her decision.

"But why so quickly?" Jasmine demanded. "There is no time to prepare properly, or have a gown made for this most special occasion."

"Mama, I am thirty years old," Autumn said, "and it is my second marriage after some rather shameless adventures. I want a simple wedding with just a few family members. Henry and Rosamund, but certainly none of their extended brood. Charlie and my two nephews. Rohana and Toramalli, and Fergus. As for Gabriel, he has no one. I want only people I truly care for who are nearby, not a great family gathering. Please let me have my way in this. When Charlie returns to court he will be able to tell the king his wishes have been fulfilled."

"Is *that* why you would have this quick marriage? For the king's sake? Could Charlie not say you and Gabriel are being wed in the spring in a grand party to which he is invited? We could bring all of the family together once again. The Blackthornes, the Burkes, the Edwardes, the Southwoods, the Gordons, the Lindleys, the Leighs, the O'Flahertys, and the Leslies. What a grand fête that would be!"

Autumn saw the hope in her mother's eyes. She took Jasmine's hands in hers and looked deep into the wonderful turquoise eyes. "Mama, there is no reason you cannot have your party, and have it whenever you want it. You do not need a wedding as an excuse to bring the family together. Gabriel and I have decided together that we wish to be wed on December first. Please, Mama, please, accept our decision."

"What will you wear?" her mother asked despairingly.

"I shall go into the attics and see if I might find a gown as my niece Sabrina did. Madame Skye had some wonderful gowns in her day, and if I find one I like, it can be altered in time."

Jasmine sighed. "You will be with child by the spring," she said knowingly. "I shall plan my party for summer of the year after, and you had best be able to travel down from Durham then!"

Autumn threw her arms about her mother and hugged her. "Thank you, Mama!" she said, and Jasmine heard happiness in her daughter's voice for the first time in a great, long while.

Autumn went up to the attics that very day to see if perhaps there was a gown that might be worn. She found trunks of old-fashioned garments, all carefully packed away, but it was a gown of pure apple green silk that caught her eye. Pulling it from the chest, she held it up to herself. The color was wonderful, and just perfect for her gardenia skin. She brought it downstairs to show her mother.

Jasmine gasped with recognition. "Oh, my!" she said. "Oh, my! I cannot believe it still exists after all these years!"

"You have seen this gown before, Mama?" Autumn said.

"Your great-grandmother wore it when she was married to your great-grandfather. It was made in France. They were wed at Archambault. Your grandmother, my mother, wore it when she wed Alexander Gordon. The marriage ceremony was celebrated here even as yours will be, and as mine was when I wore this gown to wed Rowan Lindley. If you wear it, Autumn, you will be the fourth woman in the family to do so." There were tears in her eyes as she said it. "Every bride who has dressed herself in this gown has been happy, and that, my dear child, is what I want for you and Gabriel."

Autumn clutched the gown tightly to herself. "Oh, Mama! What a lovely history. I do want to wear it, but I don't even know if it fits! I haven't tried it on yet."

"It may need an alteration or two, but if you want it, you shall have it!" Jasmine said firmly.

Autumn nodded. "I want it," she replied happily.

"Then it is yours!" her mother said.

It was decided to redesign the gown slightly so it would conform with the fashions of the day. Shimmering apple green in color, the bodice's low, square neckline became a low, scooped neckline. It was embroidered with golden butterflies, daisies, and tiny seed pearls, some of which needed to be removed and then restored to the adjusted neckline. The overskirts were looped up on one side to reveal the darker green velvet underskirt. This skirt, which had a wide panel of embroidery to match the bodice, was moved about so that the decoration showed to its best advantage, and additional embroidery was added to it so that all the dark velvet underskirt was now embroidered and glittered. The leg-of-mutton sleeves with their tiny gold ribbons were left fairly intact but shortened, and now ended just below the elbow. The gold lace ruffs that had formed cuffs were removed and a waterfall of golden lace was added to each sleeve. The wasp waist was still fashionable, but the bell-shaped shirts had to be altered to flow over petticoats rather than fit over a farthingale. Even the pale green silk stockings embroidered with grapevines and the delicate silk slippers remained. To everyone's surprise, and Autumn's delight, they both fit.

"Oh, look!" Jasmine almost sounded like a young girl again. "Here are the cloth-of-gold roses Bonnie, the seamstress, made for my hair! We didn't have fancy tailors like Monsieur Reynaud back then."

"How did you wear your hair?" Autumn asked her mother.

"The same way you do," Jasmine replied with a smile. Then she said, "I also wore my grandmother's pearls. You shall have them, Autumn, not just for your wedding day, but to keep."

Autumn cried, much to her mother's surprise. "I have always loved those pearls," she said, "I know how precious they are to you, having belonged to Madame Skye."

"You are precious to me," her mother replied. "My baby. My very last baby," and she sniffled.

Learning from his soon-to-be mother-in-law what his bride would be wearing, Gabriel Bainbridge disappeared from Queen's Malvern for two weeks before his wedding day. When he appeared in the family chapel on that morning, he was garbed most fashionably in deep green velvet, apple green silk, and elegant gold lace. Even his shoes were of dark green leather and had gold rosettes on the toes. On his head was a wide-brimmed green hat with a shallow crown and two magnificent ostrich plumes. He carried a long green and gold enameled walking stick. He winked at Autumn as Charlie brought her to his side.

They were married at nine o'clock in the morning. Outside the small family chapel with its beautiful stained-glass windows the sky was gray-white, only the horizon toward the east showing a pale peach, darker gray, and rose color. There was no wind, and while not bitter, it was a cold day, with a hint of dampness in the air. After the ceremony that made Autumn the wife of the Duke of Garwood, the few guests adjourned to the family hall, where the morning meal awaited them.

There were eggs, poached in heavy cream and Marsala wine and sprinkled with freshly grated nutmeg; salmon broiled in white wine and sprinkled with dill; a pink country ham; a silver plate of lamb chops; a half-wheel of hard, sharp yellow Cheddar, small tubs of sweet butter, and newly baked cottage loaves. Autumn's daughters delighted in the heavy cream and egg custard with its burnt sugar topping, and when the small wedding cake came they squealed with delight at the spun-sugar figures atop, demanding they each be given a figure to eat, though Autumn said no.

"I shall keep these figures," she told them, "and then one day when each of you weds, we shall have them to put atop your wedding cakes, *mes filles*. Is that not a nicer idea?"

The two little girls nodded, although neither was honestly certain it was such a fine idea. Still, they had been allowed watered wine with the feast and decided not to complain. If they did, Grandmama might not take them back to Cadby with Uncle Henry and Aunt Rosamund. Jasmine had decided she would allow her daughter and Gabriel a few weeks' respite before she brought Maddie and Margot to them. The bridal couple would depart in two days' time for Garwood Hall in Durham. In deference to the bride and groom, the guests were gone by half after twelve o'clock.

"I'll bring the children up to Garwood Hall in time for Christmas," Jasmine told her daughter. "Unless, of course, the roads are not passable." Then, as the coach pulled off, her granddaughters laughing at some silliness of their own making, she waved gaily to her daughter and new son-in-law. *Well, Jemmie,* she thought silently to herself, *I believe I have made it all right for our last bairn. Finally.* And she chuckled.

Autumn and Gabriel watched the carriages containing their guests depart and then, hand in hand, they reentered the house.

"We are alone," she said with understatement.

"Quite," he agreed. Then he led her upstairs to her bedchamber. "I will join you shortly, madame," he told her.

"It is afternoon," she responded.

"Yes, it is," he acknowledged, and opened the chamber door as he released her hand. Then, as she entered the room, he closed the door behind her firmly.

Lily and Orane hurried forward to help her undress.

" 'Twas a lovely wedding, m'lady," Lily said with a broad smile as she undid Autumn's bodice and drew it off.

"This gown, madame, *c'est magnifique,*" Orane remarked, undoing the skirt, the petticoat tabs, and the laces to draw the garments down.

Autumn stepped from the tangled pile of fabric. "Be very careful with the gown," she cautioned them. "Remember, it has been worn by four brides in my family and is almost a hundred years old."

"Never knew a gown could last that long," Lily observed, bringing a basin of scented warm water for her mistress to bathe in, a small linen towel over her arm.

Orane cocked her head at her mistress questioningly. "The shoes and the stockings, madame?" she asked.

"Most definitely the shoes and the stockings!" Autumn said emphatically with a small laugh. Perhaps one day she would amuse Gabriel by parading about in such provocative garb, but certainly not tonight. Besides, she could not be certain that the king hadn't told his intimates about her erotic love play. She certainly didn't want to remind her bridegroom of her wicked past, had he ever heard of her "stockings and garters" game. She sat down so Orane might remove them, and when she had done so Autumn rose, going to the basin to bathe herself. Then she brushed her teeth, rinsing her mouth with minted water.

Lily brought her a silk chamber robe. Autumn pulled off her chemise, handing it to Orane as she slipped into the robe.

"Will there be anything else, m'lady?" Lily asked as Orane added another log to the fire.

"Nay," Autumn replied. "You may go, girls. Good night."

"Are you certain you won't be wanting anything else, madame?" Lily said. It was after all only early afternoon, despite what her mistress might say.

"You may both have the rest of the day off," Autumn told them. "Have Becket lay a cold supper in the duke's bedchamber at sunset."

"Yes, m'lady," they chorused and curtsied before hurrying out of her bedchamber.

Autumn looked about the room. It had always been her room when she visited Queen's Malvern. Once her sisters had shared the room, and before that her mother and her grandmother. Autumn loved the rose velvet bedhangings and draperies. She loved the big oaken bedstead with its linenfold paneling headboard, and the lead-paned windows that looked out across the green park to the hills beyond. The room was a sanctuary, and now she was to spend her wedding night in it. She wondered if the chamber would ever seem the same again. Then the door in the paneled wall that connected to the bedroom next to it opened and her husband stepped into the room.

"Good night, Dunewood," he called to his valet, and then he closed the door behind him. He was wearing a silk chamber robe too.

Autumn was silent. She didn't know what to say, or where or whether she should begin. She worried her lower lip with her teeth. Except for that one time they had kissed and he had fondled her several weeks earlier, they had had aboslutely no physical contact. There had never seemed to be time for it. Then he had disappeared for two weeks. Finally she said, "This is ridiculous, Gabriel. We are not virgins, and I do not know where we should begin." She laughed nervously.

He walked over to her and undid her garment. Then he gently drew it off her. "I think, madame, we should begin this way." He stepped back and observed her thoughtfully. Then he sighed. "Yes, you are very beautiful. I can understand both Louis and Charles desiring you, Autumn. You are irresistible."

"Never mention either of those names in our bedchamber, my lord," she said, half-angrily. "Remember, you swore to me that you would put the past behind us. I cannot bear it if you do not!"

"Forgive me," he told her, "but it is difficult to do. I know I promised you, and I am trying, Autumn."

She began to cry. "How can we make love when I know you are wondering all the time if I am making comparisons? I hated what I had to do with my royal lovers. *I hated it!* I want to be loved again for myself, not because I am a beautiful or desirable creature. Surely there is something about me besides my beauty that has attracted you!" Oh, God, she thought! Her nose would be red with her weeping, and yet she sobbed all the harder, unable to stop.

God's blood, he thought, surprised. He had not realized how vulnerable, how very fragile she was. She had always seemed so strong. He took her into his arms and held her against him. "I'm so sorry, poppet," he murmured into her ear. "I would not hurt you for the world. I am a foolish, jealous man. I don't deserve you at all!" Tipping her wet face up to his, he kissed her slowly, deeply, until she relaxed in his embrace and sighed contentedly. When she had calmed herself he said, "Aren't you going to take my robe off for me, Autumn?"

"Do you want me to?" she asked. "I didn't want to seem forward." Her nimble fingers undid the garment, and she slid her hands in to caress his chest. This was ridiculous. She wasn't a virgin, and he well knew it. She was an experienced woman and she was going to act like one. If it startled him, he would soon be purring like a lion beneath her experienced touch. After all, she had had a husband before she had known her royal lovers. Who was to say Sebastian hadn't taught her all the skills she possessed? Pushing the chamber robe off his large frame, Autumn bent her head and began to kiss his chest and his torso.

Gabriel groaned, but the sound was definitely one of pleasure. "Do not stop," he commanded her. "I absolutely forbid you to stop, my bewitching wife."

She kissed him for a moment more, and then she said, "I must cease, my lord. I am frozen and want to get into bed." She took him by the hand and led him to their couch.

"Oh, yes," he agreed. "Let us go to bed, madame."

Climbing in, Autumn said, "I've never been to bed this early in the afternoon except when I was sick." She drew the coverlet over her naked body and snuggled down against the pillows.

"Neither have I," he countered, climbing in and leaning his big body over her so he might begin kissing her pretty round breasts.

"Oh, Gabriel!" she cried softly as his mouth closed over a tender nipple and he worried it with his teeth, then his tongue, and then began to draw deeply upon it. His action caused a reaction deep within her nether regions, and she shuddered. Her hands caressed his long back, finding his skin quite soft for a man, yet she could feel the hardness of his muscles beneath the flesh.

His tongue swept up the deep valley between her round breasts. He breathed deeply. "You smell good enough to eat," he told her, and lay his dark blond head upon her breasts. "I can hardly believe you are mine, Autumn. I have loved you for so long!"

Her hand caressed his head gently. "You hardly knew me," she said to him.

"I knew everything I had to know that day we first met. You were loyal and loving and brave. Two of those qualities would have been more than enough, but that you possessed all three was a wonder. And then your beauty, my darling—it took my breath away!"

"I thought you were arrogant and horrible," she told him. "There was Bess and poor old Smythe dead at the hands of your men. I hated you and all of Cromwell's men. I probably would have shot you had you not retrieved your weapon and I not been in such shock."

"You may kill me tonight with pleasure, Autumn," he said to her, lifting his head from her chest and staring into her face. "There are some who would say your wonderful eyes are witch's eyes, but I love the turquoise and the emerald orbs you look at me with, my darling." Then he kissed her.

Autumn remembered the time she had wondered what a kiss was like. She recalled how amused Sebastian had been with her over it, and how he had insisted she seek out kisses from all of her suitors to be certain he was the right one. And she had, and he had been. Never since then had she enjoyed a man's kisses until now. Gabriel kissed her tenderly at first, and then more fiercely and insistently. She felt not just passion in his lips, but also the love he had for her. Emotion such as she hardly remembered began to well up in her breast, and she started to cry again.

Feeling the wetness on her cheeks transferring itself to him, he ceased his kisses and demanded of her, "What is the matter?"

"You love me!" Autumn wept noisily.

"I told you I did," he said, puzzled.

"You really do!" she sobbed. "You really do love me!"

He began to laugh softly. "Yes, Autumn, I really do," he agreed. "Oh, sweetheart, has it been so long since anyone loved you that you believed it could not happen again? Those two nameless fellows who used you had no heart, for they are kings and cannot have hearts. But, my darling, I am not a king. I am nothing more than a country gentleman who loves you and wants to make you happy for the rest of your days." Then he kissed the tears away from her cheeks.

"Oh, God," Autumn wailed. "I don't deserve you."

"Madame," he teased her, "if this is a ploy to avoid your marital duties, I shall be forced to beat you."

"No! No!" she cried, and then she realized he was bedeviling her. "Oh, you are a wicked fellow," she said. Her heart was suddenly much, much lighter. She hadn't felt this way since Sebastian had died.

"Nay, madame, but here is a wicked fellow most anxious to make your acquaintance," he said boldly, giving her but a small glimpse of his love lance, which was obviously at the ready.

"You must kiss me again," she told him boldly, and then she sighed as his lips began to taunt her with their astonishing skill. Autumn closed her eyes and floated, as she suddenly realized she was safe again. Safe and loved. "Don't ever leave me, Gabriel," she said as she drew away from him for a moment. It was in that space of time that she comprehended that she was indeed falling in love with him, and the feelng was wonderful!

He understood what she was saying to him, and what it meant. "My father was fifty when I was born," he told her. "He died when he was eighty, Autumn. I will not leave you, my darling. I will never leave you!" Then he began to kiss her in earnest once again, and when shortly thereafter he entered her body, making them one, Autumn cried a cry of such intense joy that he almost wept that he had been able to bring her such pleasure, for she had certainly given him even more.

And afterwards as they lay contented in each other's arms, Autumn knew that she had found love once again. This time, she sensed, she would not lose it. This time the love would remain and grow. It would surround them and their children forever and ever. This time she could really let go of Sebastian. *Farewell, my first love,* she whispered in her heart.

Adieu, ma cherie, she heard his voice in her heart a final time. Then Autumn turned back to the man she would love until the end of time and beyond.

Epilogue

QUEEN'S MALVERN—
SUMMER 1663

The front lawns at Queen's Malvern were covered with gaily colored tented pavillions. The back lawns and gardens were filled with people. Skye O'Malley had borne eight children, of whom seven had lived to sire a generation of 49 grandchildren, who in their turn sired 158 great-grandchildren, 302 great-great-grandchildren, and 27 great-great-great-grandchildren as of the summer of 1663. The children of Skye O'Malley were now all deceased, the last and youngest of them, Velvet de Marisco Gordon, having died the previous winter at the age of 84. Twenty-nine of Skye's grandchildren lived on in their sixties and seventies.

Jasmine, Dowager Duchess of Glenkirk, stood proudly surveying the great crowd of Skye's descendants. There were O'Flahertys who had traveled from Ireland and O'Flahertys who had come up from Devon. The Earl of Alcester and his family of Edwardses, had come, as had the Southwoods of Lynmouth; young Earl John and her granddaughter, Sabrina, the proud parents of a little son and a baby daughter. The Blakeleys of Blackthorne, the family of Skye's second daughter, Deirdre, lived nearby and were well represented, as were the Burkes of Clearfields Priory and the Gordons of BrocCairn. There were Leslies, Lindleys, Stuarts, Ashburnes, and Leighs from Scotland, Ireland, and England. Only her daughter Fortune and her family were missing. Fortune, having crossed the

Atlantic Ocean once to reach the New World, had vowed never to cross it again.

Jasmine smiled as she viewed her many relations. The size of the growing family, and the civil strife that had plagued England in the past years had only served to separate them. Now she had brought them back together in an effort that had taken her almost two years. Cousins who had never met greeted each other with delight. Faces from different ends of the family spectrum were discovered to look alike. Kerry blue eyes were noted among many of the younger generations. There would even be some matches come out of the gathering, Jasmine suspected.

"You have done it, Mama," her daughter Autumn said, coming to her mother's side.

"I have indeed, haven't I?" Jasmine agreed, putting an arm about her youngest "The lawns will be ruined, but they can be replaced. Seeing all of Mam's progeny is well worth the damage."

"Gabriel says he is glad the gathering is here at Queen's Malvern and not at Garwood Hall," Autumn chuckled.

"Gabriel has put on a bit of weight, hasn't he?" Jasmine said.

"Marriage agrees with him, and marriage to him agrees with me, Mama," Autumn admitted. "How I love him, and I never really believed I should ever love again."

"Those twins of yours certainly came from love," Jasmine said with a small chuckle. "I've never seen such contented little hell-raisers as Jamie and Simon. God help you when they can walk and talk. Can you tell them apart yet?"

Autumn shook her head. "Not yet, Mama. They are so close that they even begin crying together. They are identical in every way, but hopefully when they are older something will distinguish one from the other." She looked to her right, where a blanket had been spread upon the grass in the sunshine. There her sons crawled determinedly toward their sisters, Madeline and Margot, whom they already adored, while the nursemaids attempted to keep them on the blanket.

Jasmine chuckled. "Just like their grandfather Leslie," she noted. "They must have their own way."

"Just like their father," Autumn replied with a smile. "Thank you, Mama. Thank you for knowing what was right for me, and making me see it through my anger and heartbreak."

Jasmine hugged her daughter lovingly, her heart almost hurting with the happiness she felt as she looked about her. There was absolutely nothing better than family, she decided with a smile. Mam's descendants had grown sizably since her mother's generation, and it might not be possible to keep them together, but she would try.

Gabriel Bainbridge joined them. Standing looking out over the crowd of his wife's family, he said, "Do you ever think our descendants will rival the stars in the sky as do those of your great-grandmother?"

Autumn looked up at her husband, her jeweled eyes twinkling with laughter. "If you wish it, my lord, then we shall have to produce more bairns than we now possess."

"Then, madame," he replied, his own blue eyes filled with love, "we had best adjourn to that delightful rosy bedchamber of ours now, my darling. Neither of us is getting any younger."

"Sir!" she cried indignantly, "I am as young as I ever was!" Then, turning, she ran off toward the house, her duke in hot pursuit.

"I don't know why those two always seem to favor the afternoons," Lily said to Orane as they watchd their master and mistress depart.

Orane giggled. "Love knows no boundaries, Lily, time or otherwise," she said. "You are married to a Frenchman, so surely you know that."

Lily's face softened for a moment. "I do," she admitted. Then her visage grew disapproving. "But a respectable virgin such as yerself should not," she scolded.

Orane's left eyebrow lifted, puzzled. "Whatever made you think that at my age I was a virgin, Lily?" she said. And with a wink she sauntered off toward a group of footmen, her skirts swaying wickedly.